Red High Heels II

Rotha J. Dawkins

ISBN: 1-891461-06-0

First printing: May 2001

Printed in the United States of America

Dedicated to

Rebekah Ruth Tredway

To the one person in my life who has hung with me -- taking the best and worst over the long haul of life. Being red-headed "Tiggers" makes it happen. You're always my daughter, friend, confidant and advisor. Thanks for it all.

You're a great bundle of talent -- just cut it loose! I love you!

Love,
Mom, Rotha

Acknowledgments

Shelba D Johnson Trucking, Inc., Thomasville, NC.
A. L. (Red) Johnson

Regis Koloshinsky, Shelba D. Johnson Trucking, Inc.,
Director of Maintenance (arranged photo shot).

Rebekah Tredway, Executive Photographer (covers).

Chad Gallimore, Model & Photo Assistant.

Agnes Hussey Stevens, secretary.

Triad Freightliner, Greensboro, NC,
owners Larry Tysinger and Ken Maynard, use of their
Freightliner for cover shot.

Also, to all of the dedicated men and women
truckdrivers all across America

CHAPTER 1

"Which is cheaper?" cried Red High Heels into the receiver, "A clutch or a tow truck?"

The man on the other end of the line at a truck stop in Cincinnati, Ohio listened carefully before he answered. "It all depends, Baby!"

"Depends?" she screamed. She was wiping the tears with a convenient dish towel. She usually cried when she was angry; that made her more angry.

"Just listen, calm down! Tell me you love me, first!" he teased.

"Oh, Early Bird, I love you!" she sniffed.

"That's better!" he comforted. "Tell me about it!"

"What happened doesn't matter. It's not how I got into the hole, it's how to get out!" grieved the red head.

1

"Well?" inquired Early. "What are we getting out of? What is in the hole and what kind of hole?"

"An asshole!" she snapped. "Just like a man!"

"Talk to me! Your car?" he patiently quizzed.

"Certainly not a car! If it were just my rag car, I'd leave it! What would it matter? My truck! My big ass truck!" she whimpered and started to weep. "Oh, Early Bird, I don't know what to do! I've never been stuck like this! I went through fifteen neighbor men helping me get out!"

"Do you have to get it before next week? I can be there then," he suggested.

"Yes! I have to get it. I can't work without it!" she moaned.

"All right, talk to me!"

"You know I wanted to put one of my trailers below the house. I need that storage bad!" she started.

"Right!" he understood.

"I had the area bush-hogged and things were perfect; trees cut, too!" Red continued, "The sun was shining beautifully. Well, Lone Wolf came to help me. He backed the trailer into a stump. When he pulled up and rolled back, the trailer went farther down the hill to miss that stump. You know we haven't had rain for two months. Right then, the bottom fell out! We couldn't even see anything!"

"You've got to be kidding!" Early groaned.

"No! It poured!" she replied. "Started thundering and lightning and flooded the area! He came out of the truck and we ran for the house. The storm raged for about an hour. You could look out the window and see the trenches of red mud flowing off

2

the road and down the hill!"

"What did you do?" Early sympathized.

"I made a pot of coffee and got us towels!" Red High Heels ployed.

"I see!" Early uttered. "You need to go on and put the pedal to it and get it on out!"

"We've tried. Every man in the neighborhood has tried. When Wolf and I returned to the truck, we kept trying to get the tractor from under the trailer," she said. "It was still raining some but I figured we'd better try."

"I can see it all now. Old Wolf had a chance to catch Red Riding Hood in the woods!" teased Early.

"Crap! It's not like that!" she retorted. "Red wasn't tiptoeing with cookies! Red was moving a rig! You men think we are dumb and helpless!"

"No, Baby. I'm playing. Lighten up! I'm listening!" he petted.

"I'm not helpless, jerk! Not at all! Laugh at me, see if I care! I'll figure it out!" flipped Red and slammed the phone to the cradle breaking off a corner. She slipped a dry tee shirt on and left, nearly snatching the door off the hinges.

"Jerk! Pure jerk!" she walked alone with tears rolling down her cheeks. "Men! Hateful, old shits!"

Red could hear the phone ringing as she went on to where the cabover was sunk below its bumper in a huge, gushy pit. She shook her head from side to side saying aloud, "Poor Blue Heaven. I'll get you out of here! In fact, if it hadn't been for all those know it all men, you wouldn't be here now! They know it all! Turn it left! Turn it right! Rock it! Jerks!"

She felt better having a hissy alone than in

front of people. It sort of seemed to lighten her load to talk to the truck. Continuing walking and talking to the vehicle, Red tried to figure it out.

A neighbor kid rolled in on his bicycle. He stopped in front of her and rested on his handlebars smiling, "Can I help you get it out?"

At first Red wanted to kill anybody that offered to help. She nearly snorted, then calmed down. "What do you think we can do?"

"Well, those old men didn't know nothing! I bet you can do it if anybody can! That's what Mama said!" he grinned. "Wanna try?"

"Maybe. There's so much water around the tires and look, its almost bottomed out. It won't go nowhere like this," surmised Red.

"Let's get shovels and dig!" the nine year old suggested.

"I'll tell you a secret!" whispered Red.

"A secret?" he joyfully got close and leaned closer toward her.

"When they built that house there," Red High Heels pointed, "They dug a huge hole. It was big enough to swallow up the bulldozer. Then, they pushed all the trash in the whole area into it!"

"They did? Wow!" he exclaimed.

"The motor weight is on the front so it could get worse! Look at that hole beside the left tire!" she continued, pointing once more, but with her foot. "Now, see that water running over there?"

"Yeah!"

"I believe it's tunneling under this truck!" she replied, "It's like an underground stream! It's rained a bunch and I don't believe it will totally stop for a few days. Anything could happen. Those people helping were just digging in deeper! Could have ruined the clutch or transmission like that!"

"That's a funny smell!" he sniffed.

"The clutch and brakes got a work out! I'm glad I quit when I did! That prissy guy said we'd get out if we kept on!" injected Red. "Get the shovels. We can test the ground!"

He jumped on the bike and was gone a short time, then returned. The kid flung the shovels off with pride. "Where do we start?"

"Here!" smiled Red as they negotiated the plan. "Let's try to move the water down hill; maybe make a little ditch. It has to be cut lower than the bottom of the tire."

"Shit!" he yelled. He had tried the shovel but his couldn't cut into the ground. It stopped. "I'll be back!"

Once more, he left, then returned. This time with a little hose and funny contraption. "Hell, I'll drain it like this! We'll pump it out!"

Again, the child started his new task. He got onto the ground in the mud trying to drain the hole. Sure enough, he had the water trickling down hill. The only problem, there seemed to be no stopping.

Proudly he announced, "That's how I drain my play-shed!"

It was as if it were a stream with no end. Red put blocks around the trailer wheels and rolled the landing gear a bit higher to keep it from hooking back when the truck rolled that way.

The kid got on his bike and pulled a little tree out of the way using his chain. Then, he removed several other objects the same way. He strutted like a peacock feeling manly.

Red found some roof material and slipped it at all the wheels. She returned to the truck and turned the tires sharply right, then eased off the clutch. It was spinning again.

"No use! We'd better call!"

As she started out of the truck, she felt movement. The brake was on, still a forward drop.

The kid yelled, "Jump! Quick!"

Red High Heels stayed on the step rails then, bounced to the ground falling backward. She watched the truck settle deeper into the muddy trench, leaning more to one side. Her eyes widened along with the young boy's, viewing more of the truck settling to one side very deep.

Once again, the materials beneath the heavy Transtar shifted, forcing the truck to bow even deeper. The rain started a steady, heavy mist. The hole started to fill, making it real juicy.

"I'm sorry!" cried the boy. "I didn't mean to empty the hole! Your truck is sinking!"

"You didn't do anything wrong! We just picked the wrong day. My driver got too far down the hill! Come on!" she ordered. They ran for the house.

In the kitchen, Red made two cups of chocolate and placed a bowl of cookies in front of him. "Call your mother."

After he finished, the phone rang.

"What!"

It was Early Bird. "I'm coming in!"

"I'm all right! Just have to get a tow truck for sure!" she tiredly replied. "I've straightened my 'drawers' out!"

Early laughed, "My truck needs servicing. Freightliner is picking it up. My plane leaves shortly.

I'll be there soon. Just hang in!"

Red whispered, "Wonderful! Want me to meet you?"

"No, I'll get to you. You have enough to concern you. Take it easy and Daddy will be home to Baby!" he whispered, blowing her a kiss.

They hung up and Red fell to the floor squeaking, "He'll be here in a few hours!"

"Who?" asked the kid.

"My boyfriend!" Red replied.

"Boyfriend? Boyfriend?" He had tears in his eyes. "After all I've done? What about me?"

"Look! You're my friend, too. He's a man!" she soothed.

"Well, I'll grow up soon!" he cried.

She put her arm on his shoulder. "Look. Me and you are a different thing; we help each other! Most people never do that! I really needed you to help me and you did!"

"Shit! That's what all women say!" he exclaimed.

"No, it's not! Look, let's call a tow service!" smiled Red, trying to humor him. She reached for a stack of calling cards then, the phone book. "This might be better."

"Shit. You'll need ten tow trucks for that! Hell, they might be better to come from the underside," he chuckled. "You know. Down yonder. Hell! The devil!"

Red gave him a dirty look. "We'll just try from on top first. Here's one. I know them!"

She dialed the number and an answer service answered, "Naturally, you can't talk to a person, it's Saturday! I'll leave a message."

Red left a message and called six more, leaving messages with each. Finally, one tow service answered.

"Yeah? Pop's!"

"Hi. I need a wrecker I think," she began.

"We don't do cars. Call Morgan's," snarled the man. In the background she heard two men arguing over something.

"It's a big truck!" she replied.

"Oh? How big?"

"An International cabover!" Red nearly begged, "It's in a hole and might be getting deeper!"

"What, a septic tank?" he growled. "Did you put it there? I hate those damn shit-holes!"

"In a way, but it's not a septic tank!" she responded.

"Good. The last pile of shit cost the bastard! I ain't getting into shit-tanks no more? I'll quit first!" he grumbled. "What kind of hole?"

She related to him how the neighborhood rescued her into the hole and explained the ground situation.

"Wuzzent no fuel tanks or explosive stuff?" he asked.

"No, just debris left around. The machine ran over it a bunch to pack it then put dirt over it!" she informed.

"All right. We'll come. Cash, you know. Probably be a hundred dollars if we don't have a snag!" he eased up and agreed to help her.

Red gave him the statistics of location and hung up.

"He's an asshole!" squeaked the kid.

"Who? Why do you cuss?" Red pondered.

"You're so young!"

"I feel like cussing, that's why! Everybody has to cuss to get noticed!" he laughed. "Besides, it's fun! The asshole? The tow people. He's going to try to take you fer a ride! If he does, I'm going to kick his ass if Early Bird don't get here!"

Red High Heels shook her head. She couldn't help but laugh. The kid had done odd jobs for her for a year. He was all right, actually company to Red, too.

About fifteen minutes slipped by until Red felt the ground shake and heard the rumble of a huge engine. From the window, she could see the boom of the wrecker. It was a huge truck to the rescue. The two waited at the porch for the tow driver.

"Hey! You called?" he smiled. He was a very handsome man of fifty. His grey hair was uncombed and he tried to shape it with his fingers when he looked at Red. "A beautiful girl like you shouldn't have a truck in the hole! Where you got it?"

Pointing, Red giggled, "Out there! Come on!"

They walked to the sad truck. It had fallen even deeper since Red had last seen it. Once more, she started to cry.

"Oh look! It's ruined! My poor truck!"

The man took her in his arms and tried to soothe her. "Honey, Superman is here! Don't worry. It'll be all right!"

The kid ran toward them and stomped the man's toe. "You old turd! Get away from her! Me and Early Bird can handle all of this! Just get your ass gone!"

Red jumped quickly. "He didn't mean anything!"

9

"Shit! Look at his britches in front! Oh yes he does!" the kid retorted. "Get your ass and that ragged truck out of here!"

The man was shocked but ran for his truck. Safely inside, he turned it around, while the kid retrieved his B-B gun off his bike and started shooting.

"Don't come back! There, asshole!"

The driver yelled, "Don't worry! Lady, your kid is crazy!" He rattled out of the drive and left a trail of mud behind.

"Why'd you do that?" screamed Red. "You brat! This is not your business! I need that truck pulled out!"

"He wuzzent goin' to do it! He wanted you!" gulped the kid. "I saw him! Shit, we ain't sharing you! The truck can stay in the hole! It's enough to split you with Early Bird!"

Red had to laugh to herself and thought, 'We ain't sharing you.'

The young boy stuck his chin out, determined. His sandy hair matched his sprinkle of freckles. For his age, he was tall and determined.

As they entered the house again, the phone was ringing.

"Hello," she answered, snatching the receiver. A tow service was returning her call from earlier. Once more, she agreed for him to help. As they waited, Red said, "All right. Now don't go off on this man. I've got to have somebody help me. I think I'll name you Lil' Hitler. Yes, that will be a good CB handle for you!"

The kid grinned. "Lil' Hitler? Good!"

A couple of hours later, a huge, blue wrecker roared into the road. Once again they walked onto the porch. The man grinned out the window through a rough beard and greasy baseball cap. His helper jumped out.

"This where the truck is stuck up?" he asked.

"Yes, over here!" Red said; they followed her.

"Damn! What 'ja do to get in that? Dig a pit?" smirked the helper and started motioning to the driver to come that way.

"What the fuck?" ranted the wrecker driver. "Damn, we gonna haf' to git another truck. One ain't gonna git it!"

Red bolted to them and stomped her foot. "Don't laugh at me! This is your business! If I weren't in a bind and others like me, you'd be working at something else! I didn't do it alone! I listened to a bunch of stupid men!"

The wrecker service ordered more equipment, then both men lit cigarettes and waited. A half rotten tree near the side of the old cabover seemed to sway with the weight of the two. A funny, snapping noise seemed to wiggle the dead twigs above and a few fell to the ground. Then, where the helper stood a big hole opened as things shifted below him. He fell down and started crawling to get away. Red wanted to laugh. Again, the ground under the truck moved and straightened the truck, but deeper.

"Jez, what is this shit?" roared the driver.

"A hole!" said Red. "The Hole! It should be all right; they pushed all the trash in the area here. It must have decayed. Maybe it's good we know now!"

"Show me where the digging wuz!" grunted Driver, giving his help a hand. "I seen wors'en this! Once, I pulled a trailer and truck and two more out of a caved in place. Had been a buildin' they'd pushed

11

the top off and left a basement! It happens!"

Two more big wreckers raced to the scene. They were followed by the highway patrol, sheriff and an ambulance. For lack of anything else to do, the emergency crews stayed to be on stand-by; they immediately realized there was no business here for them.

Naturally, the neighbors returned with their input. One woman said, "Maybe we had an earthquake! I felt something shake hard!"

"Looks like the storm up rooted trees!" said another.

"Oh, God! The Lord is coming! It says right in the Bible the grounds will open and swallow things!" She fell to her knees and began to pray.

Another started running. "Oh, Lord! We are on that ground fault line that goes around the United States! One side is going to fall into the ocean!"

As they all tried to distinguish the cause, the tow truckers gathered in a group to make a plan. Red High Heels tried to outline the filled in area as best she remembered. The sheriff made a line with yellow ribbon so they could work and urged the nosy crowd to clear out. They refused. This was new and news! Somebody called the media and they started to appear all at the same time and asking for information. Red disappeared into the house to get away, leaving the job to the wrecker service.

"They making a damn mountain out of a mole hill!" groaned Lil' Hitler.

"More like just dig in deeper!" replied Red. "People are crazier than I thought! Look at them!"

"Sure gonna make you famous!" Lil' reasoned.

"Hope not. They might make us dig out all that stuff and have it hauled to the dump. Government can do anything!" whined Red.

"Naw! I saw them do that around all these new houses they build!" Hitler informed.

"Really? Where?" quizzed Red.

"Those new, big, fancy places!"

"Good! One of our commissioners lives there. I'd better call him!" smiled Red, dialing the phone. Quickly, a man's voice answered. She stammered, "Commissioner! This is Red." Then carefully, she related the story.

He agreed to come immediately. "We don't need a bucket of worms opened. There's no law against this that I know."

"Mine was buried twenty years ago!" she said.

A dump truck of crush-run with a bulldozer behind, drove in. They unloaded the truck-loader and the truck dumped his load in front of Red's truck. The cabover had been lifted, leaving its back tires on the ground. Cables were attached in the other directions from the truck. It had taken them a lot of time to get all things in place.

Hours had passed and things seemed to just hang. They would solve one problem and start another. A wrecker had gotten stuck down hill from the Transtar in the pit. An argument started between two drivers.

"Fuck you!" said one. "Why'd you go down hill?"

"To get around to the other side, motherfucker!" he argued.

"I gotta pull your ass out now! That ain't no

13

DAWKINS

land-rover! Stupid, fucker!" the first returned.

"Who you calling that?"

"You, fucker! You!"

The man jumped from his truck and grabbed the other man. As they punched and fought in the mud, a drizzle of rain started again. The younger of the two started bleeding from the nose. He pounded the other one in the mouth with a closed fist, then jumped on top of him screaming, "Who's a fucker?"

Entwined, they pounded and rolled to the pit of the big ravine; then, both men lay in the wet, laughing and started getting up.

One puffed, "You look like shit!"

"So do you!" panted the other.

Once more, they knocked each other down and laughed again.

The wrecker man in charge screamed at them, "Git your asses up here! We got work to do! You crazy?"

They looked at each other, both saying, "I could beat your ass!" Then they laughed together and returned to their trucks.

A white Chevrolet turned into the driveway and stopped. Red heard a key in the door as she watched the men from the bedroom. She rushed toward the back door as it opened. The tall, handsome, greying man smiled his perfect smile.

"Early Bird!" Red's heart jumped. "How did you get here so fast?"

As they went to each other, he whispered, "I bought the airplane!" Their lips met. Immediately, they tasted the passionate kiss they both lived for.

"Oh, Baby," he groaned. "I've missed you!"

"Early Bird! Thank God you are here!" she

14

moaned. "I love you!"

"I love you!" he returned, absorbing another deep kiss as he felt himself starting to throb all over. Suddenly, he felt eyes on him and pulled away. "Who's this?"

"I'm the other man!" boasted Lil' Hitler. "We gotta watch her! I ran one off already today! The old hot-ass!"

Early Bird laughed and winked at Red. "So, I have competition?"

"Certainly!" responded Hitler. "Don't worry. I'll take care of things at this end!" Then, he told Bird about chasing off the tow driver.

"Let's go see what's happening out there!" Early insisted. He liked to walk behind Red so he could watch her move. Today, she looked especially good in her slim navy pants and matching blouse. The red edging outlined the petite figure perfectly. Her curled, long, red hair bounced gently. But, Red was a determined woman who was tough. He thought, 'Maybe I do need the kid to watch after her!'

Early checked with Red, "Can I handle it for you now?"

She nodded her head in agreement. "That Blue Wrecker, he's been in charge!"

"First thing, they need to run all these people off! My gosh, how many does it take? In the rain, too!" pointed out Early.

"Who is you?" asked Blue Wrecker.

"Appointed over you!" informed Early, flatly.

"Sez who?" resisted the driver.

"Red!"

"Oh! That's different!" Blue nervously grinned. "They got a mess here. The po-lease ordered

15

the hole filled before we could git the truck."

"I've never seen anybody fill a hole with a truck in it! That's a nuts idea! They had better not beat up her truck!" ordered Early Bird. "You going to keep it hanging forever? What's the hold up?"

"Nobody will listen to anybody. Now they got that pile of dirt, we can't git the truck. They waitin' fer ah-nudder load of rock!" he said.

"Have that front end loader to push that pile flat. Try to swing the front end of her truck this way," suggested Early.

They finally flattened the pile and listened to Early Bird, who snatched a helper out of Red's Transtar and got into it himself. He turned on the CB and ordered all the trucks on channel fifteen. Then, he talked their way to remove the blue International out of the messy, massive hole and back into Red's yard. Once he got out of the truck, after parking it, the crowd finally decided to leave.

News people gathered around him but he brushed off their questions with a little speech. "No big thing. Just a little rock underground that's not used to a heavy load. The rain, well, it always makes a single axle spin. Nothing to it!"

Eventually, everyone disappeared. Red was happy that Early Bird rescued her. She sent Lil' Hitler home with a piece of cake while Early found the shower.

Red filled the hot tub and lit the candles around it. She quickly touched up her make-up and found a little string bikini. She grinned to herself and worked herself into the tiny set of clothing. Her reflection in the mirror passed inspection as she turned the overhead light to very dim.

She heard the water cut off and Early rambling around. A slight smell of Oleg Cassini cologne seeped into the room. She grabbed a squirt of Chanel #5 and added a slick pair of silk lace thigh-highs to her costume. She scrambled into a six-inch pair of red stilt heels. The final touch of a puffy black feather boa gave a seductive 'come-hither' look. Happily, she struck a sexy pose, waiting, as he entered the room wrapped in a fluffy, new white towel.

His eyes fell onto his beautiful, sex goddess. It was all so perfect, like a dream. She was the most changeable woman he had ever known; so full of life, into living to the fullest, then, stopping the whole merry-go-round of the world and holding it for him. She had made his life hell occasionally but most of the time she was almost a living fantasy. She could portray womanhood completely and uniquely.

Red whispered, "You smell delicious!" She took his hand and guided him to the crystal, steaming water. Without hesitation, Early stepped into the heated pool, feeling goose bumps from the hot-cold factor. He was like putty in her hands. She could do anything. Without words, Red settled him into place and started the jets in the water bubbling. Early eagerly relaxed and closed his eyes with the pure comfort. Her lips found his and their tongues met with sensuous harmony for a very long in-depth reunion, as she leaned over the tub's edge.

"I'll be right back, honey!" Red hoarsely whispered. "I love you!"

"Never have I felt so much love! I love you, Baby!" he returned.

Quickly Red slipped to the kitchen and put a tray of Early's favorite morsels together. She always had pre-ready things that a quick microwave job would bring to life. Satisfied with the elegant tray, she returned to his side, placing the floating tray in the water before him. Removing the clear coating of plastic from the stemmed glasses, her fingers fumbled getting the cork to move on the exotic bottle of champagne. Even with no alcohol, the glamour of the thought was in the pink, bubbly grape. Early Bird took the bottle and gently poured the two glasses full.

Red flipped the boa of black feathers across his silver hair, smiling, "You know just what to do! Good?"

"Oh, yes! Very good!"

They slowly exchanged sips from their glasses and followed with feeding each other from the floating tray. Red had attached a little red ribbon to it so it wouldn't get far away. The miniature crackers with stuffed shrimp, bits of cheese, delicate breads with beef and ham dipped deliciously into the dill sauce and liquid hot cheese made hors d'oeuvre a satisfying course.

Once they finished the food, Early poured another tiny glass full and watched Red as she changed the music on the stereo. Quickly, she flipped to the floor and started seductively rotating her hips to the very slow band. She used a small part of the floor and gently threw the fluffy black cape of feathers toward a nearby bed. Early looked intently and sipped.

"Mm-mmm! That's great!"

Red continued to dance for him. Then, she put one foot on the edge of the tub and wiggled it slowly as she reached for the beautiful shoe and removed it. She turned a few turns and repeated the move on the left foot. She set the expensive posh shoes toe to toe on the edge of the Jacuzzi and proceeded to seductively remove one stocking at a time. Moving and dancing then throwing them into the water with Early Bird.

He was amused with her new, exotic dance. It was something he had never experienced before. As he watched, she gently pulled the strings to the tiny bikini bra and it fell gracefully from her hand to the carpet with about the third gentle turn. There was only the string of a panty left and Red continued by getting close to him and sitting on the steps to the tub, then rolled seductively. She stood tall, then flipped a small something in back and the cover disappeared to the floor and unveiled her full nude figure. Red eased to Early; then, slipped into the warm water.

The music mood changed to a quiet and peaceful soft piano. The new king sized bed was lavishly made with silk linens of pastel colors intertwined. Red took Early by the hand and led him to a fluffy floor mat, and with a huge, plush white towel, dried his back then wrapped it around his bottom.

She smiled and slipped into her pink, opaque gown beside the tub.

Early finished drying, found his robe and filled their glasses with the sparkling juice. They each tasted with a nod of knowing toast.

The phone rang as Early Bird sank into the plush soft nest. Red reached down and snatched the cord from the wall and you could hear its muffled ringing in the far distant rooms.

Red slid between the sheets and curled close to him. "Thanks for being here!"

"Mm-mmm. Wouldn't miss it, Baby! You're my everything!" he assured. "I never want to leave you! Come with me on the truck!"

"Shh! Shh! Shh!" hushed Red. "Talk later! Let me just hold you close now!"

Baby, I love you! Probably too much! It scares me!" he acknowledged.

"I'm trying, Early, you know I love you. Just give me a little more time!"

"Please. Why can't we just get married right now! Call a preacher, judge or witch! There's no need to wait!" he reassured. "It's just you and me! We have it all; just us and a love deeper than the ocean and higher than any sky!"

"Soon! Let me get rid of the business in New York!" she added.

"You say that, but then you don't!" he projected with disappointment in his voice. "Someday will never come!"

"Oh, yes! I promise!" she smiled.

He took her hand and fumbled at the wallet on the nightstand. Early took the huge diamond and slipped it onto her hand. "Please wear this as a promise! It's what really symbols my love. That other ring isn't big enough to neon my feelings!"

Red looked with delight. "Early, this is fabulous! I'm scared to wear it! It's beautiful!"

She held her hand daintily in front of her. He kissed it and smiled, "It's only metal and gem on your finger! Wear it for me! Your promise to be mine, all mine, soon!"

"I've been yours for a long time! I love you!"

"Just tell me when you're ready. Tell me how to make your life better and everything you need!" he proposed.

"You already make it better! It's not you; not us that makes me wait. It's all the old days that scare me!" Red sadly replied.

"Let it be over and behind you, Honey! Trust me all the way. I'll be here for you! But you have to give in and let me! Take this love I have for you and wrap yourself safely into it. I won't let you down and when I die it will only be because I have to; but I'll love you even then!" pleaded Early Bird. "I know you've felt it all with me, it's there!"

"I know!"

"Please! I'm so afraid of loosing you! Please, Baby!" he added.

"Soon! I'll do things fast! Okay?" she smiled and started rubbing his handsome, broad shoulders as he rolled over.

"That feels good!" murmured Early Bird. "You know everything! Where to touch, how to touch, when to touch! Come on! Tell me now! Let's get married!"

He grabbed her in a playful manner and rolled her over and held her hands tightly beside her face. He suddenly could see a tear roll from an eye as he sat astride her petite body. Then, it was as if she flipped from the soft, beautiful and cuddly woman into a scared, tearful stranger.

"No! Get off me!" she screamed as her feet started kicking. Once more she tried to get up but was restrained, which frustrated her to fear. "Quit it!"

Early Bird jumped quickly and moved to his side of the huge, now lonely, bed. He lit a cigarette and stared into space thinking how stupid he had been. He loved her so much and rough-teasing seemed only natural. Then, the story of her past, as the victim of a twisted and haunting relationship, came back to mind. He always had to be careful not to drift into that old history. Early felt with time he could help her overcome. Yet she could be torn emotionally like this forever.

Red High Heels pulled the sheet over herself and slid to the other side of the bed. She felt the hot tears flow as the mounting confusion made her feel completely helpless. A vision of the past snapped into her mind and she replayed its memory.

*****

"Get up bitch!" screamed the out of control man. He was sniffing and panting heavily from his last blows to her petite body. "You ain't hurt, now are you? You like this!"

He grabbed her hair and jerked her head back, then spit between her eyes. Once more, he threw her head to the floor and started to kick her, but she quickly jumped up.

"I'm up! I'm all right!" Red quivered with panic. She felt as if she were a boxer loosing a battle in the ring.

He stared at her for what seemed forever, then grabbed her again. Red tried to dodge but he caught her to the side and lifted her fragile body over his shoulder; yelling and swearing. Again, Red was at risk. He flung her to the floor; slamming her head down first and dropping the rest of her body. He stepped over and kicked the door shut behind him.

Red had heard the loud crack when she crashed to the floor and graciously passed out. Minutes later she came conscious and felt her head reeking with pain. She felt the wet hair and looked at the mass of blood on her hand.

She said, "I've got to get out of here! He's going to kill me!" Stammering, she began to scramble to her feet, "Oh, God! Help me! Please, God! Help me! I don't know what to do!"

The man returned, acting as if nothing had happened. "Did you fall, Honey?"

"Yes," she answered.

"Your head's bleeding! Look on the floor!" he discovered. "Let me look at your head!"

She let him fumble with her hair to expose the seven inches of a deep gash. Red felt sick and faint. "I'll be all right."

"You better go to the hospital! Too bad you fell like that!" the mad man grunted. "Remember not to get up on them chairs anymore. The floor's slick. Go on! Get it looked at!"

Red reached for her purse and keys as he watched. "You better tie a towel on it. Here, let me do it!"

Afraid to say no, she sat on a stool as he folded a dish towel and placed it on the spot. He reached for a long cord to tie it. Red quickly blurted, "It doesn't need to be tied!"

Realizing she was afraid, he once more laughed and snapped the heavy string together. "A person could do lots with this! Remember how you fell?"

"Of course!" she whispered, looking down, feeling like a subordinate.

"Go on! You better come back!" he snapped a beer cap. "Don't forget you ain't going no where else!"

"I'll be back!"

He sat in a chair and motioned to her with a pistol in his hand to sit. Red obliged and waited, trying to hold back the tears.

"Look, bitch. I ain't got nothin'! But, you are mine as long as I say so! You get that?"

She nodded quietly. The months of hell he had put her through let her realize why they called him Devil-man.

"It's like this. If I decide to, I can kill you. Your fuckin' family and everybody else, I hate! They ain't gonna do no more for a bunch of you fuckers than just one!" Devil laughed, "You know I can do it!"

Red again nodded in forced agreement as she prayed silently.

"You just remember, you can't get away from me! I'll track your ass down! Ain't no motherfucker going to have you, ever!" he fussed. "You git that?"

"Please, let me go! I'll be back," Red begged. "I'll be back!"

"Yeah! Nobody likes your sorry ass anyhow! I ain't sure why I do! If you ain't back soon, I'll come looking!" he warned. "Kiss me!"

Red stood in front of him and reached to placate him.

He laughed, "Go on!"

Leaving the house, Red slipped into her car just in time to dodge three fast bullets that hit the ground beside her door. The vehicle started immediately; she was grateful as she slowly drove away.

"Freedom! Oh, God! Help me!" she cried. "Please, help me!"

Red remembered how it took twenty some stitches and the concussion kept her head aching for weeks. She knew she might as well be dead as go back. This had to be it, never again! The hospital knew, by all her cuts, bruises and scratches, a fall to the floor did not the problem cause!

A counselor was called, then family, then the sheriff. All this was fine, except there was Devilman's promise. "I'll track you down! Nobody else can have you!" Red could not shake it from her mind. It was always there.

Over the months that followed he managed to stay away from her and she kept as far from him as possible. She changed up her activities and places through the assistance of the SBI. This gave her extra comfort in the hope it was over. Time set in and Devil seemed to find a life of his own. Maybe he realized for the time that it was only trouble to keep assaulting and going crazy. A couple of years finally slipped by, but Red could never forget the threats. He was psychotic in some ways and Red was afraid to reach out to another man. It was her fear, that a man would be in danger to associate with her. For a long time she stayed to herself.

*****

Red snapped back to the moment with the phone ringing. She reached for the portable beside her, answering, "Hello." On the other end there was silence. She repeated, "Hello, who do you wish to speak to?"

The phone went dead. She snapped the off button and sighed, "I wish I knew who keeps doing that!"

"I'll get you a caller-ID, then you'll know," smiled Early, as if he could read her mind. "You had any trouble from him?"

"No. I guess I'm paranoid!"

"You have a right to be! Come here, honey," coaxed Early Bird. "I don't mean to push you! I love you. I'll wait forever if I have to. You know that!"

Red High Heels moved close to him and cuddled in the safety of his strong arms. It felt good to have his care; he felt good to her body. She closed her eyes and prayed to herself, "Thank you, God, for this wonderful man!"

Early rubbed her hair gently and kissed her neck softly over and over, moaning his love for her and bringing her back to her usual strength and vivacious self. He whispered, "Red, I will be here always. Try to put all that behind us. I'm your man. I'll never harm you and nobody else will if I'm around. Just put your head on Daddy's shoulder and go to sleep!"

Red relaxed in the depth of his feelings. As she clung to him, she drifted into a deep slumber.

CHAPTER 2

The loud clammer of the air compressor flipped on as Red was fueling her truck. A young fellow walked up behind her and stood, watching. She continued servicing her Transtar in preparation for the trip. The tires on the truck were aired-up, she had already adjusted the brakes and was pulling the air-tank handles to empty any water and sludge. She then bumped into the fellow.

"Oh, mercy! You scared me, Ass!"

Her son-in-law grinned. "You can't slip up on a noisy thing like this, you walk up!"

"I know! I love all its big noises! Lucky Runner, why don't you and Kikki Dee go with me? It would be fun!" pleaded Red.

"We can't. Maybe next month. Early Bird called. Wants you to call him as soon as possible,

Lucky grinned. "When you going to hook up?"

"One day!" laughed Red. "Soon as I dump the stores! I have to do that!"

She took the slip of paper and Runner took over her fueling job as she darted to a pay phone. "Early Bird!"

"Yes! Babe, when are you leaving?"

In half an hour," she gleed.

"That will put you in Richmond about nine-thirty. Can you meet me at the Petro near there?" he quizzed. "That's easiest."

"Oh, super! How'd you do it?"

"I figured you'd be there tonight. Can you stay over?" he asked.

"Only if you beg me and have the sleeper with green lights!" she giggled.

"Perfect!" he agreed.

Red ran back to the rig feeling like she was on thin air. "He's meeting me in Richmond!"

"I knew it! Mama, you better be good to him!" Runner advised. "We don't want you to let happiness pass you by! It could! It's just that you've never been this happy as long as I've known you. When Early calls, you come alive! But, you just have to stay my fishing buddy!"

They talked until the fuel hoses snapped and each hung one up. Red saw her son-in-law drive out of sight. He was always helping and on her side. She remembered the many times he and Kikki Dee rescued her from the beast of a person that made her life a disaster for such a long time. It had been very hard on them, too. At that time, Red felt her only move was to do as Devil said for everybodys' safety and best interest. She thought that the misery was a small price, better than death. In her mind, she knew that with his out of control moments, one could easily get killed even if it were truly an accident. He was controlled most of the time when she carefully stayed. But, she finally set her mind to get away from him forever. The kids were her support; her reason to go on! It was hard to have such business responsibility and be hiding, too. Finally, time let it all ease up and drift somewhat to the wayside.

Red paid her fuel bill and rolled the stick wagon toward the interstate, trying to get ahead of the work traffic. A red Chrysler, with the top down, shot in front of her rig. She braked gently. As the car swung in and out of traffic it finally made one line of traffic come skidding and sliding to a stand-still as the horns began to blow.

From the high cabover, Red observed the little car as it crashed into the right backside of a long fifty-three foot trailer that was stopping because of being in the turning lane. The front end of the car bashed halfway out of view and the driver could not be seen.

Red grabbed the CB. "Hey, big truck. USA, come on!"

"Yeah, come on!" answered the driver.

"You the USA in the turning lane?" she asked. "A car just shot part way under your trailer!" she informed.

"Oh, damn! Thanks driver!" he nervously answered.

"Stay calm. Just park your truck where it is. I can pull right in front of you. It'll be all right. Wait for me!" said Red. She realized it would be best to stop just halfway beside him and block traffic for the accident. The other two lanes could handle the traffic. Quickly, she got into place as she phoned 911 to report the scene. As her brakes snapped on, the driver walked toward her. She rushed out of her truck carrying her fire extinguisher and handed it to the USA driver.

"Here, let me get my emergency markers. Check that car under you!"

Traffic was trying to move and look. As they moved past the scene you could see all the necks snapping around trying to nose into the event. Red slowed the traffic as she set the first triangle to the back of her trailer, then the next and the next. She was now committed to the scene and offically in charge. Another car was beside her truck so she asked the young man to take a red towel she had and motion traffic until help arrived. Immediately, the man had the traffic moving on and others tied behind them were freed to move.

The fire truck, blasting its loud horns and flashing its tremendous display of lights, rolled in beside the car from the emergency parking lane; then, the rest of the emergency crews lit the area and jumpd into action. The paramedics wedged their way to recover the driver of the car. Suddenly, a loud explosion piped through the air. People fell to the ground, covering their heads with their hands. Firemen scrambled with equipment and the blaze quieted into a vast balloon of smoke, bellowing throughout the area. It was hard to see but as the firemen controlled the situation, the smoke changed through a number of colors as it finally reduced itself to very little.

The fire chief took over at the scene and the

driver handed him his load papers, explaining each portion of the haul. His placards were fully visible with a danger sign that jumped to you.

Once everything was in order, Red High Heels was told to go on. As she started her truck to go on toward Richmond, she saw in her rearview mirror the driver of the red car with the sheet fully covering him being placed in the ambulance. Red was saddened with the thoughts of so many little vehicle drivers loosing their lives just trying to win a few seconds.

As she hit tenth gear, the road stretched before her and traffic soon settled down to a normal pace. She couldn't help but to think of how fragile it all is. One split second and anything can happen.

A huge Peterbuilt stormed the highway trying to pass her just before a narrow bridge. His rig eased right onto the middle line and just inches off the old furniture hauler.

"Hey, Red. Where you goin'?" laughed a voice.

"Ain't you awfully close?" groaned the woman as her side mirror made a snap and the glass shattered. "Hey! You've hit my mirrors!" Quickly, she slowed more to let him get off her side and away from her.

"Thought you could drive that thing!" he laughed. "You skeered or something?"

Red didn't answer. She was totally angry. He kept laughing and yelling and trying to make her react. She reached up and flipped the CB to 'off,' continuing to drive on. With the mirror shattered, she would have to get another replacement as soon as possible.

31

The area radio station stopped the music with an update on the accident. Red felt miserable hearing the information of the outcome. The announcer had said, "The twenty-eight year old driver had died instantly when he collided into the rear of a tractor trailer, relatives would be notified before realeasing the name."

Red High Heels saw a big, orange sign and decided coffee would fill the bill. It was a quick stop to break the somber spell. She ordered the coffee to go. Receiving it, she started toward the door.

A man yelled, "Hey, Red High Heels!"

Turning and looking, she didn't recognize the man. He stood real tall and big. His beard was rough, still he looked like a wrestler. With him were two skinny, young fellows grinning through bad teeth.

Everyone in the little truck stop road house watched. Red was the only woman and alone.

She said, "Do I know you?"

"Yeah! Scarface! Remember?" he tettered.

"I guess so!" she whispered.

"You wuz my buddy's girl. Me 'n Devil done time together. I heard you done him wrong!" he growled, showing a pipe in his hand.

"That was a long time ago!" she pleaded, looking around.

A man jumped up; he was about five feet eight. Scarface looked down at him and laughed, "You think you gonna be her hero, Mr. Prick?"

"No, but let the woman alone. She ain't done nothing!" he urged. "She is just trying to make a living."

"Fuck her! She's another bitch taking our jobs!" he grunted.

"Look. I drive my own truck. It doesn't take nobodies job. It's for my furniture store!" she quivered.

"Yeah?" he quizzed, walking closer to Red and reaching. "Yeah?"

At that moment, a sheriff walked in and directly to the big man. "You got a driver's license?"

"I reckon!" he sputtered as he spit on the floor.

"You didn't stop for the siren. I told you on the CB to pull over!" the sheriff argued from his well-matched, big built body.

"I didn't understand!" stammered Scarface.

"I gotta take you in; a list of charges!" he added.

"Shit! I ain't done nuttin'!" grinned Scar, annoyed.

"You're breaking parole being here with that beer! Then, you can't drive with that beer. Before this, I clocked you at ninety-five miles per hour in a fifty-five zone. There's more! We are going to check that trailer! Heard about your load!" the officer insisted.

"Hell, do it. You ain't gettin' by with this. Gimme a phone. I know my rights!" informed the man as the cop read him his rights.

Two more deputies arrived to assist Scarface out of the restaurant. Everyone was relieved.

"That was close,"said Mr. Prick. "Guess I'd have had to fight him somehow. You are Early Bird's lady, Red High Heels!"

"Yes. I'm trying to meet him in Richmond. Been trouble all the way and I'm not half way there," complained Red.

"Did you hear about that feller running under that trailer back toward Greensboro?" he asked.

"I saw it happen and stopped to help," she smiled.

"You're all right! Good you'd help! It's getting harder to be willing to stop any more!" added Mr. P. "People play games so much now days."

"We still should stop! Wasn't no trickery to this. It was a plain out wreck! That man must have been on something!" Red informed, then relayed the pitiful details while everyone listened. Then, she shared the story of her broken mirror.

"Just wait here," P said and raced out the door; then, returned with one of the cops to hear in 'mirror story'.

"Young lady, he could have made you lose it. These mountains ain't so big but not to be played with. Some of our ditches here drop off about a hundred feet off the side!"

They wrote a complaint; finally, Red downed the cold coffee and asked for a hot refill to go. Once again she was on the road, this time concentrating on seeing Early Bird.

From then until Richmond all was well. The exit for the Petro was just ahead. Her heart started pounding. She flipped the visor down and parked on the side of the off ranp, well out of the way. From her make-up kit beside the seat Red proceeded to carefully touch up.

The CB was cutting-up with all kinds of truckstop gab. Still, she heard the familiar, sexy voice call, "Red High Heels, you out there?" She waited to answer and listened again, "Come on! Red, are you out there?"

"You got it!" she excitedly spoke. "Go to twenty-five."

They flipped channels. "Baby, where are you?"

"On the ramp, coming in!"

"I'm fueling, Sugar. Park your truck to the side as you come in. There's a good spot on your left, unless you want to back into one!" he teased.

"Maybe I would like to back in, ass!" she laughed, "I see the one you're talking about, old handsome. By the way, your pants are unzipped!"

"I was just getting ready!" he laughed, looking down, checking. "No they're not!"

"April Fools!" she screamed with laughter.

"This isn't April!"

"Well, I didn't want to miss it!" Red humored and swept a big turn to ease the rig next to a moving van. Early watched and was excited to hear the air brakes sound off. Red shut her rig down for the night.

As he finished fueling, she pranced to his side, smiling her best. "Can I check your oil?""

"That's a thought!" he whispered as he pulled her deep into his arms. Their mouths met greedily and the hunger between them was apparent. Early braced her against the side of his Freightliner and felt her breast protruding against him and the heat from her mound against his leg.

"Oh, gosh woman! I forgot where I was for a moment! Come on! Let's pay up!"

They went to the fuel desk, holding hands. Several men stepped back for them to get ahead.

Early grinned, "I don't want to cut in line!"

"Looks like you'd better!" teased an old truckdriver. "If I had her beside me, I don't know if

I'd ever have gotten to the fuel desk! You people just hurry on through so you can get back to what you were doing!" It sure looked good!"

The couple blushed, clinging together with their hands. Red snuggled appropriately to Early's side and whispered, "I love you!"

"I love you!" Early Bird announced to all, flipping his credit card to the man across the counter. Early kept looking into Red's eyes. Sparks were dancing between them as they glued themselves side by side, waiting for the ticket. Once more, Red laid her head against him and put her lips on his muscular biceps, then tickled him secretly with her tongue. He felt a thrilling chill fly through his being. As he finished his transaction, he pitched the pen on the counter and reached down to Red. "I love you!"

He gently picked her up and started to exit the side door that lead to the fuel island. Someone had dropped a pool of oil in the middle of the walkway. The traction was no longer there. Early started to slide with her in 'baby bunting' position. There was no way around it. In seconds the two were near the ground.

"Oh, hell!" Early called out.

Red hung on laughing, "I love you! My Lord!"

Two men coming toward them saw their plight and tried to help. In short order, all four of them were laying in the walkway together and laughing.

A security guard came over and snarled, "Get up! Old men acting the fool! Truckdrivers! You all right, lady?"

"Nope! I'm just acting the fool, too! I'm a

truckdriver!" laughed Red.

"You can't be!" he said, astounded.

"What am I to do? Wear a wheel around my neck to say 'Truckdriver'?" gritted Red. "That's the way it is. Everybody thinks a truckdriver has to look a certain way! Not so! We come in all kinds of packages. The best ones are fools!"

The men chuckled together, feeling crazy, flat on their asses and mocking the guard.

One said, "Truckdrivers are fools!"

"Shit, yes! Pure, insane. That's why we can run all over the country with a handful of papers they call maps and security guards can't see oil in the walkway. I'd rather be a crazy fool than a stupid turd," he compared.

"Right on!" smiled Early and winked. The guard was looking the other way when he pulled the string to the man's shoe to untie the otherwise slick fit.

Red High Heels had stood in front of the man but caught the trick from Early. She quickly stood on the man's string. She kept his attention. "Never mind them. They are just beginners!"

"Yeah! We're beginners. Here!" Early pretended to hand him something and as the security man moved slightly, Red hit him in the ribs with her elbow, an intended 'accident.' The man grunted and tried to step back but with the help of the loose shoestring and somebody's foot, ended up on the walkway in the pile of people.

Then, men on the walkway crowed and onlookers stared in hilarious amazement. The most wonderful thing that could happen, happened! The security guard flipped to his ass, too!

"My, Barney, you might qualify to be a fool

truckdriver, now!" grinned one of the men.

"I ought to run everyone of you in! You knocked me down!" he growled.

"Who did? You fell on your ass!" giggled Red, trying to hold her composure. "How could they knock you down from the floor?"

"You did it!" he bitterly whispered. "Silly bitch!"

"Did you hear that?" grieved Red.

"The drivers jumped to their feet and together ranted as if rehearsed. "Hell, yes!"

They looked at each other laughing, slapping hands indicating the party was over. Each left to their own direction. Early and Red glanced back at the man crumpled still on his back on the slick walkway.

"He looked like a fool!" laughed Red.

Early found her hand and nodded, "Get in that big Freightliner, Little Girl."

He opened the door to the driver's side. Red slid into the seat and quickly put it into gear with him on the running board. He silently held tight to the rails and shook his head. She rolled the truck about twenty feet then stopped, set the tractor brake and slipped into the other seat.

"That, lady, is going to cost you!" Early teased.

"Good! Shall I do it again?" she laughed then moved to her knees on the floor and found the warmth of his body near her. She watched him trying to guide his rig into a parking spot. She stood and slipped her head behind his neck and started blowing her breath hot and seductively. Then, she took her hands and started feeling his tight muscles begin to relax as she gently massaged his big shoulders. "You smell so good! Mm-mmm, you taste so good!"

"Oh, girl, let me park this beast! I can't do both!" Early suddenly stopped half way into the parking spot. "See, I can't back in like this!"

"All right! I'll go to my seat!" smiled Red, wiggling her lips and blowing a kiss his way.

He snapped the brakes on quickly and slipped toward her. "Oh, baby, I love you so much! I want you to be happy all the time!"

"Park this thing! Please! I might go on without you!" Red laughed again. "You do make me happy!"

Again, he rolled the huge truck and fifty-three foot trailer forward then jacked it into the spot with ease. He checked everything and finished his logbook. "Only takes a few minutes for this. I can't let myself forget. Did you do yours?"

"I will now," she replied, reaching into her purse to find it.

They finished business, put things in order and Early stared at her happily. "I do have a surprise for you! Close your eyes tight; I have to lead you to it!"

He opened the drapes to the sleeper and escorted Red High Heels to sit on the edge of the bed. He then told her to look. When she did, she squealed, "Early, you little heathern! I love it!"

The whole sleeper bedroom was in green. He had green lights that cast a strange spell over the whole room. The sheets were green. The covers were green. He had green stars hanging from the ceiling. A unique sight. He reached into his closet and handed her a square, green wrapped box.

"The final touch to the suite!"

"Oh, Early. You are so great! How did you do all this?" she questioned as she flipped the wrapper to bare the white box. The top slipped to the floor and Red could see a filmy, green thing. She picked it up and cuddled it to herself with adoration. He handed her another box from the top bunk. She opened it to find a pair of six inch, green high heels. Her mouth dropped. "How did you do all this? It's so grand, so wild, so you! My sweetness!"

"Luck I guess. You said green lights! You got 'em, Baby. Now, you have to stay the night with me!" he reminded her.

"Of course! Might stay a week!"

"I could handle that!" he bargained.

"Well, I got my dog with me! It's her last trip. She has to retire. Poor Zipper! She's getting so old. I'm afraid I'm going to hurt her putting her in and out of that high cabover," explained Red.

"She's been good for you! Kikki Dee will take her, I'm sure," he consoled.

"Yes. She'll be happy there. Actually, Zipper is really her dog. She just started running with me by accident, then she was such good company!"

"Now you have me!" he looked at her longingly.

"Can I model this for you?"

"Please! Do be my guest! Let me put on the music!" he coaxed, adjusting the tape he had ready.

Trying to stay out of his view, Red slipped into the elegant Victoria Secret outfit. It was precious and had a do-dad to clip into her hair. She pushed her long, red hair up and back to one side with it, as he finished closing the outer drapes. One look and he was on his knees before her, and again with another beautiful ring.

"Red, this is for luck. It's emerald. May it give you the strength to do what you have to do and become my wife. I love you so much!"

He slipped the ring on the pinky finger next to the engagement ring. As she smiled accepting it, he turned her face gently to his and found her lips with his.

Quickly, their tongues met and they were experiencing the deep flow of passion that constantly overwhelmed them. He wanted to be careful not to rush her or do anything that would make her backtrack and take her mind to the old miserable past.

Red was happy with Early Bird, the only man who had ever truly loved her. He felt wonderful and would walk the water for her if he could. She pulled him as close as possible and slid into the bed forcing him gently with her.

"I love you, Early!"

"I love you, too, Red," he moaned as she started to undress him. He joined in to help so as to not be far behind in the nudity stage.

"Everything! Even your socks!" she teased. "Off with it all!"

He smiled and flipped his toes into the sock tops and they were off. Red kept telling him her love as she gently massaged him. She found the herbal oil in the drawer and rubbed every inch of his body. He let her have her way, to do as she pleased. Once the hand massage was complete, Red gave him a 'bosom' rub and slipped all over him with her firm breasts. In a sensous, easy manner, she built his desire to near peak. Then, she breathed her hot breath and kissed him gently over his hot body. He was about to go crazy.

He groaned with sheer joy and ecstasy. "Oh, Baby, Baby, Baby!"

Red slid beside him with great desire and coaxed him to gently roll on top of her trim figure. "Oh, Early! My love! Forever! I'll love you forever! Oh, God! Baby! You are so special!"

Early checked his speed, holding her tight, kissing her now with pure passion and pleasure. Red returned the same. They locked every door to their hearts together and closed out all else. Their love was perfect and as they gently held to each other, the final surge of pleasure filled them as they passed out with the overwhelming heat of desire. They could feel the marvelous explosion of their joy rush through their beings and their lips clung together muttering their love. Never had loving been so grand, even with each other; this time, was a lifetime magnetic overture. The birds could sing, the rivers could roll, the sun could come and go; this was a perfect moment. Red finally smiled and relaxed. Early slid beside her, still holding on.

"You are incredible! Never before have I loved like this. I thought I loved you but I love you even more!" he gloated.

"You don't know anything about love. I love you! I feel you! I can taste you! Oh, Early, it's perfect; you are everything!" she whispered. "Everything, I've ever wanted!"

"I know, darling. We can't ever loose this! Please, love me forever! Whatever it takes, I want us for always!" he panted.

"Me, too! It's right here. No restrictions. Nothing binding. It's just you and me. Me and you!"

passioned Red.

They fell into a deep sleep, locked in each others arms.

During the night Red got up, put on her clothes then walked her dog into the truck stop for the bathroom and two coffees. When she returned to the truck, Early was gone. It frightened her somewhat. Then, she heard a familiar noise outside and he mounted the steps.

"I walked Zipper and got coffee. Really had to 'tinkle'. I'm all right!" she insisted.

"From now on, late like this, I need to go with you!"

She thought for a minute. "Well, I guess so!"

He produced his two cups of coffee, too. They laughed and he galantly smiled, "It'll save getting too many coffees!"

"I know!" she gave in. "I'm just used to doing things alone!"

"When I'm with you, do what you want but just tell me or leave a note. There's no point in you doing anything alone. Can it be 'we' and 'us'? I'm here for you, Baby. Everything," he urged.

"Well, I'll try. Just remember I've got lots of years of habit!" Red High Heels uttered. She reached to him and slipped into his lap. "You're right. This is better!"

Again, their lips met and they gently rekindled the fire. He took her shirt off and melted into her passion. As he fondled her pert breasts, he could feel the rapid beat of her heart. Her skin was so soft and her nipples protruded erectly with the touch of his tongue. This discovery was new and wonderful. As many times as they had been together before, he

had never had a chance to fondle her breasts and see
the response to the touch of his tongue.   As she
exhibited pleasure, he continued looking and touching
to examine her full beauty and depth of desire.
Usually, Red wanted to give the pleasure of touch to
him.   Then, she started fondling his hair and barely
touching his ears and eyebrows as she watchd him
through nearly closed eyes.

"Early! Darling!" she moaned. "I want you
so much!"

He stretched her across the bed and slipped
on top of her. Gently, he found her and they moved
slowly   and   deliberately   in   unison,   constantly
whispering their love and both holding back of the
sheer pleasure of the moment.

"Right now!" she cried.   "Oh, yes! Early
Bird! Yes!"

"Now, Baby! Now!" he moaned as he lost all
control. "Oh, Red, I love you!"

"I love you!" she whispered and with all the
depth of passion she snuggled safely to him.

Time again passed. A strange noise in the
truck disturbed them. They found they were totally
nude and still wrapped together. Red rolled him on
his back and slipped a breath mint in both their
mouths. Again, she started to fondle him and quickly
was engaged into another intent escapade. This time
she took the aggressive role, on top. As she felt his
pleasure deep within her, she forced him to give it up
quickly.

They laughed together, "That's what you call
a sixty-second man!"

"Still good! she bragged. "I thought it was
supposed to be quick at first and last longer later!"

"Is that a complaint?"

"No! It's perfect! This you cannot do wrong!" she assured him. "This is your calling, loving me!"

"I always dreamed it could be like this!" he exposed.

"Hold me, honey!" she pleaded.

He took her into his arms and cuddled her close. He wanted her to feel safe, loved and happy. She seemed completely at ease, like the old world had fallen away and now theirs was beginning for real.

The sky above, through the skylight, was lit with all the stars. There was a flicker of distant lightening occassionally, and the wind shook the truck gently.

"Did you feel that?"

"What?"

"The cab moving? See what you do! You love up a storm!" he picked and wrapped his arms around her, snuggling close to her back. "You feel good, honey! This is everything!"

"Shouldn't you sleep? You have a delivery tomorrow, don't you?" Red quietly asked.

"No, this trailer just goes to a yard. I can take a load whenever I ask for it. I really wanted time with you. Maybe I can get a load near you!" he added.

"That would be great!' she grunted. "Let's get some sleep!"

Night, love!" he whispered, but his big hand found her breast again. At first he just touched them but somehow the hand began to fondle. Once more, he was aroused and before they realized what was happening they turned to each other and Red wrapped her legs invitingly around him. Again, their lips met.

In a flash they were on their way to the sweet land of utopia. They clung to each other, telling of their love and pleasure. And, again, they both reached the ultimate of pleasure and began to perspire.

"Oh, Early! You're killing me the best way I know of!" gasped Red, falling into slumber.

"You're the killer! I can't get enough of you! Baby, I love you!" he moaned and went into a deep sleep.

The night's storm passed through and when they awoke it was late in the morning.

"Good morning!" gleed Red, jumping on top of Early.

"Morning, Baby. I love you!"

With a breath mint, Red soaked her tongue then slipped it into Early Bird's mouth! His lips invited her into a passionate trap and very quickly they were making love once more. They touched, moaned, groaned and cooed as they reached a slow and beautiful plateau together. They could feel each others love flow, with the added heat of their love, come to a finale. Trembling and weak the two exhausted themselves to just a smile.

"I have some orange juice in the refrigrator," offered Early. "We need something to be able to get enough strength to get up."

He handed her one and took another for himself. She was suddenly quiet and strange acting. It scared him.

"Baby, are you all right?"

The tears started flowing from her eyes. He put his arms around her and patted her, trying to soothe her carefully. She was so wonderful but complicated!

"Oh, Early, it's so great! I love you so much! Please don't ever let me go!" she cried. "I don't think I could live without you now. You make me so happy!"

"Perfect! You do the same for me! Just tell me when!" he smiled and tipped her face to his. "Baby, when you are ready, I'll buy you any truck you want and we can run team!"

"Team!" she whispered. "But, I want home-roots, too!"

"Honey, you can have home-roots. Just name the town! I'll be there!" Early Bird consoled. "Early is yours!"

She hugged him tightly and laughed, "We're naked! Suppose the D. O. T. comes?"

"I'm sure they'd give us a one hundred per cent on our last twenty hours. Ready for breakfast?" he asked.

"We need to take care of Zipper and feed her," planned Red as she slipped into her button-up front suede dress, nylons and heels. She flipped her hair around, sprayed and did eyeliner and cheeks.

"That's what I love about you; a few minutes and you are ready to go!" he bragged.

"Humph! I'd better get out of here while I can!"

"Oh, really! Maybe Daddy had better get him some more of his delicious sugar!" teased Early, flattening her onto the bed again. Realizing she might be willing, he grabbed her hand and snatched her up. "Come on! We have to eat first!"

"First?"

CHAPTER 3

The three days in Richmond with Early Bird had slowed Red's business slightly but she didn't care. This time she would put it together and find a way to close out. She knew it would be a real challenge, but running team with Early Bird would be perfect. They loved each other and it could be a real advantage for her to go with him. The lonly road could evolve into an exciting daily journey. She could look after him and do the house and paper work that he disliked doing.

Red pondered to herself. What if, after a few weeks, the two of them might not like the day-to-day forever together. She had never been tied that tightly to anyone.

In regular home life, both parties go their own way by day and catch each other at night.

Truckers are gone in most families for weeks then pop in for a few days. Red had met many trucker-wives who would say that if her husband got off the road they'd end up in divorce. Most of them meant it. Their way of life was not ideal to Red High Heel's by any stretch of the mind.

Red had little experience with long term relationships. Men in her life in the past were usually business and professional people. Nothing to rave about, nothing to think about. Nice but no rockets spiking off in the sleeper. In fact, dating here and there had become such useless attempts at whatever. It seemed men only wanted a roll in the hay at their call. Being an independent woman, Red would tell them, "I can afford to pay my way. I don't prostitute for a meal! Your company sucks!"

Time after time, to appease friends, she'd go out. It was always the same and she'd get in her car and leave. Once she went out a bathroom window to get away. They were classified as jerks. Red thought it hilarious that so many men actually believed one night was a for certain sack-night. She didn't ever need sex. She needed love. Early Bird proved to be such a true love; a friend, comforter, listener, partner and lover. He was everything to her that no other man had ever been.

Driving along the turnpike inspired Red. She began to change up her plans and think about all the other states, even Canada and Mexico. Driving team would put her everywhere.

She picked up the CB. "Early, I love you!"

"I love you, Red. Take this next exit. I need to talk to you," he urged.

"You've got it!" she replied.

The two trucks stopped side by side at exit eight on the turnpike. The drivers met in front of the rigs and kissing each other excitedly..

She smiled, "We'd better walk Zipper!"

"I know," agreed Bird. "Let me get her!"

The dog happily allowed him to take her from the seat. She stared at Red High Heels with an embarrassed look, as if saying, 'Get this damn diaper off my ass! What will other dogs think?'

Red snatched the diaper and threw it into the garbage. Zipper walked to a row of trees and picked up a back foot to do her thing. Then, shuffled the grass behind her. After running around and rolling in the grass, she finally laid down by the front tire of Red's truck.

"She's finished and wants back in the truck!" said the woman.

"That's amazing! Great dog!" boasted Bird, returning Zipper to her place in the truck.

"You can put a towel or coat down; she'll stay on it until told otherwise. She's almost seventeen years old now!"

"That's old!" he grunted. "Oldest dog I ever had was seven. We'd either get rid of them, they'd disappear or get killed somehow."

"This one trains all the dogs in the family. She was trained by a big Siberian Huskey who carried her in his mouth when she was a puppy. This old dog has nearly grown up with Kikki Dee and given us everything. I know she can't live forever!"

"Letting her be a pillow-pet now is the best for her!" sympathized Early.

"We keep trying to get the old granny-girl to take it easy but she jumped on a big dog four times her

51

size the other day!" noted Red, snapping the lid from a packet of Pedigree. "This is her trip food! Expensive, too!"

Early emptied the contents into a little bowl and Red threw in a half chopped up Hershey bar. The man shook his head and laughed, "It's good we're not having children!"

"I know. I'm wierd, but you love it!"

"Of course!" he agreed. "Let's have breakfast. It's getting late already. You know I leave you the next exit or so. I just want to look at how beautiful you are. Unless, you want to go with me now!"

"Can't, honey! I've too much to do as it is!" she looked away, feeling sad, wishing she could stay with him forever. Tears filled her eyes and he could see them drop to the sidewalk.

"Come here, Baby!" he nurtured. He took her into his arms and comforted her without words. In his mind he was sending her the mortal message to hurry out of her present statis and become one with him. As he clung to her, he too felt as if the tears would fall. "I love you!"

After breakfast and talk, they had to move on. As usual it was a painstaking effort to let go; both quietly promising they would not be long apart.

Early Bird took his truck to the road ahead of Red. They found their voices on their channel and ultimately said their last heartbreaking farewell.

Early Bird found the road, leading away from Red High Heels, going on into the edge of New Jersey for a switch-out of trailers. After that, it was anybody's guess. He wanted Boston but would most likely end up in Chicago; then, wherever. Once more, he tried to call Red on the CB but he couldn't hear a response so he forced himself to focus on the work ahead. He'd call Red at his next stop.

Red heard his last CB message. His unit was strong 'send out' but her response was not heard. She said, "Well, Zipper, Daddy's gone now. He'll call later. We've got to get these next three hours behind us."

Things went like clock work. The store was open and Puss was her usual happy self with everything in order. She waved as she saw the truck swing in. Red backed to the door and rushed to her.

"Let's start sending the orders!" Red suggested, hugging her friend-employee. They rounded up the delivery people and got deep into it. As the day moved on, a third of the truckload was scattered into houses around the Island and the bank-roll became thick.

"What are we going to do with this?" asked Tiger Puss, showing the hefty money bag to Red. "We probably have delivered fifteen thousand today and I already had eighteen thousand and change."

"Put it in a bank-bag and deposit it. Do the checks separate. We'll U. P. S. the cashier checks and certifieds to the manufacturer." Reaching into the drawer, she ran her finger over the edges. "The people at home need their share!"

"I did a lot of credit cards too that went to your bank. It's probably about fifteen thousand, all in all!" noted Puss.

"Keep quiet about it," urged Red. "After all, that's not profit!"

"It's still great!" Tiger bragged. "I'm the best!"

"Of course you are!"

"Actually, we're the best team in this business!" added Tiger.

"Sit down. No, stand up!" giggled Red. "Let's finish and go eat!"

They assembled everything in order and left. Red was trying to pick the right moment to tell Puss her plans of closing the store.

"Wonderful new ring!" spoke Tiger. "He's nice to you!"

"We need more time together!" Red started.

"I can handle this. All you have to do is bring the furniture!" she mused.

"He wants me with him all the time!" informed Red.

"Let him help you!" Puss passed the buck.

"That's not what we want. We want to run team all the time!" stirred Red. "I love Early Bird!"

"Maybe, but what about Devil? Did you forget his promise? He'll not let you go! He might get crazy!" reminded Puss.

"Screw him and his horse! I can't live my life around his hell! That's history! He's moved on!" cried Red.

"You hope!" she gloomed. "He's subject to…"

"Hell with that asshole! Whose going to tell him? You? Damn not living! I'm having Early Bird and as soon as possible!"

"I hate to disappoint you, but Devil has been circling this place and we've had a bunch of hang up calls," replied Puss.

"Well, it's been years since the ordeal! He'll leave me alone. This has nothing to do with him!"

stormed Red. "I can handle my life!"

"All right! Just so you know! Remember why you opened here?" she reminded. "To get away from Devil. Just think about it! If he finds out you have someone, I'm telling you, he'll go nuts!"

Red went about working and the days to follow were spent with the pit-of-the-stomach feeling. She was once more living in the old fear. Not only fear, but when would Devil surface?

She didn't have to wait long. The next week, he caught her on the phone.

"Don't hang up!"

"What do you want?" Red coldly asked.

"I owe you some money, remember? I want to work out payments," he sugar-coated the game.

"Forget it. I don't care about that!" she tried to dismiss him.

"I miss you. I love you!" he injected. "I'm sorry things were not as you wanted. I know you don't want me, but I just had to tell you. I was bad to you when I got drunk!"

"That's over! Let's just leave it buried!" said Red. "I have to go. Take care. Good-bye!"

Red was alone in the efficiency apartment she had set aside from the rest of the furniture store. Even so, her room and the kitchen were still a part of the total facility. This was a second store quite a distance from the main, long-established business. Often, Red would open a 'six-months-sale-place' to move extra merchandise and aquaint new faces to her operation. Even with all the trouble in her past with this out-of-control fool, she still served her customers well and they liked her.

Long ago, the constant fits and comtemptious

rage expelled on Red from Devil seemed to have run its course. He had been her man. Just after Red's miserable divorce, Devil devoted attention, fun and laughter. He seemed brilliant and was packaged into a trim, handsome physique. As with all relationships, people look, act and dress well. Cater to the friends and family trying to win approval. It didn't take long for this man to have the world eating from his palm. He was a true Jekyll and Hyde. One minute, he would be wonderful, the next, at the drop of a word, Devil could snap.

Over a very long time, he brutally harassed and beat Red to keep control of her. It was natural and easy for him; he was the perfect, experienced manipulator. Injecting fear into the basic tactics, he knew just how to work Red.

She remembered him badgering, 'You ever leave and it will be the last thing you do. If you put me back in prison, I'll get you! Ain't no difference in killing one or twenty. Fuck! They can't kill you but once! If I decide to snuff you out, I'll kill everybody I hate! I hate your kids, your sisters, mother and you! You think you have everything! I can do anything to all of you. Before it's over, nobody will ever have anything to do with you and I could enjoy seeing you in jail! That's it! You fancy people in jail!'

He would usually grab her by the neck and squeeze until Red would nearly loose her breath. On several occasions like that, Red would have blurred vision for days, severe headaches and not remember most normal things. When she'd recover, she would plot within herself about how to get away. Within the fear for flight was always the implied threats to her family; but, they were not just threats. They were real promises.

The abuse was not unlike what other women experience. The abuser finds the vunerable areas and that's where he hits. Red would run, but he'd force her back with denial, promises and threats. In the end, the conclusion would be the safest place for her was continuing the risk rather than the alternative of not knowing what he would do next.

One night Red had been to the limit and ran. In the process, he went on a public tangent and fought with the police. When he was arrested, he ended up with time in jail. Red got away and sought new resources in New York. This gave her time to rework her life and pushed him into going his own way.

Red made it a point to steer clear of Devil and he had to oblige or be in violation of parole. Police in the big city seemed different than those in a small community. They deal with so much crime that a criminal would be another number to them; not a person, not a face. He couldn't get to them with threats and lies; they knew his type.

The phone rang again. "Furniture!"

"I saw you at the diner. I started to come over!" said Devil and laughed into the phone. "I'll always be here!"

Red slammed the phone down and sat quietly. "He's back! Puss was right!"

She locked the doors carefully and went to bed but couldn't sleep. Much later, her helpers noisily returned from a delivery. She drifted off when she heard them on the stairs to their room.

That next day, orders were delivered and at the end of the day Red went to the main store. Puss and Chocolate had brought a nice late lunch and were laughing and planning.

Chocolate smiled, " What's wrong, Sister. Looks like you lost your best friend! Don't forget, we're here!"

"I know," strained Red through fear while turning away. Quickly she took a damp cloth and began wiping furniture.

"She's house cleaning! What's wrong?" demanded Puss. "It's big! Gigantic!"

"Nothing!"

"I know you! Yes there is!" insisted Chocolate.

"It's Devil!" injected Puss. "That's it! He's bugging her!"

"I'll be all right!" said Red. "I'm closing the stores soon! I have to get away!"

"Do what you have to do! I don't blame you. That man's a fool," soothed Chocolate. "When they're possessed like that, you just have to stay away from them. They'll kill you! You come home with me tonight. You know you're safe with us!"

The day went on. Late in the afternoon, Red looked up and to her amazement, she saw Devil in front of the store, getting out of his car. Her heart nearly stopped.

"Puss, look!" she pointed. "I'm gone! I'll be next door!"

Red fled from sight when the front door opened.

"Hello, Puss!" he smiled broadly, looking around.

"Hi!" she returned.

"She here?"

"No! She went…," her voice trailed off.

"Shut up!" he yelled. He proceeded to look through the store, then he sweetened his voice. "I have some money for her. Here, give it to her! Gimme a receipt! Eight hundred dollars! I told her I wanted to pay her back. Tell her that!"

The phone rang and Chocolate answered, "Furniture!"

"Chocolate?"

"Yes."

"It's Early Bird. Is Red in?" he asked.

"Yes, Miss Beasley. Your set will be delivered soon. They should arrive in about fifteen minutes. Call us when they get there," she replied, trying to give a message without saying.

"Something's wrong?" he asked.

"Yes! Call when they get there, please! I know you've waited a long time," she covered her tracks.

"Want me to call the police?" he asked.

"Certainly! That would be nice!" Chocolate smiled through her fear.

"Don't hang up! Keep talking! There's a phone next to me!" he determined.

Immediately, he dialed long distance to order the police and Chocolate went into the colors of the furniture as she hung on. When Early returned to her line she said, "Yes, I appreciate your order. Red should be there on the delivery, too. I need her to call in. A friend of her's wants to talk to her."

"Really?" Bird asked as he put two and two together. "Are you all right now? It's that fucking Devil?"

"Yes!" she smiled. "I need to go."

"I'll call later!" Early insisted. "Take care of

her for me!"

Chocolate cradled the phone as the police sirens screamed into the quiet. Then, the four cars roared into the parking lot. Police jumped out and began looking around.

"What's happening?" Big Mace demanded, his badge glistened in the sunlight.

"You crazy?" asked Devil with a grin. "I just wanted to buy something here! I owed some money. See! My receipt!"

"All right! All right! Move on!" Mace ordered.

"I'm leaving. I ain't done nothing wrong!" he smirked. He hit his fist on the show-case, smashing the glass. The blood dripped from a small cut and dropped to the floor. "Look at that! Tell Red I'll see her! You understand. I will see her!"

The police let him go and turned to the two women. They tried to explain the situation

"Where's her court order?" asked Big Mace. "We can arrest him!"

"That won't be necessary! He'll leave me alone!" Red tried to pass it off as she emerged out of a huge oak wardrobe.

"Red, are you all right?" Mace quizzed.

"I guess so. Like thay say in the south, You can't arrest somebody for thinking!" she sighed.

"You have a court order. He's to stay away!" the police officer quibbled. "You cannot give an inch! I'm talking to him! He has to understand this is a fact. With criminals, you just simply cannot let them get by with anything."

"He'll never leave me alone!" urged Red. "He just wanted to let me know that he can come if he pleases!"

"That's it…if he pleases!" raved the cop. "I'm talking to him." He bolted out of the door to confront Devil.

As he walked up to a police car, the policeman angrily insisted that Devil spread his feet and lean on the car. Devil had slipped into his 'nice-man' facade for the moment and cooperated.

"Let me talk to him," delivered Big Mace. The man let loose and walked away. "You know that you can be arrested for calling, coming around, or generally being near Red High Heels!"

"I ain't done nothing! Just paying her back some money she's bugged me for!" muttered Devil, looking down.

"Stay away from her and her property! Do you understand?" insisted Mace.

"Well, fuck you! Motherfucking cop! You been over here fucking her! I know! I've watched you!" ranted Devil with his face turning red.

"That's not so! I've never had anything to do with her!" Mace succumbed to his accusations.

Devil had put him on the defense and was thrilled with finding his weak spot. "You son-of-a-bitch! I'll go tell your Captain, your precinct and the whole world!"

"I've never been involved with Red!" denied the cop truthfully. "I just know her from the job!"

"The job! It's your fucking job to come 'check' on her every few hours? I see you drive by!" Devil gleed with his victory and started for his vehicle. The cop let him go.

Red had followed Big Mace and heard the story. Tears gathered in her eyes as she stood in the big parking lot watching everyone leave. Devil won again! Once more, Red realized the cops couldn't be counted on; not in a big city either. She was out on a limb again. Was the only way out to kill or be killed? Funny world!

"Red!" Chocolate called out. "Telephone!"

It was Early Bird, concerned and nearly crazy. "Baby, is everything all right?"

Red relived the emotional combat to him.

"Honey, be careful! Call the S. B. I. again! You have them!" Early urged. "I'm in Texas now but I'll come if you need me! I'd like to kick his ass! The cop, too! You've been through enough! Get rid of that business and come with me!"

"I'm working on it!" she whispered.

CHAPTER 4

It had been a long wait getting into the yard to pick up the loaded trailer. The winding road that led into the tile plant was difficult to maneuver with a fifty-three foot trailer. You always had to drop one trailer and pick up a loaded one. Early Bird had hauled many loads from this tile plant and it was always the same; delays and more delays.

Knowing this, Early planned a strategy to keep from going crazy. He would bring his next meal, check in to wait and spend his time catching up on his paper work.

Eventually, he heard his call on the CB. Grabbing his paper work, he rushed into the office to sort out the details. He thought about Red and was looking forward to calling her as soon as he returned to the real world. This place seemed to be a world of

63

its own.

The dispatcher motioned to Early Bird, without words. They put the plan into motion giving him assignment of a certain trailer. His company hauled many loads from there daily. The trailers were heavy with tile; a driver always weighed his load before leaving the yard.

Picking up the papers, Early went to his bobtail to locate the load. At the far end of the rows of loaded trailers, he found a new one with the corresponding number on his paper work.

Automatically, he backed under his trailer, hooked up and drove to the scale. He waited in the truck for the numbers.

"Shit!" he groaned. "Overweight again!"

He slammed the door of his truck and stormed back to the dispatcher. The man smiled, lifting a brow, "What's the problem?"

"Overweight! Damn, it's too much trouble to haul like this, a few pounds but 4,000 out of this hole?" Early Bird complained, "I just don't like it! The D.O.T can smell a tile load, I believe!"

"Augh! Go on! You'll be all right!" urged the dispatcher.

"Let me call my company!" Early retorted as they punched in the call to his own administrative dispatcher. "They have it 4,000 pounds over! This is Early Bird!" he grunted.

"Take it on! We'll be responsible if there's a problem. I need the load!" he soothed.

"All right! I still don't like it!" Early went on. "Why do you let this keep happening? One day, the D.O.T is going to fine you real big!"

"We need that load now! Just come on!"

insisted the man and hung up.

"Fools! Damn fools!" moaned Early as he stepped up to his big Freightliner. Again, he popped off the brakes and eased toward the tiny building at the side of the gate. Flashing his papers, the guard motioned him on. Once he got to the main road from the out-of-way tile distributor, Early started the long, heavy pull up the long hill. The new Freightliner jumped into a low gear and didn't hesitate. Once to the top, it would be a similar grade to go down on the other side. After this, the posted signs looked like snakes identifying the curved road.

Early was alert and assisted his wonderful rig to nearly float through the over rated path. He found the radio along the Mexican border to be filled with static. He pushed a cassette in that played odds and ends that Red had put together for him. It was a bit comforting.

The big truck rolled on with ease until Early came up behind a slow car. He had to brake quickly. He felt something happen. He heard a thump.

"Oh, no!" Early screamed. "Oh, no!"

In his side mirror, he could see the trailer leaning to one side and the wheels were a few feet off the ground. As he maneuvered the rig carefully, somehow he managed to get the trailer back on the ground. He grabbed the strap for the horn and the lady in the four wheeler pulled off the road to let him by.

The big Freightliner rolled on but there was no place to stop; no safe way to get off the road. He slowed a bit, trying to keep going until he found a pull off.

Each time he'd find a curve, he'd try to shift

the weight in the trailer to even the load. Throughout the hectic forty miles, each curve became more and more dangerous with the shifting and sliding of the load. Suddenly, he felt a big thud and heard a crash in the trailer; the blood rushed to his head as he once more saw his trailer lift off the ground and start to turn over.

"Please! Truck! Come on! Help me!" he cried out. He shifted the gears and swung the rig to pull the trailer out of the bind. He felt perspiration running down his face in the effort to save the load. It happened! He managed to stop the truck across an intersection. Although it was partically in a ditch, he had finally stopped upright. He sat trembling, feeling numb and crazy.

"Oh! Thank God!" he breathed. Locking down the brakes, Early went to the trailer. He had to break the seal and opened the door. Then he understood what had happened. When they loaded the trailer, the loaders placed the pallets of tile in the middle of the trailer. They assumed the weight would hold them in place. Nothing had been tied down.

"Shit! This is nuts!" he groaned at the scrambled, heavy load. He couldn't move anything now. He'd have to call in. Somehow, it was almost as if this load was doomed.

With his satelite communication system, he punched in his request for help. He poured himself a Coke and waited until the system beeped and pushed out his message.

Finally, he was told help was on the way. With this notification, he added to his request for additional help of a forklift and several men.

The tow-truck came, but they were paralized

totally. The load had to be mostly removed to recover the truck. At that point, Early realized what a spot he was in. Soon after, a half dozen Mexicans appeared to hand load the project.

The big tow-truck called for additional trucks. They had to hook lines of support to the major areas of the trailer to keep it from flipping over during the removal of the load. This was not very safe for anybody. It was possible the total combination could turn over at any point.

To complex matters even more, the gigantic shining rig was quite close to the edge. It was certainly a case of one false move and it could be over. The highway department sent help to secure the traffic out of range of the incident. The crews solemnly set to the slow tedious task until the big Freightliner and the trailer were able to find a safer location to reload the tiles.

Early Bird felt grateful that he and his new truck, along with a big load of Mexican tile, didn't hurle over the massive cliff. All this created by people short-cutting their job. Now, he had to deal with the D.O.T and no telling who else. He stood by, picking his one tooth that always seemed to give him trouble at times like this. People had come from the "woodwork", it seemed, to make a crowd, all talking and surmizing the situation. Bottom line for Early, he was all right now.

"Gimme your license, health card, log; you know, all of it!" the uniformed cop demanded.

Early Bird thought he could have mentioned it was a nice day or was he all right or how lucky he was. Not at all, he was all business, as if jail time might be a solution. He handed the officer everything needed and waited. "I believe I have it all for you."

"You stay right here and I'll be back when I verify this!" he insisted. "I mean, until I tell you differently, stay right here!"

Early knew to keep his mouth shut with this one. He must have gotten out on the wrong side of his bed, was Early's conclusion. He shifted his feet and leaned against his huge, perfect fender. Early watched a beat up old Ford pick-up sway to the side of the road and a very thin and small black haired man jumped out as if a Jack-in-the-Box. The fellow ran frantically to a nearby Ranger, nervously talking. He was squeeling and waving his arms.

"Senior, ze beeg truck...et push me from da road! I bleed...see? Dee beeg monster...Et vent, *whoosh* and den *bang*! Et keel me! See...et *whoosh*, like dees!"

The officer looked at the man and walked to his truck with him. The old truck had been in many incidents. Early Bird could not be absolutely positive with all the hell he had been through, he could have hit the fellow's truck. He started to look for signs along the road that distinguished the fact that he was in the state of Texas and not Mexico. He didn't remember the road to be out of the country. He knew for fact, in Mexico, he would be on the way to jail, just because he is an American. That is the way they do it; strictly for money.

The officer, who had his papers, walked over. "Mister, you just may be in some massive trouble! That fellow says you hit his truck! That would be hit and run, wreckless driving, no tellings what!"

"I don't think I hit him! I was trying to keep

my wheels on the ground. I was watching my mirrors. I never saw anybody in front of me!" Early defended himself. He wanted to go, and he wanted to do what was right. He was telling the truth.

"Think?" growled the big Texan. "You're supposed to know!"

"I didn't hit him!" asserted Early. He stood near the big cop. "Sir, I was doing everything I could to save the truck, the load and everything around me. I have never seen that man or his old truck!"

"I needed to ask. Let's look at your truck."

Early joined him as he looked over the big rig. Every now and then, the man would grunt and talk to himself under his breath. He didn't rush; he just ambled slowly and carefully. Suddenly, he stopped, "Look at this. What is this?"

Early dropped to the ground beside him to look. He felt like his rear end had been kicked up to the back of his throat. His ears started to ring and his head thumped. He could see a smear of yellow, about the middle of the handsome white trailer, but felt relief, "I guess that's the sign I mowed down. It probably saved me at one point! I remember when I hit that. I'll pay for it!"

The D.O.T. officer kept checking the rig for damage but couldn't find another point of trauma. Again, he walked around the truck to be certain; then, he scooted under, on a little set of wheels from his car. As hard as he tried, he could not find anything that put the rig on top or against the other truck. Ordering Early again to come with him, he snarled, "These little bastards! Always trying to get money! That's why I like to see them go on up into the states! Now watch this!"

"Et ess zee bad hoppen! Zee truck go, *whoosh*!" the young Mexican kept trying to finagle.

"Come, let's look at your truck," urged D.O.T., ushering the man to the truck. Early stayed back.

The fellow said, "Look, ez red paint! Zee truck ez red!"

The experienced older officer smiled, "Yes...Et ez red! Let me take a sample!"

He took his finger and touched the paint to find it wet, then showing how it stuck to his hand. "You little fiend! I ought to shoot you!"

The Mexican started to run, but Early Bird restrained him with one hand.

"He's all yours!" laughed the cop. "What do you want to do with him?"

"Maybe pinch his damn head off!" stormed Early.

"Go on and let the trooper have him! We can make him an example!" promised D.O.T. They cuffed the fellow and seated him in a patrol car. "Maybe we should have him load the trailer back by himself."

"I need to get going! Here comes the men that can get me loose! If we don't get it moving, I may be here another day," complained Early openly.

"The tile plant is sending inspectors here before you can load," informed D.O.T. "We have been after this tile plant for a long time. Now we have something that will put their dicks-in-the-mud! Bud, you're not the only man that has been through this. Last week, an old Peterbilt went over, right where you nudged that sign. That driver had his wife with him and they both died in the wreck. We couldn't prove how the truck was loaded. We suspect that the load shifted, just like yours!"

Early Bird realized then, the reason the cop was so stern was for good reason. Now he understood just how truly fortunate he was. He thought of Red and was happy she wasn't with him. She could have been driving. Red loved to drive in odd places. At that moment, he swore to himself to never let his beautiful woman ever drive in risky places. Still, it wasn't the place; it was the load not secure. As the truck moved, the load shifted and threw the trailer off balance.

His patience was wearing thin. Early went to the Freightliner and found his computer and sent a message. He took a quart of skim milk and down it while waiting for an answer. When the message came for him to call in, he picked up his cellphone.

The dispatcher, at JOY Carriers, was having a general fit. He was laying it on about the late delivery and many other things.

"Tell you what, Mr. Asshole, I can't get it off the ground! You think you can do it? Come get the shit! I'm tired of your crap! You get this load! I'm dropping this damn trailer here and I'm leaving this mess!" Early shouted in the receiver as both parties missed purposes.

"Early, you can't..."

"I can and I will!" Early hung up. "Ha! I'm done with this tile-hole anyhow! Screw him!"

He went to the police for his papers and clearance so his truck could leave. It took only a few minutes until Early Bird was on the back of his truck disconnecting the lights and air lines. He grinned to himself as he heard the screaming of the computer, begging him to respond.

"Keep squalling, prick! I'm gone!"

Early knew the tile company would return the JOY trailer to their lot at the plant. D.O.T. would see to that. In fact, the trailer needed to be checked out, since squatting the ditch and getting a couple holes ripped in the side from impact. All that would be on the almighty tile plant. He wondered if he had recourse anyhow.

"Son, please, let me talk to you!" the old man from the plant insisted as he appeared.

Early jumped off his bobtail and reached out a hand. "I'm Early Bird! I sure got into a mess!"

"I'm real sorry, Son...Real sorry! Listen to me, please!" he nearly had panic in his voice.

Early loved hearing him on his knees with remorse. He reluctantly offered, "All right. You know I could have been killed! Not to mention JOY is upset!"

"We'll pay for your time! I have another trailer ready at the plant. Please take it! We're going to loose this account if you don't. Look, I can give you a thousand dollar bonus if you can just let this go! Please, son, I have a lot of people depending on you. If we shut down, all these people won't have work. We have our problems but we don't mean for things to go wrong. You've been here before. You never had trouble then!"

"Well, that's right!" agreed Early. "My dispatch knows about this!"

"He ain't the one I'm scared of," whimpered the man. "It's the people that distribute!"

"Look, I don't want your folks in trouble. I'll take the load but I want to check it out! You'd better make all the drivers check this stuff out. I wouldn't have pulled out without it being secure had I looked. They shouldn't put the seal on it like that! After all, this isn't secret shit!" Early informed.

Down deep, Early Bird knew his dispatcher had fixed the deal. Somehow, he felt like a little boy getting his way. That was the greatest part of his arrangement with JOY Carriers; they would come through for you. Even though he knew he had acted a bit "assy", it brought his dispatcher's attention alive and alert.

As Early backed under the new load and hooked up, he remembered his order to be able to check this load. He smiled gently at the young Mexican helper. "Speak English?"

"Yes, sir!" he announded clearly.

"Cut the seal!" demanded Early.

"We can't! It's a law!" frowned the black haired fellow.

"Do it! I have to look!" Early stated.

The helper looked across the road and caught a nod from his boss. He quickly flipped a tool from his pocket and snapped plastic strap. Early helped him open the back doors and smiled.

"Perfect!" What a lovely load!"

Again, he signed a paper and climbed into the truck. He adjusted his log and sent the dispatcher a message. Early stepped out of the big Freightliner and walked around to check things better. His load couldn't move this time and the weight on his papers was realistic. After stepping behind a bush for a few moments, Early was ready to go.

Once more, he was motioned to leave and slipped the brakes off and started to ease on. He felt all right now and glad this trip would end well in spite of it all. He knew the road ahead and planned to drive to a better area to get some sleep. Actually, he was technically almost out of hours anyhow.

Three hours later, he arrived at a good truck stop. It was still Texas. Once he had a shower, he'd call Red High Heels. He was hungry, too. It didn't take long to feel like a different man. He found a table in the restaurant, picked up the phone and dialed Red's number in New York. To his amazement, she answered on the first ring.

"Hello, Sugar! That was fast!" Early delighted.

"Oh, Early! I'm so glad it's you! I've missed you so much!" she nearly cried.

"What's wrong?" he questioned, sensing her anxiety.

"Nothing, I just miss you! I'm scared I'm going to fool around and loose you!" she admitted.

"Never, Baby! Never!" he soothed. He told her about his escapade of the day and she filled him in on her data.

They ended the conversation with 'soon-plans' to see each other and lots of sensuous, private talk.

In the days to follow, Early Bird rolled many miles, dropping the tile trailer; then, picking up his next assignment, heading for Memphis. He was glad to get to headquarters for JOY. He wanted to pick up some papers for Red and check out insurance, too. The last Texas trip was one where they needed all details, since their trailer was damaged.

Early thought he would be heading for New York or North Carolina but he was sent back to Alabama. He hated to disappoint Red. It had been eight weeks since he had seen her. He tried to call her every day and Red understood. Her life was hectic, too!

Again, he picked up another load near the yard and smiled when his dispatcher sent him a message that he would take that load to its destination and he'd work him to Atlanta. This meant he'd head in the direction to see Red. He started to ask for time when his computer answered his request. "Put your truck in for service and time off."

He smiled happily as he directed the big red rig with JOY Carriers boldly displayed. The southbound sign jumped in front of him. Early eased left onto the big road with the fifty-three foot trailer following his command.

Traffic had been unusually heavy for a Thursday. Dispatch had changed his destination with the load to meet another truck and trade-out, then head back toward the mountains of Tennessee before Atlanta. He took it in his stride. Early had learned to accept the changes. It was part of trucking. Sometimes he referred to his "dispatcher" as the "old woman". Once he made the comment to the dispatcher himself and was slightly embarrassed. Yet, he grinned, "Well, you people in dispatch are like a woman, always changing your mind!"

The man had replied, "I guess that's right, not that we mean to change up. Somehow, it just happens. We don't even like to re-route but often we have to!"

Early always felt it was a sign of confidence in him; that JOY Carriers could select him to run a more complicated route. He knew trucking; it had always been his life. Now, he wanted to run team with

75

Red High Heels. Early knew JOY would gladly add her to their roster. They liked teams. Maybe it was too much to expect of Red.

Lots of women go with their husbands or boyfriends. Maybe not all the time but some of the time. Early could daydream about how alive it would all become. It was always perfect, the times Red went on trips; even when she followed in her rig. There was a deep longing for the companionship. The past with Red had kept him into the dream of forever; new places, ideas, and pleasures that he had never expected.

"Red," Early Bird said aloud, "Just trust me! Me and JOY can give you the whole world! Look at it!"

Early Bird watched the sky ahead of him. It was only black and white. The technicolor had faded with the day and as night started to take over, things seemed more solemn, yet bleak. He turned the heater thermost a little higher as he felt a slight chill go through him.

The clouds seemed to meet in the middle between the cut away trees that lined the edge of the road. The CB squawked and a voice squealed, "Hey, JOY. Carriers! You got your radio on?"

"Certainly. Come back, driver!"

"Yeah, big man, this is Pro-rate! Where you heading?"

"A few more exits, about time to shut her down for the night," answered Early.

"What you hauling? Cigarettes? Heard JOY got that big contract!"

"Not cigarettes. I think it might just be fertilizer. You know, shit!" answered Early, annoyed with the inquiry.

"Where did you say you plan to stop?" he irritated.

"I didn't say where! Why?" replied Early.

"I just thought we could stop together. It might be cold later. I ain't got any heat in this truck. I could bunk with you. That's a mighty nice rig!" he invited himself.

"I don't think so. Get you a motel! I drive for a living. I don't let people in my truck!" the tired man corrected. "You'll have to find somebody else!"

"I could make it worth your while, GOOD BUDDY!" the voice replied in a more feminine manner.

"What?" snapped Early Bird. "Did you say, *"GOOD BUDDY?"*

"That's right!" gleed the voice. "Would you like to be my "Good Buddy" tonight? I love big ol' boys!"

"Hell, yes! Right up here is a rest area. I'm going in! Come on!" blasted Early with anger.

"I'm right behind you, *GOOD BUDDY!*"

Early was steaming and ready to kill him. He said aloud, "The damn queer! Pervert! I'll kick his damn ass. Bastard! The sorry prick!"

He was so angry, he was all over the road, but managed to roll into an open parking spot. The rest area was nearly full. Apparently, other drivers had heard the conversation on the CB and were out of their trucks, waiting to see the "good buddies" arrive. This made him even more angry. "The fucking jerks! All of them! Want to see some action? By gosh, you'll get action! I'll bust that fruit's ass!"

He reached back into the sleeper and grabbed

a small pillow and shoved it into the top of his shirt for tits. Red High Heels had left a big brimmed hat. He grabbed it and wrapped a handkerchief around his head then plopped the hat on to keep things in place. he tied a loose sheet around his waist and hoped he looked, at a distance, like a female.

The other trucker drove up beside him. All Early could see was another Freightliner. He stepped out of his truck and switched his hips as he went to meet the other driver. He knew he would kick the man's ass.

Just as Early Bird pulled his fist back, he caught his Uncle Mule Train's voice. "Hello, driver!"

"You old fart! I ought to kick your ass anyhow!" laughed Early.

"I bet you would!" laughed Mule Train. "I knew you would stop fast if I called you a "Good Buddy!"

The two men shook hands and laughed together. Mule stared at Early Bird's strange outfit. Early defended himself, "Like my skirt and hat? Designer garb!"

"Shit, a Good Buddy special! Hell, you thought you really had one!" shrieked Mule. "I ain't so sure about this!"

"See all those drivers watching? I did it for them!" Early smiled. He grabbed his uncle and flung him into a big embrace as if he were kissing him. "It's been over eight weeks! Darling!"

Mule, knowing Early was giving the other drivers a show, played along. "Sweetheart, I didn't know you cared!"

They fell to the ground, laughing with the horse-play.

"Can I sleep with you, Baby?" begged Mule Train for all to hear.

"Oh yes, Honey! We might stay here a week!" Bird answered, trying not to laugh.

"I might get hungry," Mule replied, trying to keep a feminine voice.

"Daddy has plenty for you to eat!" crowed Early.

"That does it!" rebuked Mule. "Get off me!"

"Hell, no! This is fun!" teased Early as his big hat and hankie rolled off his head. "Come on!"

The two got up and went into Early Bird's rig. They had a big belly laugh. Mule grinned. "That skinny fellow was really looking. Wonder if he was a "gay" or if he had never seen one?"

"Who knows? Takes all kind! You know, I was really pissed because you wanted to know what I was hauling; then, you add the "Good Buddy" to it and I was wild. I couldn't catch your voice and I hadn't seen your truck."

"I knew it was you when I saw that JOY Carriers on the back of the trailer. Something about that red Freightliner that says 'Early Bird'! It puts off a foul odor, too!" smiled the older man.

"Ass, you're going too far!" laughed Early.

"Where's Red High Heels?" asked Mule. "Thought you two were running team?"

"Not yet. She has to close down that New York shit! I sure do miss her. It's been over eight weeks!" longed Early.

"Tell the dispatcher you have to go there!"

"He knows! I'm heading that way. Several loads ago, he told me to put it in the shop and take time off, but with it came another trip! I think I'll

79

have somebody take his wife away from him for a few weeks! Bet that would kill him. They don't understand!" wished Early as he crushed a plastic cup with coffee still in it. The liquid dripped into his lap.

"That's a hell of a way to cool off," observed the uncle.

"I worry about Red. She is so independent. I know she loves me as much as she can love but there is a problem in her past that she still fights!" shared the man with grief. "I don't know what to do. My instinct says to get up with that bastard and go off on him. She says to leave it alone, that time will take care of it. Time doesn't though. I will think everything is all right, then it all comes up again!"

"Maybe she still secretly loves him. Sometimes that is how women are. A man that treats them like shit, they love them! Never underestimate a female! Red knows you are a victim of her love and you would walk the trees for her beautiful ass!" cautioned Mule. "You can't let her rule you! Shit, women just roll us up as putty in their hands and manipulate us as they please. I've had it happen to me a hundred times! Let her think there is another woman!"

"I can't do that! It's no game. She is afraid and afraid for me. From what I have heard, she has reason to be afraid. I thought maybe I could help her most if she would just come with me!" explained Bird.

"I see. I guess she is caught between the devil and the deep blue sea!"

"You can say that again. I feel so frustrated because I don't know what to do. Right now, I just try to be patient and wait. I love the woman, there just couldn't be anyone else for me. You know Red. She can run that truck with the best of 'em and then tackle everything else that comes her way! Last week, going to New York, they pulled her over for a routine check at the tunnel in Baltimore. She slipped on her red high heels and when the D.O.T. opened her door and looked at that beautiful leg, he melted. She said he told her that he needed her to back the truck over by a building to be weighed. She must have thrown that pretty smile on him about then. It was pouring rain, too, she said. Her mirrors were fogged and there was a crowd behind her. She knew she had to get out to look where to back, it was her blind side anyhow."

"Another D.O.T. walked up as she started out the truck. They both were watching Red and the rest of the traffic was stopped around them. The officer with the higher rank told the other one, "Tell her to put her legs back in the truck and get out of here! A furniture truck won't be overloaded anyhow!" She heard him and carefully climbed back up in her crazy cabover. I told Red she could get out of anything with that high cab and heels!"

Laughing, Mule replied, "That's like the fellow that had his truck to break down in the country way away from everything. He went to a farmhouse that was a mile or so down the road and asked the farmer if he had a phone so he could get help. The farmer said he didn't but he would drive him to town the next day and he could stay the night at their house. So, the trucker did."

"That was good of the old man!" smiled Early.

"Well, the farmer showed him to a room and told him he would be welcome to breakfast with the family the next morning. He said that he had three

81

daughters and his wife was a great cook. They loved to have guests because not many people got that far out to visit them. Well, the next morning, just as he had said, his wife had gotten into the kitchen and cooked ham, bacon, grits, eggs and biscuits. The perfect country breakfast and it smelled great. They had filled their plates, then he looked up the stairs to see the oldest daughter descending the steps in a flowing thin, pink robe. Her breasts were proudly half displayed and he was in awe. He gulped and said to the farmer. "Please pass the puss-kets!"

The two men crowed together. That was the wonderful thing about Early's family, at a weak moment, one seemed to pop up and console you with care and humor, and often wisdom.

"I didn't plan to stay here tonight. I don't feel safe in some of these rest areas. This one has too few lights. I need a shower; I'm going to that truck stop up the way. I want a decent meal, too. I ain't got all thay much fuel!" hesitated Mule Train.

"Fool, you have no choice. Get in front so if you do need fuel we can get you fixed up! Check your gauge!" ordered Early.

Mule Train left for his truck and looked at the gauge. "Damn, Early! It don't register!"

Bird pushed the "on" button of his CB and answered. "Get your stick out, you cheap ass. Might as well do it now! I got a hose and bucket."

"Yeah, we had better. This thing will never start if it runs out, the antique bitch! It's as old as Red's truck!" Mule moaned back over the speaker.

Another voice came on the radio. "Hey, driver. I'll be right there. I got fuel for you! Just wait, you're in the rest area?"

"Yeah, two Freightliners, just as you come in," answered Early since Mule had already left his truck. He saw a big, funky six wheeler coming toward them. It was an old oil truck but you could make out the lettering to read HOMELESS OIL.

"Hey," greeted Homeless.

"We need diesel fuel!" announced Early.

"I got it! This is a new business for me. I got this old truck and I plan to use it as a trouble truck. I got everything on it. I can change tires, fix an engine. Got good lights. I have really put it together," he insisted.

"Is it legal?" asked Early, not wanting to get into some kind of problem. He remembered that fuel has federal tax and if you don't have the right color in the tank, you are in trouble if you get caught.

"Of course, I ain't that stupid. I own a service station back there. My wife runs that. I just ain't happy with all the trucks that run out of fuel here. You can't hardly start one with a jug of fuel, especially if they run out. Some trucks just have a hell of a time coming back; the bigger, the harder!" he said, blinking his near black eyes. "I think I have a great idea; on the road service station! Neat, huh?"

"Well, it depends what it costs me!" grinned Mule Train.

"Tell you what I'll do. I'll charge for the fuel by the gallon and you can get underway!" he smiled.

"How much a gallon?" asked Early.

"Two bucks and fifty cents!" he answered.

"Are you nuts? Two fifty!" muttered Bird.

"Ain't no station for fifty miles either way!" grunted Homeless. "If you are out, you are out!"

"He ain't that damn 'out'! Man, you're really

trying to put a real one on folks!" grumbled Early Bird. "I have a lot of fuel. I can just give it to him!"

"Yeah, but I came here to help!" uttered the fellow politely.

"You did that on your own. We didn't ask you!" revealed Mule Train.

"All right. Look at it like this, Uncle. He is here. So if we paid a road service fee of twenty dollars and got twenty gallons, the dollar and fifty isn't quite as bad!" Early insisted with a mental change of figures.

"That's still high!" blurted out Mule. "Screw it!"

"How about buy twenty-five gallons at $2.25 a gallon?" struggled Homeless. "I can't do no better! You might be right. Maybe I am too high. Look man, my old lady thinks this is the stupidest thang I ever done! She hates this truck and everything about it. If I make this job tonight, I might just get some poon-tang! She cut me off three weeks ago!"

"Oh, hell! That's different! Let me get on the CB and see if anyone else has a problem! I sure see where you're coming from!" teased Mule Train taking a liking to the man's sad situation. He winked at Early Bird.

"I tell you what. I might need a fuel filter. You got one? Old Red gave a couple mean gulps and hesitated back down the road," Early related.

"Oh, yes sir! I have just what you need for that purdy Freightliner. I'll do right by you! Mister, can I pump you some fuel? I'll even clean the windows!" pleaded the man.

"Of course. Pump me fifty gallons. That ought to get you some leg!" laughed Mule.

"Will it ever!" gleed the man, jumping up into the air. "Whoopee!"

"Fifty gallons will probably get him leg, tit and arm pit!" laughed Early. Finding his way back to his truck and getting to his CB so he could announce to the other drivers there was a service truck in the rest area.

No sooner had Early finished the announcement, three other drivers were heading toward the trucks. He slipped his tire checker into his belt and locked his doors behind him.

As they joined him, each started talking together. One was nearly out of fuel, another had a heat gauge problem, the other one needed his reefer checked. Early beat his tires and threw the stick back into the side box on the cab. They talked to Homeless as he fueled the tank of Mule Train's rig. Quickly, the man replaced Early Bird's filter and the two paid him and were on their way.

Homeless was happily into working on the other trucks as they groaned out of the rest area.

Early said into his microphone of the CB, "Darn, I forgot to ask him if he had a shower in that mobile service station!"

"I hear you!" laughed Mule. "At least we were able to help his home life. He probably was going to be real 'homeless' if he didn't make it pay soon!"

"It's really a great service! He has to make a little with it or he can't be out here. I like to help a man that's trying!" replied Early as they settled in to run the next stretch of road for a better spot.

"He is all right!" flipped Mule. "Just hope when he gets home it won't be like the poor old drunk!"

"Yeah? What?" asked Early, knowing full well Mule had something going on.

The CB buzzed and then he heard Mule Train break into one of his old fashion songs:

"You dumb fool, you crazy fool!
Can't you ever see?
That head on the pillow in my room,
That's only a big cabbage head
Your granny sent to me!
(The man answered)
Now, I have been drunk many, many times,
and I have been down very low!
But, Honey, a cabbage head with a mustache,
I ain't never seen be-fo!"

Mule always sang crazy things and this one was perfect. He had a good country voice and you couldn't help but laugh.

"Where did you get that one?" shrieked Early.

"Heard Uncle Charlie singing it when he was on the john!" laughed Mule.

"Hey, Mule! Watch out! Something is wrecking ahead!" stormed Early. "Stop! Now!"

Both Freightliners stopped immediately and watched.

There was still some light in the sky ahead. You could see an overpass over the road ahead. A small vehicle zipped passed several others up there and the sound of sirens were in the air. The flash of bright silver went out of sight. Instantly, the tattered wall of the old bridge gave way and a big bus dropped from above. As it rolled over to the ground, it landed on its top. The lights went out and smoke started.

Without words, Early and Mule Train jumped from their trucks and raced to the broken up vehicle. Early could see the sign that read 'County School District'. Then he heard crying children.

There was no other traffic that stopped and no other help. He knew he needed to alert the Highway Patrol for major help. He cried out, "Mule, get the doors open! I'll get the call made!"

"Yeah! Hurry!" screamed Mule.

Early Bird made the call as fast as he could and called out on the CB to anyone coming into the area to help. He jumped out of his truck and slung flares into the road behind Mule Train's rig. Early ran back to the bus.

"I can't get the doors open!" cried Mule. "The kids are going crazy! They are toward the front. I can't get them to help!"

"Mule, get our fire extinguishers! Quick!" Early pleaded. "Let me try!"

Through the window, he saw bodies all over. The bus must have been full. They were all ages. He looked at several in front of him and yelled in Spanish, "*Agase para tras! El vidrio abietro!* (Get back! Open the windows!)"

Early got a little result from a young girl, "Meester! Pleeze! My seester!"

"Open the windows! Get those that can help to go out the windows! Hurry!" Early Bird urged. "Here! Push here!"

With one more hard jerk, and great relief, the door finally clicked and he pulled it open. Blood was everywhere amongst the cut bodies. Early yelled, "Get out of here, fast...If you can move, get out of here! Use the windows or doors. Go! Go so we can help! *Vete de agut rapido...Si tepuedes mover, vete de agut. Usas las puertas ventanas. Vete. Vete y nosotros podemos alludar.*"

He would yell his warnings in English and followed with Spanish.

"Meester! My seester!" replied the girl again. "Help her1"

Early looked and knew the child was dead the girl wanted to help. He said, "Go on! I'll bring her!"

Mule Train had returned with the extinguishers and had sprayed the engine that had a bit of smoke seeping out and the area where fuel might have slushed.

The inside of the bus still had lots of smoke and fumes. Early was forcing those that could move out and it left about ten children laying in the tangled mass on the tattered roof. The driver was still buckled in the seat belt and hanging with blood flowing from his left arm.

"Mule, let's look at the driver!" Early decided.

They made their way to him through the mass of books, papers and clothing. The people laying around needed professional medical attention. Once they got to the man, Early spoke, "Can you hear me?"

The man sputtered and whispered, "Oh, God! Oh! My children!"

He seemed to pass out again, but they knew he was alive. The bus had hit on the right side first in the fall as it skidded onto its top. Then the man moved slightly. "Help me!"

"We will! Can you move? How about your hands?" questioned Bird, following by asking about his neck, if he could move or feel anything; then, his legs that were entwined with the steering and seat. He kept saying it all seemed all right. Early found a tee shirt to wrap around the man's arm and tied it tight.

"Mule, when we take this seat belt loose, he's going to fall! We have to catch him!" worried Early. "He's going to weight like three hundred pounds!"

"We can't get him like that! We had better wait! I'll find something to put under him! We could break his neck!" whispered Mule.

"You're right! Why doesn't help come?" appealed Early. "I called! Please come!"

"Remember, that mechanic said it was a long way from everything. That overpass ain't got roads leading to down here!" adduced Mule.

As the men began to pray to themselves, a vehicle with bright lights rolled up, shining its glory over the scene. The children from the bus were huddled into a spot at the edge of the bridge where Mule Train had herded them. They put their hands over their eyes and cried out together.

Then, the sirens from both directions came screaming to the massive wreck. Some went to the children, others went around with flares to add a safety feature. Police cars moved into place and the big fire truck came to take control of the school bus. A paramedic from the fire unit rushed to the front doorway that Mule finally had gotten open. He squeezed inside, "We are here to help!"

"Thank God!" said Early. "He needs to be moved! Want us to get out of here?"

"Sure! Thanks! We have equipment...," he started.

"I know!" acknowledged Early. "Come on,

Mule! Let them handle it!"

The two men eased out of the bus and let the emergency crews take over. It was a heavy situation. The firefighters checked the bus for spills and possible danger of fire, then sprayed some sort of chemical around. The ambulances rolled in to collect the children and cars of other people rushed, now to the accident. You could hear the crying of parents and children and the devastatation of those who received news that their loved one was critical, yet three were pronounced dead and sheets covered their faces.

Time went on for hours. Everyone was trying to get all the people from the bus to account and transport them somehow. The news media finally arrived at the scene to film and photograph. Early and Mule stood back watching them working to capture the scene for the public. The authorities told the story related to them by the two truckers.

About one o'clock in the morning, they were finally able to get their rigs back on the road. They had forgotten about being hungry, tired and dirty. The two trucks puffed on up the long grade that was ahead of them. After more than a half hour, they could hear activity over the CB which indicated a truck stop was near. Soon, they were met with familiar bright lights and a flashing sign inviting them to come rest. It was like an oasis for certain.

They popped on their brakes in the fuel island and inserted the pumps. Early looked at the sign that read, 'diesel fuel $1.10'. He smiled, thinking about the man earlier with his old truck. His price wasn't all that bad.

"Hey, Bird!" grinned Mule. "We did good!"
"I know!"

They were glad to be at the truck stop. They both still had blood from the accident on their hands; but, they felt good knowing they were there when needed. This was putting Early with little sleep, but sleep was nothing now. It hurt to remember the black-eyed girl pleading, "Meester! Help my seester!" He would see the tiny face of her sister for a long time as she lay lifelessly before him.

Mule wasn't being his crazy-self now. He remembered how he had to gather the children to safety and put one in charge of looking after them. He would never forget the shattered bus and the children left at his feet that could not get up. He had picked up a little book from the side of the road. Opening it, he read, "The Lord is my shepherd; I shall not want. He maketh me to lie down in green pastures; he leadeth me beside the still waters. He restoreth my soul; he leadeth me in the paths of righteousness for His name sake...Yea, though I walk through the valley of the shadow of death, I will fear no evil, for thou art with me; thy rod and thy staff, they comfort me."

He walked over to Early Bird, "Are you hearing this?"

"Yes," whispered Early Bird and as Mule continued reading, Early joined in from memory. Together, they quoted:

"Thou preparest a table before me in the presence of mine enemies; thou anointest my head with oil; my cup runneth over. Surely goodness and mercy shall follow me all the days of my life; and I will dwell in the house of the Lord forever."

The two quietly hung the hoses and went between the trucks. They both had a lump in their throats and tears in their eyes. They hugged in broth-

91

erly fashion. The scene was still with them; maybe it always would be.

"Children, little children!" Early Bird stammered.

"Sad, very sad!" Mule lightly answered.

They walked silently into the building and asked for a shower as they paid.

"Did you hear about that bus wreck?" asked the man as he gave change.

They shrugged their shoulders.

"They said on the news that two truckers got there first and saved a bunch of the kids! They kept it from blowing up! Ain't that great?"

"Maybe it is!" smiled Early.

"Yeah!" grunted Mule.

"They have to be heroes! Real men!" smiled the fuel island clerk. "That took real stuff!"

CHAPTER 5

It had been very cold in New York. The blizzard conditions made work almost impossible. Red had sent most of her help home. She sat down and stared into space. Catching herself rehearsing a conversation with herself, she laughed, "Hey, Zipper! Come here, you precious dog!"

The little, big earred, skinny dog came obediently. She stood at Red's feet looking up with a dog smile on her face.

"Thank the Lord for you! You have to stay close. If anyone catches me talking to myself, they'll think I'm crazy! Even if I am, I don't need to admit it! Tell you what; if we can start that truck, we're going to North Carolina before it gets too late. It's just mostly lots of snow. The closer to the city we get, the better traveled things will be. You game?"

The dog wagged her tail in agreement.

Red secured the store and threw what she needed into her old Transtar. It had started with no hesitation. Once she put the dog in the riders' seat, she climbed into the cab to back out.

"This is slick!" muttered Red. "Good! There goes a sand truck!"

There was no traffic and visibility wasn't great. She whipped around in the road with a big, slightly sliding, U-turn. "Oh, mercy! We won't do that again!"

As she got farther from the store, the visibility lessened and the snow began to get deeper. Red knew this was the one chance to get herself and Zipper off the Island. The weather forecast was grave conditions from the next day forward for at least two weeks. She had to beat the storm. At home, thermometers would read about sixty degrees and no snow.

Red just eased on to find the west bound side of the Long Island Expressway. Traffic there was considerably light. People were using their heads and going home. Oncoming traffic on the east bound six lane road was bumper to bumper. Suddenly, Red saw a small car sliding into the middle, between the two roads. Somehow, he expertly slipped through all the vehicles as if he were Dale Earnhardt running the last lap in the Winston Cup.

"Atta, boy!" Red exclaimed out loud. "Leave 'em in a puff of smoke! Keep moving or they will be up your tail!"

Smiling to herself and happy there wasn't a big pile up, she slowed more and tried to exercise even more caution. Along the sides, you could see the piles of snow from the week before still on the road way edge. The plows were working fast and the sand-trucks were about a mile ahead of her. This was wonderful; as if they were laying a royal carpet just for her and Zipper.

The snow nearly stopped and a slight drizzle of misty rain began. The lines of lights facing her from the other side were all but at a standstill. A truck was coming up behind her fast. She hung tightly to the steering wheel and anxiously waited for him to pass.

The CB blasted a deep voice, "Hey, Stick-hauler! Got 'em on?"

"Come on!" she answered.

"Where you going?"

"Home, if I can get out!"

"I'm headed for Virginia. Get in behind me. I'll run front door!"

"I don't want to go that fast!" Red informed.

"Me neither. I just wanted to catch up with you! Come on!" he insisted as he passed her. "Wow! You sure are a perty little thang! I don't want you to get into a problem alone. This stuff is dangerous!"

"I know!" Red supplied.

They were running together with the man reporting to her how the roads were ahead. It was a great help.

He yelled, "Slow up! They stopped with the sanding of the road up here! We might get into ice!"

"Watch out! Here comes a four wheeler sliding everywhere!" Red warned. It was too late. The little pick-up slipped into the side of Red's truck. She felt it shake as it slung the little truck forward. The driver must have hit the gas and was thrust out of control into the back tires of the trailer of the front-door truck. Red had eased to a stop and watched the slow motion happening before her eyes. The little truck then slid off the road into the middle and rested against the guard rail. The big rig in front of her was swaying from one side of the road to the other.

"Hang in driver! Let up off it! There's ice underneath! Take your time! You'll get it! Easy!" she whispered, consolingly in the CB and trying to help him not to panic.

Everything was quiet; whatever was going to happen was somewhat left in the art of the way the front rig could maneuver, along with sheer luck. The trailer went left and right; then sideways, then, back to the left, almost straightening out. There was nothing to hook a tire into. It was a thin sheet of black ice laying on top of a bridge that seemed to change all factors. The driver was nearly helpless. At the end of his ropes, he was sideways, sliding west bound. Suddenly, he saw the line of cars all over the road and on the sides. As the truck started for the trees, he gave the wheel a big turn and brought it to rest. He was relieved at first, then jumped from the truck to see what had happened.

Red eased her truck a little closer as a police car that was in the area threw on his lights and stopped by the big rig, jackknifed in the middle of the big six-lane.

"That took a lot not to hit all these cars!" said the officer. "Is anybody hurt?"

"No. That truck back there hit my trailer!" the driver said.

"He hit that woman's truck first!" replied the cop. "Are you all right?"

As Red walked up, she shook her head that

she wasn't hurt, but sighed, "I really thought his rig was gone! The pick-up is over there. He hit me pretty hard and glanced off, I guess!"

A man with a handkerchief wadded around his bloody nose walked to them whining. "They pushed me off the road, officer! Fucking truckers! They think they own the damn road! My truck is ruined! It won't start back and God only know how bad I'm hurt! I'm off the road!"

"Get in the back of my car!" ordered the officer. "I'll call for an ambulance!"

He didn't have to call. Bright lights were on the way and you could hear the blasting horns. They looked at the big rig stretched across the road, trying to determine the next best move.

"I wouldn't have given you ten cents for this truck about five minutes ago!" teased the policeman gently. "What do you think?"

"I wouldn't have either," replied the trucker. "I can get it out of the road. Man, am I lucky! It didn't touch the tanks and I didn't hit anything else. I guess that pushed up stuff on the road edge saved me. Let me check the trailer!"

The three of them went to the spot where the pick-up hit. It showed the paint from the pick-up and it had cut the outside front tandem tire.

"Let me write this up for your company! Let's look at the other truck, too!" offered the policeman.

"I can see he about knocked my bumper off. It's hanging out pretty far. Look here. He hit the quarter side, too! It really isn't that much. I can go on. If I don't, I might sleep in this truck for a couple weeks!" groaned Red High Heels.

"I'm an owner-operator. I can get it out of the way. We really need to go. She's right!" begged the other trucker.

"Tell you what. Let me quickly write this report for you while you two get ready to go. Let me have your license," offered the tall officer. His breath blew a cloud of vapor with each word. Both handed him their license. "Go on and get that thing straightened up and come back here. We'll be in the car."

Another patrol car arrived in time to order the traffic to stop for the rig to be turned around. It only took the driver a few minutes to circle the huge International out of the way and park it in the paved shoulder area not far from Red's rig.

It didn't take the officer long to put the data together and release the two trucks. The man from the four-wheeler was being put into an ambulance unit. He was yelling at the truckers, "You son-of-bitches! I'll get you! Run me off the road! Fuck you! I'll get you both! You can't run away from my Uncle Louie! He's the Mafia! He'll fix you bastards!"

"Shut up!" demanded a uniformed woman as he was rolled into the vehicle on the stretcher. She shrugged her shoulders and smiled at Red. "That's an asshole!"

The two trucks waited for the ambulance to clear the area and the two drivers fixed their log books then returned carefully to the road. The man said into his CB, "I guess that killed almost an hour. I have a weather band. I just listened to the report. It sounds as if things will be a little better as we go. We only have a few more exits left of this bad weather. Hey! Look, there's the salt and sand trucks now!"

"I see them!" Red answered. "Just take it easy. You can't make up lost time. It'll eventually eliminate itself. I just want to get where I'm going in one piece! My trailer is almost empty. Mostly pads, straps and a few return pieces!"

"I'm totally empty. I couldn't get a load out of here. Nothing moving because of the weather!" he replied.

They finally got to the exit that would take them through the Bronx and on to the New Jersey Turnpike. The traffic was moving well, keeping the roads open. Sand had already been heavily laid. Both drivers hoped with every time the wheels turned that things would keep moving. A taxi flew past the two trucks and found a patch of ice in the road and began to slide. He lost it and went on over the side and down an embankment.

"Did you see that?" asked the front truck driver.

"Couldn't miss it!" Red answered. "Keep going! That's history now. There's a cop not far behind anyhow. They might have to get him from below."

"I heard that! Real stupid!" growled the driver.

"Taxis in New York know one thing. Go! Just come on, let's ease on!"

The driver obeyed and they were finally facing crossing the George Washington Bridge. There had been an accident on the top level but Red had taken the lower level because she thought the roadway would be clear. The other truck had taken the upper level. Actually, in a joking way, he had told Red he would race her to the other side.

"Hey, big truck! I'm going on! I won! How beautiful! The Jersey Turnpike sign! I told you to take the lower level! Oh well, hang in and have a good trip!" Red teased.

"Hush woman! Don't you leave me! If you do my Uncle Louie will fix you! He's in the Mafia!" laughed the driver.

"Oh! That's right! I'll head for the T. A. at Elkton, Maryland. There's no stopping old Blue Heaven now!" giggled Red. "Take it easy!"

"All right. I'll be on that way in a few!" he grunted. "Oh, damn! There's another pile up! These stupid jerks! They gotta fly! Red, can you still hear me?"

"Yes!"

"I may never leave this now! Have a good trip! Remember you are the best one I ever got in a jam with!" he snickered.

His voice trailed off and Red wanted only to concentrate on driving. The snow started coming down just as she approached exit fourteen. She could see many four wheelers pushing their luck with driving too fast. Staying in the road and on the paths made by other vehicles was essential. Snow was almost blinding with the huge flakes rapidly coming at her. The windshield wipers were working as fast as possible to clear a view. Visibility was reduced more by the fog created by the moving traffic. Red was glad to be up above most of it in the cabover.

She continued carefully at about 35 to 40 m.p.h. "Zipper! You all right? This is a slow trip, Baby; we can't stop! I'm sure glad I put your diaper on you. Maybe we'll get on out of this soon!"

The little black long-eared dog got out of her

seat and moved over toward Red on top of the motor box cover. She sat looking out the windshield as if she approved of the big snow. Zipper lapped coffee from Red's cup.

"Sorry it's not very hot! You can have it all now!" Red smiled at the little beast. "I love you even if you do take my coffee."

Gently, the little dog went to the edge of the sleeper finding her favorite kind of candy; she brought the bar back and dropped it near Red for her to open. The woman smiled with enjoyment. "You're wonderful! I am so glad I have you with me. At least if I break down, I have you to keep me warm. You know what? I believe we're running out of the storm now!"

The lady trucker reached for the Hershey bar and started to open it for the dog. After breaking it into pieces, she smiled as Zipper hesitated. "Go ahead! It's yours. I'm on a diet!"

The dog laid down, looking at the bar of candy sulking. Ears straight to a point, she glared, then squinted her eyes at her master as if to say, "I don't eat alone!"

"All right then, Bitch! I'll eat the nuts! I keep forgetting and buy you male Hersheys. Next time, I'll get them without the nuts!" she laughed and picked up a piece to bite the almond out. "Actually, I believe you like my teeth prints!"

Zipper kept eating the candy as Red served her bit by bit. The dog happily wagged her tail. Once the treat was finished, she settled back into her nest in the back edge of the sleeper. Red glanced as she sighed with a big puff and closed her eyes.

"You're getting so old, I'm going to have to

retire you. Maybe Kikki Doo will take you for a while," Red muttered.

The weather lightened up and Red drove on into the Elkton, Maryland truck stop. She was glad to fuel, although she still had half-full tanks. In bad weather, or really anytime, she preferred to run off the top of the tank. You never know when you might get stuck. while the fuel poured, Red took Zipper to the 'pet-walk-area' and let her do her thing. She put a towel down for the dog to return to. That was routine that seemed to work with Zip. Once a towel was in place, or a piece of clothing, the dog returned there and waited.

Everything seemed fine with the truck. It was colder now; Red was glad they had a fellow to assist. She returned her dog and moved the truck into a parking spot. It would be best to go on and eat, then she could get on home.

Inside the restaurant the big table was nearly full. A driver called out, "Hey, Red! Come sit with us!"

The waitress brought her coffee as she dropped beside him. The woman brushed her half-wet hair with her hand and smiled, "Big Thang! How great to see you!"

The man looked tired, but put an arm around her, giving her a big hug. "Miss Red! Where you going? South, I hope!"

Early Bird's Uncle Thang had lost weight and his hair had turned a bit whiter. Yet he looked good. He drove his own truck the last she had heard.

"South it is! I barely got out of New York! It was icy, then came snow!" she reported. "I knew home would make it possible to work. Maybe I'll go to Atlanta for a trip. A store there needs some stuff."

"Hell, you might not go anywhere for a few weeks. I came up from Charlotte. They supposed to be getting the same thing!" informed Big Thang. "You're sure dressed warm!"

"Heck, yes! I've been in an accident and through hell getting to here!"

A voice behind Red called out, "I told you, you wouldn't get away!"

Red looked to see the front-door trucker from the Long Island incident.

"Pull up a chair!" she invited, intruducing him to Thang. Everyone around introduced themselves to each other. "I'm amazed you got here!"

"Not as amazed as I am!" he groaned. "They closed the top level of the bridge right after we crossed and I barely made it to the Pike. I heard on the CB they shut it down just after I got through. Once I got to Exit 9 they were starting to put up baracades to block off exits there. I expect it's mostly shut down now. There are so many accidents they can't get through. I heard one north bound truck say he had been in one spot for an hour waiting to get moving. Who knows what happened!"

They each ate and made calls. Red wondered where Early Bird would be. She took the chance that he could be reached by his cellphone. Lots of the time, he would be too far from receiving towers. The call seemed to be going through. "I think I am going to reach Early!"

To her disappointment, the service answered, telling her to leave a message. As her face dropped, she whispered, "Early, this is Red. I'm on my way home. In Elkton at the T.A. now. Leaving soon. Plan to go on home without stopping. I love you!"

She hung up the phone and stared.

"Poor thing, still craving that old Bird! I'm here now, Baby! Let Uncle Thang keep Early's girl warm!" he picked with her.

"Hateful!" sneered Red. "I'll tell on you!"

Everyone laughed at the teasing as the intercom called out, "The driver of the blue cabover International parked at the garage, please pick up the first phone and dial six."

"Oh, Lordy, that's me!" worried Red. Obeying the call, "Yes, you called me on the intercom...the truck at the garage!"

"Can you come here soon?"

"I just got my dinner!" she begged.

"This is urgent!"

"Be right there!" She hung up and started out. "Guess I'll have it cold again!"

"I'll eat it for you," grinned Thang, grabbing her meal.

Red went to the garage and her truck. Another truck was into the side of her trailer. A new driver had backed into it and taken a hunk out of the metal in the middle.

"I'm sorry!" cried the young black fellow. "I thought I had plenty room. I did until the trailer twisted and I couldn't see! I'm so sorry! It's slick there beside your trailer!"

At first Red was annoyed, but she felt empathy for him. "This is called a learning experience, I suppose. I'll bet you slid some on that ice!"

"I reckon!" he stared miserably.

"This is my second accident for the day!" she

complained. "That will have to be patched!"

"The company has insurance!" acknowledged the driver.

"Well, I don't know that we need to get 'a piece of the rock'!" she smiled. "Get that guy from in there!"

He returned with several men from the building that worked on trucks. One looked and quoted a price, "Probably take about four hundred or more!"

"No it won't! I have a man down home that can patch it for very little! Park your truck and let's go inside!" demanded Red. "It's too cold out here!"

"I'm too nervous!"

"Yes, you can do it! How long you been driving?" she asked.

"This is my first week!" he hung his head embarrassed.

"Y'all go on, we got it!" Red urged. As the others left, she smiled. "Look, I'll pull my truck into that spot in front there and you just ease into this space. You can do it! Everybody has to start somewhere."

"I'll try!" he grieved.

They moved the rigs and returned to the table in the dining room. "Look what I found!"

"Ted, that child ain't ever shaved yet!" teased another driver.

"Oh, hell he has! Got his first close shave today!" smiled the woman and winked at the young driver.

"That's right! My first one today!" he grinned for the first time.

"My truck was in the way and I had to move

it," Red advised, not embarrassing the young man.

He turned to her and whispered, "What about that?"

"Forget it! I'll trade some hot rolls and jelly for the repair. Just get out of the truck and look if you need to from now on! Do like me, I like to be a 'forward driver' as much as I can. It takes time to get the hang of backing in at truck stops. I look at the new rigs and nearly die! It took me time to get over the fear of backing into something. Then, suddenly, I decided I had better learn to put it wherever I had to. It's mostly in your mind!"

"I believe that's right. Anyhow, here's how to get in touch with me if it costs you!" He ordered dinner and wrote down the phone number for her.

Red had noticed her truck seemed cold when she got in to leave. She drove out to the highway, then turned around and returned to the truck stop. She reached down and turned her electric socks to medium. Throwing a puff of the feather-quilt over Zipper, Red went to find Big Thang. "I started out and I don't have much heat! I'm already about to freeze!"

"Let's go look!" grinned Thang. "This might cost you!"

"In that case, I'm coming along!" laughed another driver.

"Me, too!" quibbled another.

All the drivers at the table filed out behind the pretty redhead, then gathered at her truck. Thang had one man to get in and turn it off. They did all sorts of things until they figured what to be the verdict.

"Sugar, I believe she's low on water. Let's pull it into the garage and find out. Want me to take

106

her for you? Go on in the building where it's warm!"
Big Thang caringly offered, "Find out which door!"

By the time the truck rolled around the
building, the mechanic was motioning to Thang; he
watched his commands. Red and the other drivers
were waiting in the trucker's lounge.

About half hour later, Thang and the
mechanic walked to Red like two brain surgeons, very
somber and patient. The mechanic spoke, "We
drained the radiator. I had to replace the top hose. I
flushed it and got all the crap out of it. Then, we put
Al-Kool in to keep things open for the next year plus
new anti-freeze. You had better be glad you checked
it. You didn't have enough coolant to be driving in
Florida. Don't you check that?"

"No, I have you to do that!" replied Red. "I
keep my stuff up. They replaced a bottom hose a few
months ago. He said he put the antifreeze back in. I
figured it was all right!"

"It is now.   That will be $124.00 for
everything!" smiled the mechanic.

"Can I give you a check?"

"No. Got a credit card?"

"Yes, but..." she started.

"Take her check. Her company does business
here all the time. We put her last Michelins on that
tractor!" ordered the boss.

"That's all right. Let me give you cash!"
smiled Red, not offended. "I know I needed this!"

She finished paying and tipped the mechanic
who had gone overboard to help.

"Girl," grinned Thang, "Early should look
after you better. I thought you were going team with
him!"

"I am, soon!"

"You ought not be out here by yourself!" he cautioned. "Well, you need to remember, if your water is low, the heater in your truck won't operate well. If it gets very low, that engine can get ruined. Keep an eye on the heat gauge all the time."

"It hadn't shown any different!" she replied.

"That's good!" Big Thang cheered. "Tell you what, this old truck will freeze you to death anyhow. It's getting colder outside now. I'm going to put a piece of plastic over the bottom half of the radiator front. That will keep the wind from blowing through. It might push the heat hand up, but keep a close eye. If the heat hand rises much, then stop and take half of it off. You know what to do! You need to get a weather-front!"

Red finally got back on the road and was happy with the truck being so warm. The gauge was all right and she sang her way to Washington, D. C. and then on through Richmond. This trip she stayed on I-85; her usual route would go through a slightly, more mountainous, area.

Getting home was most important. Red drove without stopping again. The sign for Greensboro always made her feel the trip was over. As it jumped before her, she knew she had just enough energy left to get to High Point.

Pulling into the parking lot of the Hardee's on Highway 311 was wonderful. Everything was closed and quiet except for the motors of the other trucks. Zipper again got up and waited beside her. Red knew she had to at least let the dog out. As Zipper ran to the familiar grass, Red found a phone.

"Hello?" answered a sleepy voice.

"Hey, Kikki," started Red.

"I'll be right there!" the daughter excitedly replied. "Oh, Mama! I'm so glad you're here! Early Bird called and said he'd be here tomorrow!"

That put Red High Heels in the clouds. "Come on!"

In less than ten minutes, the girl drove in front of the rig in her Mercedes yelling, "Let's go, Mom!"

Zipper jumped into the car and flew into Kikkie's arms. "I'm keeping her, Mama. She needs to stay with me! Poor puppy, out in trucks!"

Red was glad to hear that and didn't say anything. She knew the dog couldn't handle the road anymore and it was hard on her getting into the high up truck. No more was said. They each found their beds for the rest of the night at Kikki's beautiful suburban home.

The next morning, Kikki sneaked to Red's room and opened the door. Red awakened to the bright sunlight as three dogs flopped all over her.

"Oh, mercy! Help!" laughed the woman, feeling like a child. "Get these wild, stinking creatures off me!"

The basset hound rolled over onto her back, close to Red and shut her eyes; Zipper was wiggling and rolling, while the big, overgrown puppy of a dalmation rolled and tumbled, trying to find Red's face to give sloppy dog kisses.

Kikki plopped into the middle of everything on the king size playpen screaming, "We've missed you!"

The energetic dogs jumped and played, then roared after each other out of the room and down the stairs. You could hear them growling and rolling together in the living room.

Kikki whispered, "Those two missed Zipper!"

"I know. We miss you, too! If I let Zipper stay with you and your pups, will you treat her right? You know she has all her peculair ways. You can't get her off her cycle of exotic items," the mother indicated.

"Nobody can do better for her than me, not even you; unless you get her out of that truck. She deserves to be able to flop and play. She is so lively with these other animals. They love her, too! I know you think you need her with you, but her age is against her. Technically, she would be over a hundred years old. This settles it. We out vote you, five to one and Zipper votes with us!" cheered Kikki Doo.

"Don't get your drawers in a snitch! I totally agree with you!" beamed Red.

"Oh?"

"See how agreeable I am! You're right!" Red sneezed big. "I might be getting allergic to the little 'puss'. By George, I am starving! Let's go eat a horse or two!"

"Get your butt up and let's get with it. I gotta get to my store sometime today. I have a thousand things going on!" ordered the beautiful, shapely, young woman.

CHAPTER 6

Red was proud of her talented daughter. She was always there when she needed her and always would come through to help Red. The many times Red had called on her, there was never a hesitation. As the girl left the room dancing with a blanket, the mother marveled how fortunate she was to have such a wonderful friend who had been there from her first breath. These feelings were natural, creating a mutual exchange.

As soon as they could get their faces on and decide how to dress for the day, the two women started out the door. The phone rang in the distance. As she slipped back inside the house, Kikki reached for it quickly.

"Mama! This is yours!" she called with that special tone in her voice. "It's my future Daddy!"

Red High Heels squealed and ran for the phone.

Kikki extended the receiver. "Let's put it on the speaker so I can listen in!"

"Early Bird, where are you?" Red breathed seductively.

"Just out of Atlanta! I have a drop at the JOY Carriers terminal. Once I switch trailers, I will be on my way to you. I am so glad you got out of New York. I worry about you, Baby! Go with me for a trip. We need some time together!" he pleaded his case.

"We can think about it. When will you be here? I'm with Kikki now. We're leaving for breakfast, then I have to get the truck backed in and loaded at the manufacturers' on the south of High Point. I can leave my truck there," smiled Red.

"Don't load yet. Just park it for a few days!" he pleaded.

"I love you! Just hurry and get here! No, get here safely," Red demanded.

"You know I can hardly wait to touch you! Promise me some extra time!"

"You got it! I'm so thrilled you called," she sighed.

"I'll see you in seven or eight hours."

"Want me to meet you part way?" asked the woman.

"Maybe I should call you when I know the final plan," replied Early Bird.

"All right, call my house after four o'clock. I need to get myself together. I haven't been home yet," informed Red. "There's never enough time."

They were excited by just simply hearing each others voice. It wouldn't be long before they could once again be together. He had a days work ahead driving to North Carolina. Early knew it would be best to have her meet him rather than take the chance of running into the complications of her busy routine. He wanted her away from everything.

"I'm sure glad for you!" encouraged Kikki. She drove on to the nearby Waffle House. They went inside and exchanged pleasantries with the many people who knew them both. Kikki delivered Red to her truck and waited for her to start the blue International.

"I need to get the air up. Here, drop this deposit bag at the bank. I need to just go on home. I'm not loading yet!" confessed Red. "I need time with Early Bird. It's been so long since we were together."

"It's your fault! All you have to do is make it happen!"

"It takes two," Red mumbled.

"Here, take this with you. It's your birthday present. Don't open it until you see Early. I'm gone! I love you, Mom," Kikki said tenderly, reaching for her mother.

Hugging the girl, Red whispered with a tear in her eye, "Thank you. I love you, too. I'll call you!"

She stood by the truck and watched her daughter drive out of sight. Red walked around the truck, checking tires and the security of her rig. Everything was in order, it seemed. The main things to check would always be the CB and television. If they were there, nobody had been in the truck. Tires were up, things were all right to go home. With only an hour drive ahead, Red still entered her particulars into the log book. She actually liked the little journal.

Many times she needed it as a reference as to time and place. Throwing the log onto the dash, she adjusted her seat then got back out of the truck to grab a "to go" cup of coffee. It was a little stretch of the legs to walk across the street for a cup for the road. She realized she missed Zipper already and felt lonely.

Upon returning, Red sensed something was wrong. Just a feeling; she jumped into the seat and looked into her mirrors checking the side door lock. It was in place. Suddenly, she caught the shadow of something under her truck. At first, she assumed it might be a dog. A horn blew slightly, then the figure fled behind something else out of the sight of her mirrors. This troubled Red High Heels. She thought to herself, "Always something stupid."

She sat for a few minutes to think. Behind the parking lot she connected to a fleeting shot of a familiar pick-up truck. There were two men in it. then it hit her boldly. She said aloud, "Oh, no! Dear God, please let me be all right."

Quickly, she locked her door and crouched down in the seat while Devil and his pal drove away. She felt better with them gone. She knew she had to get away as fast as possible. She had checked the truck out and was ready. She pushed the brake knobs and put Blue Heaven in gear. Watching her trailer, she stopped instantly and jumped out.

"That sorry jerk! I can't believe this! Deliberately unhooked my trailer! Oh, Lord, if I had dropped my trailer, I would be in a mess," cried Red. She felt the tears of anger swell in her eyes as another truck pulled in beside her. The driver came to her when he saw her trailer hanging by almost nothing.

"Damn, can't you get your truck under it?" he

smiled.

"It's not that. I nearly drove out from under it! I almost always back up before I take off after I get out!" whimpered Red and shaking like a leaf.

"You sure are lucky! What happened? Got an enemy?" he asked.

"I guess I am lucky. It could have been curtains!" she added.

"Yeah, but some asshole did this, didn't they?" he sympathized.

Shaking her head, Red opened her side box to get out her crank for the landing gear.

"Wait. That trailer is all but off the truck. I'm amazed it's hanging. Let me help you. If you touch anything, it might drop. I'll chock the trailer tires first," he planned.

"I did throw the air on the brakes of the trailer and the tractor."

"That will help. It might be alright, evenso, you can't take a chance," the driver told Red looking her over.

She followed him to the edge of the road where a pile of blocks and pieces of railroad ties were stacked. He smiled, "This right here will get us what we need."

Two more men came to their aid. They were watching from the restaurant across the street. Once they realized the score, they ran to help. Without words, they pitched in and grabbed blocks and ties to place supports behind the trailer.

"See, you have yourself a set of false legs. I'm glad you didn't have those landing gear legs all the way up," sighed the trucker.

"I think we should add a bit of support with

blocks on each side of the trailer, too," one man suggested.

"Not a bad idea. The truck might've loaded her back anyhow, but it sure isn't worth the chance. I don't see how she didn't drop it! She must be lucky!" smiled the driver.

"I can't believe this!" cried Red.

"I can believe anything. People will go to any lentgh to antagonize someone! Somebody is pissed at you," one of the men pinpointed.

"I saw them drive off. I also saw a shadow from under the trailer. He must have pulled the pin-lock open while I went for a cup of coffee. I just didn't think they would do me like that." Red put her hands to her eyes and brushed away the tears and gritted her teeth. "I get so mad. When I get angry, I always cry."

"I'd be more than mad. If you would have lost it, I bet it would have been something else. You're ready; go on and slip it under the trailer. Don't stop until you hear the lock click!" ordered the helpful driver.

"Maybe you should do it. I'm so upset I can't drive," the woman pleaded.

"Glad to!"

He eased slowly into the seat; things seemed to stay in place. He scraped the gears finding reverse then let the brakes off. Quickly, he slipped the truck back under the trailer; the loud snap of the connection was like music to their ears. Setting the brakes again, the driver jumped from the cabover and started putting the stacks of materials used back to the edge of the road.

"Want to save one of these for a "memorial" keepsake?" he laughed.

"I really prefer to forget but I bet I will back up from here on!" Red sniffed.

When the men finished putting everything in order, Red asked to pay. They had a fit, telling her not to insult them. They wanted her to have breakfast with them. She agreed, needing to straighten out her nerves. After a short time, Red excused herself to leave for home.

"Girl, don't forget to back up!" teased the truck driver.

"Shut up! Smart aleck!" laughed Red and went her way.

This time, things went smooth and she rolled onto I-85 southbound. She couldn't dismiss the fact Devil and his buddy tried to sabotage her rig. They were subject to do anything. More important, it scared her for him to know she was in town. From the depth of her stomach she felt sick. Just when she thought it was over, she found it really was not. The concern was almost too much. She planned to call the S.B.I. to let them know. Maybe they could help.

Without much thought, Red drove into the small city to find a payphone, then dialed the code number and the phone beeped. She gave the verbal code name. "Red Cobra," she said.

A familiar voice replied, "Where are you?"

"In the shopping center with my truck," she replied.

"Are you all right?"

"Yes, just scared!" Red shivered as she answerd.

"Need to see me?"

"I guess not. I'm just panicky. Devil, you know the one, he found my truck today. I saw him and someone else!" blurted Red.

"That's going to happen. Did he bother you? You know there is the court order!" Cobra reminded her.

"I just saw him, he had somebody to pull the pin-lock on my truck. I nearly lost my trailer. It would be a real mess if I had not seen his truck and managed to stop short. I mean, it was within a hair!"

"Maybe you should come to the meeting place. Why don't you stay at the shelter while you're home?" suggested Cobra.

"I really can't. I need to leave my truck somewhere. I'm going out of town for a few days then maybe it will all blow over," the woman cried.

"You can't afford to take it lightly. On the otherhand, we need more to prove he did that to your truck. That falls in the category of "chicken" work. He's a real low-life to torment you. I hadn't heard from you in a long time. I thought it was over!"

"I thought so, too. Looks like I would be the least of his concern. He has girlfriends I hear. Is my room at the building still there?"

"Yes. As far as I know, it will be there for as long as you need it. What do you want to do?" he asked.

"Just to let you know. I feel better talking to you. I guess I had better start praying!" she wept openly.

"Stay in touch and be careful. Don't be alone at anytime and mail in a daily journal of everything that happens. Don't forget people like him are so spiteful they want to ruin you. He could try to set you up. Just stay ahead of him. You are smart enough to know you need to keep yourself around people. Take the truck to the garage and we'll check it for you," Cobra suggested.

Red knew this would be the safe thing to do. A deputy took her to her car after she delivered the truck. He had received a call from Cobra prior to her arrival.

When Red drove into her own driveway, she decided to hide her car. A neighbor had a big garage and had let her use it before. As she started to walk back home, she again caught a glimpse of Devil's vehicle. She fell flat to the ground watching him slowly drive by. She knew he would turn around and slip back by. She didn't move. She didn't have time to run to her house. As expected, Devil drove back by, looking for signs of her. He boldly pulled into her driveway amd looked the house over carefully then left. Red would not have been surprised had he gone in. This probably meant that he figured she was not coming home. Hiding inside from him would have been hell for certain. She didn't want to get up. She felt like her legs were made of rubber.

Fortunately, the neighborhood dogs knew her well enough not to bark. She knew to take the moment and move fast. As she closed the door behind her, she heard a truck drive into her yard; her heart fell to the floor. She didn't know to bail out the window or roll under the bed. A grinding noise let her know it was the propane gas people making a delivery. This was good. He wouldn't come with them outside.

She took a fast shower and grabbed a new piece of luggage to gather some things to wear for the next few days. She would meet Early Bird soon. The phone frightened her with its buzzing.

"Hello!"

119

"Baby, this is your ticket to heaaven! Ready for paradise?" teased Early Bird.

"Yes! Oh Honey, I just got in the house. I changed it all up and I am ready!" shouted Red almost out of control

"Are you all right?"

"Of course, just want to get to you! I will meet you half way. That will be faster!" She whispered, "I love you so much. I need you!"

"I like that!" he cooed. "In fact, I crave that. I love you, too, baby."

They agreed on a meeting place and Red grabbed her case and locked the door behind her, feeling relieved. She turned her beeper to vibrate and grinned to herself, thinking Early would pick at her about having a beeper viberate in her pocket. She remembered him taking it from her before and telling her he was all she needed. It made her feel good to think about running into the safety and solitude of Early's wonderful strong arms. Still, she couldn't ruin their time together worrying him with Devil's pranks. Besides, she felt the old tormenter had to let go since he knew it would cause him trouble. He had just wanted to aggrivate her once more she hoped, for old time sake.

Again, she got into her hidden car and took a minute to think about the best route to be certain she was not discovered. As she started to back out, she again watched Devil's pick-up truck drive into her yard. She silently thanked God to have gotten in and out and best of all received Early's call. She eased the car back in the garage. Fortunately, her friend had left the door unlocked so she entered the house to use the phone.

Once more, she called Red Cobra to tell him Devil was at her house. She waited in the neighbor's home until she watched the sheriff car arrive. After a few minutes, both vehicles left. The sheriff deputy was following the pick-up and the two were moving out. This was Red's clue to move it quickly.

Taking a new route toward Charlotte was easiest for her now. After about a thirty minute drive, she felt home free. Going in her car anywhere could be risky with Devil tracking her. Now she wanted to place her mind on Early Bird and forget everything. Finally she appeared at their appointed spot before Early arrived. She would have time to settle down and make a few calls.

She phoned Red Cobra to let him know her whereabouts and current plans. He had to know or he might send a posse. Cobra informed Red that the sheriff had arrested Devil for driving drunk. He had gotten ahead of the officer and started speeding.

"He broke into jail for tonight. Get your ducks in a row!" the agent told her.

That was good news. Maybe Devil would give up or not bother her anymore. Red wondered how much longer she'd have to escape his wrath.

The big red Freightliner rolled into the huge parking plaza. It stopped in the fuel island. Red stopped everything and ran from the building to fling herself into Early Bird's arms the minute he stepped to the pavement.

Their lips met and Red High Heels felt him pull her tightly to his muscular body. He was moaning as he hungrily thrust his tongue deep into her mouth. She ran her hands across his broad shoulders and then his hair. She nearly fainted with his touch of ecstasy.

The two openly held on and reached for the satisfying flow of tender love.

"I love you!" she finally sighed.

"I love you, my darling. I have missed you more this time than ever!" Early quivered. He held her at arms length and looked deep into her eyes seductively smiling.

"Get the fuel! No, let me!" she smiled and grabbed the huge nozzle.

"I'll do that, honey!"

"Go to the bathroom! I know you need to. That's the way you are. See, I already have to tell you when to 'wet'!" she teased.

He laughed and ran for the "john". She had both tanks fueling when he returned and was starting to wash the windows.

"You are the partner I need! Ready for teaming with me?" he winked. "Don't answer; know I'm ready for you anytime."

"When I go back to New York, I'm selling the store. This time I will. I love you. This is all I need. You," Red promised as Early held her behind her fanny while she worked on the windows.

"I want to check the oil, too!" Early said.

"Mine or the trucks?" she laughed.

"Both!"

They finished and parked the truck then Early went in for a shower. Red found a special card for Early, thinking about the future of the night. She felt wonderful and safe.

"Dumb ass, you could have the world if you'd just do it! You want love, here it is!" grumbled Red to herself. "You're too stupid to just grab it! Early is a true man. Self, why don't you just let go of it all and fall as hard as you can?"

An older lady was nearby hearing Red talking to herself. The woman smiled, "Don't feel alone. We all talk to ourselves. I've been running with my husband for ten years, but I think people just talk to themselves anyhow. You can talk to me if you want."

"I'm at a point of running team with Early and have things that I have to do first," replied Red. "It's making me nuts!"

"Honey, my first husband was a trucker. I never went with him. I was always sorry I didn't. He wanted that more than anything but time ran out on us. He had a heart attack one day when he walked in the house from a trip and fell over dead. I guess that's the only thing I really regret. We loved each other and I could've gone with him some. It means a lot to these men, even if you don't drive."

"I have my C.D.L.," bragged Red proudly.

"Then, honey, go with him. I married a man my husband worked with. His wife had cancer and died several months before my husband. She didn't go with him either. One day he told me he needed me to go out on a short run to deliver some garden soil, you know, in bags. He had to do it at a time we were supposed to celebrate our first anniversary, so I went. He opened a wonderful new world to me. There was a splendid new relationship we found together and it has been that way ever since. Just something very special about being there for him!"

"You just got a good whiff of diesel!" laughed a bald man as he walked to her and put his arm around her waist.

"Maybe. I was just telling her how much it means to me to go with you," said the lady, blushing.

"I was talking to myself and she caught me!" Red informed. "She thought I was crazy."

"Pretty Lady really thinks this is fun! I believe she just loves to sight see, but sometimes she hates it," he continued.

"When do I hate the road?" argued Lady.

He grinned, "When we're home. She plans everything to get back out."

Early Bird set his shaving case on a nearby rack. "That's what I want my Red to do. Love the road, almost as much as she loves me."

Red put her arm around the handsome husky man and replied, "I like the road. I have been on it by myself for quite a while. It isn't like I don't know. Look here, I have my negligee!"

Red cracked her huge purse open for him to see the delicate lace in the shadows of her paperwork. Early looked and was instantly aroused with the thin silk and the aroma of Chanel No. 5.

"Oh, yes. She'll love the road! Do we have time for dinner?" Early Bird teased lifting an eyebrow seductively and winked.

"Probably should. We may never get back out of the truck," picked Red High Heels. "Maybe you people could join us."

"That would be great!" squealed the other woman.

The four enjoyed a leisurely dinner with conversation. Truckers have a way of finding mutual friends on the road. When they meet even later down the road and over the years, they remember each other. It makes for a strange and interesting network.

Hand in hand, Early and Red arrived at his truck. He helped her leap over the driver's seat and into the place for a passenger. Without words, Early closed the curtains of the big Freightliner's enormous cab turning it instantly into a cozy apartment. He reached for his beautiful lady and slowly drew her to him. Welcoming her into his home, he lightly kissed her on the neck.

She felt a tingle run through her. Quickly the need of the recent time away from him made her shiver.

"I want you forever, Early."

"I love you, Red and I don't ever want you to leave me. I need you more than ever. I just think it would be so much easier if I had you here all the time. When we get tired we can take time out. Please, Babe, stay forever!" pleaded the man.

They had been chasing each other all over the country for several years; all along, he would beg her to go with him. She always had something in the way of their dream.

"Maybe we just want to hold each other. You know I love just being here with you. I love you all the time, not just when I have you in bed. I just want you forever. I want you to marry me and let me be what you need. I love you; all of you!" Early declared.

Red felt the tears trying to surface. He was so wonderful, never demanding and so easy going with their relationship. She loved that about him. He didn't care about all the money-hungry devices that rule the average person. He was simple in his needs. He would give her the world if she would take it and protect her to the finish. He would melt all the hell away that she had to go through if she would just let him. He would go that extra mile just too be near her. He wanted only her, other women were people to him.

Everything was wrapped into him as a perfect man. The special devotion was what Red had never had. He accepted her for herself and never tried to change her to be different.

Early loved Red, she was so unpredictable and exciting. The woman had a mind of her own and great talent. She found answers to problems as they would come up. She had worked at something all her life. Having a furniture store full of stock and keeping up with all mystified Early. She was a business woman, then on the other hand she was just a good woman; one with the simple needs of wanting to share life with him. At times he felt selfish expecting her to drop that world for his. Loving her was a mystery of life that one would never be able to explain. It was astounding how she could be so feminine yet still do a man's job, too. She was a little person, soft and sexy; everything he could ever want. More importantly, she had the want for him.

"Turn your head!" smiled Red. "How can a girl get ready for bed with people looking?"

He grinned and turned away, watching her in his mirror. She carefully slipped her shoes off and dropped her tiny, short skirt to the floor. Folding it carefully, she placed it over the back of the seat. Her suit jacket had four buttons that gave no problem and she dropped it with the skirt. Gently, she eased out of her sheer pantyhose, leaving her in an elegant burgandy, lace panty and lace bra that matched. It thrilled him to know she wore this for his benefit. Red reached for her purse to retrieve a thin fabric set and changed the already dainty panty for an even more sheer and exotic high-cut pair. The day bra slipped to the floor with a simple snap then was replaced with a soft, velvety sheer-looking thing you still couldn't quite see through. The luminous garment gave Red an innocent, girlish look.

"You done yet?" Early stuttered.

"Yes, honey. I forgot to potty!" she teased.

"Well, now what?" he asked, amazed and trying to think of something.

"We're backed up at a field. Nobody's around; I'm going under the trailer," she informed, slipping on her high heels and coat.

She wasn't gone long and returned yelling, "It's cold!"

He laughed. "We'll get a truck with a bathroom built in if you go with me. Any truck you want, you can have."

"I like this one! Know what I like best about it?"

"What?"

"You!"

Early had moved to the sleeper area and kicked off his shoes. He held the covers for her to slide beneath. He smiled at her teeth chattering from the cold. He slipped into his pajamas and laid beside her. "Want the front or the back?"

"Maybe the top!" she laughed.

"Top bunk?"

"No, love! The top! Like this!" she giggled, jumped on top of him and eased her lips across his. "I love you, Early."

"I love you, too!" he whispered and rolled her over.

"You've lost weight!" noticed Red.

"Not much. I've been exercising and missing meals. But mostly, I've been grieving over you and worrying, too," admitted Early.

"You worry about me? Now why?"

"You are out there on your own, baby. I need to be there for you. You're in my mind all the time. Don't you realize just how I need you?" asked the man.

"No more than I need you. Hold me, honey!" she whispered and snuggled into his cradled arms. He felt so good, his smell was blending with her's and becoming one.

Early placed his lips to hers and gently moistened them with his tongue. She closed her eyes, letting her spirit meet his and soar into the intricate spiral of ecstasy. Together they found perefect harmony and their love was so abundant. Holding on and touching was everything. He was so patient and gentle, with total control and understanding. He was careful not to let her feel she was under any pressure, and many times Red would stop in the middle of heaven and drop him from the cloud. Even that made loving her more real and exciting.

"I love you! Early, I love you!" breathed Red excitedly.

The night was spent reviving every morsel of love they shared. From time to time the two lovers talked about the time away from each other. Nothing mattered, they were together now.

"That trailer. You know, the thing you hauled in here behind this love machine. Is it loaded?" asked Red evetually.

"Trailer? Do we have a trailer?" he teasingly mumbled.

"One's back there; got JOY Carriers on the side!" she panted.

"Oh that. Let's not talk about it," he whispered.

Knowing he was teasing, she continued, "Are you loaded?"

"Yes and no!"

"What kind of answer is that unless you count air?" spouted off Red.

"Yes, I'm loaded; no, I don't have to deliver it until I want to!" he eased her mind.

"I have a delivery outfit, too!" she picked.

"I'm sure you do! I really brought the trailer as an excuse to get away before you totally kill me!" he reflected. "I believe after a few days here I'll just disappear into thin air or fade away."

"We'll both fade! I'm going in the truck stop for coffee," Red announced. "I can't believe its eleven o'clock. This is another day. How time flies!"

"You hungry?"

"Just for you!" giggled Red rolling to him.

The truck didn't move for three days. This was their home of the moment. They needed each other with time to share.

Ultimately, they decided to go back to work. Red would go back to the big city. Early had a Charlotte drop. He wanted to go up the road with Red and her truck. That was always exciting. He could pace his trip to make it possible.

Red knew she could load in one day; orders were ready. One phone call would set the stage. It was neat to walk into a trailer with nothing but pads, straps and maintenance items in the morning; by the afternoon, it would be loaded so tight you'd have to force the doors closed. The manufacturers always told Red she carried two loads in one trailer. She'd defend herself with, "You like to load like it's a flat-bed." It took effort to fit furniture pieces like a puzzle. She always had to oversee the job to control her orders making certain what was on her invoice was correct. Loading special loads was more difficult than backing in, grabbing a ready load and leaving.

Early knew Red had to get her trip arranged. He planned a day away for his own delivery. As tough as it was, they finished their last cup of coffee to say their good-byes.

"I think I should just take you with me!" Early smiled.

"You should go with me!"

"Oh, God, woman! Leave me alone!"

"Then get out of here!" teased Red.

"I will!" flashed Early grabbing her for an on the road special kiss. Again, they melted into each others' arms as if they hadn't seen each other in a thousand days. They felt the rush of love again fill their being.

Without words, they walked silently to his big red Freightliner. Early unlocked his cab, opened the door and picked up his wonderful lady and slid her into the seat. She didn't object. By the time he was inside the truck, Red High Heels had removed her coat and little dress and was lushiously swaying her perfect body, showing a set of exquisite lace high-cut briefs and a matched top that made her breasts pop like two soft velvety mounds. He could see the shadow of her small pink nipples through the thin lace. He watched her ease to the bunk and turn the covers back. She commanded him with the slightest movement of her hand to come to her.

Early dropped to his knees before Red and

pulled her warm flesh next to himself. His lips found her neck, she grabbed his hands and moved them to her buttocks. The feel of her skin was enticing, lighting him as though he were on fire inside.

Red's seductive eyes flashed desire. Early gently placed his open lips on hers and thrust his tongue into her mouth, feeling the movement of her tongue on his. She stretched her shapely legs around his waist and moved provocatively. Red grabbed the front of his new plaid shirt and yanked it impatiently, tearing the fabric and sending the buttons pinging around the sleeper. Early unsnapped the small bra top and let it fall as he reached for her perfect breasts with his moist lips. Red unsnapped his buckle; then, he finished removing his trousers for her.

The woman rubbed her chin gently over his slightly hairy chest as he carefully removed her string of a panty and his own briefs. She felt his pulse tingling and her own deep tintinnabulation. The overwhelming power of desire was at its peak. They continued to boister each others fantacies, giving way finally to the sweet ripple of every muscle in their bodies as they committed their fevor. The deep endulging union left them both faint, yet surging as if on a plateau above them with a mass of trumpets playing "Taps".

They clung to each other, receiving the total sensation of freeness in their love. Their lips met gently as they murmured, "I love you!" In the glory of it all, they soared emotionally from the urgencies of the moment into a flight of spiritual climax. They forgot everything for the challenge of this ultimate affirmation of love.

As the perspiration rolled from their bodies,

Red last remembered covering them with a sheet. The Freightliner's climate-control kept them in perfect comfort as they melted the hours away in bliss.

Sometime later, Red and Early were jolted to reality with the banging on the door. They both found it near impossible to respond. Finally, Early knew he should peek out. When he looked, he saw a man in uniform and a paper and pencil.

"Shit, it's the cops!" he whispered loudly to Red. Where's my shirt, honey? Oh hell, you tore it up!" Finally he rolled the window down and said, "I'm in the bunk."

The security guard displayed a psychotic attitude and replied, "You truckers think you can just park anywhere, now don't-cha? I git tard of making you move. You right on the scale!"

"I'm not on the scale unless I got towed onto them," reasoned Early.

"I know you got a bitch in there with you. She a lot lizard?" he scoffed.

"I'll be right there!" Early hotly screamed. Red found him another shirt. He threw it around his shoulders and crammed his legs into the pants from on the floor. As he was sliding into his shoes, he bound outside the big red cab and stood over the short man.

"Texas, I saw it on your truck. JOY Carriers know you're on this wild tangent. You'all been drinking? They told me this rig ain't left the lot in almost a week. What's going on? You on dope?" accused the guard.

"Look, I'm about ready to clean your clock. I'm not on the scale and I don't have a whore with me. I'm taking a few days off that I have coming. Being an owner-operator gives me something. What makes it your business?" Early snarled.

"Tell you what makes it my business, Texas. You been here too long. I saw that truck shaking like it wuz in a wind storm! That wuz a lotta hours back. Hell, you might've died with a heart attack. You ain't all that young. That girl met you here," continued the guard.

"It's my business. Get back in that store before I kick your damn ass. I haven't done anything out of the ordinary. You're just a nosy jerk! Leave us alone!"

"I can make you move from here!" he pointed to his badge. "I got the right to enforce the law."

"Look, just leave us alone and go get us a couple cups of coffee!" Early Bird pulled out a twenty. "Please!"

The security guard smiled big, took the money and left. Early returned inside the Freightliner. He looked at Red under the covers of the sleeper with a big smile on her face. She said, "I heard it all. Old Ass, just nosy!"

"I guess so. Want to stay tonight?" asked Early.

"Might as well. It's too late to do anything else but stay," whispered Red. "I want some coffee. Think he'll come back?"

"Sure!" replied Early as a knock sounded from the side of the truck. "Better slip into some clothes, honey. He is nuts, and might sell tickets in the truck stop."

Red sat up and put on her coat and high heels.

Early opened the door. The man handed him the coffee and craned his neck to see who was in the sleeper. Red moved into the passenger seat. Her red heels were sexy and the full length white mink coat made for an ensemble that was rarely seen at truck stops and practically never in a place the guard would frequent. He concluded there had to be something fishy about this deal.

"Why you dressed like that? Just movie stars wear fur and stick heel shoes like that. This is a cover!" he excitedly jumped. "That's right, she is famous!"

"All right, just don't tell nobody. JOY hauls for movie stars," teased Early Bird.

"Yeah! I heard that before! Yeah! You'se carrying a movie star. Maybe you both are movie stars! I gotta go. If you need anything, let me know. My name is Private Eye. That's an undercover name. I have to be careful and not let anybody know the real me. Like you, you have to be careful. Wow! Movie stars! Just wait till I tell my wife!" he jubilantly squealed.

"Tell you what. Let Red step out of the truck and give you an autograph and I'll take your picture with her!" urged Early.

"Oh, God! You will do that?"

"Sure!" Early licked his lips and chuckled. He caught the shock on the beautiful woman's face.

"I don't have anything on under this coat! I'm going to kill you," divulged Red coolly.

"He won't know!" snickered Early.

"Fine, I'll flash him when I get out!" snapped Red as she carefully stepped out of the truck.

The man looked at her as if she were the only woman he had ever seen. "Wow!"

Red wrote her name and "good luck" on the

paper he extended. She grabbed her lapels and pretended she was going to remove the coat. Early rushed to her and covered her with his arms. They laughed but Early tripped and they stumbled to the ground with Red's coat slipping to the side, revealing her naked fanny.

Private Eye gulped, and screamed, "Citizens arrest! Citizens arrest! You're naked!"

Early found his feet quickly and thrust Red into the rig. He started begging the man to let it slide. After a long time, he once again convinced the man that movie stars are different.

Red High Heels was on the war path and ready for action.

Early knew words would only get in the way. He found her moving lips with his and quitened her anger. They once more slipped into that special paradise where Red had learned to loose herself with him.

"My movie star!" whispered Early.

"My leading man!" Red whispered, feeling the tingle. The heat of loving returned again. Red rolled on top of Early and jerked off the shirt. The buttons again flew around the truck.

As he quickly kicked his pants off, he muttered, "You sure are hell on shirts. Guess I'll know to get disposables!"

Early returned to her web that he was wrapped into. This was everything he desired. Soon, it would be forever. With his eyes shut, he fell prey to her every whim.

Love was a plateau unto itself. The two were auspicious. It was almost impossible to pull away.

CHAPTER 7

The seventy-nine International and the new Freighliner were like old lovers in the edge of the turnpike parking plaza. They glistened in the early morning sunlight as if to come alive with the rising sun. Both trucks were soon to go separate ways from this point. A door opened on the cab of the big red Freightliner and two happy people emerged. The man helped the woman down the steps and then pulled her tightly to himself. People around them merely went about their own business.

"You make any day beautiful. I really love you, Early," smiled Red High Heels pertly. "I'm going to miss you more than ever. I never realized how astounding love really is. Compared, I guess I haven't loved at all before you."

"Tell me about it!" chuckled the man. "Say

you promise you'll get things all worked out soon."

"Promise!" exclaimed Red. "I want to run with you. We can make it work. If things get too closed-in, we'll just pull over and take a walk. We're going to be the super-team!"

"I don't think anything can take me far from your sight!" declared Early Bird. "Let's get our coffee and check out the plumbing."

"Sure! Let's eat outside here. It feels so good. Once I leave for New York, I could be in my rig for three to six hours. It has been like that at times. You know how the city traffic can get."

"Yeah, how well I know. Glad I'm heading toward Philly!"

"See! You're already glad to get rid of me!" pouted Red.

"Not hardly!" Early denied, ushering her into the big rest area building. They agreed to meet back at the trucks.

Red returned first, then began checking her truck. Finding a trailer light out, she decided to change it. Her tools for quickie repairs were beside her driver's seat and a bulb was with it. Early had told her often that bulbs blow in groups. Now she assumed she would be going all over the trailer lights since this second one was blown. "All lights must burn" is the D.O.T. rule.

When Early Bird reappeared, he looked carefully for his beautiful trucker. Seeing the edge of a furniture pad sticking out from the back trailer tire, he tiptoed to check it out. Easing behind the furniture trailer, he saw Red's legs, indulged in black slacks and red heels, sticking out from under. At first, she was singing a little weird song she had learned from Mule

Train:

> "Oh the rabbit and the possum,
> Went down the hill a fightin',
> The rabbit jumped in a crack,
> And burst his sides a laughing!
> Big eyed rabbit, hoopity high
> Big eyed rabbit high
> Big eyed rabbit, hoopity high
> Big eyed rabbit high, high, high!"

Suddenly she was quiet and said out loud to herself, "The wrong bulb! Might know!"

Early had to dodge the sliver of lightening when it flew past him, landing in a nearby bush. The woman was aggrivated with her finding but continued to work on the wire set-up. He could see the dust and pieces of wire dropping onto her chest as she readjusted the connection. He slipped toward her, setting their coffee and sandwiches on the pad. Crawling beside Red he said, "Let me do that for you!"

"Look, being a man doesn't make you the one who has to wire this durn rag. I drive it, I'll fix it!" she exploded.

"Oh, woman, don't get touchy. All you need is the bulb. I have one in my pocket!" he offered.

"You don't" Red smiled.

"Here, I had it left over from my truck. I just changed the same bulb. I knew you had one out so I saved it for you!" He handed her the item, not daring to interfere.

"Here, then do it! Guess this will be one of your chores! I'll be the cook!" teased Red, calming.

Soon, they forced their way into their trucks to join the rat-race. Early turned off the Pike toward Philadelphia. Both lovers felt the lonesomeness in the pit of their stomachs. After CB "good-byes" both flipped the dials to channel nineteen. The traffic had picked up all over. It was going to be one of those intense travel-days.

Ultimately, Early Bird reached his destination and dropped the trailer, receiving orders from dispatch to go about thirty miles bobtailing and pick up a load for Alabama; from there, he would most likely head for Nevada. That seemed to be the rule for these trips. It was a sad grind without Red, but he liked the big miles that JOY Carriers allowed his rig. They didn't make you waste much time.

Early could run as much as he desired. He never understood the people who constantly complained about not being home every week. It was not possible to get long runs and hang around the house. As much as he loved Red, he still had old reality knocking on the door. He had to make a living like everybody else. Early settled in for the days and weeks of long, hard driving. He was ready to deliver dispatch their next request. The big, red Freightliner rolled endlessly and its' big engine proudly boasted its power. The long nose guided the balance of the train-like rig west and south, keeping with his heavy schedule. Sometimes, Early almost imagined his truck to look like the smooth bounding of the JOY Carriers logo, such a dramatic and elegant silver fox. Being an owner-operator gave him the best of the trucking world. He had trucked in every possible way but this suited his fancy. He could customize his comfort and travel with pride.

Red caught a traffic snarl just before the George Washington Bridge. This was an intense one. She could see the smoke of an overturned vehicle ahead. The loud blast from the fire-squad was coming from behind her. There was no place for a big truck to go so she prayed somebody would let them through. Maybe a life might need saving. Still, the four-wheelers seemed to only be interested in holding their place as if they may never get to the other side. Red tapped her horn and motioned to a car beside her to pull in front of her rig. Once it moved, the traffic opened a small lane to let the emergency vehicle through.

Six hours for this trip made Long Island a welcome sight. Red drove into the parking lot to find waiting faces grinning out the window. One of the delivery men opened her cab door.

"We wondered if you wuz getting here!" he said.

"Traffic! Wild traffic!" muttered Red, pushing him out of her way. She disliked her male help assisting her from the truck. "Here, take this key and open the trailer."

"We been delivering all morning," he whined.

"Yeah, and you'll deliver all afternoon and maybe half the night!" Red stated. "You've been on vacation while I was away."

"Naw! We done delivered da big bedroom and a couple sets," he tried for approval. "I took that funeral home order; that big one. I ought to get a big tip!"

"Tip! That's all in hell you jerks think about...Money. Then you blow every cent you can get, find or steal!" growled Red.

"Ain't no reason not to. I just drink a bit of beer once in awhile. By the way, we got some more

141

hanging up calls. Your old buddy, Devil, rode by this morning," grinned the helper as if happy to report the bad news.

Red went on declining to comment. The day passed too fast and with the evening there would have to be more deliveries that would go on into the wee hours. People in the area didn't care when you delivered as long as they received their orders. In this, Red was crazy. She would go into any part of New York. Her help called her "nuts" or "lucky". They were always able to get the jobs done without incident. If someone complained to Red that she was taking chances, she would say, "You only live once. Besides, nobody wants to aggrivate a redhead."

The wind picked up and rain drizzled lightly as predicted. They drove on to Brooklyn anyhow. Protocol would have them stop for dinner and Red would allow her helpers a beer, but only one. Deliveries would be made. It went smoothly and tips for help was over-abundant.

Once back to the store, they drove into the big parking lot and ambled into the store. One fellow lit a cigarette and Red came to a hissy.

"Damn it! Go outside! You know you can't smoke in here!"

She unlocked the front door for him and half apologized, remembering how she had slaved him all night. Standing outside with him, Red saw the light in the sleeper of her truck was burning. She sighed, "I can't believe I left that on. I didn't! There was no reason to have a light there. I arrived during the day."

"Maybe it wuz jest on!" puffed the man.

"No, I didn't do that. Somebody has been in my truck!" Red flipped.

For the moment, she thought about Devil and that it could be possible for someone to be inside the rig. "Go call the police!"

"Police? You stupid? Ain't no reason to bother them!" he grumbled as he went stomping inside.

It only took the patrol car minutes to arrive. They were aware of Red's continuing trouble with Devil. "How do I get in this thing?" smiled the young cop, looking up at the cabover. "I've never done this before!"

Red told him what to do and pushed him up from the backside into the passenger seat. She in turn climbed into the driver's seat. Immediately, she saw the missing radio and the scrambled inside. "Oh, no!"

"What?"

"You don't think I keep my truck like this?"

"Let's do a report. There has been lots of this lately."

The report was filed and another hour was killed that should have been spent sleeping.

Red flashed, "I know who is behind this!"

"You are probably right, but you can't be certain!" he sympathized. "Get a copy of the report tomorrow. Well, later. It is tomorrow."

Feeling violated and angry, Red trudged tiredly into the store. For the rest of the sleepless morning, she stared at the ceiling trying to plot a plan for stopping the trouble. She decided, getting rid of her stores would be the answer, yet running wasn't her chosen style. She had already ran once to survive, now she would have to go again. Tears filled her eyes antagonizing in her turmoil.

The next day she felt even worse and more

worried. She knew Devil was on the warpath and it wouldn't stop. He would do everything to intimidate and threaten. Once he had told her, "You can't stop me! I am there when I want to be. Like a thief in the night, I'll get you. You'll never be anything, you ain't gonna be nothin'! I'll get you put in jail if I want to and nobody'll ever speak to you. I'll make people despise you. Your family, friends and business contacts will hate you. When I'm through with you, you'll be nothing and have nothing. Do you understand? You're nothing!"

These words stuck in her head. He was proving he could sneak around like a serpent, taking her pride to destroy it. For five years Red had fought to keep him away. Just when she thought it was over, it was happening again. He was to be feared, he was a true criminal. As well, he was handsome and charming and could make the world believe in him. It was crazy, how he was isolating Red from her people, forcing Red into a paranoid state of existance. She had to keep an eye over her shoulder and hope nobody would get in the way of a bullet designated for her. Once more, she pulled herself within the confines of her fears and prayed for the best. Few could understand her situation, most did not want to be involved. Others were as fearful of Devil as anyone else he pledged his wrath; a walking time bomb.

A tall gray haired man walked into the store. He had an accent and looked over every inch of her showroom. Red thought it peculiar. He was very business-like and well-groomed. After a short time, he asked her to talk with him in private. Red knew this was good or the end of her world, she obliged. He proposed to purchase her business; additionally, he

144

wanted to know price, availability and other details.

"I don't know, let me think about it," Red High Heels responded as she showed him out.

"Here's my card. Call when you are ready," he suggested calmly.

The redhead watched him get into his shiny, fancy car and drive away. She filed the card with her most carefully hidden papers, thinking long and hard. This could be the answer; then, she worried that it was too good to be true, too simple. She calculated, probably a trick of some sort. Finally, she forced all the negative thoughts out of her mind and left for her second store. She was in the process of closing it. This was the first step anyhow to change. That store was far away and rather secluded. She arrived and ordered her help to load a lot of extras into the extra drop-frame trailer, so by the first of the month this would be vacated. There was much more inventory than Red had realized, however, the other store was boundless with space and would absorb what wasn't sold in the storewide sale.

It was a Saturday night. She felt at odds with herself. There was that un-told rage in the pit of her stomach; the feeling you get when you feel something is off balance. The big, full moon didn't make anything better. The weather was as unpredictable as a woman's mind. It was snowing heavily again on top of the last months snows and bad weather. The freeze didn't let up. Even when the sun did shine, it never seemed warm. Red went to the nearby diner for dinner and ordered her favorite prime rib. Just when she was being served, the hostess brought her the phone for a call.

"I thought I would catch you there!" Early

Bird feverishly alloted. "I had to hear your voice!"

"Wonderful! I love you. We're moving the store from way out on the Island. I'm getting rid of it!"

"That's my baby," he whispered seductively.

Red was glad to hear his voice and finished her dinner quickly so she could receive his call again back at the store. They talked a long time but Red never brought up the story of her problems. She couldn't worry him with something he couldn't do anything about. It would change, she would make it happen. Early had the safety of his job, the responsibility of the truck and his personal well-being to keep him busy. This was not the time to bring up trivial possibilities. Besides, Red figured that Devil had had his fun with his latest agrivation. It would all work out. Getting out of New York would end Devil's rage she consoled herself. Nobody could take Early Bird's love from her.

The days ahead engulfed routine work and fighting the ten inches of snow that paralyzed the city. In many ways this was good. It let time set in and made things seem back to normal. Red then assumed the "Devil-thing" must be over. She knew that JOY Carriers had Early Bird running south and into California. This was best, too. She didn't want him involved. He always wanted to kick-ass but that's a man thing that wouldn't solve this.

Most of her helpers from the south had been sent home on the bus. They needed a break and this was the best time. Her New York crew could handle the slower version of furniture sales. Even so, people were still finding their way to the showroom.

Red wasn't certain her truck would move in

the deep snow. She stood at her front door watching other rigs as they carefully moved on in the slush. The Transtar had not been started for a few days. Snatching her keys, she headed for the old International. She always talked to the vehicle.

"Well, Blue Heaven, let's see if the old shiny 290 will kick off."

It was icy and slick getting into the rig but she managed. Knowing that it would have to have starting fluid, Red took the can and found the little hole devised for this purpose then sprayed a good amount.

"That should do it!" she muttered. "Now, come on, Baby! Kick over for Mama!"

It didn't take much effort and then, Old Blue blew out a huge puff of smoke and the engine was giving its best to reach an even rhythm. She gave it a gentle assistance with holding the fuel slightly to it. The old truck quickly warmed enough to be left to idle.

"You take your time and I'll go inside. I want you ot have a chance to eat a little meal of petro! Bless your little fuel pump! I'll be back!" sighed Red.

She jumped from the rig happily. It was a wonderful feeling for the moment. The store would be closed the next few days so this would give her some time. Red got her things together and gave the truck time to warm well. Once back into it, she noticed the buzzer for the brakes was still on and the air was barely up. She moved the air buttons and pumped the brake but nothing changed.

"I guess you have water in you lines! Can't do nothing without that solved."

Red High Heels went into the store and phoned the mechanic in North Carolina. She relayed her situation.

In a slow drawl, the man suggested, "Go out there and beat that foot pedal up and down. It's probably got ice in it."

"It's been running for about an hour."

"That's not got nuthin' to do with this. Got some de-icer?" he asked.

"Probably. I buy all that junk when I sit around the truck stops," she asserted.

"Take your connection to the trailer and pour some of that into the air line going into the trailer. You know, the hole in the glad-hand," he explained. "It would be good to have it in the line anyhow. I wondered if you were moving. Nobody else from here can get their trucks started. Get your idle stick out and let it run tonight if you plan to go anywhere."

"I might just come home if I can get out!" stated Red.

She went back to the truck and banged the pedals again but a bit harder this time. Nothing changed. She found the juice that was appropriate for the glad-hand and poured some into it. It seemed a strange thing to do. It was hard to know if any was going into the lines but the stuff seemed to disappear. Back into the truck she jumped and rubbed her cold hands. She laid her head on the wheel to think, finally the air buzzer stopped and she looked to see the red light had disappeared.

Happily, she squeaked, "You old, faithful angel!"

Red was going to go home. She made a short note for the help and went to the truck. The North Carolina weather had been much better. It was a handicap to try to work in this weather. Ice was all over the parking lot, making it very difficult for customers.

As she started to drive off, she caught a movement in the little sleeper. She glanced back and saw a foot in a heavy boot sticking out. Her mouth went dry and her heart started to race. She knew it had to be the "enemy". She thought, 'Oh, lord, why now?' Trying to remain calm, Red talked out loud to herself as if she were alone.

"Dang, I forgot my money bag!" she said and quickly opened the door and jumped to the ground. The door to the store was locked but she had the single key for it in her pocket. By racing to the building, Red had given herself away. She managed to get the key into the deadbolt lock and open the door.

Looking back at her truck still running and ready, she caught the glimpse of a big arm with a little pistol pointed in her direction. She fumbled to get inside with the key. As she did, she heard a shot ring clearly, then two more. She remembered to lock the deadbolt on the inside then ran from the window area. Another shot was fired, then there was silence. It seemed forever. Red was hiding under the shelving while calling the police; she was so stunned, she couldn't talk. All she could do was beg, "Help!"

Red dropped the phone, letting it dangle to the floor when she heard her truck leaving the yard. Her head started to spin and a big ache struck. She fell to the floor in silence.

"My truck!" she mumbled, trying to recover from shock.

She heard the police banging on the front door and crawled in that direction. Forcing herself up from the carpet, she unlocked the door. The police barged in, with guns in hand, searching everything.

"No! Not the store...My truck! He stole my truck! He shot at me!" blubbered the redhead through fear. "Do something! He got my truck!"

"Calm down!" reasoned one officer.

"Calm down? Are you nuts? My truck is gone! That's my life!" cried Red in panic, breaking down into a nervous cry. "My truck! Please, help me! Find my rig!"

Her old friend from the beat reached for her hand, "Red, we will find your truck. It can't disappear from here that easy. Give me the information so we can look for it."

Still in shock and a frantic terror, Red gave the information as best she could. Her insurance papers, in the store files, concluded all data. The truck was immediately reported stollen.

As the police covered the lot and building for clues and information, Red was relieved that her purse had fallen from the cab when she got out. Although it had gotten run over by her old International, important papers and money were there. Everything else became flat from the ordeal.

"Are you sure you didn't give anyone permission to use the truck?" asked the officer.

"My God! What will it take to get you people on my side? Somebody steals my truck and shoots at me and you want to know if I let them do it? I can't believe this. That bastard has badgered me, stalked me, phone me, humiliated me; you name it, he's tried it!" screamed Red in anger. "I have no rights! The rights are for your sorry criminals. I don't matter; they come first. Don't hurt their feelings or accuse the guilty; it might cause a lawsuit!"

"You have to be careful who you take up with!" replied the cop.

"You aren't no different than Devil. You let him get by with this. You're too chicken shit to stop him!"

"Lady, we can only take the report and check it out. If we get the evidence then his ass is mine!" imposed the policeman. "I don't commit the crime, I try to enforce the law. You have evidence?"

"He shot at me! The truck is missing!" stung Red.

"This is a bad situation, I'll inform you its history. The man she refers to is an old boyfriend..." started the other cop who was familiar with Red's case.

"Maybe the truck insurance will help out," guessed the cop.

"I don't have that kind of insurance, just on other people. The rig isn't all that valuable to insure but it will cost plenty to replace. Please, I need my truck!" Red started crying again. Her shoulders shook and she felt totally lost and intimated.

"We have everything. Maybe it will show up. I'm sorry," spoke the old officer friend. They looked around more and gauged several bullets from the tar-like walkway. As Red watched them, she knew Devil was the one. His technique was written all over it all. The scare tactics, stealing the truck and shooting to scare her. The cops would never believe her. She thought, 'Why would they, they are men like him and men always stick together. This is something else! My truck and trailer are gone. How am I going to get this straightened out?'

Red daydreamed that maybe he would simply

abandon the truck, just do this to let her know he could. Maybe he would get caught. Then, he could wreck and get her in a lot of trouble. Her head hurt and rang. She felt like dying. She said, "How do I ever get away from this?"

The phone rang and she picked it up. "Yes?"

A customer wanted to know if she would be open the next day. This was an urgent order, too. Red High Heels started to compose herself to try to carry on. She agreed to meet them since her transportation home had taken flight. Red grabbed a hand-truck and started moving furniture around then she laughed, "Yep, I at least have a truck. A hand-truck!"

The shock of it all started to blend with the rest of the hell she had been put through by Devil. Red couldn't help but to reflect back to the very beginning. He was so wonderful, people thought. Then, that personality changed into a strange series of mishaps. Things would disappear. He borrowed money without planning to pay it back. He insited that she wanted everything for herself, including all things that belonged to her, from her property to jewelry and anything of value. Then, his next step was playing the fear tactics. He began to threaten her life and that of her family. Red lived in fear. Many times he would hit her and force her to do whatever he said.

Although he was involved with shady deals, he never included Red. People would come around and he would go away with them or talk away from Red. One time he confessed that she was just a 'front' for him, his patsy. She would make him look good to his parole officer. Sex was not his thing, from the beginning. He was hell bent on making money in every way and taking anything from anybody that was around.

Each time Red would try to get away from him, he would beat her and threaten to kill her. She believed he would. More important, she was embarrassed for being such a fool to get involved with such a maniac. As time went on, her options got slimmer and running was nearly impossible without miserable consequences. She ran various times but would be forced back. Red couldn't understand how someone, such as herself, could get paralized by such a situation.

Many women get hooked into such situations. When you can look at it in the light, most of them are case-similar. Embarrassement and being a trusting fool makes this kind of captivity more possible. Red thought after all she had done before now, her dilemma should be finished.

The worse part of all, was there seemed no place to turn. The victim is marked by the aggressor and people turn their backs. Red's fear now was not like in the past. She was angry. She knew all this was his ploy to try to get her back under his control. This could never happen again. Death would be better than never knowing when someone was going to go off and expell their inner-rage upon you. Red also knew that in his mind he had a concept of her as a threat. Beyond all this fear was Early Bird. Such an opposite, yet at times, Red questioned Early and his motives. it was difficult to love and be loved. The scars of this kind of terror were lasting. Red watched for any sign of force and arguing was scary to her.

The S.B.I. at home had finally helped her. Where were they now, she thought as she stared into space for hours.

The night came and went. There was no sign of her truck and it all became more frightening.

About eleven o'clock the next day, without sleep, Red let into the store the policeman who was knocking on the door. He was shifting his feet and mumbling.

"Come in! Have you found my truck?"

"Damn, it's cold!" he replied. "Here, I brought you some coffee."

"Thanks. Sit down!" suggested Red, hoping there was good news.

"There are several trucks left on the side of the road on the expressway. Want to ride with me to see if one is yours? Don't get your hopes up. I think they all got stuck in the weather last night. It was brutal out. One truck is blue."

"All right, I can go. Here is a picture of the truck and trailer. Did you see anything like that?" she asked.

"Truth? I can't tell one from another. The D.O.T. is looking for it. This photo will help. When it's found, you know that is a federal crime to steal an interstate rig? The word is out everywhere. I know you can't hide a truck like that here very easily," he said.

"Do you think it is still in New York?" quizzed Red.

"If it's not found quickly, it will probably go to a shop where they chop them. They are looking hard in Brooklyn. Come on!" replied the cop.

There were seven trucks at various places on the L.I.E. but none even resembled the old cabover International. This made it more impossible to believe the truck would be found. Red started thinking about replacing it.

Several days passed, then a call came in at three o'clock in the morning. Red grabbed it, thinking it was Early. He hadn't called for some reason and this concerned her, too. After she answered, a strained male voice spoke in a whisper. She could hear paper crinkle.

"Red High Heels?" it said.

"Yes!"

"Listen carefully. I know where your truck is located."

"Oh, God! Please help me!" trembled Red in tears.

"It's in Greensboro, North Carolina. You have to go there. Don't get nobody involved or you won't get it. Do you understand?"

"All right. Where is it?"

"Go to your home down there and I will call you. Give me the number."

Red called out the number and the phone went dead. She was stunned. She could walk right into a trap but she decided to go. Once on the plane, Red felt better. At home she could get a gun for a little protection and check in with the S.B.I.

Red High Heels made certain she was near the phone and at each ring she would catch her breath and begin to shake. On about the twentieth call, the smothered voice began.

"This Red?" he asked.

"Yes!"

"No tricks, hear? Just go get your truck. It's parked in the Friendly Shopping Center lot near a bank. They have a pick up tag on it so you'd better hurry. Your key is in it, I think," he whispered.

"Why are you telling me this. Suppose I get the cops?" she asked.

"Personal reasons! Just go soon!" he uttered. "Don't get no law. You don't need to."

"Is this a trick?" asked Red in fear, yet happy for the news.

"Just get your truck and shut up. Don't tell nobody you got a call. I'm the only one that knows where it is right now. I stole it from Devil. They were taking it to Florida. Just go!" he hung up.

Red was scared but had to try. She bounced out the door and drove the hour to where her truck should be. When she saw the big beast sitting there, her heart jumped. It even looked all right. Still, the situation was too strange to be true. Then, "possession is nine tenths of the law" was a familiar saying. Red stood beside her car and stared, trying to see if someone was in it. It was too risky. She went to a phone in a nearby restaurant and dialed 911.

After explaining the situation, a car was dispatched to the truck. The sheriff and a highway patrolman arrived at the same time. Red walked to them, "I called you. I was afraid to get in it!"

"You better be glad you didn't get caught driving this thing. We had a watch for it. This is the one from New York?" the trooper snarled. "The only trucks that get stolen around here are these furniture wagons. Usually, they leave here loaded and you find them empty. This has been gone a week. They had time to do whatever and dump it. That's what they usually do. Your agent says this is spite work. Don't matter. It pulls the same amount of time. I have to go over it and make a report. Got your license and truck papers?"

"Here's my license. The truck papers are inside but I have the truck and trailer titles, too."

"Good!" he responded and started his investigation. After an hour of checking and looking, he made a car-radio call. Soon a D.O.T. officer and drug dog arrived. They continued their trail to search for who was responsible.

"I know who did it! I saw his foot in New York. He shot at me!" Red exclaimed.

"Well, you have to refer to them as suspects. We already talked to him. He has fifty people saying he was here when the truck disappeared from New York. Even his mother says he was with her. That doesn't mean he didn't have it done. Somebody did," D.O.T. injected. "This is a slap in the face for us, too."

"At least you can have your truck when we release it. We need to open the trailer. I hope things are all right. Did you have a load? It seems full!"

"No, I was coming home; pads, straps and six pieces of furniture. We come back empty, usually," supplied Red.

Everything finally checked out. The rig was dusted for fingerprints and turned over to the owner. Nothing had been done out of the ordinary, other than smoking. The cops kept all the cigarette butts, drink bottles and trash in the floor. Red checked the tank and found it nearly empty. They had been filled in New York so it made it easy for them to get the truck south. As the police told her, it takes times for the A.P.B. to get into their nationwide network.

It felt strange getting back into the seat she had decided she would never see again. Everything looked wonderful. Things were mostly like when it left. Just location changed. Red was more than grateful to whoever called. It must have been another of his victims. Even so, Red got ready to leave and headed for the first fuel stop she could find. She left her car in the parking lot. In fact, she didn't care if she ever got the car. She had to have her truck.

"Blue Heaven, I thought you were gone to the glue factory. Thank God you are here!" said Red aloud. She was glad too it was returned with the police checking it out.

At the fuel island another furniture truck drove to the pump beside her. She hung the nozzles and went inside. She had carefully locked her doors now and would do so in the future even for a moment. What a risk. Open doors are forever a no-no.

Old Blue was thirsty. Everything else was all right.

Red drove to Elm Street and found the I-85 sign and followed it south. Soon, she backed her rig into a new location she found for parking; she was back to the old days of hiding the truck. Red felt this would be best at least for the time being. Although Red was excited to get the Transtar back, she knew this might not be the end. Devil didn't give it back and she had no way of knowing how it would effect him. With the rig safe, Red retrieved the car and worked on getting her orders in together. She made it a vivid point to always have someone with her. There was no reason to take chances again.

Not wanting to worry everybody, Red kept the details to herself. Kikki Doo was the only one she felt that she could trust. Her daughter was angry.

"You had better be careful! He is crazy!" she steamed flatly.

"At least I got out of the truck. Suppose I had driven off!"

"Oh, Lord, you might have gotten killed. He shot at you so he had a gun!" grieved Kikki.

"Wish they had caught him with that gun in NewYork. That is a seven year prison term for somebody like him!" Red revealed. "But, Devil is slick and gets by."

"One day, he'll meet his match. He will just do anything. I can't understand how he is so lucky. He gets by," cried Kikki. "You don't deserve to have to go through all this. Please be careful. You are the only mama I've got."

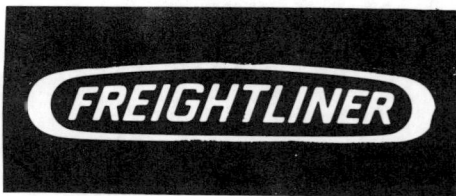

CHAPTER 8

Early Bird was tired of not being able to get in touch with Red. She had become so strange; one day telling him how much she loved him and then disappearing. He was determined to put a stop to it or just let her go her own way. Love shouldn't be so painful. He finished fueling and was leaving Memphis to find Red. His truck could be serviced later.

Finding a phone, he pressed the numbers of the calling card and the call went through. The phone rang twenty times which irritated him tremendously. Four weeks had passed since he had had a decent conversation with his woman. When he could catch her with a call, she seemed to be hiding something. He had to find out, once and for all.

He cradled the phone and walked away, then turned around and tried again. He mumbled out loud,

"Hell, I want to know what's wrong!"

"Hello," answered a sweet voice that melted all his suspicions.

"Honey, I'm in Memphis!"

"Coming home to me?" she sighed.

"Want to meet me?"

"I will. Where?"

"Greensboro," he answered.

"That's lots of driving for you," Red whispered. "How about I take a plane to catch you part way. Then we could come back together."

"No, I'm coming in," Early decided. "I can handle it. I'll call you later. This will give you more time. I'll run on in and leave the truck at Tri-Ad Freightliner. You can pick me up there."

It was settled.

Early felt better then returned to his truck. When he got inside a young woman was sitting in the passenger seat. He was startled. Not having his door locked was stupid.

"Hi!" she grinned through thick lips and flipped her hair.

"What're you doing in my truck?"

"I need a ride. Thought you might help me. I broke down, me and my boyfriend. That car over there," she grinned.

Her clothes were fairly decent. She didn't look like a lot lizard. Maybe she did need help, he surmised.

"I just need to get to the next town about twenty miles. I live there."'

"Get out. The company won't let us have riders. I could loose my job. Here, take this. Go get a cab!" he said, throwing her a ten dollar bill.

"I don't want money. I just want to ride!"

"I've got to go! Go on and get a bus or something," he insisted.

"Can I do something for you?" she asked.

"Hell, no! Now get out before I call a cop!" he angrily yelled. "Go on!"

The woman laughed real big and flashed a badge. "You said the right thing, Big Boy!"

"That would be entrapment!"

"We've had trouble around here with some trucker that has been picking up women and taking them off. Happens about once a week."

"I wasn't asking for anything. Why me?" asked Early.

"You were here!" she giggled and jumped from the truck.

On down the road, Bird wondered if she really was a cop. He didn't have time to find out. She could have been; then, she could have been a dope carrier or maybe even a female rapist, he mused.

Weather was in his favor and so was traffic. He put the pedal to the metal and made history. He stopped for a rest and grabbed a snack. Arranging the final plans with Red, he dashed into the rig and kept trucking.

Early felt good seeing the big sign for Freightliner on I-40. It wasn't very late as he had first thought it might be. Red was in their parking lot waiting. He stopped. She came running and jumped into his lap. For a woman who had been acting cool, she sure got hot.

She grabbed him tightly and gently slipped her tongue across his lips and whispered, "I love you and I missed you. It's been miserable. Hurry, I got us a motel across the highway!"

"Get in, I'll run this to the back. I'll drop the trailer for them. I have a little oil leak that needs checking. They know what to do. Get off me, woman, and let me get out of here!" Early teased. His old Red was back. Maybe he had just gotten lonesome and imagined things. Red had a lot of pressure on her he knew. Not like just plain trucking, she had to make all her decisions alone.

When she opened the room to the big hotel suite, Early was totally pleased. She had decorated it for his late birthday and had everything seductive and soft. She took his bag and dropped it on the luggage rack as she led him into the huge bathroom. The Jacuzzi was ready with bubbles and scented water. Bits of snacks were beside the big tub.

"Wow, woman, this is what I call heaven on earth! I sure am glad this happened before I got too old!" he whispered while removing his clothes and joining her in the elegant pool. The lavish fixtures and plush carpet fitted the dream style. Early reached for Red High Heels and gave her the kiss they had so longed for. The soap in the water had made it very slippery and they both ended up in an underwater embrace.

"Now I look like a drowned rat!" laughed Red. She surfaced and made herself a bra with soap bubbles. "I don't care though. My baby is finally home. Thanks for being here."

Suddenly tears filled her eyes and she turned away slightly.

"Honey, I will always be here as long as you want me!" He melted with her tears. It amazed him that she picked him to love, but he was thrilled. He wanted to do the right thing with her and support her efforts. "I love you, darling!"

Only moments separated them from their first passionate reunion upon his return. Early helped her from the water and carried her to the big king-sized bed. Their lips met and they felt their temperature rising. He slid his hand gently across her shoulders and smiled.

Early whispered, "For as long as I live, I will never have enough of you. You are my every dream and my hopes. Paradise is only in your touch, your eyes, your soul and your heart. I never knew what love and loving really could be. You give it all to me. You are not just beautiful, you are creative and unique. I love it all and all of you."

Red looked radiant, a real perfect woman. Her tears moistened her blue eyes and made them glisten. A sparkle slipped through as she reached under her pillow.

With her red hair dripping wet, she looked childlike and gave him a strange smile. "Give me your hand!"

She took the left one and slipped a beautiful diamond ring on the third finger. His jaw dropped with surprise.

"This is a token of my love and adoration. Early will you marry me soon?" she whispered. "You are all I could ever want or need. I want to do it all together."

He chuckled as he grabbed her. "I was engaged to you I thought. Now I'm double engaged. Of course, we will be married anytime you say."

The suite had been rented for two days and they took full advantage. Both occasionally surfaced to call work and home. The rest of the time was spent loving, talking and cooing; a utopia of its own. Finally, they had to come off the cloud and deal with the rest of the world.

Early picked up his truck and followed Red to where she had her rig hidden. It was then Red told him about her recent confrontation with Devil.

"I'll kill him!" he declared.

"No, its over now. He won't bother me any more," cried Red. "They had evidence but nothing real. I just dropped it all. He will leave me alone now!"

"He had better. It would be best for me to just go look him up. He's the kind of bastard that can't face a real man. He just wants to mess with people smaller than him; women and kids. That bastard!" Early raged.

"I couldn't tell you on the phone. I knew it would make you crazy and you'd come home. You can't change what you are doing." Red shared, "I got away from him and I have my truck back."

"I love you and I just want to tear him apart for all he has done to you. Animals like him need to be shot! Couldn't I just go beat him up?" Early begged.

"No! Just please, leave it alone and let it go away. I can't afford the publicity for the aggravation. This is his last shot at letting me know he can be there. I feel more secure now. I am almost out of the other store and then I have a buyer for the main one. Once my ducks are in a row, I will be with you! Yippee! JOY Carriers, here I come!" Red giggled.

"All right, tell me everything from now on. Don't get cold on me. I can handle anything as long as I know you love me. I'm tough, and I won't just go off half-cocked!" promised Early.

"Good! I don't want you half-cocked!" Red laughed again.

They settled in each others' arms and felt the flow of near static excitement rush over them. Their lips met and Early coaxed her to be ready to run to New York the next day.

"We can go through Virginia together, at least," he begged.

"How about the weather in New York?" she asked.

"It's going to be good for the next week. They had a big rain that cleared things up and got warmer, too!" he told Red.

"All right!"

A day later they were again on the road. It had been a perfect stop. Early Bird was more in love with the woman than ever. Red was happy knowing she would soon rid herself the burden of the furniture business.

Red threw the furniture orders in a Ryder truck so she would not have to use her own truck. As well, she preferred driving rentals in the bad weather. This truck seemed to take forever to get going and it wouldn't do more than 60 m.p.h. down hill.

"Hey, girl! Can't you kick it a little more?" Early teased on the CB.

"How about I drive that and you take this?" laughed Red. "Better still, I have been figuring out a new device; a road hook. I can hook a furniture strap to this and the other end to yours and you can drag me to the turnpike."

"Sounds good but let's let somebody else try it

first!" laughed Early. "Why don't you drop that truck in the city and go with me a few days?"

"Maybe I will. You must have been reading my mind. That would be super!" answered Red.

The plan was set. She would spend a few days in the middle of her problems and then catch up to him wherever his destination required. Red didn't care where.

Once they left each other at the usual place on the turnpike, both drivers had easy traffic and found their destination with ease. Red wanted to drive team anyhow to make certain that was what she really did want.

Driving alone was lonesome for Red. She now missed her little black dog that had gone for years up the road with her. That was a great companion, never an argument, just always there.

Red had a strange feeling, like something was going to happen. Maybe it was just missing Early Bird and Zipper. She remembered her last trip that the dog spent with her.

* * * * *

The traffic on the Sunrise Highway was ripping. People were rushing from work to whatever would be next. Red High Heels had her blue International going slightly ahead of the flow. People in Long Island don't seem to know about speed limits. In fact, Red hardly ever saw signs regarding speed; it was as if they had vanished.

Zipper's window was open enough for her to hang her snout out. 'Must feel good,' Red thought. Then she said, "Sit Zipper!" The dog obeyed and wagged her tail with pleasure. Red threw a Hershey Kiss which she gulped down.

Behind her, Red High Heels could see a maze of flashing blue lights. They were moving fast, coming her way. The blinding glare made it impossible to know exactly what it was.

"Durn it, Zipper! I'm going to get a ticket. That's a pile of cops!" yelled Red. "That might be m y C.D.L., too!"

She had eased off the accelerator; the flashing lights bore down faster. Over the noise of the Cummins, she could hear blaring horns and sirens.

"Lord! I might as well find a pull off! I've had it now!" cried Red as she pulled onto the ramp leading off Sunrise to the service road. "Oh, God! Here they come!"

The blue lights were on her tail flashing as if flying. As they passed by the big rig, Red High Heels could read on the side of the big truck and several cars, "Lindenhurst Fire Department."

"Oh, thank God! Fire department!" laughed Red nervously. She snapped on the air brakes and grabbed her truck-dog. "You must have had your toenails crossed, pretty girl! I forgot the police here have red lights. At home they're blue!"

* * * * *

Red remembered the details of that day completely. Zipper acted as if she could have told her so but had not been asked.

Red paid the last toll to get into New York. The six wheeler cost as much to take over the bridges, tunnels and roadways as her furniture truck. They charge by the axle. Her rig had a single axle and the trailer did, too.

There was still ice hanging off the overhead roads that reminded you it was still winter. Ice slicks would form under these making slick spots on the cold road. Red had decided to call the D.O.T. and suggest they sand these spots again. A car not far ahead of her nearly wiped out as it braked coming across one of the ice patches. She made the note into her tape recorder.

Once back to the store, Red gave instructions to the New York crew. They would deliver all the orders in the one-way Ryder van then return it back to the company in two days.

The sky looked the gray that comes with the preliminary of a storm. Red's neck hurt too, a sure sign.

Early called to tell her he was still working in the northeast. He was going to Canada and then return to upper New York. It would take him a few more days.

Later that afternoon, Red received a call from Kikki Doo, who was so upset as she babbled into the phone.

"Mama! I'm so glad I got you!"

"Are you all right?" quizzed Red.

"Yes, but I don't know how to tell you!"

Red could hear her crying over the phone. Her sobbing was increasing. The mother wanted to cry with her. "What is it, Baby?"

Finally, Kikki managed to force herself to whimper, "It's Zipper."

"Zipper?" Red felt her heart race and swallowed, trying to hold strong.

"Yes, Zipper! Mama, she died!" she burst

out. "Zipper died!"

"Well, honey, she lived a long time. At least she didn't go through an awful end, did she?" Red forced herself to stay calm.

"No, she just fell over in the yard. Lucky Runner found her when he came home from the store. What are we going to do?" cried the young woman.

"Have her cremated and we will make a grave wherever you think is best. Kikki, she lived seventeen years and had a good life. That's a long time for a dog and to be in such good shape for so long. At least she didn't have to suffer. It's funny. I had her on my mind today. We'll miss her, but she gave us her best!" consoled Red.

"I know. I just wish you were here!" cried Kikki.

"You have your husband, sugar!"

"He's not you! She was *our* dog! It's like a baby died!" wept the girl.

"When I come home, we can have a funeral," whispered Red.

"We'll go ahead and do it! He took her to the vet already," managed the girl.

"Need me home? I can come!" Red carefully mentioned.

"I wish you would come!"

Red hung up to call the airport. She had just enough time to catch a plane. Six hours later, Kikki was greeting her at the airport in Greensboro.

The ashes of the dog was in the trunk of the car in a box. As Red dropped her carry-on into the back, she glanced at it.

"Is that Zipper?"

"Yes, Mama. I didn't have time to go home.

I wanted to make sure we would have her for the funeral," smiled the girl as she swished her long red hair that fell casually around her shoulders.

They drove homeward, planning the final service for Zipper.

"I already told everybody. We're going to have an early morning service and breakfast after. I guess about fifty people will come. Zipper liked the morning best!" she planned.

The next morning, very early, about the time it started to become light, Red had to be dropped off at her truck with the ashes. Lucky Runner set them in the floorboard of the cabover.

"Zipper would want her final ride," he grinned. "You know Kikki! Your rig is her house!"

Making closure seemed important for everyone. Zipper was different. Red drove the now tractor-trailer-hearse and parked in front of Kikki's beautiful, modern home. All the guests had arrived.

The men took the ashes to the backyard where everyone had gathered. The tears were flowing; it was a true trucking memorial. Kikki sang a song that Zipper used to love. Then, she had Red to talk a few seconds and the package was put into an urn, then covered. It was over, but they all knew Zipper would live on through their memory.

"A truck dog is different. They give you protection and companionship like no other. We did it all together!" Red smiled as she placed her long stem yellow rose at the base of the tomb.

After breakfast, Early Bird caught her on her cell phone. "I can't believe you are in North Carolina!" he exclaimed.

"Had an emergency. A funeral!"

"Oh, I'm sorry. Who?"

"Zipper!" Red answered.

"That's terrible. You all right? How about Kikki?"

"Of course, just had to come for Kikki. She was so upset! She had to see Zipper after she had died. We did a funeral."

"How sweet! I should have been there."

"I just flew in to be here," said Red.

"I'm in Greensboro, now! Can I come over?" Early surprised her. "I got a load this way."

"I'll meet you in High Point, same as usual!" She screamed.

Borrowing a car, Red met Early and they returned to the house. While he checked out the burial sight and dropped one of Kikki's roses at the base of the urn, Red readied herself to leave out with him. They planned to run team for a week. She would test it in a different way now.

Red had a ton of stuff to be absorbed into the big Freightliner. The funeral procession seemed to follow them to the truck to see them off.

An old friend of Red's giggled, "I can't believe this is you going out in this huge thing! I had heard you drove one but I never paid any attention to that. Sure is different seeing you get in it for real! Don't it scare you?"

"No! At first I nearly died when I drove. All that power and sitting up so high! A cabover like I have is a worse feeling than a conventional; straight down. Men always tease me saying I'd be the first at the scene of a wreck!" answered Red.

"I could never do this. I could dig riding in one. It's probably like a bus!" concluded the friend.

Several other women had to get in the big clean cab and look around. They were laughing and joking. Early Bird found it not funny having a bunch of nosy hens clucking around but he kept quiet and helped them in.

"Red!" giggled one refined attorney's wife. "Do you do 'it' in here? This is like a room!"

"I swear to God!" gruffed another. "It is a little, miniature apartment!"

Two of them jumped into the nice, cleanly made bed and ruffled the covers, getting dirt in the floor. They jumped and giggled as they played 'discovery'. Early Bird had it just 'so', especially for Red. He had even slept on the top bunk saving it.

"Look! Flowers!" snickered one woman.

"My lord! Look, pink lights and listen to that music!" crooned another.

"Shit! This fool has a bunch of gifts wrapped for the pussy cat!" jeered another.

"Oh, hey! Dig this, the smelly stuff. Oh, God, he is a sexy fool!" whispered the first woman.

"Look at this! He must wear silk pajamas!" faintly smiled another.

"Oh, my God! This is fantastic! Oh, God, this is the most sensuous place I've ever seen! Makes me hot to be in it! Oh, Red, how can you ever drive this! I'd have him in that bed all the time! He's a damn looker! Look at those big hands!" informed another woman.

All the women tried to get to the door to check out his hands, then, as they filed out of the truck , stricken with total awe and romantic fantasies, they glanced directly to check out Early Bird's crotch.

The next group had to drift through the truck

as if on a paid tour. They too were excited and talking rapidly. Once more Early was putting up with their giggling and snide remarks for the sake of his woman. A truck was home to him. People wouldn't go jump into their beds and act stupid, he surmised.

He warned, "Be careful. The maid got out in Washington, D. C. Red expects my home to be perfect!"

Red winked approvingly to Early Bird and whispered, "I love you!"

He thought to himself, 'You might not love me if one of those bitches pisses me off!'

Once again, the women were shrieking and groaning.

"Oh, this is terrific! My God, a feather-down comforter! Ahh, it's so silky and soft!" gloated one.

"Lord! Look at that refrigerator! Bet he has champagne!" she moaned as she tried to figure out how to open it. Red flipped something to reveal the contents.

"Oh, shit! Shit! Jesus!" wildly hollered another. "Look! That man has caviar and filet mignon!"

"Hell! Look at this! Damn it! Avocados, shrimp, dips!" groaned a little lady.

"This has got to be the height of damn sexy!" hollered another. "He has teeny, raw oysters! How fabulous! I'll bet she uses a pure gold fork and feeds him these one by one! Can't you just see him rolling them around his cute mouth!"

"Oh, God! Shut up! Big Dan wouldn't roll a McNugget if it were sitting on his pecker!" revealed the first woman.

They all laughed and agreed their lives were

simply hum-drum in the posh way they were accustomed to and settled with.

Red's eyes lit up as she smiled, "Ain't this special? I mean some kind of special! Home in this big, sexy truck with my Baby. You just can't imagine what it's like to make love and be totally in the nude in that wonderful nest. The engines purr while you do it and you go crazy. Sometimes the truck rocks so hard the police have to get the emergency crews out to kept it from flipping over!"

"Oh, God! How wonderful! I haven't had that much excitement since my children were born!" remembered a lady.

"Me neither!" agreed another, sitting on the side of the bed. "Tell us more! What else do you do?"

"We ride everywhere, see everything and make love all night long. We scream when we reach our climax and begin all over," Red replied. "When I do it, it has to be in the truck or trailer or on top of a load of Kotex or something special!"

"You screwed on top of a load of Kotex? How appropriate! The fuckin' things!" grieved another woman, daring to be a real heathen.

"Oh, yes! We carry all kinds of stuff in these trailers! Once we even had a load of condoms!" teased Red High Heels staying in earshot for Early Bird. He laughed with the story. He knew Red was playing a number on the locals from the country club set.

"Do you think your man would let us rent this truck some night? I don't mean to drive! To do "it"! Maybe we wouldn't need Viagra!" whispered one lady.

They were all eyes on Red, waiting for an answer. She paused with thought, then answered, "No, he couldn't do that. You have to have a C.D.L."

"A what?" they asked in unison.

"A commercial driver's license; C.D.L." smiled Red. "You have to have a C.D.L. to make love in these."

"Oh," groaned one woman. "Charlie Boy is going to buy one next week and set in the backyard. I'll rent it out to all of you!"

The women left the truck and Early got into the passenger seat. They could hear the women raging on about wanting to make love in a truck and they clung to the men available.

Red smiled, "I've got to drive?"

"Yes, baby!" answered Bird. "It's the least you can do for this audience. Let them see you drive off. Give them the horn! That should dry their drawers! The dirty old broads!"

Kikki Doo and Lucky Runner waved and blew a kiss as they watched Red ease the beautiful, glistening rig into the road and roll on out of sight.

"Perfect!" smiled Early as she turned off the signal light and settled down. He picked up his computer and punched in his message. They waited for a return answer.

They were near Spartanburg when the traffic came to a total stop. Red patiently waited. Someone on the CB was informing the world an accident happened in a construction zone earlier in the day that had created the mess. The one lane would eventually let you through.

"Want me to take it a while, honey?" asked Bird.

"Yes, I could take a break!" smiled Red as she snapped on the brakes and jumped from the seat.

Early had plenty of time to get in place, fix

177

his log and buckle up before the traffic inched on. It was an hour back up but once through the mess everything became normal.

"Traffic is just part of it!" he grinned. "Not my favorite, though!"

On down the road, Red made sandwiches and snapped the tops of the Cokes. "I'll make coffee to go with that cake I brought!"

"Sounds great!" agreed Early Bird. "Hang on a minute. I'm getting off here. There's a lake just around the bend!"

He found the beautiful view and stopped the truck.

"Oh, honey! This is awesome!" exclaimed Red.

"I always thought I'd love to put my feet in that water!" shared Early. "It reminds me a lot of a place at home. Here's a rule for us, we need to stop for our meals. I don't want to run while we eat. It only takes a few minutes and we need to get outside the truck some. Your old women friends thought we'd never budge from here, just stay in the sleeper!"

"I know!" Red recalled. They ate, enjoying the beautiful lake to the side. Another truck pulled in behind them as they started to get out.

"Hey, Early Bird!" yelled a tall trucker.

Red could see JOY Carriers on the side of his trailer after she had jumped the ditch. The man ran to catch up.

"Damn, am I glad to see you!" he extended his hand and Early connected with him in a friendly manner.

"How have you been, Diesel Chaser?" Early smiled, "Have you ever met a taller Texan, Baby?"

"No!" laughed Red. "How tall are you?"

"Six foot, nine!" Diesel grinned. He was very clean cut with big shoulders and wearing the usual hat and cowboy boots that screamed TEXAS! Early Bird and I lived two miles from each other. I was with the Texas Rangers for years and retired early. Got tired of law work. Two years ago, Early helped me get with JOY Carriers. I love this road. Nothing like it!"

"I know!" smiled Red.

"Now, how would a peach like you know about the road?" he quizzed.

"She's an old truckdriver from the word go! We're running team this week. Preliminary to a permanent thing, I hope," uttered Early. "She still has a business in New York."

"Girl, you'd better grab this old bird. The women in Texas would chew the rubber off his tires if he'd stop!" bolstered Diesel.

"Let 'em!" smirked Red.

"You wouldn't care?" the man quizzed.

"No, they'd just end up with black teeth," teased Red. "Of course I care!"

"I'm the one that has to worry. This one has men wanting to kill for her!" humored Early.

Red flashed him a strange look as she thought of Devil. She felt herself shutter with fear as tears came to her eyes. She became quiet and walked faster toward the water to leave them behind, talking.

"What happened, Early?" asked Diesel, puzzled by Red's abrupt change. "Is she angry that I stopped?"

"No. It's a long story. The poor girl has been through a real bad situation. Years ago she knew a man and got into a thing. He was bad news but he masked his true self for a long time. He used her for his patsy. You know the kind," filled in Bird.

"That's always rough. some women never get over that sort of thing. Once they spend time being beaten, stalked, threatened and generally humiliated, they live in fear. Early Bird, you are a better man than me to take that on. She's beautiful but is it worth it?" inquired the ex-ranger and United States Marshall.

"Oh yes, she's worth it all. I love her!" Bird acknowledged.

"Never underestimate a criminal mind. I dealt with them until I retired. They make a plan and find the victim. She'll have to absolutely stay clear of him," informed the friend.

"She's out of it with him; been away from him for many years. Still, she remembers. She's paranoid about the matter. I see it when we are at her home turf," rambled Early.

"She probably needs medical help to get it behind her. I've seen these cases. Just when you think it's over, something happens!" suggested the friend.

"She's trying hard. That's why she waits and postpones going team. She said that she won't put me or the company in jeopardy. When she's on the road with me, everything goes all right," said Early. "I still think I should go find his ass and beat the hell out of him! That might fix it for her!"

"You could do that, but it wouldn't stop him. he's one of these possessed freaks. They have a screw loose and don't want to let go. He has deep-seeded reasons for hanging on. Once I knew a man that did everything but kill his wife. His quirk was she had a tattoo on her ass and he would imagine that someone else saw it. It drove him crazy until he finally got drunk enough to go after the wrong fellow who had never seen that tattooed ass. He pulled his gun out screaming, then the fellow got shot dead!" remembered the ex-cop.

"My God, don't say that!" Early feared.

"Face it, friend. You never can call a card when a fool plays it. I had no choice but shoot the man!" returned Diesel Chaser.

"You killed one?" gasped Early Bird.

"I had to! That's the problem with domestic disputes. Nobody wins. Once a person gives in to their fear, they're caught in a web that's hard to untangle. Most of the time, the victim is right in believing it's life-or-death. They can loose it all and die, too! It all depends on their ability to find help and get totally away," shared the lawman. "Psychotic bastards and fuck ups!"

"Red told me some of her thing. I try not to pry. It only reminds her of the old miseries connected to it. He nearly killed her once and she had to adjust her whole life. She lost a lot, but she's strong and has managed to pull herself out of it," Early said.

"Just don't ever think he can't fuck with her. he will die to try," Diesel warned. "Just be very careful!"

"I still should kick his ass! Just because it needs to be done. If he ever bothers her again and I find out about it, his ass is bought and paid for!" Early promised.

"Tell you what. I'll be right there with you, if she means that much to you! I'm just a phone call away!" smiled Diesel as he shook Early's hand, sealing a promise.

When they caught up to Red beside the water, she had her shoes off and was in knee deep. "Early! This feels good!"

The two men laughed and watched. Red saw a little frog on a rock jutting up and reached for him. As quickly, she stumbled and immersed herself completely. When she bobbed back to the top, she held her hand out, squeezing the frog to display her successful catch.

"Tonight, we'll have frog legs under glass!" she laughed putting the frog into Early Bird's pants while she hugged him with her wet clothed body.

"Woman! Why you little hussy!" screamed Early with laughter. As he stood to the slippery edge, Red forced him into the water with her. They both were swimming as they fell into each others arms.

"Come on in! It feels good!" yelled Red to Diesel.

He kicked off his shoes, socks and shirt and walked to his hips into the water. "I ought to have a swimsuit!"

"We don't!" giggled Red. She reached for his hand to keep him from sliding into the water.

The three of them squatted to be neck deep and discussed everything from world problems to trucking, then family and old times.

"This is wonderful!" gasped Red. "To just be somewhere in the world free as a bird and stop. Certainly gives you time to smell the roses and reach into yourself!"

"It does!" agreed Early's friend. Having met Red and connected with the two as a couple made him happy for Early while reserving a small concern for the lovely woman's situation. He had to find a way to talk to her. "Red High Heels! I've talked to you on the CB once!"'

"I remember now! I was on my way to New York and running up I-95 with Mule Train. He introduced us and you passed my little old ragged Transtar," giggled Red.

"That's right! You're sharp!" he replied.

"Mule Train is such a nut. He told me you were a Texan with a ten gallon hat and a two quart head," she mused.

"You know him! Always something going on! I don't think you could phase him with a stick of dynamite!" laughed the lawman. "Don't you get afraid out in your truck alone?"

"No! I just do what I have to do!"

"She's nuts, too! On the one hand, she's wild and free: then, sometimes I see a dark side that I can't reach!" muttered Early.

Red dropped her head as the truth stung. She wanted to yell, only because it was true. Clearing her throat, she said, "I'm doing better, Early. You've given me a new world and I'm hanging on."

"Early told me about Devil. Has he bothered you lately?" asked the ex-ranger as if interrogating a subject.

"He's alive! That bothers me! It's just I feel threatened. I don't know how to explain it. It's like something deep tells me someday, someway, he'll get me! The bad dreams just never go away!" she meekly related.

"I understand," soothed the man.

"We need towels!" sniffed Red as she jumped to the dirt path and ran to the big Freightliner. She quickly changed into dry clothes and found two beach

183

towels for the men. Dripping wet, they were walking toward her.

Snatching the towels and pitching one to Diesel Chaser, Early shivered as he dried then wrapped himself in the towel. "You know something girl, you're going to be my death! I can't keep up with you!"

Red listened to the men discuss the rearends of their trucks and soon they were ready to hit the road, refreshed and rejuvenated. Red marveled at how unique it was to run into one of Early's special friends. She had heard a lot about him. They said their good-byes and returned to their trucks. Each had paper work to look after.

Early Bird put the heavy loaded rig into gear and started gently rolling back to the service road. He switched on the CB, "Hey, Diesel Chaser, you ready?"

He didn't answer.

"Big Diesel! Got 'em on? Thought you were ready!" he inquired.

Again, there was no answer. Early had run with the man before and knew he was usually ready before he was. At least he would come back on the CB. He stopped on the side and yelled again, "Hey, Diesel, you coming?"

Once more there was no answer.

"Red, something's wrong! Hang on!" he ordered and backed the truck to near the front of the other Freightliner. He opened his door and jumped out. Red was ahead of him.

Early ran to the driver's side and opened the door in time to hear Diesel Chaser scream, "Oh, God!"

"Red, get the cellphone and call 911! Give them location and tell them to hurry. She stopped at the steps and punched in the number. Quickly, she talked carefully to the voice on the phone and asked for assistance.

Early moved the big man to the outside of the truck to arouse him and started loosening his clothes. He ripped the shirt open and unbelted his pants.

As he came to, again he was screaming with arm and chest pain. "Early, I'm dying!"

"No! We have help coming. Lay down and try to relax!" he demanded. "You'll be all right! We're here!"

Red ran to Early's truck to retrieve the emergency kit. She found a bottle of aspirin and poured a few in her hand. Running back to Diesel, she sat on the ground beside him. "Here! Swallow these! Have you ever had any pain like this?"

He shook his head 'no' and managed to get the pills down. He drank a little water she forced on him. His pain was something Red had never seen the likes of before. She knew it must be his heart, probably a heart attack.

A highway patrol car roared onto the off-ramp and the distant sirens were coming closer.

"Hang on Diesel! They're almost here! Just be seconds!" Early pleaded with his friend as he held him tight to the ground. "Hold on friend!"

"Oh, Early! This is killing me!" he moaned.

Red extended a towel doused with water. "Here! Bite down on this. Don't talk! Maybe we should..."

The ambulance swung off the interstate with a fire truck on its tail. They drove to the scene and jumped to work. Early and Red got out of their way and joined the highway patrolman. The paramedics expertly began to stabilize the huge trucker in a short period of time. They hoisted him into the waiting ambulance.

The sirens blasted a big sound, screaming loudly, as they roared away with Diesel Chaser in their care.

"Man! This is something! Where they taking him?" Early Bird inquired.

"Hospital's at the next exit," answered the patrolman. "How about these trucks? Was he with you?"

"In a way. He's my long time friend. He has to be all right. This is awful!" Early muttered.

"He's getting the best care possible. Why not drive to the hospital? I'll show you. There's a big lot across the street where you can get both trucks in. Sure can't leave them here. Follow me!" offered the man.

"All right, Red, take our truck. I'll bring the other one," Early decided.

They followed the cop, parked and raced for the electronic doors of the emergency room. The ambulance was still in the drive and Diesel had been rushed inside. It was a long wait until the doctor had a nurse usher them into a small, private room with desk and chairs.

"You may have saved his life," he began, "Calling so fast for help and giving him aspirin! He's being admitted for tests and all the necessary treatment. He managed to sign himself in. Lucky, very lucky. Most truckdrivers are some place where help is a long way away or passes out and doesn't get help. He nearly had a major problem."

"Thank God!" breathed Red. "I'm so glad we

were there! He's such a good person!"

"You people acted so quickly, it may have very well saved his life, even extensive heart damage. Knowing what to do is vital and not panic. At any rate, it made things easier on him. Those aspirin checked the blood flow. We'll know more later. Everything depends on his tests," smiled the young doctor. "The man is lucky. You should call his family."

"I will! I'll call his company, too!" replied Early Bird with relief.

"Stay in here. Feel free to use the phone. You can see him soon. He's having his first test," whispered the doctor as he was leaving the room.

"I'm sure glad we were here!" Early smiled at Red. "You saved my old buddy!" Early scrambled through his own wallet to find phone numbers. "I've got to call his wife. If anything happened, she'd be crazy!"

Quickly the woman was on the line, listening to the course of events. She handled it as well as could be expected. "I'll leave now. I can drive it in six hours or less."

"Just be careful. We'll wait for you!" promised Early and hung up.

"What about your delivery?" reminded Red.

"I'll talk to JOY. We're not that far from Atlanta. I'm going to the trucks. I need to check on his papers. Wait here for the doctor!" Early ordered.

"Fine. Here, take the cell!"

He kissed Red on the cheek and disappeared. Once more, there was a long wait. Red relaxed in a reclining chair and fell to sleep. Early organized the truck situation before returning and contacted the

187

company by satellite.

"It's all set. We'll take both trucks to Atlanta. He was scheduled there for tonight; we'll be on time and can still come back here. We'll switch trailers and head back north. They want us back here with him!" Early tiredly smiled.

Red put her arm around him as the door opened. It was the doctor. "If that old hellion of a friend would settle down, it would make it easier! Go talk to him! He can't leave here! He says he has a delivery to make!"

"Where is the old hoot?" asked Bird anxiously.

"Come on!" ordered the doctor.

They followed him into a room to see Diesel Chaser limply fussing and growling. Several nurses were attending to various phases of his induction.

"All right then, be a naughty boy and it'll hurt," snarled a frustrated nurse. She turned from Diesel as if he could no longer hear. "He's trying to give his own orders!"

Laughing, Early added, "He's an independent fool! You'd better straighten up! They brought you here for a reason. You could have died! Don't put God to the test!"

Diesel looked pale, then smiled, "You're right! What about my load, Early? You called?"

"Certainly. Just take it easy now. You have more tests and need to rest. Red and I are going to run both our trucks to the terminal in Atlanta. We'll grab a shower and come back," filled in Early Bird. "Your wife will be here soon as she can drive it. She's fine and on her way."

"You think of everything! Thanks, Bird!"

motioned Diesel.

"Take it easy! Cooperate with your harem. Everything's cool!" Red insisted.

"You two didn't need my problems!" Diesel Chaser muttered.

"Hush! What's more important than you?" smiled Red as she leaned over, kissed his cheek and patted his hand. "That will have to do until your wife gets here!"

A male nurse appeared with a gurney and a clipboard that would keep the patient occupied for a long time. They bid farewell and left for the trucks to complete the mission for JOY Carriers.

"You trust me to drive this?" Red smiled with concern, yet excited.

"You can do it."

"But this trailer is fifty-three feet! Mine is only forty-five," she stuttered. "Got a long nose here in front, too!"

"You've been driving my trucks for almost two years, baby!"

"Yes, but you've been with me!"

"Just get in it and follow me. Put the CB on Channel twenty-seven!" he ordered.

Quickly they were down the road and back on the interstate.

"I love it!" giggled Red in the CB. "Forget the cabover!"

"You're doing great. When we get nearer, just remember to swing wide, girl," he advised.

It took less time than anticipated. It was very exhilarating for Red to be behind the wheel of such a massive, wonderful truck. It made her old Transtar seem like a toy. Early had patiently guided her during their romance to be able to handle his rig. For all the right reasons, it was important that she master the long hood and fifty-three foot trailer. As they occasionally surmised, in an emergency, Red could drive. This emergency had tested her ability.

Once the trailers were delivered, the company took possession of the truck belonging to Diesel Chaser. They would service and take care of it until he could return. At least it was safe and could instantly be back in service. Atlanta was his home base now anyhow.

Red and Early completed their job and once more backed under another ready trailer. Early smiled, "Go for it, truckdriver!"

"Did I do all right?" she smiled.

"Of course, the best! Go on back to I-85 and let's find the hospital," insisted Early Bird.

Red maneuvered the rig cautiously through the heavy Atlanta traffic and put the nose north. She was comfortable with her new found love, Early's truck. There were so many wonderful features that made driving so much simpler. The cruise control and air ride were a world of difference. Red felt much less tired not being beat and flipped around as with the old cabover Transtar she had driven for years.

Red drove the return trip to the hospital while Early Bird slept. She knew they'd stop but the load would require immediate delivery. As she snapped the air buttons, Early mumbled then sat staring at her in the visor mirror.

"I feel like I've died!" he grunted. "I cannot believe we're here. I've never been able to sleep with the rig moving. Baby, you're as smooth as silk! Guess that's another thing to love about you!"

"Just like my professor," said Red as she parked exactly where the truck had been before the trip. "Let's check on our boy!"

Early found the room easily. Diesel's wife walked in behind them. Her face was white and she stared. Red immediately took the woman's hand. "Have you been here long?"

"I just got here! Where is he?" she let the tears in her eyes dribble to the floor uncollected. "Will he be all right? Oh God, I've been crazy!"

"We just got back from Atlanta. Had to get the trucks there. Early, go find the doctor," ordered Red. "Sit down. He'll be all right!"

Even so, Red cuddled the woman into her arms and consoled her with sympathy and understanding. She continued to cry as she let the exhaustion and anxiety flow through the tears.

When the doctor came into the room, he observed the unnerved spouse. "You'd better straighten up. That old, tough toad is on his way here!"

The wife smiled big, wiping her eyes. "Oh! Thank God! Let me fix my face! He would die for sure if he saw me now!"

"He had a close call. You're going to have to make him change his ways!" replied the doctor watching the wife.

"He doesn't smoke or drink! What's left?" she blubbered

"The eating habit!" he returned.

"Oh, that! Yes, I suppose too much junk food on the road," she acknowledged. "I'll work on it!"

The door swung wide and the mobile bed wheeled beside the flat sterile one in the room. Diesel was smiling as the orderlies attempted to hoist him. "That won't be necessary. Hold the buggy still!"

Everyone watched him slide to the other bed and snickered when the night-shirt slid up to expose his privates. Not concerned, the big man grinned. His feet came to the very end of the bed. He quickly pushed himself to a more comfortable position and looked from one person to the next. The hospital crew exited and the others gazed with pride that their friend was hanging on.

"Well, now you've really seen me," teased Diesel proudly, referring to his exposure. "Hospitals! How can they expect a man to wear a dress?"

His wife flew into his arms and gabbed about all they would do to keep him well. Realizing their mission was complete, Early and Red gave an update on the whereabouts of his rig and started to leave.

"Hey, Early Bird! I owe you my life again. If you ever need me I will be there. That goes for you both," sadly Diesel rendered. "I mean that, I've done it all! Listen, this shows how short it could be. Get it together, you know, running team. Us old men need our babies with us to keep us straight. My girl might run with me now!"

"Oh, can I? Oh, yes! I'm going everywhere with you!" insisted his wife. her eyes glowed and she kissed him as the door closed behind Early and Red.

Quietly, Early took Red's hand and they returned to the big Freightliner.

"Thank you, Babe, for being with me!"

"Thank you! We do need to be a team! It is more important than I could imagine. Any of us could be out like this and anything can happen. I suppose it happens every day," replied Red.

"Guess all this is so personal that nobody hears about it. The news can't tell of these happenings. Life is so fragile. A person really needs someone to count on. You can count on me. You know that?" Early questioned.

"I know! I'm all yours. You can count on me!" she whispered.

"But you still have that old baggage, that fear. I need you with me all the time. It's the whole package I want for both of us. Can you ever make the break?" he stared at her with hope.

"I'm trying. This is what I want! I'll be your best teammate! Promise! I have to get rid of that other stuff, the store, the trucks, and furniture. I'll be here soon!" promised Red.

117 N. Mountain St.   Phone
Cherryville, NC 28021   (704) 435-3072
              Acting Director: Gert Fisher
              Curator: Martha Beam

Discover the World of Trucking

Visit

C. Grier Beam Truck Museum

Truck history is preserved through the story of Carolina Freight Carriers, founded by Grier Beam. A real must to see and experience!

CHAPTER 9

The load was just a matter of switching trailers. Early had awaken about five o'clock to get to the location in time and be first in line. He insisted that Red stay in the bunk and catch up on some lost bed time. He also desired for her to rest, think and learn to enjoy team driving. Being a team was the goal, maybe he was nearly compulsive. It was a special dream with no reason that it couldn't happen She had everything it took for being the perfec partner.

First of all, he loved her so completely that being near her all the time was ultimate! He could handle day in and day out, nights and the road with another person. The limitations inside the cab could be overcome by real special understanding. A well planned reason for doing; and, the ability to give and

195

take would make it possible.

For Early Bird, he could love his lady anywhere; but, she was so good on the road. They teased each other with careful tenderness. They both respected each others private moments. Everybody needs to have a little break from the other.

"I like my own shower room!" Red told the fuel desk lady one evening. "I'm crusty from being on the road. We had to load it off today! I really need a real butt kicking trucker's bath all by myself!"

The woman handed them two sets of towels and two sets of keys. She twisted her nose and grunted, "Ain't nothing to me if you go together or not!"

Early Bird was amused. He'd knock on her door teasing. She'd yell, "Go away! I don't need any!"

Separate baths gave Red a chance to refresh and come back to her best self. It made her feel good to get nice and clean and dress up just to excite Early Bird. The touch of Chanel 5 especially turned him on.

Then it would be dinner, talk, sleep. awake early and hit the trail. It was always different. Truck stop food was becoming tasteless and Red had other ideas. Sandwiches were simple but good down home food was better.

"See that store up there? Let me out!" she demanded.

"I don't have a place to get off!"

"Circle the block!"

The light started to change as he said, "I don't know if I can!"

"Circle the town!" growled Red. "Just let my butt out, if you know what's good for you!"

He stopped in front of the hardware. She grabbed her purse and giggled. "Get back to me when you can!"

The gleaming rig groaned out of sight. Early tried to find a spot to park, then spotted a fire department, pulled off and went inside for information.

They greeted him heartedly and urged him to back in beside their building.

"We never use that area. It's graveled. One of the boys will drive you back to the store," mused the Captain. "Women sure have a mind of their own! Sure not like us!"

"When Red has something on her mind, it is now!" laughed Early Bird.

They found her at the check-out with a pile of cooking utensils and a Coleman grill. As she paid, Early reached for the stack of items. "I don't know where we'll put all this!"

"You'll find a way," she promised. "Once we get rid of the cartons this comes in, it will be half this size. Besides, I need to feed you better. We'll end up like your buddy Diesel, clogged arteries and such. We're dumping all the damn potato chips and candy when we get to the truck. I'm going to a grocery store to re-stock, too!"

Once back to the fire station, the fire crew was outside admiring the big, new, red Freightliner. Several of the men were underneath the cab checking the layout of the air suspension. One shrieked, "Wow, this is some ride! We have trucks, but nothing like this! Freightliner built all our trucks, too!"

Proudly, Early informed, "We have lots of miles to roll. Your trucks are geared to get your stuff where you have to go! Can I look over your equipment?"

"Certainly!" agreed the Captain. "Let your lady take her things into our kitchen and do whatever she wants to get them ready for the road."

"Oh, thank you!" cheered Red. "I need to scald it all and get the papers off. You get fifty dollars of packaging and ten dollars of merchandise."

"That's what my wife says," agreed the Captain. "We're having dinner soon. Want to eat with us?"

"I don't want to put you out!" resisted Early Bird.

"Never! Sergeant cooks enough for an army. Some of the wives may come, so there's always plenty. I think he has a pot of chili and beans," informed the Captain.

"Sounds fabulous! I could make some of my special cornbread. I can send Early across the street for stuff I might need," Red offered.

"Good! That would be an even deal. Let me take you to the kitchen, then see what you need. Actually, we keep nearly everything."

Red found all the makings and soon had enough cornbread to feed another army. As the hot bread came from the oven everyone gathered with additional guests and served themselves. The Sergeant said a nice prayer before talking started again through the smacking lips and chewing.

Dinner was perfect; it was like heaven to Red and Early. A real home cooked meal found in the most unique place. They agreed to stay the night beside the firehouse and used the company showers as special guests.

An old man that had walked to the fire station and made himself at home said it all. "They look after me, just like I'm one of them. Ain't nobody a stranger here. Their duty is fires and the community. They're best with both, if you need 'em; they're right there! I live in a room up the way. They feed me 'cause I ain't got nobody. I weighed about a hundred pounds when I first got to talking to 'em. Now, I'm about to be fat!"

In the night, the fire trucks rolled to a call. Early got out of the rig to check it out. From the front of the station he could see bellowing smoke not too far away. All the trucks were out and he heard sirens in other directions seemingly going to the fire. He slipped back in and told Red he would be back. Quickly, he tugged on his boots, grabbed a coat, then walked to the scene and stood back watching.

The old hotel that had been made into a rooming house was well into flames. The firemen expertly had the hoses in place and were attending the scene. Early could hear them calling to each other as they smoothly began to control the fire.

Suddenly, two firemen burst out the front door each carrying a person. They laid the bodies to the ground for the paramedics that were waiting, then rushed back inside. Another fireman joined them and the spotted dog sitting beside the truck followed. Once more, they returned with people coughing and crying. Again, they returned into the three story old building and found another group of people and led them to the street.

From above, an old man was waving and yelling on the top floor. Early heard the Captain say, "Keep it going here. I've got to go up!"

"Let me, Sir!" pleaded one of his men.

The Captain swiftly rushed into the building and was out of sight. Another fireman, who had been inside the structure, yelled, "I'm going after him! It's bad in there!" Then, he bolted through the door.

The other firemen kept fighting the flames, keeping pace while every on-looker frightfully stared with concern for the firefighters inside. It seemed forever until the men joined the man at the top floor window. The untamed flames seemed to engulf the area suddenly as the aerial truck sprayed from overhead. The crackling fire and smoke was overwhelming.

"That building is not stable! We'd better get the net!" screamed a wet fireman. The word became an order as a group instantly stretched a big netted contraption below. One fireman jumped and rolled from the catch to the ground. The Captain was having trouble with the victim. He was refusing to jump. Then, it was like the man fainted and the Captain wrapped himself around him and the two dropped into the big hoop together, bouncing like a 'tigger'!

There was great relief and the crowd cheered as the above structure crumbled out of sight. Then, the next floor roared as it fell into the one below with an eerie crash. Again, flames swooped the whole structure and the smoke swirled thick and was almost overbearing in every direction. The people who had gathered, once more moved back, giving the firemen a greater fire-line.

As paramedics readied various individuals rescued from the building, ambulances on stand-by received them and left screaming for medical facilities. The Captain had scratched his head somehow and a medic was trying to hold him down long enough to pull it together.

"Take care of him!" demanded the Captain. "I had to knock him out to get him down here!"

Early Bird could see it was the old man who had come to the fire station for dinner. He could sense the Captain's concern and expertise. The Fire Chief arrived and stood by his car watching. Everything was in order, the only thing that could be done now was maintain the fire and keep it from spreading. It was amazing that the firemen had emptied the building of its people and two little dogs as well. Their contents and personal belongings all burned. The trucks of equipment and well-trained men may have not only saved about twenty lives but most likely that whole area of the town.

Early Bird returned to his truck and sat in the driver's seat unable to sleep. The fire crew was still out and another one would replace them. He wished there was something he could do. The sky started to lighten. He could see cars coming to park at the firehouse. Men walked past his truck going into the station and returning immediately wearing fire gear. They piled into a van and started for the fire. Later, the Captain and several men returned.

Not wanting to be in the way, Early went to the kitchen to tell the Captain thank you for his hospitality and good-bye. A lady had coffee ready and was starting to plan breakfast.

"Where's that woman of yours? I'll bet that 'southern belle' could make us a hell of a breakfast! I want some biscuits and gravy!" smiled Captain.

"I'll get her!" Bird smiled. "Some fine firefighting! Never thought I would ever see such, like in the movies!"

He returned with Red excited about getting to cook again. She took over the kitchen and the women who had arrived were happy for her help. It wasn't long before the tired firemen showered and sat at the table to be served.

After the prayer, the Captain smiled, "I thought the old man was going to get us killed. He wouldn't jump! When I heard the squawking of the floor and a slight vibration, it was time! I punched him a little so I could grab him and go! I knew I would have to bring him down. Poor thing, he was so confused. That old man is about eighty or so."

They talked about the fire and planned to return. They knew it would be a several day job with extra time and help. The Chief came in and sat with the others. Red automatically served him a breakfast.

"Captain, you are quite the hero!" Chief accessed.

The man blushed and brushed it off. "Any idea the cause?"

"Sure, they found a hot spot in the main wiring. Guess it arced and with the dust of time, the old building blazed. It was its time to go," he answered.

"What about the people living there?" asked Captain.

"The mayor was there. He said the churches will take care of them for now."

The meal and dishes were finally done. Early and Red hit the road again. This had been an interesting night but the rest was something to be desired. Red put the big truck into the road and headed east. With few words, Early Bird fell fast asleep in the bed. Red was a smooth, steady driver and there was a long stretch of interstate ahead. The radio gave the details of the fire; soon the station finally dropped from range. Red found another one with soft music.

The scale house was closed for repair, so all trucks rolled on. Traffic was light for the time of the day and made it all the better. More familiar names of towns and cities were beginning to appear. Red saw a sign for a truck stop at the next exit several miles away. She knew JOY Carriers fueled at the T. A. This would be a good move. She had driven about four hours and Early had snored the whole trip.

"Honey! Wake up!" she yelled.

"I'm awake! Haven't shut my eyes!" he mumbled.

"I know! Poor thing!" she consoled. "I have only been driving about forty-five minutes!"

He jumped straight up! "Oh, hell! It's almost eleven-thirty!" We're late! Damn, I'd better let them know!"

"We need fuel, I think!" she mumbled as she snapped on the brakes.

"You hussy! You were teasing me! We are right next to the drop! I ought to spank your fanny! But I'd better kiss you! I screwed around last night at that fire. I couldn't have driven it!" Early praised her.

"See! I am worth it! I love driving this thing!" she uttered. "Let's throw the nozzles in and hit the bathroom!"

"You got it!"

They were arm in arm as they separated at the facilities. Fueling was always a together project. Red insisted on doing her part, although at times she'd pitch a hissy about the fuel cap being on too tight.

"Tell you what, Big Man," she squinted her eyes and glared at him across the truck, "You be in charge of the driver side tank and I'll fuel the other one! I'm durn tired of struggling to get that stupid cap off. I told you I hate that kind of business. All you men are like that! One of these days you are going to strip the threads trying to show your masculinity with a fuel tank lid!"

The man didn't comment. It was safer to let it drop and promise her the tank of her choice; one of the honors of team driving. Even so, he smiled to himself and made note not to touch her tank.

"The oil was just a little low, maybe you should look," Red informed. "I washed the windows, too! What were you doing?"

"You wouldn't want to know! Here, I did bring you coffee. I guess you want to eat after we go deliver this. All we have to do is switch trailers."

"Good! I'll test out the new stove! I saw a rest area sign a little ways back!" she gleed.

This all took a minimum of time and the rest area was overlooking a very scenic valley. Early stretched himself beside the truck and was then instructed to put the gas cylinder onto the little two burner grill. He set it up on a picnic table in front of the rig and Red laid out a plastic cloth with various items. It looked like "hell's kitchen" to him.

"Honey, take that bucket and get it full of water for me," she ordered, pointing toward a nearby fountain.

The man obeyed and returned to an orderly batch of vegetables cut up into a big bowl. Red scooped a pot of water and put it onto the grill to heat. In a pan she flipped in some butter and the cut up onions. The smell immediately brought all eyes upon them. A couple of rigs were parked next to theirs. One man could only lick his lips.

"Invite them to eat if you want to. There's plenty," she smiled, throwing rice into the water and sprinkling in salt.

With slight objection and "I don't want to put you outs" the men joined them. One fellow had been on the road only four weeks and was basically lost. He had taken a wrong turn and didn't know how to get back. He actually couldn't read a map. Early and the other driver told him what to do. When Bird wrote the instructions in large letters, Red whispered to him, "Honey, he's just lost, not blind!"

"I wrote them big so he could find them. These kids just take off not knowing. God pity the trucking companies. I'll bet his dispatcher is going nuts. He's afraid to call in!"

"No kidding! I wager he has never shaved either! Think of it, drive off to the end of the world in a big rig; never having done such before. I heard him say he was twenty-one. He still has nerve!" smiled Red looking at the thin, tall young-faced fellow that she classified as a child. Then she addressed him, "You young'uns have more guts than I have, getting out in a beast like that!"

"Nobody wants to drive flatbeds. Ain't many drivers anyhow back in Montana. I wuz supposed to drive around home then this feller got sick and died, too. He wuz off in the truck and went to a doctor but he still died. Fell over dead buying gas. I had to do it. Ain't much of a truck either. I had to replace a hose yesterday!" he grieved.

"Here, you'all sit down. Lunch is ready!"

urged Red as she made the plates full of the steamed rice covered with sautéed chicken and vegetables with sour cream gravy. Her salad was big enough for the Jolly Green Giant.

Early was proud to share. It felt good to him to 'father' this young man and befriend the other. The team thing was better every day. He looked at Red and smiled, "Somebody want to say a prayer? We have a lot to be thankful for!"

"I will," smiled the young fellow.

The whole transaction may have taken forty-five minutes. The cooking time was no longer than in a restaurant and the food was heavenly. Red was wonderful in the fact she liked to mingle with people. 'She would probably talk to the devil if he horned in,' Early Bird had thought.

"See that pole down there?" Red giggled. "Race you to it!"

They both cut out running. Red took it slow but she caught Early at the bottom. She jumped onto his back. He lost his balance and they rolled into the grass. He quickly found her lips and showered his kisses on her. Red pulled him tight and panted, "Not here!"

"Why not? Just a 'quickie'! Nobody would dare come down, besides I have my coat and now I'm hot! Oh, my love! You are the best woman alive! I love you so much! Please make it all happen soon!" he whispered.

"I really want to, Early! I love you, too!" Red gleamed. "I enjoy you so; being together gets better every day!"

"We are the best as a team! I want you forever! Honey, let's get married today!"

"Not yet. Wait until I get out of the store! Know what? I've enjoyed this so much I nearly forgot everything. That's crazy!" she murmured, rolling beside him in the green grass.

"Oh, no! That is good! I'm counting on you, Babe!" he cooed. "Here, let Daddy hold his Baby!"

"Early! Take it easy! It's broad open daylight and on the side of this big hill! Somebody might see us!" she argued as she opened her lips, melting as his tongue slipped deep into her waiting mouth. The soft maize sundresss conveniently fell away and Early had already removed her tiny bikini leopard panties. She pulled one of his hands to her breast and reached for his groin gently. As the zipper of his pants grizzled, Early took the lead and gently forced her flat to the ground. Red's bottom settled into a pillow of cool grass as Early Bird reached for her warmth.

"I love you, Red! Oh, God! My Red! I love you!" he exclaimed as they both fell quivering together deeper into the soft grass.

"I love you, too, Early!" sighed Red as perspiration dripped from his handsome chin onto her dress. "You're heaven!"

"Shhhh!" whispered Early. "Don't move!"

Red obeyed.

Early Bird motioned, "Shhh. See!"

About fifty feet from them, a big bear was leading two cubs across the path. She was moving slowly with big flops and her babies were running on all fours to keep up, their fur glistening in the full sunshine.

"Oh, lordy!" whimpered Red, "Bears!"

"Keep calm!" whispered Early again. "They

don't know we're here!"

About that time the mother bear stuck her big dog-looking nose high in the air and gave a growling bark in a very low tone. She had spotted them. Early took Red's hand and motioned for her to ease backwards up the hill toward the truck parking. When they slipped about another ten feet away, he grabbed Red's arm and made her move faster from the big grizzly. Once nearly to the red Freightliner, he stopped and paused to see the family of bears had two more to join them. They were no longer concerned with Red and Early.

"That was close!" Red stared in fear. "A big bear!"

"Close! That could have been tragic! A mama bear can be very protective!" revealed Early. "Look! Isn't that cute?"

"What?" asked Red. "Oh, no!"

"They found 'em! Your pretty little panties I hung on the bush!"

"Dang! Those were my favorites!" pouted Red.

"Mine, too!" laughed Bird watching the young bears throwing the tiny undies around as if afraid of them. "At least you have your dress!"

"That's for sure!"

"Come on. We need to hit the road!" urged Early.

With everything in order, Early slipped into the driver's seat and whipped the rig back to the big road. Red stepped into the sleeper to change into fresh clothes. Months before, Red had insisted on the full length mirror. She had closed the curtains then set about finding another sexy, comfortable little dress.

As she inspected her petite body, she peeked at her backside and screamed, "Oh, Early! This is awful! Look!"

Without thinking, she stuck her buttocks out from the partition. Early Bird took a quick glance and started laughing so hard he could barely drive. The more he thought of it, the funnier it was. Just outside the soft drapes was that cute rearend for all side traffic to see.

He yelled, "We're going into a weigh station!"

"It's not funny!" she snapped.

Continuing to tease her, Early said, "Oh damn, we're going to be inspected!"

"Oh gosh, Early Bird, did they see my butt?" panicked Red.

Early saw a pull off and whipped the rig to a stop, smiling. "Yes they did! I've never seen a green 'hinnie' before! Too bad it's not Saint Patrick's Day!"

"Hateful! You get me on the ground, loose my best panties, grass-stain my ass and then laugh at me!" giggled Red. "This isn't a 'chicken coop'!"

"Come here, honey. Daddy can rub you in the nice sheets and erase the grass marks!" Early teased as he moved into her direction.

"Quit it! Stop right there! You're not erasing nothing! Go drive!" she demanded with a grin. "I can take care of my own tail!"

"She's got grass on her ass...but I love her!" he sang as he put the truck back on the road.

"He's a jerk with a smirk...but I love him!" returned Red with glee.

Happily, Early continued toward the Memphis signs but a lump collected in his throat knowing that soon this wonderful trip would be over. This drop there, then probably to Charlotte, NC and his woman would leave him for her own life. His mood changed with the thinking. Early became silent.

The radio played George Jones singing , "He Stopped Loving her Today" then another thing about "How do I Live Without You?" It made him want to cry to think this would ever end.

"Penny for your thoughts!" Red broke in.

"A thousand dollars if you can fix them!" Early Bird sadly replied. "Anything, baby, just stay with me! It's so good out here with you."

"I know! I'll get it together. Honey, you know I have to go back and close the store, straighten out my furniture bills. I can't just walk away on a cloud. How long would it be before it started to haunt us?" reasoned the redhead.

"I'm selfish! Honey, you've put me off so long. I can't loose you now. Life slips away. Both our children are situated and it's just us. Money doesn't mean anything if your life has no real meaning. I've been there too many times. I'd have a hard time living without you in my life."

"Stop worrying. It is only you I love. This is what I want. I know it's hard to get into somebody else's soul and totally believe. I'm sorry I have been so afraid to cut loose and trust you. I never meant for it to hurt you. Still, we both had to be completely certain of our love. The sex is just a part of it; it's that down deep feeling of loving and wanting that rules the true soul. Call it anything, but the bottom line is love, just that simple -- LOVE!" Red proclaimed.

Early took her hand and kissed her fingers one at a time. "Girl, I have had a lonely life. Even

210

when I was married, it was just a thing that was supposed to happen. I worked and she did her thing. I reckon we would have separated eventually had she not died. There was no room in her life for me other than to provide her with all the things she needed. I turned my head for the children's' sake. I knew she was one of the many women who shelled out the loving for her convenience and needs. I was just a dumb ass. Maybe I had my mind on my trucking company a lot, but I thought that was part of it. The better you do, is best for all. Maybe it was just me!"

"You can't blame anyone. Just the fact that people are different and some people want things that others don't need. Nobody can make sense of unfound love. Love itself gives in only to total dedication. If we're desperately seeking it, we can make mistakes or jump too quickly. Maybe we have to learn from those old pains. God, look at me! How crazy could I have been with going through all that time with Devil. Never in a million years would I have ever thought I could have been sucked into such a thing. That was not even about love. He pretended so, but there was no relationship. We didn't have sex! He somehow manipulated a control over me. He threatened me and I let him nearly ruin my life trying to protect my family," Red remembered. "I couldn't get away until he bled my money and extorted my soul as he kept me captive. I was his victim. I was his patsy. I was the biggest fool in the world."

"Red, that's over now!"

"No, it isn't! As long as I live, his mark is there!" she cried. "It's like the mark of the beast!"

"I'm here. Remember Diesel. He is still one of the finest law men in the world. He's like a tiger!

211

He and I will pay that bastard a big visit if he ever bothers you again!" growled Early Bird. "My friends are your friends. We are everywhere!"

"You don't understand. He is like a nightmare. You never know where it comes from," she whimpered.

"We have to go beyond this. Just close your store out in New York and you will never have a problem with him again!"

"See," she blurted out, "He threatens to kill my family and do stuff to them. Once he kidnapped Zipper. The poor dog was missing for about a week. I had her at my son's house. He really shouldn't have known where she was or even where my son lived, for that matter."

"That was probably an easy thing for him to do to make you think he could screw you around! You let his 'people' and spies know that the Bird and Tiger are here. He's a dead son-of-a-bitch if he ever bothers you again! Get that message out! You know how! Stop right now trying to handle him from fear and succumb to his garbage. You have the right protectors with you now. I love you. This can't go on, hiding from this predator. Baby, look at me, you have me and thousands of truckers that I know all over the country. We are there and there's nothing better than a good ass kicking. We'll track him and give a dose of his own. This kind of a prick isn't a man. He stalks the weak to survive. Real men hate a low-life like that!" Early Bird rendered. "He's put you through too much already. Just leave it to us."

"You still can't realize what it's like to have someone beat the hell out of you for no reason and threaten..."

"He had better live somewhere under a rock where we can't find him.   Yesterday has already happened, but this is now!" declared Early.

Another George Jones tune cried out for them.   "She's my rock and I ain't going to throw it away..."

The load was actually ahead of schedule. Early   Bird had poured the fuel to it during the upheaval of discussing Red's problem with Devil. He knew now these fears kept them separated. Always the excuse was her business, but underneath it all, she finally admitted her greatest fear. This made sense that she could never relax except away from home in his truck. He understood her struggle, trying to keep ahead of that crazy man.

Early wanted Red to know he would never hurt her and she could count on him to be there. At least, recognition of the problem was the first step to solving it.

Early smiled, "Baby, you can't fight this battle alone! I love you and I'll do anything to make your life perfect. You deserve only the best!"

"You're the best!   Thank you, Early, for loving me. I'm sorry I've been so nuts. I'll dump that New York store in a couple of months," promised the woman.

Early Bird rolled to the dock that had been assigned to him over the CB. He got out, unhooked the trailer, then pulled out to pick up the loaded trailer for Charlotte.

Somehow, they both felt a let down, knowing this trip was almost at its end. They needed to go separate ways on a positive note. This was a goal for each of them.

"I'll get you home soon. It's been a wonderful time for me," smiled Early Bird.

"Yes, out of this world for certain. I love you," nodded Red.

Early rolled under the big fifty-three foot trailer and hooked up again. He heard a continuing leak after the air brakes were locked in. "Dang, I have a big air leak!"

"Wonderful!" smiled Red.

"Girl, we need a better location to break down."

"Not really," she pouted. "We can always make the best of it. Let's check it out."

"It's the foot valve, I'm sure. I'll need to have it fixed," he managed.

"Can you still drive with it?"

"Certainly hope so. I guess the air is up enough. We'll make it to Freightliner in Greensboro. They can service and fix this. It shouldn't take long," Early surmised.

Although it wasn't a problem for the moment, an air leak could change at any time. They dropped the Charlotte trailer and picked up an empty. Once at Freightliner, Early was told it would be a day, maybe two.

"Let's go visit Kikki!" spurted Red.

"Can't we just get a motel near here?"

"I just thought home would be nice for you," injected Red.

Early won. They were picked up by the hotel limousine and ultimately ushered into an elaborate suite. Red smiled at the elegant surroundings. "You know how to spoil a gal!"

"Anything for my baby," he muttered as he

flipped the bellman a healthy tip. When the door closed, he took Red by the hand and pulled her to him. When their lips met, the zippers started zizzing and clothes fell to the floor.

The hot tub was bubbling briskly; and heat from the steam was stimulating as it puffed at them. Red led Early Bird down the emerald tile into the vapors where they found marvelous seats neck-deep in the water.

Early took Red gently in his arms and rubbed his body next to hers. He lived in constant arousal. She had a great, strong, muscular figure. He felt her round buttocks as he explored her neck with his lips and tongue. Red moaned and whispered, "Careful! I might go on without you!"

"There's always plenty more!" he groaned loudly. "Oh, Baby, I love you! You're everything!

"Darling! Oh darling! You're wonderful! Come on now!" she breathed.

They slipped between the sheets and found perfect paradise through their love. They both moaned and screamed out together.

They collected themselves and gently returned beside one another in the bubbling pool still with their lips entwined.

"I'm hot! I've got to get out!" Red gasped.

"Are you all right? Let me help you!" Early offered. "Give me your hand. You look faint, honey. Are you all right?"

"Yes, help me to the bed!" she breathed. "I love you!"

The kingsize bed was lavishly sheeted with lilac satin. Red looked so tiny when he placed her in the middle. He slid beside her and pulled the covers over their unclothed bodies.

"Want some water?" he tried to help.

She accepted, then pushed herself into a propped position in the huge bed, trying to regain her composure.

"I'm just too much for you!" he grinned, rubbing her hair.

"Humph!" she laughed, sliding down to take a nap with him enveloping her in his arms.

Several hours later, Early was talking on the phone beside the bed when she once more drifted back to reality. He was ordering a rental car as he watched her fling the fluffy covers. Red jumped out of the nest and marched to the bathroom to do her makeup and hair.

Early had already showered and dressed. "Just name it. Where do you want dinner?"

Red hastened to join him; they found a great restaurant nearby. "I haven't had seafood in ages! Look at that Alaska King Crab! Oh Early, they have West Coast Quilsene oysters, too!"

The hostess seated them in a secluded booth. As Early held Red's hand gently, he marveled over the sparkle in her eyes. He felt good, his true reason to live was finally coming to him with this beautiful, talented and complicated lady. He flipped his hand to the waitress signaling no liquor.

The woman eased close to Early Bird, looking into his eyes. "Not even one?"

"No, we'll have dinner!" he said flatly.

"Okie dokie! I'll be right back, sweetheart!" whispered the thin blonde seductively. "Don't worry, for you sugar, I'll do anything!"

Once she left Red said, "Am I crazy? That

216

chick is laying it on you!"

"Aw, she's just doing a job," Early Bird replied.

"No she's not. That girl over there just took that table of men drinks and didn't flop on them," retorted Red High Heels.

"My baby's getting jealous?" he teased. "Forget it!"

"Hell, no! She's all over you like I'm invisible!" snapped Red. "I hate that! Believe me, I read her loud and clear!"

The woman returned with her pad and pencil. She moved as close to Early as possible then sat on the edge of his seat. Pushing against him she said, "Ready honey? The steak is great!"

"We want Alaska Crab," he started.

"I would have thought a hunk like you might need a big piece of meat! Like putting coal in the furnace!" she laughed at her own observance.

"We'll have the crab to start, then West Coast Oysters, baked potato and maybe a salad to pick on," intervened Early quickly.

"I get off work in forty minutes," she whispered to him, reaching over, rubbing his cheek. "You're a real hunk! I love big men!"

Early was uncomfortable and blushed. Red lifted an eyebrow, despising being ignored. It was out of line completely. Red wasn't a woman who would let it go. She stood up in front of the woman, "Hey, who do you think you are? We're customers!"

"Sit down!" the waitress finally acknowledged as she flipped her hair and eyelashes. She licked her lips for Early to see and winked.

"I'll not sit! You dumb bitch! I don't take

217

this kind of treatment! He's my man and with me.
You act like I'm nothing!" Red excelled.

"Nothing? Right! You're nothing! I'm Miss
Daisy Queen 1998!" she bragged.

"Well! No shit! Miss Daisy Chain!" Red
High Heels purred angrily.

Red stepped back as the woman tried to place
a blow to her face. That did it. Suddenly, without
more, Red High Heels was on top of the blonde who
had tripped to the floor. She grabbed her, rolling her
over, face down and entangling her arms behind her.
Then, Red saw the perfect blonde hair that had flipped
so flirtatiously and grabbed it with one hand, giving it
a big twist. As it disconnected from the woman's
head, she started to laugh, "Daisy Chain, you're not
even for real! How about those big tits?"

"Please, let me up!" cried the girl.

"The tits. They yours?" asked Red.

"No! They're false; rubber!" she moaned and
kicked. "Let me up, bitch!"

"Yeah! You can get up! If a man had you,
he'd end up getting into a drawer with your spare
parts!" growled Red. "This is stupid!"

The restaurant manager was staring as they
both got up from the floor. Early Bird was gawking in
amazement.

"We'll leave!" he offered.

"No, sir, everything will be all right!
Please!" smiled the small dignified man. "We've had
trouble with this one before. She's my niece!"

The waitress left the dining room and
stomped into the back.

"I'm very sorry!" apologized Red.   "I
shouldn't have snapped!"

"No, I'm sorry! Dinner is on the house!" the man apologized in return.

The couple returned to the candlelight meal that was extraordinary.

For the most part the team trip had been perfect. Early would go on up the road alone and Red would return to her life to make adjustments. As they held each other for the last time, they could feel the deep need and want for the perfect team-life together. Making a truck their home would work! That was the goal, the dream, the plan. Nothing would stand in their way.

Red stood by her car at the overpass and waited for Early to enter the ramp then move on out to places unknown. Delaware would be the first drop. He had picked up a load in Thomasville.

Red watched the big, red Freightliner as it rolled toward her. She smiled, waved and threw him kisses. The tears slipped down her cheeks as she knew there would be weeks before they would hold each other again. She watched until the grand rig was out of sight.

"I love you Early Bird," she yelled.

As Early shifted the gears, he could see his gorgeous redhead on the bridge ahead of him. She had positioned herself for this final glimpse. He wanted to pull over and wait for her until she'd join him but he knew that would be juvenile. Red had to do it this way. It all seemed too perfect! He waved and blew the deep horn. He tried to watch her from the rearview as long as he could.

"I love you Red High Heels!" he yelled as she disappeared from his sight. "I'll love you forever!"

CHAPTER 10

Red had to pull it together and return to New York. She had a good store manager yet operating by occassional phone calls could often be costly. The phone was busy for sometime before her call went through.

"What's happening?" asked Red when the familiar northern accent greeted.

"I don't know! Are you ever coming back?" asked Tiger Puss. "We need some special orders. I've called them in."

"I'll be there tomorrow. I'll put them in a rental truck. See how happy I can make you!" humored Red.

"See that you do. People keep calling for their orders! Oh, by the way, some man keeps asking about buying a truckload of furniture. What do I tell him?" groaned Tiger.

"Sister! Girl! Calm down. I'll be in there tomorrow night!" assured Red.

"Don't leave me hanging like this again! I thought you went completely crazy! I've put about thirty thousand dollars in my safety deposit box. I didn't know how to handle it. That couple picked up their houseful," Puss continued. "Anyhow, I was worried. You don't hardly call. Love has ruined you!"

"Never worry. I can handle things!" Red insisted.

"You'd better hope so. That damn Devil keeps calling here. One night he followed me almost home. He scares me! He might think I'm lying for you!" the woman nearly whispered. "Hold on, let me get the other line."

Red waited a couple of minutes and then the line went dead. "Durn, can't she use a phone without cutting me off?"

She dialed, after a while the answering service came on. Red left a message, "Since you don't want to talk, ass, I'll see you tomorrow!"

Quickly she put her plan into full gear and left the rent truck to be loaded at Oak Ridge Manufacturing. The orders were ready, plus extras.

A young man at the furniture plant agreed to give Red a ride to her car. He smiled quietly, "You hear from Devil-man anymore?"

"No," said Red, not wanting to hear his name.

"I heard he was wanting you back," he informed.

"That's just stories. He has his own life now,

222

besides, he also has a girlfriend," remembered Red, hating his name, hating that she ever knew him.

"That's the talk. He said he ain't done with you. I can't blame him though. You're good in this business. There ain't no other women that can work like you. You sell lots of furniture," he replied.

"Not for long. I'm going to quit!" Red defended herself. "I'll be better off out of it and away from any chance-meetings with Devil. I already started moving one store into the main one."

"Need help? I could go for a short trip!"

"Really? Well, all right! Meet me back at Oak Ridge in four hours!" answered the woman as she got out of her car.

She made a phone call and her hairdresser; Mr. Tony, said, "Well, come on! I know you need a cut and style at least!"

While he finished the lady in the chair, Red went next door to her favorite local restaurant, *Kathy's*, and ordered the famous chicken pie and coffee. The owner herself brought the lunch and sat down.

"I just took this from the oven. We've missed you!" blinked Kathy. "Is that good?"

They talked a while and once more Red heard the rumor that Devil was wanting her back. This scared her even more. Still Red assumed it was just talk. Then, her mind drifted back to the last several months. She remembered the times Devil had tried to catch up to her. She knew she'd better check in with the S.B.I. for double safety.

At the beauty shop she called the agent, "It's me, Red."

"I haven't heard from you in a long time. I

had hoped it was all over, finally," he greeted.

"It is and yet isn't. He's telling people he plans to get me back. There's no way!" Red stormed.

"Good! Just keep somebody around you at all times. Hire a bodyguard if you have to. Just be careful. He's capable of anything. A man like him doesn't take rejection well," he cautioned. "Sometimes they want to make their move after they feel the heat's off."

"That's what I'm afraid of. I thought he'd leave me alone but I still have that old fear!" uttered Red. "I just went through hell before!"

"I understand. Just stay around people and keep in touch. We'll check on his whereabouts," promised the agent. "There's nothing tangable to deal with. If he follows you, that's stalking. If he touches you, that violates his court order to stay away from you."

"I just wish he'd disappear!" grimaced Red.

"Do you have a gun?" he asked. "Might be a good idea."

"Oh, no! No gun, that's out! Too much can happen with a gun around. I couldn't kill anybody anyhow and I don't believe in idol threats," rallied Red High Heels.

That old feeling of "something's-going-to-happen" deepened. The old paranoid thoughts filled her mind and Red became engulfed with fear. She wished she had never let Early Bird leave her. He would help her close the store if she'd ask. Somehow, it was hard to ask another person to drop their life to fix hers. She pushed the worry aside to pace her plan for getting out of the the big city.

Riding to New York was easy. The helper

could drive the rental truck to free Red to get the heavy laiden tractor back to the city. Everything was moving to par. Keeping busy and unloading the stores was most important. Finally, the trip of twelve hours was behind them.

"She in?" asked Devil on the phone to the new helper.

"Yes, who's calling?" he asked as he threw a cushion back into a sofa.

"I just wondered if she got back!" Devil said.

Red looked at the young man and snatched the phone from his hand, "Hello!"

"Hi, baby!" Devil panted. "Been a long time!"

"Don't call here, please!" Red screamed.

"I'm sick! It's my heart! I'm flying home. I just wanted to tell you I love you and good-bye!" he pleaded.

"That's bad. I'm real sorry!" sympathized Red reluctantly.

"You don't care! I could die!" he tortured. "You never cared!"

"I don't want you sick. I hope you'll be all right," Red sighed.

"I won't bother you anymore. I'll probably die anyhow," he said.

"People have heart problems and get all right!" Red encouraged.

"I'm leaving all my stuff to you! I just want you to know. Bury me in a simple way. Just remember, I loved you more than anyone," he added, trying to make her feel guilty.

"I hope you'll be all right. Go on to the doctor, get one here!" she suggested.

"I'm leaving for home. I want to die there!" he meekly pondered. "You can get you somebody else now. Maybe that cop!"

"There's no cop in my life!"

"Yes there is. I know you see him at the store all the time! But it's all right. I ain't going to be around. Oh! My chest!" he screamed loudly and hung up the phone.

The line went dead and Puss walked over. "You look like you saw a ghost. What's wrong?"

"That was Devil!" answered Red. "Says he's dying!"

"Good! The bastard!" cringed Puss. "What are you talking to him for?"

"He's sick! His heart! Says he's in bad shape," Red informed.

"Great! I hope his ass dies!" Tiger Puss snorted. "The son-of-a-bitch deserves it! He's a walking time-bomb anyhow!"

"Well, he'll leave me alone maybe," Red continued.

"Yeah? Like calling you now? You are nieve! He called you! He follows me! I don't believe anything he says and you had better know he's slick. He'll do everything to get to you. That call was just to get information! You wait and see!" growled Tiger, lifting her eyebrows. "Sick? Yeah! He's sick all right!"

The orders were delivered and everything seemed normal. Red called the man who wanted furniture and agreed to meet with him. The next morning he came to the furniture store as planned. He was a handsome, tall, grey haired man with an accent. He walked through the store and selected a truckload, then offered to purchase everything.

It seemed unreal. He said, "I'll pay cash as each load gets in my store. You'll have to move it since you have trucks."

"Let me bring a load first. I'll inventory and we'll think about it," smiled Red nearly unstrung.

"I want you to work for me, too. Tell me what you need!" suggested the man. "Here's my card and I'll wait to hear from you. Bring me that first load tomorrow."

He left Red in a state of shock and confussion. Tiger Puss observed the last part of the conversation. She quizzed, "He wants your store? What are you going to do? Close this?"

"I'm going to take him a load of furniture tomorrow!" Red dismissed the conversation.

As planned, Red delivered the load to his store then caught a ride to her main store. She drove in her delivery van to her second store. She had a month left on her lease and knew that would terminate that location if not sooner. She had a sleeping room there. She needed to go there to make plans to close. She slept there quite often.

It was a Friday night, and cold, too. The snow was still around the houses and fields. January would always have ice around the area at night. The weather was again starting to change; sleet and snow were mixed. It looked like a storm for sure.

Red sat in her vehicle a minute and stared at the display of furniture. It had paid well to have this store. She thought for a moment she saw someone move inside. Then, there was no sign of anyone, even so, it might be one of the workers. Again, a shadow moved behind sofa; she could almost feel someone watching. The tiredness of the long, hard day was catching up with her, now she was imagining things. Nothing moved anymore, so she resigned herself to believe it was nobody and if it were, probably one of the employees. She gathered her belongings to go inside as she had done for a couple of years. Her key to the door was in her hand. Carefully she found her footing along the icy walkway and fumbled with the lock.

* * * * *

At almost the same time, Early Bird had just backed to another dock in Seattle, Washington. He had been running hard to stay busy and with racking up good miles, he'd rack up the money. Once he dropped the trailer, he went inside to call his dispatcher in Tennessee.

The man who answered his call was irritable and snapped, "Where the hell are you? Thought you'd have called someone!"

"Are you nuts?" growled Early, feeling shot down since by his figures he was two hours ahead of schedule.

"Oh, hell! This is Early Bird! I thought you were Trail Blazer. That son-of-a-gun has yet to call. He's late and Toronto is about to go crazy!" the man complained with apology. "That is one of those loads that, if it's late, they may not pay!"

"Oh, grief!" sympathized Early, "That's what I just dropped."

"You are always ahead of schedule. Trail usually is too. Maybe something happened!" suffered the dispatcher. "I'm worried!"

"He'll be there, stop worrying. You know him!" Early tried to console him.

"Let me get this other line!" the man stammered, leaving Early still connected. "Where you been, Asshole?"

Early smiled to himself and hung up. He'd let them have a little private battle and would call back after a shower.

He liked the posh terminal in Seattle. It had so many neat features. Being able to do his laundry was a real plus. The company was definately driver orientated. They had a small company store that covered little needs and gifts, too. He used the Floral-Fax and ordered flowers for Red to be sent to her store the next day. Then, he bought himself some new socks and a company tee-shirt for Red. His late lunch was ready when he picked it up.

The phone table was well lighted and seating comfortable. It made driving for JOY Carriers a real positive experience. One felt as if they cared. Even the smallest terminals had scaled down comfort stations. In return, each driver was expected to clean after themselves.

Not only did JOY Carriers have all this, they paid well with no hastle. Early had heard many drivers complain about their companies not paying immediately and he knew it could happen. Still, often drivers dream of one contract but reality on paper was slightly different. Every driver is individual and each company is too. Knowing what is expected of you is first important, then doing it makes a number one set up.

Early found he got more out the job by cooperating and using understanding and forethought.

Sometimes he would get stuck on a two day lay over in some weird place. He always had things to do to make it go easy for him. One time he fell onto a 'trailer-moving' deal that paid big bucks, another time Red met him about three hours from her house.

He picked up the phone and dialed a bunch of numbers to finally reach Red's cell phone.

As Red started to enter the store she heard her cell phone ringing and rushed back to her van to drop the arm load into the floor. Quickly she grabbed the phone, "Hello?"

"Glad I caught you. I'm three hours in a different time zone! Guess where?" Early smiled.

"Where?"

"I see your old favorite space-needle!" he teased.

"Oh! You're in Seattle!"

"Yes!"

They talked over each others week of accomplishments and plans for the future.

"I'm going to sell 'him' my business," assured Red proudly. "I have to take it all to his store. Isn't it great? One load has already gone."

"Just be careful. That ice is bad and keep yourself bundled up. Don't get sick on me," he hesitated. "Why don't I take time and come help you?"

"Because you hate furniture!" she picked.

"I love this furniture getting out our way! Honey, I'd do anything for you!" Early insisted. "Even load furniture!"

"I can handle it!"

They hung up and both pondered the days long ahead. Early entertained a surprise visit and Red could only plan a fast sell-out. Once more she collected her things to go back to her store. She marveled at how great it would be with Early Bird all the time and forever. She hoped it could always stay wonderful. She said aloud to herself, "I'll do everything to keep our love good! I love you, Early Bird!"

Out west, Early Bird spoke aloud to himself, "My redhead, I'll do it all for you. I'll keep our love safe and pure. I love you, Red High Heels!"

* * * * *

Red entered the store. A note on the counter jumped at her. It read, "Gotta go home. Have an emergency. Taking a 3:00 bus. Will be gone a couple weeks," signed, 'Us' P.S. Took $500.00 each."

"Well, that's fine!" Red said. "Who gives a flying flip? The big ass babies prove to me everyday they're not worth all this!"

Red dialed Tiger Puss at home. When she answered, she seemed upset. "God, I'm glad to hear from you. Everything is nuts! I gave the new boy a key and told him we'd be closed for the next two days. I have to take my son to the doctor. He got hurt playing soccer. It's always something. I made you some cookies. They are on your desk top. Hell, I forgot to ask. How did your delivery go?"

"Great!" answered Red. "They had about twenty fellows to unload. I left the truck so they could get it into their warehouse. Quite an operation. I'm tired. Sure takes a lot out of you loading and driving. A jerk pulled in front of me and I nearly busted his ass!"

"I don't see how you have the nerve to drive that big thing and in this weather! It's supposed to snow all night!"

"I see the moon is full and it looks cloudy!" injected Red.

"Oh, by the way, 'old asshole' called about when you left. He never believes me. He said he's going into some hospital. I still don't think that's no more than an excuse. Why don't you come over to our house and stay a few nights. I have a bad feeling!" entered Tiger.

"I'm fine. I have a lot to do here. See you Wednesday," said Red wanting to just order a pizza, jump into bed, shove her head into television and not think about anything else.

She called for the pizza then entered the kitchen to wash a few left over dishes. Once the pizza arrived, she threw her big coat back on and went back outside to the van for some papers. Locking the dead-bolt, Red started toward the small bedroom apartment. The shadows on the walls reflected with a turning car outside the big windows showing a figure of a man it seemed. Her heart jumped for a moment, then she recovered, trying to brush it off with being only an illusion.

* * * * *

Early Bird felt wonderful! Everything was working out perfectly. He would rest a bit and then head for New York. A surprise visit it would be. Even if just a short moment, he still had to see his wonderful fiancee. Hard running for about three days would get him there. His load in Montana would take him on north. He had to check the road condition to find out if he would need chains. Getting over the Cascades was not always easy. He thought too, maybe he should call back for a southern trip. However, he had always just driven wherever.

The only problem with going south, it would mean another week or so before seeing his woman. He checked the weather and found the roads to Montana would be closed and that might mean more delay. He was forced to call his dispatcher.

"Right after you hung up, I had a load to Portland that needs to get there in the morning. Do that for me!"

"Sure!" agreed Early Bird knowing it would be best in the end. At least he could get somewhere and work his way as he could.

He walked back to his truck to find the sleeper and would rest a while before the trip. He started singing a song he made up one time:

IN SEARCH OF RED HIGH HEELS

(Chorus)
        I saw her in the distance
            my heart flipped a thrill
        I looked that woman over
            and saw her Red High Heels!

        That night I tossed
            Oh, God how I turned
        The name of my beauty
            I never had learned.

        I couldn't eat and

I could hardly sleep.
Lord, I beg hard for mercy
All I could do was weep!

I pictured that long red hair
falling to her shoulders
The swing in her move
just purely knocked me over.

A tight, sexy skirt
beneath a business suit so real.
And the strangest touch of all
was seeing those Red High Heels.

I'll search here and the whole world over
I have to search for this four leaf clover,
She wasn't a mirage, she truly was there
I know she'll be someplace, and find her with
care.

One special day, I was staring
while pumping fuel,
In the truck right next to me
I saw those Red High Heels.

Her beautiful legs ascended
She came walking up to me
My heart stopped, then pounded--
Red High Heels became a reality!

After Early sang his original, he dropped off
to sleep. The last thing he remembered was the
picture of his beautiful woman smiling happily across
from him. He could always see this image in the pale

darkness that seemed to almost make her come alive. He was satisfied knowing that very soon, he would touch her again. Even more, they would run team-- Red had promised. This love was so perfect it nearly scared him.

* * * * *

Red watched the slight pinging of sleet fall on the big plate glass windows. Her new parka was still close around her and she dropped the wad of keys into the pocket. She studied the shadows in the room; everything seemed too quiet. The round, full moon had slipped into the low ceiling of clouds and the temperature had dropped. She felt herself shiver as a pang of uneaasiness came over her. She thought of Early Bird and how he would change her whole world soon. It usually eased her anxieties to play with his memory.

The wind outside was snatching loose items and flinging them around. Relentlessly, it gave a deep groan and she could feel the cold coming through the glass. Red wished she had stayed at the other store; her apprehension was the weather.

When she reached for the pizza, suddenly there was a tremendous noise and in a flash, someone jumped her from behind. She felt the tight squeeze around her shoulders and groaned, "Oh, God!"

From the shock, her head felt like a bullet had struck her. She felt it thumping with fear that forced a sudden rush of blood. Soon, her nose started to bleed. There was no getting away from the hold. Quickly, a fist came across the side of her face, glancing off her left ear. It should have knocked her out but she could not let that happen.

"You cop-fucking bitch! I'm going to kill you!" screamed her old terrorizing preditor, Devilman.

"Devil! Oh, I couldn't figure…"

"Shut the fuck up! I saw you and your cop! You cop-calling whore! You fucking snitch! You love that motherfucker, don't you?" he ranted as he pushed her, grabbing one arm. He took his booted foot and kicked her hard, forcing her into her bedroom. "I wonder how many times you fucked him here? Tell me! How many?"

"Never! I swear there has never been anything going on with me and Big Mike!" she cried.

"Tell that shit to someone that don't know you! Tell me the truth! Are you fucking him or not? I saw you and him with your heads together grinning like two 'in heat' hogs! Does he make you hot? Tell me, does it make you feel good having that damn blue uniform rubbing all over you?" yelled the man frantically. His face was as red as a chicken's comb; as he spoke, his alcohol-breath slopped drops of saliva around. "You simple bitch! Do you think I believe you? I saw you talk to him just this very morning! Didn't you?"

"Yes, but nothing personal!" she reasoned.

"Don't lie! I saw you!" he graveled.

"I did talk to him!" she admitted.

"About what?"

"His wife ordered a chair. I told him!" Red remembered.

"Don't give me that shit! I ain't buying!" he argued. "Here, take those pants off!"

"No!" cried Red. "Please, we've never done

anything wrong!"

"You cop chaser! I'll find out if you did anything! Get those pants down!" he ordered.

"Please! Please! Don't make me do that!" begged Red. "I swear. We haven't done it!"

"I'll find out!" he squinted his beady eyes.

Again, his big fist connected to Red's chin. Red could hear a slight snap and she knew her only defense was not to pass out and to keep him looking at her. She fell against the wall stunned, nearly dazed. She was seeing things in twos. Her head spun but she could not let herself loose consciousness.

Immediately, she had to fight the nauseating feeling. She managed to see the full moon drift in and out behind a cloud outside. She remembered how he had always gone crazy on a full moon. In the many years past, way back when she had been his prize "patsy" and possession, he usually flipped on the moon. It could be anything that would trigger his mood. He would throw his psychotic fits to manipulate his prey.

Her back was still to the wall as she propped herself against it. He stood in front of her breathing the fire from his bloodshot eyes. For a moment, he almost smiled, but then, he returned to his demands. "Get them off!"

"I can't do it! No! Please!" sputtered Red.

He reached to the woman with both hands and grabbed the front of her jeans. This night, Red was only wearing jeans and panties. Lots of winter days she'd put on three layers. The front snap gave way to the angry jerk and he gruffly had her exposed as he ripped whatever was in his way. She could feel the air to her skin. She wanted to die. She felt so small and violated.

"Please, I'll do anything but this!" she sobbed. Tears rolled from her face to the floor. Red remembered that resisting was not good but she couldn't let him rape her. She was feverously trying to think of a way out.

"You fucking whore! You been with that cop! I saw you, don't deny it!" he continued as he struggled in his pocket.

"No! I told you! No! I wasn't with anybody. Please don't!" she cried.

"You cunt! You think you're better than anybody! Ha! You ain't shit! Say it! Let me hear you say it!" he pushed at her with his arm as he opened a six inch knife.

"I'm not shit! I'm nothing! You deserve better than me!" she forced herself to blare out. He had chased her with guns, beat on her, cursed and humiliated her in the past but he had never threatened her with a knife. Red was desperately afraid of knives. She cringed at the thought of what he might do.

"You slut, cop-fuckin' tramp! I'll see if you fucked him or not!" he slobbered madly. He quickly used the knife to ripped a bigger opening in the jeans and cut the crotch from her panties.

"All women are whores and bitches! My mother was a bitch and a slut! I used to see her and the old man fight all my life. She went to church to get laid. The old man said so! You try to be so society and hi-faluting! You are a sorry slut, too!" continued the raging man. "I hate you! I hate all women. Fucking bitches ain't good for nuthin' but puttin' a bastard in prison! I done spent my time there! I know how to do it! 'Time' don't bother me! You can go cry to the cops if you want to; like they say, 'If you can't to the 'time', don't do the crime!' They won't hold me and I'll be back!"

Red High Heels couldn't believe this was happening, but it was. She tried to think, "I'm sorry!"

"Sorry for what? Dumb cunt, yeah, you are sorry! Cop-lovin' snitch! That's you...A snitching snatch! Love, ha! Ain't nobody loves nobody but themself. I seen it all my life! If you fucked that son-of-a-bitch, I'm killing you and then I'll get him!" shouted Devil-man.

Red fought the panic coming over her. With the locked-in situation she couldn't get away from him; it might even make it worse. With no place to run, no way to hide, she could only plead and beg for his mercy. He was sneaky. Still with the knife in his hand, any move could be tragic.

"Do you like this, bitch? Don't you just love me looking at your necked ass? Maybe I'll spank you! That's it; I'll spank your pink ass and turn it beet red!" he howled with delight.

Red cringed but hoped a spanking might be all. She felt the tears rolling down her cheeks and cried, "Don't spank me!"

This gave him great pleasure. He roared, "Come here, bitch! Say it...Please, Daddy, don't spank me!"

The woman felt the grip on her wrist as he jerked her from the wall, ordering her to repeat his words.

"Please, Daddy, don't spank me!" cried Red meakly. "Please!"

"You little bitch! Words won't help now! You've been real naughty. I know you fucked that

239

cop!"

"No, sir! I didn't!" she crumbled.

"Come here!" he sat on the chair and threw her across his lap and started spanking her with his hand. Red was screaming with the pain. The knife dropped at his feet as he started paddling with both hands. "Does this feel good?"

"Please stop! No! Please quit!"

"Oh, we like this! Makes a woman hot to be spanked!" he gabbled. "You want to spank Daddy now?"

She didn't know the right answer, so not answering seemed best.

"Answer me, bitch! You want to spank me?" he roared and grabbed her by the hair, pulling her head back, forcing her to look at him.

She whispered, "No! I don't want to hurt you!"

He pushed her from his lap to the floor; standing over her, he gave her a big kick with his big shoe that landed in the ribs. Then he screamed, "No? Fuck you! You'd love to do it! Say it! Let me spank you!"

The victim quivered with pain and torment staring back. Her hair had been jerked by handfuls making her scalp burn. "Please! I'll spank you! I'll do right, too."

"Get up you spineless little beggar. You ain't got no guts! You'll do everything I tell you and that's how you are. You're a bitch! Say it! Say you're a bitch!" he forced.

"I'm a bitch! A real bitch!" she stammered as she got to her feet and leaned against the wall.

"Right! Now, I want you to spank me just

because you are skeered to. You try anything and you're dead. Sit in that chair; I'll bend over your knees and you spank me! Not hard, bitch. You hurt me much and I'll choke you! I love this!" he muttered. "Spank me, make my ass red!"

He dropped his bottoms to the floor and bent over her lap. With contempt, Red followed his directions, taking her hands and smacking them against his buttocks. He loved it; he started moaning and reached for his privates to fondle himself. Red wanted to throw up but forced herself to control her fears. Suddenly, she saw a hammer on a nearby table. She remembered hanging a picture the day before. As she continued to spank him, she tried to conjure how to get to the weapon. Then suddenly, he dropped to his knees and managed to relieve himself from the excitement.

Red focused on the hammer and stood to retrieve it. As her hand brushed it, she felt his hand around her leg and she fell to the floor, pushing the hammer from the table where it slid under the bed.

"Bitch! You damn, fuckin' bitch! Look what you did to me! You liked that?" he yelled as he drooled and sweated above her, he pulled his underwear into place, then his pants. He stood up and went to the mirror, adjusting his hair with a comb. "Get up! Pussy!"

Red obeyed, glad it was over.

Devil sat on the chair for what seemed forever. He stared into space as the perspiration poured.

The phone rang in another room. He looked at her and shook his head 'no'. Once it stopped he stood again then walked to her. "You cop fucker! I know!"

He began his fit all over. He rushed Red again as if she were a rejected rag-doll. Suddenly he spit in her face several times; she was crying with humiliation. He slung her against the wall so hard the pictures and a mirror that were hanging came crashing down. She could see his knife on the floor; at the same time, he caught her gaze on it.

"Please, let me go!" wept Red. "I'll leave and never tell anybody!"

"Cop-fuckers don't keep their traps shut! You'd have that big motherfucker here in a minute! Bring him here! I'll make him suck my dick!" laughed the warped man. "You bitch, when I finish with you nobody will ever want you! Spread those legs. Let me look at that cunt! Spread 'em!"

"Please! Please! Don't make me do that!" pleaded Red.

"Shut up, bitch! Spread 'em. I'm going to find out if you fucked that bastard!" he screamed.

The woman meekly put her feet apart with her trembling body against the wall. Tears flowed gravely to the floor as she waited his command; she had no control of the situation or her response. For the first time in her life, she felt this was near the end of it all. He picked up the knife and place it between her feet.

"I'd better tie you up. Got some rope?"

"No, maybe in my van," she hoped he'd slip up and she could run.

"Fuck it! You ain't going no where. You're stuck! Look at that sleet! Hold still! I'll find out what you're doing!" Devil growled. "You cop-fuckin' whore! When I'm done with you..."

His voice trailed off as he sadistically slapped her with his open hand to the side of her face, then coming back with the backhand blow to the other side. He enjoyed this, tormenting his victim. Red stood as still as she could to each blow and felt her face, neck and ears begin to sting.

"Please! Oh please, don't do this to me!" she whimpered again.

"Shut the hell up! You ain't hurt are you?" he grinned as he turned up a bottle of liquor and downed a big slug. He reached in his pocket and poured some pills in his hand and washed them down with the booze. "Want some of this? It might make you feel no pain!"

"No, thanks," Red whispered.

"Too good to drink with me?"

"No, I'm just not thirsty!" replied Red feeling her lip swollen almost double.

"Fuck you, anyhow, no need to waste liquor on a cop's whore," he grunted. "Hold still now or I'll kill you, bitch! I'm going to find out about you right now! Spread it more!"

She had to obey so she moved her feet a bit. Red shut her eyes and waited. This would be the worse thing that had ever happened. She knew fighting him would make it worse, if it were possible. She waited, it seemed forever.

She felt him enter with a big, fast gouge! She screamed, "Please! Don't hurt me! Please!"

Quickly, she opened her eyes to see him remove his hand and start sucking his fingers. Then, he repeated this several more times. Red watched with contempt. It was as if she were looking on. She felt the pain each time he grasped her and pleaded for mercy and prayed.

He violated her with his rough fingers. She knew he was trying to taste a man's secretion that wouldn't be there.

"Please! I haven't been with anyone!" she cried.

"All right! So you ain't fucked today. What about tomorrow?" he toyed. "Cops! Women want them!"

"Look! There's no cop with me! Please believe me!" she sputtered as he slammed his hand against her ear.

"Bitch! Shut up! I'm not done with you yet! Spread those legs!" he bellowed as he picked up the knife.

"Please!" Red squalled. She obeyed, trying to keep her legs together and feet apart. A knife was her greatest fear--she saw him slide it around in front of her face. Being cup-up was her greatest fear. "Please, Devil, just let me go!"

"You'd better beg, you sorry bitch!" he sneered.

Suddenly, he took the knife and stabbed her several times in her thighs between the legs, then he put the knife on his finger and inserted it into her vagina. Red knew this was it! Her mind raced and she cried, "Oh, God! Please help me!"

"God! You bitch! I ought to take this and slit you up to that lying tongue! Does that feel good?" he terrorized her. "I'm going to kill your lying ass! Tell me now. You hooked in with that cop? Don't lie; you got this one chance and you better tell the truth. If you lie, I'll split you all the way to your guts!"

Red felt the liquid run down her legs and the

pain from the stab wounds. She was powerless. It seemed her world was ending. She looked at her arm and realized there was an open gash still bleeding. To speak could trigger her death. She prayed silently and thought of Early Bird and her daughter. She couldn't die like this, with a knife inside her.

The over-powered woman stayed tight to the wall and cried out, "Oh, God, please help me! Please tell him, God, there's no cop! Oh God have mercy!"

The tears continued to drip to the floor and blood kept seeping. Devil listened to her wailing and plea to God. Finally he removed the knife he threatened to kill her with; then, threw it deep into the wall. Turning from her, Devil stepped aside. Red realized the blood spatters on his torso belonged to her. She didn't move. She waited. She heard him start to cry.

"What am I doing?"

Shutting her eyes, she thanked God and pulled her torn clothes around herself as best she could, saying, "I need to go to the bathroom."

Devil sniffed, "Go ahead. Don't try nothing funny!" He reached over and jerked the telephone to pull it from the wall, then slung it through the doorway.

Quickly, Red slipped into the bathroom and checked herself over. Stab wounds to her legs were like swollen punctures. She washed herself off gently and straightened out her face and hair. Her eyes were not as bad as they felt but her head throbbed and ached all over.

"Hey, bitch! Get that door open!" ranted Devil again. "Git in that kitchen and cook something. Do you think you can handle that?"

"Yes! Certainly!" the woman replied walking in the hallway meeting him face to face. He grabbed her and slung her through the opening to the small kitchen. She managed not to fall. The keys in her coat pocket rattled together and her wad of money in the hidden pocket in the back flopped, reminding her that he'd take the over $10,000 if he knew about it. It wouldn't buy her out of the situation; he'd only take the money, laugh then continue to satisfy his sadistic nature. She kept her coat on for protection.

"What you gonna fix?"

"I have a nice prime roast, potatoes and green beans. All I need to do is warm it in the microwave," stated Red. She didn't want to complicate things with real cooking.

"Fine, git it!" he sat at the corner table and watched her quickly make a nice plate for him. "Make two. Eat with me!"

"I was," whispered Red, hoping it would start easing the revolt going on.

Once the meal was before them, they started to eat in silence. A fire alarm sounded outside and trucks started to run. He jumped from the table and ran to the showroom window.

Red quickly removed her stashed money and slipped it into a frozen pie in the very back of the freezer compartment. Then she grabbed every knife she could find and threw them into the trash, covering them with news papers. As she heard him coming back, Red tried to act as if she were going to see the firetrucks. She was grateful for the interruption that allowed her that much.

"Forget it! They ain't coming here! We're all alone!" he said as he elbowed her in the ribs. "Sit back down and eat!"

They resumed the meal. He smacked his lips as if he hadn't eaten in months. He grunted and groaned with pleasure. At least he was calm; maybe it would somehow end.

Once more, he started fussing. Red tried to change the order of conversation but he stayed with it until he exploded, constantly humiliating and threating her. Then he grabbed Red by the throat and pushed her to the floor crawling on top of her. His hands were squeezing her neck and the weight of his body was on her chest. She couldn't breathe; feeling the surge of blood in her veins she passed out.

He slapped her, spit into her bruised face and roared, "Wake up, bitch! I ain't done nuthin' yet!" Continuing to hit her with both hands, he grabbed her hair by handfuls, pulling it over and over, still screaming, ranting and raving.

Red was seeing double through a bright, crystal tunnel as she started to come around. "Please! Stop! Please, oh God, help me!

Devil was huffing as he stood. "Git up! Git up, bitch! I'll kick your sorry ass! Git up!"

Trying hard to focus and obey, Red struggled to her knees. He yanked her and with his fist connected under her jaw with a loud *splat*. A push put her crawling to get out of the way. His foot flew toward her as she raised enough to miss a blow to the throat. The big coat absorbed most of the kick. He kept hollering, cursing and accusing as he hit, shoved and kicked her all over. The woman rolled herself in a ball with her face down; this was easier.

Through the swollen eyes Red watched him pick up a huge, sharp butcher knife that somehow she had missed hiding. He snatched her hair, chopping off handfuls from time to time. The room was a mess with hair and blood everywhere. He carried on for hours until near daylight.

Red had taken the beating like most people couldn't; even that angered the wild man. He stormed, "What the fuck is wrong with you? Don't you know how to die? God! How stupid! Maybe we'd better try something else! Where's your fuckin' gun?"

"I don't have one!" she mouthed through her busted teeth and bleeding nose.

"I ain't believing that!"

"Can't have one up here!" she forced.

He picked up a dish towel, wrapped it around her neck and jerked it from side to side. He laughed, "You think you can shut your cop-loving mouth?"

She whimpered, Yes!"

"Who you going to tell about this?"

"I had an accident! That's what! I'll not talk. Please let me go! I won't say anything!" she begged from her knees.

"I'll kill you if you put me in prison! I got friends, too!" he bragged. "I can get you from anywhere!"

"I know! But, I'll tell you what. Just go on and kill me now! Get it over with! I'm too tired and hurt too much anyhow! Oh, God! Forgive me for all the wrong things I've ever done! Let my blood flow on his hands and my spirit rest in peace. Please God! I can't do this anymore!" Red High Heels resigned. "Oh, God! Let my kids know how much I love them. I've tried to spare everyone all this. God! Please have mercy! I'm ready to die. And God, let Early Bird know I truly love him and he was all I ever wanted!"

Devil stepped back and balled a fist that landed on her check. He came back with the second one. Red somehow saw the clock and realized the ordeal had been going on for over six hours. She was too worn out to care. She gave way to the bright light that quickly turned black, spitting blood as she fell out and wilted.

The wild man shook her severely. Blood was pouring from her nose and mouth. He saw her eyes almost in a stare. He just knew he had killed her when her bladder emptied through her torn clothes. He dropped her fragile, limp body to the floor then sat in a chair staring with tears streaming from his eyes. He muttered, "Bitch, you made me kill you!"

She no longer moved. He pushed her around but there was no signal of life. He heard the keys jingle in her coat pocket and retrieved them. He'd have to get her out of here where no one would find her soon. He wouldn't be connected if he moved fast.

The whole area was buttoned up with bad weather. He opened the dead bolt on the door and went to his vehicle to start the engine and get it warm. He hated the nasty cold; it ruined everything. Then again, tonight, there would be nobody to see or hear anything. "

"Red deserves it all! Snitching bitch running with cops!" he babbled openly.

He rolled her body into a furniture pad and threw it over his shoulder. She seemed heavy and floppy; he dropped her into his pickup seat.

Easing along, he finally reached the exit on the L.I.E. The road ahead was filled with red lights that made him nearly panic. Taking the exit, he knew he had to dispose of the woman as soon as possible. Anything could happen. Then, the rattle from Red's keys shifted his memory to her truck not far away.

"That's it!" he gleed outwardly to himself. "Her trailer! Best place in the world to dump her ass! Be best for that fuckin' cop to have to drag her dead ass around! I can't wait until he finds her! This is all his fault!"

He could almost feel the eyes of her cop friend inquiring about his beloved Red High Heels. It excited him to think this ending would be so devastating to those who knew her.

There was no one anywhere around Red's store. He found her trailer key and opened the door. He then quickly collected her body and threw her into the heap of furniture pads. Devil grabbed a couple of them and dropped them loosely on top of her. He stood staring at the heap.

"Ashes to ashes, dust to dust! You got yours, baby, fuckin' with the big boys. I just couldn't let you go. You probably knew everything. It was all a matter fo time," he said in slight sorrow. "You were at the wrong place at the wrong time. You're actually a good person; for that I'm sorry. It's too bad for you! Early Bird! Who is this Early Bird?"

He jumped from the trailer, closed the door as the keys fell into the ice at the opening. He kicked them aside. He threw the pickup truck into a spin as he tried to speed away. The rearend slid around and hit the landing gear area hard. The shattering metal, lights and plastic was left behind. He had to move on and fast.

CHAPTER 11

Early Bird had been sleeping about an hour. Suddenly, he jumped from his bed; it was as if something snapped. He felt sick and rolled out of his truck in his underwear and barefeet. The heaving started; he got no farther than the fuel tank. His guts were burning, his head swimming. Finally, he sat sweating on the cab steps. It was almost as if something jerked him from his sound sleep.

"Something's wrong! Dead wrong!" Early proclaimed out loud. "It's Red High Heels! She's in trouble! I know it! It has to be!"

Getting back into his Freightliner, he slipped into some clothes, then went into the truck stop. The phone quickly buzzed, Red's phone. But there were no answers at any of the three numbers; that wasn't normal, nor did she answer her beeper.

251

His next call connected with his friend Diesel Chaser. Early heard the sleepy voice, "Yeah? What in hell do you want?"

"Diesel! It's me, Early Bird! I need you!" he begged.

"Tell me about it!" replied the friend, knowing it was drastic.

"Well, it isn't exactly for sure, but in my gut! Red High Heels is in trouble!" he registered.

"If you think that, a gut feeling is a true feeling! Let's go! That old thing is like a built in radar!" acknowledged Diesel.

After a few minutes, Early agreed to fly to New Jersey to meet with Diesel. They both would hang up working until they knew Red High Heels was all right.

Early situated his truck with a driver he had known for years; the man would run the rig to keep JOY Carriers on time. Early Bird took a taxi to Sea-Tac Airport and talked his way onto a flight that was late leaving for Chicago with connection to Newark where Diesel would be waiting.

As Early Bird started down the ramp for the plane his phone rang. It was Diesel, although he hoped it was Red. "Hello?"

"Hey, Buddy, what's happening?" the voice quizzed.

"As we speak, I'm getting a flight to Newark; it's Delta's flight 108. Gotta go. Check the airport!" Early replied.

"All right! I'll meet you!" Diesel acknowledged. "Delta 108!"

"Right!" said Early when his phone quickly disconnected.

The pretty stewardess greeted him smiling. "Mr. Bird, you need to get your seat belt on quickly. We're ready to taxi."

At the same time the door slammed, engines revved and the huge Boeing jet began to back from the terminal. It taxied to the runway and was given immediate clearance. The thrill of the power loomed before Early Bird as the nose took to the sky, assending with speed through a cloud then leveled out. Early felt the landing gear bang into place beneath him.

Once more the stewardess came to offer a pillow and drink.

"Coffee would be fine!" he muttered, relaxing somewhat.

"I'll sit next to you when we get underway. A night flight doesn't require as much service. Where are you from?" she flirted.

"Miss, I have to sleep. I'm meeting a dectective on the other end to help me find my girl. Red High Heels is missing!" he blurted out almost frantically.

"I'm sorry I just saw you had no wedding ring!" she pulled away.

"See this?" he held his hand up. "She gave me this engagement ring not long ago. She is a special woman. Nobody can ever take her place. I will love her until the day I die! We've been through so much! Well she has, there's an old boyfriend who keeps after her. I'm afraid I left her one time too many. She's tough, but she's as fragile as a baby. Oh God, I called this one wrong!"

"That's too bad! Maybe you're reading more into it!" she softened.

"No! I know! A gut feeling! My baby is gone!" His eyes turned red as tears trickled down his cheeks. "I should never have left her. She insisted, but she needed me and I wasn't there. Whatever happens is my fault!"

"Don't think like that! You need to sleep if you can for the time ahead. Could I get you some Tylenol or something?" she smiled with sympathy. "I wish I had a man that loved me like that!"

"It doesn't come easy. In a million years, there could never be another Red. She's the kind that does everything as right as she can," Early Bird remembered.

"I'll be your nurse. Get comfortable and try to rest! Here is the Tylenol. I'll get you some milk. Don't drink coffee. It'll only keep you awake," she consoled. "Now, shut your eyes and take a couple deep breaths."

When she returned, he felt a little hopeful. He watched her pour the milk into a glass. The Tylenol and milk seemed to settle well as he tiredly volunteered to sleep.

*****

On the other end, Diesel Chaser checked his rig into the nearest Freightliner shop. He had already made the last delivery. They would give the big truck a 100,000 going over; he'd put lots of miles on her in a short time. Now, renting a car and meeting Early Bird at Newark was next priority

As he wheeled into the airport parking, Diesel knew there would be a wait. It had been about five hours since he had last talked to Early Bird. He couldn't help but wonder what was to be ahead. It was certain, something wild was on the wind. Red wouldn't leave Early with no word, no plan; he knew her that well.

"Yep! Something's coming down!" Diesel Chaser announced out loud as he followed the signs that led to the baggage area for Delta.

A filthy man staggered to his car. "Man, I look after your car for ten dollars!"

"Get away from my car, you drunk!" he growled, throwing his special I.D. into view.

"Oh, shit! Fuckin' shit! I ain't meaning nuttin'!" he groveled and rushed away grumbling. "Cops! A nudder cop!"

"You'd better get out of here!" Diesel called behind him as he parked.

Finding the tele-view of the arriving planes he settled to wait in a conspicious spot for the incoming plane, writing notes would settle his nerves and pass time. He hated waiting, but as a private investigator waiting was a major part. Diesel wished he had something to go with, more than 'Red High Heels is missing.' Timing could be virtually everything. If Red left on her own, it would be different. Early and Red had been there for him; now he would return the gesture.

His gut feeling was like Early Bird. "Red was gone! But why? How? Where? With whom? Something was definately odd," he mumbled.

The announcement for gate number 72, flight 108 blasted on the system. He nearly jumped to meet Early. Now, they could get it together.

Early Bird smiled big; he was the first passenger to disembark. They shook hands, slapped each other on the back with the happy reunion. As quickly, the despiration in Early Bird's eyes showed the old retired detective the adamant concern. They skipped the small talk and got straight into the problem. Early Bird brought him up to date.

"I think she's had more problems with that fellow, Devil. She didn't tell me everything. I suppose she thought I'd be angry or wouldn't understand," Early injected.

"She's right!" smiled the friend as he directed the way to the vehicle in the parking plaza. Early had a small duffle bag and personal case that was slung into the backseat.

"Want me to go to Red's place now?" Early quizzed.

"Let's call again!" planned Diesel. Early handed him a list of phone numbers with his cell-phone. None of the calls connected. Each rang about twenty times. They both shook their head in dismay.

"Let's go!" Early Bird nearly screamed with fear. "We've got to find my baby. I can't let nothing happen to her. I was a fool not to see what she was going through!"

"That's history. We'll find her!"

"If it's not too late!" Early Bird worried. "Let's hit the pike and go through the tunnels of Manhattan; in Lincoln and out Midtown to Long Island. The heat of the city will make it easier driving!"

"Right! There'll be a greater chance of traffic over the bridges."

"Hell, if we get caught in the city, we can take the train!" reminded Early.

Conversation, plans and some hours put them

onto Long Island. The time of day and the weekend helped the easy passage through the roads and streets.

"Red loves this nasty, old city!" commented Early.

"God pity her!' laughed Diesel. "Then, she loves you, too. The woman may be a bit crazy!"

"That's what is so exciting. She's different and independant. That's what scares me. Red's not as tough as she thinks. Under all that outside positive toughness, lives a sweet, gentle girl that is just as fragile as crystal. She is as vulnerable as anyone and can be hurt, killed or any other form of tragedy as the rest of us," Early sadly portrayed. "I should be there!"

"We are here, old tiger's friend! You and the tiger will kick ass and stop that son of a bitch! I promise, Red will be all right once we're there!" Diesel soothed. "Where to? We need to start from where you last had contact."

"That's out East to the end of this road!" Early directed. "I hope it isn't the end of her road!"

"Shut up! Quit crying now. We're on the trail. We have to think clearly!" replied Diesel Chaser, stepping on the accelerator. The vehicle slid a bit so he had to let off. "Let's eat!"

"I'm not hungry!"

"We'll get something to go and eat enroute. We still have an hour of driving. You can't do what's ahead without food," the detective commanded as he left the road for an open diner nearby. He knew the Island, too; in his past, he had covered territory here. One job was a double homicide that he preferred to forget. Another time it was a huge heist of jewelry. That might be at the top of his list of exotic complicated jobs. He remembered well how he had tracked an Oriental prostitute that led him right to the head of smuggled, stolen diamonds and precious stones. What started with seemingly nothing took several years to a big finish.

Diesel was well equiped with knowledge and experience. Retirement was a word used by others, he was as good, probably better than ever. Now, his friends were in trouble.

*****

The sleet, snow and wind had let up. Devil was gathering his duds to leave the area. he cleaned his dishes and called to a helper, "Hey, Snag Face!"

The fellow came to the door, "Yeah?"

"We're going! Git 'cha shit together. You driving the pickup and I'm in the tractor," he said. "Put the 'stuff' in the clocks. Hurry, we can be home before morning!"

Another helper walked in. "What 'cha doin'?"

"None of your fuckin' business! Here's three hundred for your pay. We'll go down south; you've got some trucks coming in," Devil barked. "Git the loads off and into the warehouse."

"How do I check all this stuff? Sold some yesterday!" Helper replied.

"Just do it!" Devil freaked. "Do it!"

"I thought it was my turn to go home!"

"Shut up! You'll go when I want you to. You got money and things are set," Devil screamed.

"But..."

"But, hell! Just do your job!" yelled Devil totally irritated.

"I have things. _"

"Fuck your things! I'm burnt out on your mouth!" he screamed at the little man. He watched the fellow wilt against a chair. He was in his late thirties, small featured and a couple inches over five feet. In the time he had been working, he was reliable, but now Devil thought he wanted to run the show. He had begun hating him several months prior, figuring he was stealing from him too like all the rest had done.

Helper had been slapped around many times before by his boss. Devil was the kind that bullied his help and kicked them around. The atmosphere was right for hell to break loose. The little man spoke carefully, "I'll do whatever you want."

"Of course you will, you thieving bastard! How much you stole from me?" screamed the paranoid man, nearly out of breath and eyes bulging.

The fellow trembled, "I don't steal! Man, I do the best I can!"

"Fuck your best!" snarled Devil. "You spying asshole. I see you watching me. Who you spying for? The cops?"

"No! Honest! If I was in with cops would I smoke dope? Would I shoot up? Please, man, don't do this! I just work! I try!" he cried, throwing his arms up in defense.

Devil kicked the fellow between his legs and watched him drop into the floor squealaing, grabbing his groin. Once he stopped rolling, the big man grabbed him by his braid and jerked his face back, pulling him up to a chair and throwing him into it. Through gritted teeth and red face he yelled, "You lying bastard. I'll fix you! You're a no good, sorry, son of a bitch!"

The man was small and helpless against a mad man. He had seen Devil's wrath before; this time he was totally out of control. His eyes met Devil's squinted, probing eyes.

"Oh, God!" Helper cried as the big fist came across his face. He felt his head swell while tumbling to the floor. The big shoes kept kicking him in the legs, stomach, then the ribs. The blows were constant; he was forced into a corner with no way out.

The other helper stood by and watched. Snag Face was afraid he'd be next; he said nothing, he did nothing.

"You lying thief! You'd steal from your mother! Ain't that right? I know what you've been doing! All of you are just alike!" he ranted. "You sorry bastard!"

Devil looked in the direction of Snag and laughed. Snag managed an approving smile. The final blow came with the big foot to the little man's throat. The blood spirted from his nose with a big snap that dropped the fellow limp to the floor. He moved no more.

Devil and Snag stared in disbelief. They knew Devil had crossed over the line.

"He wudn't no king or nuttin'! You saw it. He tried to get up and tripped over my foot!" insisted Devil.

"Yeah, something like that. I really didn't see it!" Snag's mouth became very dry and stuck as he tried to speak.

"Get it straight...We found him here!" Devil intervened. "He was just laying here like this. I'll bet that fellow that used to work here came to beat him up!"

"Yeah, probably!"

"I know enough about you to send you off forever! Just back me up and it will be worth your while; trip me up and you'll end up like this! Call the cops!" Devil demanded.

That part of town became another murder scene with a little known victim that seemed a nobody. The policeman in charge uttered, "It doesn't really add up. He works for this man and yet they don't know much about him. Before it's over, I'll bet we come up with somebody that loves him. These two tell the same story so far."

His partner smiled blankly, "A story is only a story; a fact is non-changing."

The crime scene was closed off with yellow streamers; eventually the body was removed while the investigation continued.

*****

Early Bird felt uneasy. It had taken almost two days to get to Red. Now they were nearly an hour away from her. He felt a tinge of excitement just thinking about his redhead. It would be necessary for them to find Red's stalker and put their 'word' on him. She need not got through anymore hell because of Devil he surmized.

"We'll find that bastard!" mumbled Early.

"Right! She's probably all right. Maybe it's been a miscommunication; still, we're going to kick his ass and take her out of New York," promised Diesel.

"Son of a gun! There's my baby's wheels! That's what she drives!" Early sparked, while eagerly stopping the rental car next to the long van. "This is great!"

Early Bird slammed his door behind him and ran to the front of the store. He waited for his friend to catch up while he pounded desperately on the plate glass.

"Hold it, Early!" ordered the old detective. "Hold it! That door is ajar! Look!"

He took out his handkerchief from a long established habit, then his old service pistol. Early turned white as he looked deep into the store and caught a glimpse of a stool overturned. He felt the hamburger catch in his throat and he began to shake.

Early stuttered, "D-do y-y-you think sh-sh-she's all-all-all right?"

"Stay behind me and be quiet!" demanded Diesel. He opened the door carefully and let the weight of it swing wide. They both eased quietly into the building. There was no noise other than a radio playing in the distance. Items were piled out of place. The business area and showroom were untouched. When they entered her bedroom there was immediate evidence of a fight; red hair was in wads in the floor of the room; things were scrambled and clothes were thrown around. A liquor bottle was on the bed, and blood spots around.

"Jesus! Something's wrong!" Early cried. "She keeps things neat! That's her hair! Oh, God!"

"Keep quiet and calm down!" whispered Diesel exiting that room and tiptoeing down the hall toward the kitchen. When he entered he stopped short. "Wait there, Early! Hold on! Go call the locals!"

"Is she in there? Please, let me look!" Early

Bird begged as the tears fell uncontrollably. "Oh, God! My baby! Is she? Is Red..."

"Hold on! I don't see her, just a mess!" answered the detective. "All right, look. Don't go in! Don't mess with anything!"

As Diesel stepped aside, Early Bird could see the vomit and blood spattered. It was before them; a crime scene. Knives were laying around along with more wads of hair and pieces of fabric. One broken off finger nail rested on the table top in a smear of blood, as if she had tried to pull herself up.

"Look here!" Diesel yelled as he squatted over a couple of big shoe prints made clearly at one end of the room with bits of prints that were scrambled all over. "A big man was in here. We have to call the police here fast! This is a job for them!"

It was only minutes before a dozen squad cars roared into the parking lot; uniformed men and women along with plain clothes personel were bounding through the door.

A man with lots of clout and metals took charge, "How did you get in?"

They spilled the earlier story from the time of leaving to find Red and walked in on this. They too were given the third degree about who they were. Once the police were satisfied with the story the missing woman became ultimate.

"Where could she be?" asked Early. "Maybe she walked out or ran! She could be out there somewhere in the cold!"

"We'll look all over the area!" muttered the busy cop snapping orders to different police.

They combed the area but there was no sign of Red High Heels and no one had seen her. There was no exact time set for the trauma that apparently had occurred.

After hours of investigation, the police were ready to leave with their report, plus an APB for the missing Red High Heels. Early and Diesel would have to leave Red's unattended business to continue their bewildering search.

"Where to now?" asked Diesel. "They're throwing us out of here! They don't know any more than we do. Look!"

Early caught the drops of dark red in the ice on the path where he pointed. "She left the building; didn't she?"

"Yeah! You better believe it!" replied Diesel motioning to the head detective and pointing. "See that?"

He grunted, "I'll get a lab sample." He ordered the medical team to remove a chunk of the ice. "Glad you found that. She, or somebody, left here bleeding. Maybe somebody broke in and robbed her. I think she fought back; by the looks of it, probably it was someone she was acquainted with. Most often it is!" he shared out loud, nearly like he wasn't aware of anyone else.

Yellow ribbons were put into place. The detectives ordered Diesel to report anything they might discover.

"Don't get in over your head!" suggested the officer. "You men are too involved with this woman to think clearly. Leave the job to us. Look around but call us when you need to. Here's my card."

Early and Diesel were allowed to take Red's briefcase as they referred to her huge purse. The police amazed them with that. Once down the road, they pulled off to talk and plan.

We'll get a room to work from. I want to go through her purse!" suggested Early Bird. "She has a lot of money around her. We need to find out about that. There's calls to make, too!"

He started the car and moved on until he found a hotel on Route 110. It was convenient to the Long Island Expressway and Red's main store.

*****

It was a strange cold. The total darkness was surely purgatory. Growing up, Red had been taught there was a heaven or a hell. Later, she had heard there might be an in-between space where you wait for the word to go one way or the other. Would God call or would it be Satan?

All the pain had turned into a total numbness. The feeling of life had left her; there was no surge of energy, only a lifeless state of being that had to be a form of limbo. An awareness of time or who she was didn't enter into her soul. It was just the coldness of nothing. Red High Heels drifted unconscious again.

Once more awakening, her brain tried to function and give life another spurt. Yet, everything seemed so far away. She tried to lift her head but the weight of it was too great. Her tongue felt thick and her mouth was as if it were glued shut. It was hard to tell if she could see or maybe in purgatory there would be no eyes. Red tried to moan but there was no sound; she felt limp and motionless.

She fell back into a deep slumber and drifted into a sub-conscious dream. The technicolor scenes were somewhat splotchy with vivid faces. A pretty red headed girl was running to her with arms outstretched, crying, "Mama, don't go!" Her hair was long and her strong, muscular legs pushed rapidly toward Red. The vivid image kept coming closer. Red recognized her from some place but still couldn't totally connect. Again, the angel-like beauty whispered to her, "Mama! I will always be here! I love you! Please don't go!"

The soft image reached for her, sitting to the ground beneath Red; yet, whimpered through her words and tears while clinging to Red's legs.

Another image filtered through. A huge bright light like from a stage; no, there were two lights together. Then Red thought she could hear the deep rumbling of a far off engine. The black shadow of a huge man's figure was walking toward her. It kept coming closer and was soon very close. Red wanted to hide, who was this man? Suddenly, she could hear a comforting voice call out, "Red, I'm here! Please, open the door! I'm here!"

When the figure stopped before her, she could see a handsome face, a smile and tears when he whispered, "Please, Red, don't leave me! I love you so! Come back, I can't live without you!"

The man fell to her feet and reached for her hand but she couldn't touch him. The reach was a little too far. He cried out again, "I love you! I will always love you! Please! Baby, come back!"

The bright light turned to darkness as the two images faded and Red High Heels started to awaken again.

"I am alive! Oh, God! I am alive! I'm hidden out but I'm alive. Please, God, help me! Kikki Doo and Early find me! Please find me!" cried Red

High Heels. The numbness was fading in her arms but with checking herself, she felt her face was like two sizes. She couldn't move her mouth without severe pain. Her right hand finally manged to move and discover for her. There was a flaking-like crust on her face and in her hair.

Red High Heels started to remember some of her dilemma. It was not clear, still her store was the last place she could recall. It was a mystery where she was, furthermore, how she got here. Discovering she was wearing a coat gave a first clue; then, beneath her was cloth, tons of cloth. She felt and tried to sniff. Maybe it would come to light. She rolled over in the thick mass.

"That's it! Furniture pads!" she thought to herself.

Forcing the one eye that opened slightly through the swelling, Red could see two circles of very dim light above her. It looked like a hazy halo and quite high up. Pulling her thoughts to coordinate her surroundings and the happening was too much. It wouldn't come together. She felt tired, so tired, and she was beginning to feel pain in her legs, head, jaw and even personal places. She wondered if she had been in a wreck. Once more she slipped into a light slumber for a few minutes.

The place seemed colder, she thought about food but decided it was all too much effort. Again, Red High Heels shifted herself to a little better awareness and searched her memory for her plight. She gave up on remembering things; she wanted to know where she was now. The rest would come later.

The determined woman finally pulled herself up to a sitting position against a wooden wall. She assumed she was near blind and would never be able to count on seeing anything again. The darkness was strange. Taking her time, she found a loose paper towel in her pocket. She was glad to feel its texture, then wiped her wet eyes. It smarted to rub so she dotted them until they felt a little more comfortable.

Putting her napkin back into her pocket, she found a package of some sort. Wiggling the paper, she knew it was something to eat. Her habit of carrying something in the food line in her pocket was handy now. As she emptied both pockets she realized there were a couple of candy bars and a pack of peanut butter crackers. She carefully placed them next to the wall so she could find them.

Red felt around her and dragged herself to touch the freight that was several feet from where she had been laying. Immediately she felt the plastic cover over a stack of sofas.

"This is a furniture trailer! It's real! It might be my trailer!" she mumbled.. Once more she crawled in another direction and found the deck of the forty-five foot wagon. Feeling around, she discovered several familiar things. A cooler was before her, she hoped it had water. Lifting the lid, she felt again and found a drink of some sort.

"I always have a flashlight...here! A flashlight for sure!" she gleed. "If it turns on, then I will know if I'm blind or not!"

Red struggled to get the switch to flip on. She ached all over. She had never hurt like this before. It was as if a freight train had run over her. With the snap of the light, there was just a slight hazy light. Red rubbed her eyes and felt tears flow. "Please, don't let me be totally blind!"

Again, she became tired but adjusted the furniture pads to be more comfortable and covered all herself and settled back.. She seemed to have no strength or stamana. Once more she fell asleep. She knew there was no way out without someone opening the door. She would wait. Sooner or later someone would have to come.

*****

Having been dismissed by the police, Devil and Snag quickly rushed for his truck. The older man wasn't new to the dark side of life. He had committed many crimes over the years that cost a great deal of money; all his life paying his way out of trouble. It all seemed to lurk over him constantly. He could be home minding his own business, but a knock on the door could change everything. Sometimes it was the beginnings of the deal of a lifetime and others were just a stupid scam. He would try many; other times he would just let it go. Money was the ultimate. Such a Jeckel and Hyde, he was. His temper operated on a scale from one to a hundred. On 'one' he was the nicest man you could meet, but about 'fifty' on the scale was when Hyde broke in. He was never to be reasoned with and his control went out the window.

With the one problem out of his way, his thoughts flipped back to Red High Heels. She had to be dead in that trailer where he put her. Still, it bothered him now. If she gets tied to him, then it would be a greater problem with this last little bastard getting himself killed.

This woman was of no use to him. She shouldn't have made him mad. There had been a time that he needed Red. He could talk her into getting the things he wanted and she was so stupid. She had the two qualities he liked best in women; she had money and she was so afraid of him she had to pay out. It didn't take him long to separate her from everyone who was close to her. It put her alone and nobody would take a chance being around. He thought to himself, "You redheaded bitch, you caused all of this! I'm glad you are dead!"

He drove his rig into a shopping center and told his helper to get out.

"You ain't gonna leave me here?" he trembled.

"Naw! We in it together! I gotta go pick up a trailer. I bought it last week. Red High Heels is going out of business and I bought one from her," insisted Devil.

"I can't believe she's going to quit!"

"She and some cop are doing their thing. That bitch always loved a cop! Don't you remember how she always had them around?" growled Devil. "It don't matter...I got me a real woman now! This one is better than that damn Red. This'un just helped me to pull a truck-heist in Chicago. She likes to smoke grass and shoot-up a little. She's like a woman ought to be. She has a million dollar machine between her legs and knows how to use it! They call her Ball-breaker!"

"I reckon that's good!" replied Snag.

"Yeah! Ballbreaker and I are going to do it! We're going to get everything we want and nothing will stop us!" declared Devil. "Unhook that trailer and let's go get that other one."

The helper dropped the landing gear, disconnected the light and air lines, then pulled the pin lock. The trailer made a big thud as it let go of the tractor. The bobtail rolled back toward the road.

"When we get to Red's place, I'll back under it and you roll up the gear about half way. We'll hook up better when we stop down the road. I don't want to get into it with her and her asshole people!" planned Devil.

*****

"I have my shower. You about ready?" asked Diesel.

Early Bird was sitting at the foot of his bed. The suite of rooms would be perfect for ordinary business. He wanted to run as fast and as far as he could. Everything was so strange. Something happened to Red and he knew it was greater than anyone would say. The cops always hide the facts and the fat woman has not sung yet, so it wasn't over. He called several people who knew Red or worked with her and all of them brushed him off.

"Tiger Puss?" he asked.

"I'll put her on," answered her husband.

"Oh, hello, Early Bird!" she could smile through a wire.

"I'm looking for Red. Know where she is?" he quizzed.

"We were all taking some time off with the weather being so bad. You know her. Maybe she went to North Carolina. She'll do that without saying anything about it!" she tried to defuse him.

"It doesn't make sense. She left her car and purse at her other store...Not where you work. The place was unlocked and a mess. We had the police there but she was gone!" whispered Early. "I'm worried. I know something is bad wrong."

"God! You are right!" she cried.

Early discussed each detail, trying to fill her in and trying to search for information or a tiny clue. They both concluded that a search should be done on the store she managed. It made sense for Red to return there. Still, her car was at the other place.

It was strange and out of whack. Everyone assumed that Devil had to be the maniac that broke in on her yet; they really didn't know. It could have been some stranger.

Early focused on Diesel as he dried his hair. "Old man, get ready! Puss is meeting us at Red's store near here."

"Great! You're getting to be a good detective! I know we will at least be where some kind of information will pop up. Right now, the least little thing might be the missing piece!" Diesel ployed.

"Well, think about it! We just assumed what happened to her out there. Maybe somebody made her go there or made her go somewhere else. Her transportation was with them!" Early guessed.

"Do you think it was for money?" Diesel muttered.

"I found a piece of paper in her purse dated three days ago. It showed credit cards and checks that were deposited. There was a copy of the deposit slip and it would have been sent to a bank in North Carolina. The cash amount she had scribbled in this...Look!" extended Early as he held a paper. "I've seen her handle her money. She gets the cash in money orders or takes it to the companies down south. There's no money in her purse to speak of. Red always had a handful of ones, fives and tens."

"This sheds a different light! Do you think she had this much cash? According to this, she probably had over thirty thousand dollars. That is a bunch! A crazy person would nab that in a heart beat!" winced Diesel.

"She hid her stuff...but she might have had it on her!"

"Did other people know about her money?" asked the ex-cop.

"She knew better than that! She always acted like she sent it off to a bank. Her manager knew what was going on and helped her keep things out of sight. Lots of times Puss put Red's money in her home safe," Early Bird informed.

"Money is certainly a motive...sex is a motive...jealousy is a motive...fear is a motive!" insisted Diesel. "Now we need to know what was the motive and a lab report on the blood."

"Don't forget, the hair that was scattered all over the place. I know that was Red's...you do, too. She was the victim...my baby just might be dead!" cried Early as he wiped the tears with a wash cloth. "I love that girl so much!"

Diesel patted Bird on the shoulder, "I love your Red High Heels, too. We will find her! Early, don't give up! There is faith until the end. We are a long way from the end! Come on, let's go meet that lady!"

Early forced himself to brush his teeth and dress warmly. He knew the cold wouldn't let up. The days had rolled into one big nightmare and the time kept dragging. They left the hotel.

*****

Red High Heels finally woke up again. The furniture pads were warm as long as she captured her body heat within her little tent-like area. She felt her face and realized it wasn't really her face. It was real big and her chin seemed to hang loose.

She reached for the bottle of water again and tried to drink but part of it rolled into her lap. The bit that slipped down her throat tasted good. Fumbling, Red opened the crackers and forced a piece into her mouth. She was unable to chew so she let it soak in her mouth until it had melted enough to slip down her throat. She repeated this until she finally digested three and followed it with water. Red felt a little stick in the 'cooler', then discovered it was s sipping straw when she put it to her mouth. She happily thought, "What a wonderful victory, a straw!"

Little things that go by so meaningless everyday became huge boulders in the deep, cold darkness of Red's purgatory.

*****

The police in two different precincts were puzzled. One group had to deal with a near homeless who had been snuffed out. Most likely, the fellow had a drug problem. The lab had discovered drugs in his system; lots of alcohol and he was a smoker. There was nobody yet to claim the little, cold body on the slab with the big tag around it's toe. It lay there amongst many other odd bodies.

The discovery pointed to a simple argument between drinking buddies and a homeless would have lots of buddies like that if he had access to a few dollars and a place to stay. Some homeless fall out in the shelters and some stay borderline. In the winter they like to find a savior. Devil was his hero; he took him in and he tried to be worthy.

For all practical purposes, there certainly were more pressing problems in the precinct than this nobody that was living on the line. The busy precinct was called for a huge bus accident that had a big number of people involved. Then, a woman was at gun point in a restaurant where an intruder was pulling a robbery. Several blocks from there, a three-house fire was raging. A couple of boats in the harbor had cut loose and washed onto the shore, tearing into a huge home nestled over the water. Then, at the edge of the district, a news team was broadcasting the tremendous vehicle pile-up that cut the power to forty thousand residents. And, the switchboard kept lighting up.

At the other precinct, some miles away, two officers were getting off shift. Here again, many emergencies were being reported and the officers were moving out in the many various cars to attend the many traumatic pleas.

"Let me brief you on this missing woman!" yelled one detective to a new comer.

The fellow pulled up a chair and poured both of them coffee. He listened intently as the story unfolded.

"I know her. My wife bought our bedroom set from this woman. That's the one," he supplied, looking at the photo the man showed him.

"Her friends believe she has been abducted and I do, too!" the tired, dark eyed man concluded. "They are trying to check into what has happened. I didn't tell them but from the looks of things, there was lots of blood and hair around; all her's. She was murdered! It wasn't a pretty scene. The body was gone. The weather hurts; absolutely nobody saw anything."

"Did you check the area?"

"Everywhere within a certain radious. There was one intruder and it had to be a man. Knives were around but we can't get a clear fingerprint. We found prints but in a business location it's hard to get something definate. Got any ideas?" he asked.

"Let's hope it solves itself! If she's dead, maybe someone will find her. I'll send her picture out on the system. Who knows, she might turn up. The longer the wait, the chance is less we'll locate her," whispered the officer. "My wife will certainly be torn up. She liked the lady."

"Do everything you can. She still may be somewhere hiding from her assailant. If she is, she could die from this damn cold!" grimaced the other detective.

"I thought of that...We'll keep the search going!"

*****

Early Bird and Diesel drove to the back of Red's building to meet Puss. She was waiting in her car. Once inside the building, they began the search. It was obvious that nothing was distrubed; everything was the way it normally would be. The upstairs apartment, where Red usually stayed, was neat with only a pair of boots in front of her bed. Her pictures of Early Bird were in place and the radio had its usual station, playing quietly.

"Look here!" noticed Diesel. "This note pad. See the scribbling? Look, the first three calls have messages and names. This one has a number."

"That's a customer. They own a flower shop," discovered Puss. She looked the page over. "That next thing is a hang up...so is that one. See that? She was drawing a 'devil' picture. He probably called. Look at this! The words 'heart attack', then she marked through it. That's strange."

They went to Puss' desk and found a note from Red. "Gone out to the other store. I'm delivering another truck of furniture next week. Keep cool. I'll be back whenever. Red."

"That settles that. She did drive out to her store. Somebody followed her or walked in on her!" determined Diesel.

"Where is her truck? That extra trailer is here but her big truck is gone!" said Early Bird.

"She left it at that place where she's selling her extra stuff. When they unload, she picks it up. I know it's there!" Puss insisted.

"Can we call?" questioned Diesel.

"It won't be open," she replied.

"Let's ride out and check. Maybe Red went to pick it up!" grieved Early Bird.

"She just wouldn't in this weather. Here's the address and a key for here. Do whatever you think is best. I'll wait at home in case she calls," Puss said and left in her husband's Mazda.

"What next, boss?" Early quizzed. "We have to find her. If we keep looking, something will turn up!"

"Sometimes it's best just to wait. This is the

phone she would call first," informed Diesel.

"Let's make sure her truck is over there!" cried Early, frantic with dispair.

"We should stay put!"

"But suppose she went to her truck. Maybe she got a way there somehow! Please!" begged Early. "I just have to know. She loves that old truck and would naturally check on it."

"Come on! It's a dead end!"

Diesel hurried to the place where her rig should be.

*****

"Damn, it's cold!" blew Snag as he returned to the big, white Kenworth. "I hooked the lines into place, too! Gimme a drink!"

"Git it...It's back there in the sleeper. Jack Daniels...Best friend I ever had!" laughed Devil. He put the truck in gear and shared a big gulp from the same bottle. "The cops here don't pay no attention to booze like down south. People here are used to drinking. I got a ticket last week in Winston Salem for having a beer. The fuckin' cop just has to get him a quota. My lawyer will get it changed. It don't matter about tickets for drinking. A laywer can do anything you can afford to pay for. I got enough money. I get by real good!"

"They's put me under the jail. Hell, I just don't even have a license no more. I ain't got no car," sipped Snag. "I lost 'em a couple years ago. So, you drive without one; what they gonna do? I ain't been caught."

"You're right. A license is a lotta trouble.

278

Just another way for them to find out what you're doing. I hate all that kinda shit!" mumbled Devil as he drove down a dark street then through an off-beat side road. He felt the bobtail slip and then it moved the other way. The cab was out of control and slipped around again. "Oh, shit! This motherfuckin' ice! Hang on! Damn!"

The truck could not be controlled. It was sliding at it's own free will. It went into a spin that forced the rear single axle over the edge of a curb and into a garbage can that went sprawling. Once more the vehicle slid sideways and seemed to gain momentum as it slipped slightly downhill on a deep sheet of ice. The darkness interrupted the tilt-a-whirl motion occasionally by a flicker from the street lights.

"Damn! We're gonna git killed! You son of a bitch!" screamed Snag. "Oh, shit!"

As he yelled, the motion took his careless body into mid-air and slung him around; first, into the windshield that cracked with his weight and the cold, then he sailed back into the open sleeper. Devil held onto the steering wheel. For once in his life, he had no control of things. "This could be the total end," he thought, then screamed, "Hold on! Damn it! Hold on!"

The fellow was petrified as he was tossed so aimlessly.

The big truck kept sliding; it somehow stayed on its wheels. When it came to the end of a block it bounced off a light standard and changed directions to another street. The right light of the cab went off with the trauma and Devil could hear the cracking of the frond end. The new glide of the big truck sent the mass helplessly toward a gas station, numerous feet away. As Devil watched the gas pumps loom in front of him, he frantically grabbed the wheel but to no avail. A big bucket was in front of the truck that had been filled with the station trash. When the cab crashed into it; it forced the simplest slide that put the tractor into the edge of a building.

"Oh, shit! Oh, fuck!" exhilirated Devil. "Shit! It's over! God! Oh, hell! We're lucky we didn't hit those pumps! It would probably have blown us all the way to hell!"

The other man didn't answer and Devil reached back to shake him. As he touched him, he felt the erie dampness from his blood. He turned the cab light on that still was operating and looked at the fellow. The man's eyes were near closed and he didn't move.

"Holy fuck! Snag! Hey, asshole, wake up!" panicked Devil. "Hey, man! Don't do this to me! I need you! I love you, motherfucker! Come on, you can't do this to me! Not now! Ain't I been good to you? You bastard! I give you everything you want...I always did!"

He stared at the figure flopped before him in the sleeper. Not wanting to touch it again, he resigned himself to another 'dead one', and sighed, "What the fuck is next? Pricks die just like that! Fuck! I didn't kill your ass! You just died with an accident. I wouldn't kill my butt-hole buddy! Damn! Damn! Damn! Like I ain't got enough trouble as it is!"

Pounding the dash, he jabbed a piece of broken glass into his hand and screamed out as the blood poured, "Son of a bitch! Damn it! Look what you've made me do, Snag! Just look! I'm in a fix for real! If this truck don't move, you bastard, I'm gonna dump your ass behind the wheel and say you stole it!"

As Devil toyed with that idea, he got out of the truck to see the situation and what it would take to get going. After instpecing things, he found a box of something like rough gravel and poured it around the tires. "That's salt! Fuckin' salt! Salt! Shit, it burns like a mother, but the tires will roll!"

He danced around shaking his hand from the intense stinging. His blood smeared from place to place as he whined and jubilated. "Well, I'll move this bitch if it'll run!"

Not remembering if he turned the ignition off or not, he started to get back into the cab. His foot contacted with the icey step, then slipped from under him. Devil fell hard to the slick coated cement. His head flopped against the ground, almost enough to knock him out. Feeling stunned, Devil sat up cursing, "Shit, what in hell's going on? Maybe the witches are out!"

He stood, grabbing the side of the truck to hold himself up, remembering everything had a coating of ice. Struggling to boost himself into the cab, Devil landed back in the driver's seat. "Shit! Shit! Shit! What a bitch! I've got to go get that trailer before someone finds Miss Red High-Falutin' Heels!"

Devil's mind drifted to the blackened moments of his entanglement with Red. She deserved her ass beat; she was always a thorn in his side. He knew she'd be like every other woman. She'd never keep her mouth shut. At a time, he figured he probably loved her but they say love and trust are the same. Trust was not part of his make-up.

"How do you trust anybody? They always rat

you out or frig up something," he said aloud, squinting and staring blankly into space. "They'll never connect me! Most men would've had to have some of that 'cooter' and leave evidence. That's the best thing I have going! A woman can't trap me; they can't get 'Trigger'. Red was good like that. She didn't want sex. Just cops turn her on."

He cleared his throat and spoke in a voice that seemed foreign, "I didn't mean to, Red! You just piss me off. It's like you just can't let go. Your grip is deadly. You might know shit that could fix me. You wanted me to be straight, not drink...You said I could be a good man. I tried! I really did, a little. Reckon I should have left you alone. Maybe things would be different!"

A bright flash of light brought him around. A police car rolled up beside the bobtail stretched across the lot, haphazardly. Devil looked in the sleeper at Snag. The truck was running and hopefully would find traction.

"Hey there!" yelled the sheriff over the engine noise. "Are you all right?"

"I hope so. It hit ice and got into a slide. Nothing damaged, just scared the hell out of me!" answered Devil. "I've got to get back on the street! I have to get my trailer."

"Give it a try!" screamed the cop. "The main roads are all right!"

The tires would only spin.

"I got a chain. Let me hook it to you. Once it catches something, I'm out of here!" grimaced Devil.

They finally got the bobtail back in service and parted ways. By trying to find enough rough spots, the cab eased along.

Devil looked back into the sleeper and caught a glimpse of the big lump there. He spoke aloud, "You fucker! You got me into all this! That cop would have shit if he'd found your dead ass! I'm dumping you right up here!"

He stopped the truck to the side on a main road and was ready to make his deposit. Geting on his knees in the passenger seat, Devil grabbed his corpse by both feet. Quickly, Snag sat up laughing and screamed, "Boo!"

"Damn!" flared Devil sinking into the seat. He, at first, thought he saw a ghost!

CHAPTER 12

Early Bird and Diesel Chaser found the blue Transtar nestled by the building at the loading dock. It was covered with ice and looked so desolate.

"It's empty!" blared Early enthusiastically.

"How do you know?"

"Her truck squats like a woman when she's heavily laden. I've got keys, let's check it out and take her home," smiled Early Bird feeling better being around Red's big wagon and rig.

"She's probably locked it all over! We could set off an alarm," warned Diesel Chaser.

"I know what to do. See?" Early smiled extending a wad of keys. "These are trailer, truck, house, store...All her keys! This one is to her chastity belt!"

Opening the door of the trailer proved the van

to be empty. The men got into the cab to check if retrieving the truck would be possible.

"Let me shoot some starting fluid to it!" ordered Early finding the can in the sleeper. "Looks like Red's prepared! She usually is!"

Diesel watched Early give the vehicle a huge squirt and became somewhat dizzy from the fumes. He snorted, "This old thing isn't going to start!"

"Just watch!" frowned Early Bird as he turned the key in the ignition and pressed the starter button. After a couple of groaning tries Early waited for a few seconds.

"I told you! It's awful cold! The air lines are probably frozen, too!"

Early tried the starter again, patted the accelerator and finally the big monster reluctantly grumbled, as she fired. The big engine moaned and argued but soon settled down to a good, healthy putter. The air buzzer screamed with the warning light staying bright red.

"That's my girl!" bragged Early as the rig began to build air and the motor warmed somewhat. "Look here! Gloves! My baby looks after me! Have a pair!"

Flinging his partner the needed warm mitts Early Bird then readied a log book. He waited for the cabover to thaw. They watched a big bird try to land on a nearby roof top. It seemed as if he skidded and flipped over.

"Did you see that?" laughed Diesel. "The gull nearly landed on his hinny! I'll follow you in our car!"

Early shook his head and began to ponder his memory. "Where can my baby be? You can't leave

me Red! Baby, I love you!" His mind trailed off to
the first time he saw her. She was broke down on the
side of the road in Virginia and was wearing her red
high heel shoes. Her red hair glistened in the fading
sunlight. He remembered her very white skin and
happy smile, even in stress. That night he thought an
angel had appeared; then she spoke to him. She acted
as if he were her knight in shining armor. She was
beautiful, gentle and reached to him with her soul. He
felt that old tingle and he wanted her forever, right
then. Red never played games. She was always
"herself." She could do anything about, if she set her
mind to it. It seemed that over the years, catching
each other here and there, everything mellowed with
each time they met.

"Just   when   you   think   everything   is
perfect...Something seems to jump in the way,'
groaned Early out loud. He watched the rental car
behind him, making certain it could stick with him.

*****

Red had managed to find a hammer. She put
it to her aching, swollen mouth and felt relief from its
coldness. It was difficult to remember anything; she
just wanted to be warm and feel no pain. Again she
tried to roll into a ball and make the world go away.

The pile of furniture blankets were like a
cloth igloo. She felt air from a crack in the trailer.
She could almost make it out with one eye; giving
what seemed a slight, out of focus view. Things were
coming together a little more. This had to be her
trailer door and she knew it was closed. She knew she
couldn't get out.

Red remembered the time when her dog was missing for a couple of days and for some reason she walked by the trailer and heard her crying. It was a hungry, happy, thirsty dog that leaped to freedom. Red knew now she'd have to wait for help.

She tried to remember more; again it came slowly. "I was thrown in here! That's it! Now I know!"

Immediately, she felt panic-stricken.

She muttered aloud, "Devil! You old maniac! You tried to do me in! I hate you! You tried to kill me! Well, son of a bitch!"

Tears filled her eyes and made them sting from the trauma. She knew she had to straighten up and get tough. Devil would be back...He always had to go back to the scene.

She'd stay warm and think.

*****

Meanwhile, about a mile east, a bobtail made its way.

"We're two blocks away now! Snag, git your ass out, then hook the lines up to the trailer. After I back under it, roll up the landing gear!" ordered Devil.

"Hell, yeah! It'll be a cinch!" the helper answered, looking at the trailer as they drove into the lot. He started getting out once the truck stopped.

"Check the side door; make sure it's closed!" demanded Devil.

"Sure thing!"

Devil moved the truck into position as Snag raced to the side door, nearly falling on the thick ice. Devil stopped and watched from his mirror.

Inside the forty-five foot trailer Red High Heels heard the bobtail. She knew, by the sound of the engine, it was not her truck. "It has to be Devil returning," she grunted.

Feeling her blood rush she moved into a perch behind the pads and waited where she wouldn't be seen. Footsteps came closer, making her heart leap as she heard the side door rattle while it was being opened. She ducked down and wiped her eyes gently.

"Open that door ass-hole!" she whispered as she waited.

A loud screeching noise brought the door to a full swing open. The light hit her eyes as the figure looked into the door.

"Shit!" It's loaded!" gleed Snag; then, let out a blood curdling scream, "Damn! Oh, hell! Oh, damn almighty!"

Red had flung the hammer as best she could. It connected to the side of Snag's head. He screamed more profanities, raced back to the truck and jumped into the passenger side.

"Get the hell outta here! That fuckin' trailer's haunted! Something came flying over me and knocked me in the damn head!" He rubbed the place and felt the blood oozing. "Look! I'm bleeding!"

"Shit! Chicken shit! It ain't no 'haints'; something fell!" laughed Devil. "Whinny little prick!"

"Ain't either! Besides, there's a lock on the pin. You got a key?" Snag retorted, still nursing his head.

"A lock on the pin? Well, that bitch!" roared Devil. "We'll have to git a torch or something!"

He put the bobtail in gear and started to leave when he caught the glimpse of a blue Transtar only a half block away. He knew it was Red's rig.

*****

Early Bird was glad to arrive at the store. He decided to park the rig beside the trailer. At a glance in his mirror, he saw the signal on Diesel's rental car following. Swinging wide into the lot of the big furniture store he made eye contact with a bobtail backed in front of Red's other trailer. That seemed unusual. He flipped the rig around in front of the other truck and started backing into place. The rental car stayed out of the way near the trailer.

Devil saw Red's truck parking in beside him and nearly froze. "Snag! You know that man?"

"Naw!" he yelled. "Let's git outta here! Come on, this is trouble!"

Playing his cards for a bluff, Devil released his brake and rolled the bobtail past the big truck and threw up his hand, waving. He headed out of the lot seeking his way toward the expressway.

Early Bird jumped from the tractor, leaving it running, and piled into the rental car with Diesel Chaser. He was as white as a sheet and out of breath. "Follow that truck! That's the problem! That's that bastard! See! It has North Carolina tags! Come on, Diesel! Haul ass!"

Without words, the big detective fell on the path that had been made by Devil. They upgraded their plans as they established a pattern of pursuit. The bobtail had caught traffic lights, helping the rental car to be hot on their tail.

*****

Hearing the commotion, Red High Heels stood quickly. "Early Bird! You're here!" She knew his voice; she could hear her big, wonderful truck running. The trailer door was unlocked and flew open with the wind.

The light seemed so bright as it flooded inside. "I'm not blind! Thank God! Oh, God, thank you! I'm not blind! Please help me now!"

It wasn't easy, but Red's adrenaline took over. She found her way out of the door and glimpsed quickly at the distance. It had to be Early Bird speeding away chasing after the bobtail that had driven away. She cried, "Oh, honey, don't do anything crazy!"

Her rig was calling her as it sat proudly waiting. Red cast aside the pain she suffered with each step and pulled herself into the tall cabover. She read the log book that guaranteed her Early Bird was the one she had seen; he had found her rig. With natural instinct, she popped the air button and eased the truck in the direction of the expressway. She had a little quicker route with the traffic usually heavy at this point. She'd try it. Now, she was excited. With real luck she would cut off a bit of extra time and traffic and catch up.

Early Bird didn't want the bobtail people to notice them so they kept a little distance, waiting to get into inevitable traffic snarl ahead. Diesel was used to pursuit, so he stalked their prey, waiting for the right moment. They ultimately caught up with Devil's bobtail, still keeping a safe, inconspicuous cover.

*****

In the bobtail, scooting frantically, Devil screamed wildly, "You little prick. Why didn't you git the key from the trailer? I put 'em inside that frickin' door! You know all the keys would be together! When I dumped the bitch in, the whole wad was together...I could have gotten the damn pin collar off!"

"Hell, I can't read your mind! You said to close the side door and you'd back up and for me to finish hooking up the shit!" reminded Snag.

"Shut up, you stupid asshole. You ain't nuthin' but a pussy. You bang your head and you come running back crying! Fuck it! Little girl! I reckon you backed up to 'em all in jail. Bet you loved it!" argued Devil, trying to throw the guilt trip on Snag.

"I ain't done no queer stuff!" cried Snag miserably, rubbing his bleeding knot on his head Red had made with the hammer.

"You'll suck my dick if I tell you to, won't you?" laughed Devil.

"I don't think so!" replied Snag.

"I'll show you 'good buddy'. I'll break you in!" Devil growled, trying to force his control. He looked at Snag whimpering in the seat across from him. As he did, a car stopped suddenly in front of him.

"Look out!" screamed Snag.

Just in time, the bobtail slid and Devil had to take it to the emergency lane, missing the car ahead of him by a split hair.

"You son of a bitch! Git outta here! You're the one that's 'hainted'! It's been bad luck since the day I met you! Git out before I kill you!" roared the mad man.

292

"I ain't got no place to go...No money!" cried Snag. "Please!"

"Git out!" yelled Devil, reaching into his pocket, producing a knife.

The thin fellow tried to open the door when the air brakes popped on. He fumbled in fear, wishing he had died.

"Hold it! Sit down! I ain't gonna hurt you!" Devil's split personality changed up. He watched behind him in his mirror and could see a car pulling in. "What now? More cops?"

*****

"Damn! Did you catch that?" Early Bird stated as he watched the truck veer off in front of them.

"Yeah! The fool about rear-ended that car! Perfect! Now, it's time to move in on him. He's off the road! I'll get right behind him," Diesel replied. "Hang on a minute!"

He maneuvered around the cars in front of him, parking off the road behind the bobtail

"Early Bird, wait it out! Don't fly crazy! Promise!" pleaded Diesel.

"No, I'm not going to fly crazy! I'm going to get that bastard now! This is the end of his screwing around with our lives!" Early Bird jumped out of the car and ran to the side of the truck in front of them. As he opened it's door, Devil had started out.

This surprise appearance asserted both men face to face. Quickly, Early realized Devil held an open blade in his hand. Backing away to achieve some space between them, Early asked, "Where's Red

High Heels?"

"Who?" laughed Devil, flipping the shiny spear side to side in an off handed but threatening manner.

"Red! You know! The woman you stalk!" Early growled.

"Oh, you mean Miss La-de-da Red High Heels. You her cop?"

"Where's Red?" Early yelled angrily. "That's all I want from you!"

"You ought to know!" laughed Devil, taking delight that the man was looking for his woman. "Can't you keep up with your pussy?"

Early lost it all and lunged for the other man. They were close in size and a good physical match. Devil never fought real men, just women and the weak. Bird knocked Devil down with the weight of his body; then rolled over to his feet. When Devil stood up, Early was ready. He came up under Devil's chin with one fist, pumped a hard blow into the gut, then followed with a nice kick in the groin. Devil went down cursing and wailing.

He rolled back and forth spitting and shreaking. Cars easing along slowed to watch the uprising that could have been a perfect scene for Madison Square Garden. After heaving, the man got to his knees and started to stand. "So you're Red's new cop? She ain't yours...She is anybodies! You'll see! You know how women are...Put a dollar in their hand and you're king!"

"Best you shut up! I do know about you! Why do you keep giving her problems, chasing after her?" snarled Early Bird. "Leave her alone, now and forever! Where is she?"

"Fuck you!" growled Devil, rubbing his cods.

"Fuck you and the horse you rode in on and the horse's horse, too!" clipped Early Bird.

"Early, let's go!" interviened Diesel Chaser. "This isn't getting you anywhere."

"No! I want to know where Red is! Tell me! Where is Red?" You were at her store...I know you know!" Early stormed. "Tell me or I'll tear you apart! What did you do to her?"

"I ain't telling you nuthin'. Ain't my problem!" snickered Devil.

"Then get up and look me in the eye and say that!" Early Bird pressured.

Devil jumped in front of Early and danced awkwardly, like a frog leaping around. "Can't keep up with your bitch? Tough shit! It ain't nuthin' to me! She's nothing but a slut!"

Early had all he could take. Once more he grabbed Devil by the arm and snapped it behind him. With a squeeze, Early flipped the man to the ground. Before Devil could recover, Early pulled him back to his feet and laid another blow under his chin.

Devil stumbled, then took his head and roared toward Early Bird who ducked out of the way as the other man stumbled head on into the ground and lay awkwardly while people getting from their vehicles stared.

Early felt a surge of satisfaction and glared, anticipating the next move. He laughed out, "Seems you're looking for a reason to die!"

"Oh, hell," moaned Devil loudly, rolling into a ball. "Oh shittin' hell!"

"You got it if that's what you want," Early Bird scoffed. "Where's Red High Heels?"

The traffic noise buffed the rumble of the big blue Transtar coming behind them. The stop and go traffic moved to its usual pace.

With blood seeping from his cut chin and tongue that he had managed to bite, Devil saw his knife and rolled to grab it.

"Don't try it!" Early Bird cooly commanded. He held his Davis .380 automatic in place and stared. "Get up fucker and keep your hands up! Over your head!"

*****

With eyes swollen and aching all over Red had to find Early Bird. It didn't take long to clear the short-cut that led onto the expressway, specifically where she calculated the others could be intercepted.

Luckily, traffic was moving, allowing her to clip along with her wonderful, old International. For a moment she thought maybe she should have gone west bound instead of east but then the traffic began to slow somewhat and vehicles were off the shoulder.

Red High Heels was excited suddenly; right before her eyes the bobtail and car were on the side of the road. As she moved a little closer, she realized Early Bird was standing with a gun. She signaled, then stopped in the lane beside the rental car and jumped out, not feeling herself touch the pavement. She rushed toward Early, then caught a glimpse of the figure of Devil in front of him.

"Early Bird! Please! Oh, Early! Please don't do anything to ruin our lives! Early Bird!" called Red in tears. "Early Bird, it's me! Red High Heels! Early! I love you! Don't do it!"

Hearing her voice, he turned to see her running toward him with out-stretched arms. It was like a mirage; the woman he loved, his Red High Heels. When he saw her tattered clothes, wrecked hair, bruised and battered face, he nearly went crazy. Diesel saw her, too, and rushed toward Early Bird and Red.

"My God! My Baby!" cried Early Bird as Red fell into his arms. He looked into her blackened and bruised eyes; and realized the cut-up coat and hair torn out at places from the roots. The blood all over her was dried and matted. But, most of all, she was alive. His lips found her swollen, cut, still bleeding lips. Early kissed them softly.

"Early Bird, I love you! Don't do anything to take you from me! He's not worth it!" cried Red, feeling safe in his arms.

"Oh, Baby! My girl! I love you! He'll never hurt you again!" Early Bird held her tightly with tears of love and empathy flowing. "I love you, girl!"

Devil looked on as the two lovers were reunited. He squinted his eyes with hatred. "I should have killed the bitch! I'll git her! I'll git you!"

He backed up to the bobtail, found his footing to the top, then squeezed into the tractor. Flipping the air button, Devil crammed it into gear. The truck rolled and jerked while he cursed his way down the shoulder. Without concern, he stuck the nose in front of a moving utility van, forcing his way onto the road just before an overpass. He murmured angrily, "Fuck you! Git outta my way! Those son of bitches will pay for this!"

Snag sat quietly for lack of knowing what to do. He had watched the ordeal from the side mirror

297

with a personal satisfaction of seeing Devil get his sophisticated whipping, yet he had to concern himself with his own safety.

Devil looked at the small fellow and barked, "You laughing?"

"God, no! Where did those shits come from?" he quivered.

"Red's peter, I reckon!" groaned Devil, rubbing his chin. "That fucker packs a damn wallop! He had a gun! Did you see that? The weak asshole pulled a gun! I wish the law had come!"

Snag thought out loud. "YOU? YOU? You wish the law had come?"

"Yeah...They're hell on guns! That asshole would be in jail now! Think I'll have him arrested for assault!" snarled Devil. "Wouldn't that be a crock?"

"I wouldn't do that! There's too many witnesses!" reminded Snag. "Besides, a lot has happened. Hey look behind us!"

*****

As the bobtail had taken off from the group, several cars of police arrived to the scene. Early and Red were still holding on.

Diesel Chaser intervened and explained the situation. He was saying, "We really are not certain of anything!"

With a pen in his mouth and a puzzled look on his face, the cop watched the weak woman stand on her own as Early Bird raced to the Transtar. In the maze of confusion Early put the truck in gear, yelling, "I'll be back!"

Diesel, not wanting Early to get into more

trouble, raced for the slightly moving International, jumped and began to hang from the side steps and rails as the machine began to plunge back into traffic. he yelled to the cops as he watched Red slip helplessly to the ground, "Get her to a hospital! Please!"

"Early, come on...Pull over! Red needs you!" Diesel bargained. "It won't help to go after that dog!"

"Buckle your seat belt! This is going to end tonight! Did you see my baby? He neary killed her! Now it's his turn!" Early promised as he wiped the foam from the edges of his mouth. "He did it to her! I'll do it to him! I'll kill him! He nearly killed Red High Heels!"

"That you don't know for sure! Suppose something else happened!" Diesel tried to reason.

"On my life, I would swear that he did it! We'll find out!" stormed Early. "The truth will come! I'm going after it!"

Behind them the red lights from pursuing trooper cars had forced traffic to stop and was weaving their way toward them. Two cars flew past and one ordered them to stop, as he stayed on their tail.

"Pull it over, Early Bird!" Diesel sadly demanded and flipped his badge into view. "Pull it over. Don't make me arrest you! The law has to handle it now!"

Seeing the close flashing lights, Early Bird slowed the roaring Transtar. Diesel got onto the CB and advised the lawmen they would find a spot to stop.

Ahead of them they could see the other cars in pursuit of the old bobtail. Diesel was grateful for the rescue. Chasing a truck in this traffic and bad weather conditions was not his favorite mission. At anytime the big machine could slip or jack-knife and take half a mile of vehicles with them.

Early Bird collected his anger and began to re-enter reality. He gave way to returning to the original scene with the policeman in charge. The cop held the cab door as Early placed his size twelves beneath himself.

Diesel smiled, "This truck will be all right here for a little while. I'm going back with you!"

The officer, turned the car east bound and talked to the other patrolmen at the scene with Red. His radio crackled from time to time but it didn't interrupt the project. They had managed to run Red's big truck quite a distance, so it would be a little drive.

"Oh, hell...I don't really know who is who!" he objected in the hand phone. "I just have them with me, not under arrest!"

"I'm a truck driving, semi-retired marshall and this is my forever friend, Early Bird. We're the good guys!" informed Diesel Chaser. "My pal here just went nuts on me! His lady friend had a problem with the fellow that you people are chasing in that bobtail. It's quite complicated!"

"They just told me the woman is being sent to a hospital. She's in serious condition. What happened to her? They can't get her to respond for some reason. My God, she just appeared on the side of the road they thought. She can't talk...Something is strange!" he interacted as he observed the badge Diesel displayed.

They hung tight as the car skidded and flopped around the road as if on a life and death mission. The big officer glued his eyes ahead and turned on the siren to recapture his tracks.

Beyond the resting place of the old Transtar,

and the chaotic scene of emergency vehicles with people scrambling around trying to give aid to a small brutally, beaten woman, the police were still in pursuit of the fast rolling white truck. From time to time, the big awkward machine would slip and nearly turn around but each time luck would let it recover. The cops were loosing ground in the heavy traffic and conditions. The bobtail was almost out of sight.

From the cab side-mirror, Devil could see the red flashing lights behind him. Snag watched in fear and wished he knew how to pray. "Hey, get off at the next off-ramp! They might loose you!"

"This bitch is too big to loose...Get ready, I'm puttin' it in a spin and when it stops, we gotta run like hell!" Devil tormented.

The cars below seemed to manage to get out of the way as he drove nearly on their bumpers. Once he tapped one small car; it lost control and exited the roadway into a spin.

Devil loved that and laughed huskily. "That was great! Watch this!" He drove up onto another car and the driver raced to the shoulder before he could connect.

"Losing your touch?" snickered Snag as he got out a rough rolled cigarette that gave off an old familiar scent. "Here, this will calm you!"

Devil let off a little and sucked the weed extra hard. Coughing he exhaled then handed it back. They exchanged the weird cigarette; a warm feeling lightened their depression. Devil returned the bobtail to a faster pace. He laughed and started singing, still watching the lights in the rearview that seemed to go together in a wide line that flickered.

"I done and out-run the bastards! Cops can't

drive...They don't think either! Can't shit a shitter! A bunch of dumb asses! Here, git me about five of those pills! I need somethin' more than that pot!" ordered Devil, slinging a small can-like container he had plucked from under the edge of the seat.

"Wow! This is good stuff. I still like the 'white shit'!" giggled Snag handing Devil about eight pills and a beer from under the sleeper mattress.

"That's my boy! Got that beer on hand! I believe you could shit a beer if you needed one!" Devil crowed loudly and slapped the dash with his fist. Several lights went out with the blow. It didn't phase him and he continued laughing and making light of the police. "That cop's done gone now! We got it made!"

"Yeah! They gone!" shrieked Snag as he turned up another beer and downed a handful of the pills.

The large intake of pills seemed to take immediate effect. Devil yelled, "Wheeee! Fuck 'em all! Wheeee! Watch that asshole in the blue car!"

"That ain't blue...It's grey!" coughed Snag until his eyes turned bright red and water rolled down his cheeks.

"Piss on the color...Just watch this!" hollered Devil. "Yippee! See if that damn Yankee knows how to play chicken! Us down-homies knows just how to play it! Yippeeeee!"

He whipped the partial rig to the back of the beautiful car then eased onto the bumper. As he stepped harder on the fuel pedal he began pushing the vehicle. He let off a bit to gain a seperation; then, he poured the fuel to it and banged into the rear of the car, making it wobble in the road in front. Once more, he slipped a few feet behind the vehicle and then he came back into it with a thunderous bang. He hit it this time at an angle on a curve. The car was sent into a spin off the road, leaving the traffic pattern. It was too dark to see just what happened; Devil switched lanes and laughed hysterically.

"That takes talent!" giggled the half-stoned helper. "I never could drive like that! In fact, I ain't s'posed to drive...Ain't never got no license!"

"No, shit! You been driving all this time like that? You could get me into trouble!" Devil started to flip. "You silly bastard!

Realizing he had opened a fresh can of worms, Snag snickered, "Naw, I wuz kiddin' you! I got license in my suitcase!"

Devil glared and moaned, "You shit! Watch this!"

He was in a lane next to the curb lane and began to roll toward the cars in the right lane right under Snag's seat. He banged each one that didn't move out of the way. You could hear the bumpers crunch and the vehicles lost parts as they pulled off the road. Once next to a little Volkswagon, Devil put the pedal to the metal and darted in front of the little bug. He screamed and laughed as the little car spun out of sight.

"You damn stupid Yankees! All of you! Kiss my damn ass!" Devil screamed as a big truck pulled into the road from a side ramp that shot traffic in his path.

"It's a gas truck! Stop!" cried Snag. "Don't hit that fucker!"

"Oh, damn! Oh, hell!" screamed Devil.

You could hear the screaming of tires...Big

tires and little tires. The gasoline truck was on a down hill roll and unable to change his course. The cars in the mass managed to shoot out of the way into other lanes but the bobtail had spun sideways in the road. An overpass was just ahead as the back axle hit a vehicle beside it. This slowed the wreckless truck somewhat and it changed directions.

"Oh, damn!" screamed Snag. "Don't brake it no more! You're going to kill us!"

"Fuck you! You need to die! Hang on, asshole!" yelled Devil as the rig rolled back and forth, spitting its anger as it surged once more into traffic.

"Oh, God! That wall!" cried Snag. The door flew open on his side of the truck and he was airborne.

The bobtail kept skidding until it's front tire found a hole and it began to roll. The smoke immediately filled the cab and flames ignited.

With a final grumble, the truck became suddenly deadly quiet with a blue and orange flame flashing quietly through the broken windows.

CHAPTER 13

The weather had cleared and the morning came slowly as the light finally peeked through the window. Early Bird lifted his head where he leaned onto the hospital bed that was still empty. His friend was asleep in a big chair across the room. He could hear his easy snoring.

Diesel groaned and turned, "Better try to sleep, Early Bird."

"I dozed a little...But I've been trying to pray. I thought Red would be back here before now," he stretched.

"She went to x-ray. Hospitals take their time!" Diesel supported.

"It's been over five hours. Something's wrong!" Early worried, looking at his watch.

"Probably not. Early Bird, get it together.

You need to; so when she does get back here you can be her support!" smiled the friend, yet knowing his words were on deaf ears.

Early Bird was usually very conscious of his appearance. Now, he was wrinkled and the blotches of blood, dirt, grease and all else didn't phase him. The tear in his pants had gone unnoticed. Finally, he took a comb from his pocket and stood to a mirror above him. Once his eyes focused on his image he grinned, "Wonder who that bum is?"

"Some fighting butthole I picked up from the road. See, you do look rough. I'll get some stuff to clean up with," proposed Diesel when a nurse swished into the room wearing a crisp, starch smelling uniform. Her face lit up with a smile as she snatched the drape cord to expose all the window and the top of a nearby tree.

"I'll get you some things to shave with. You've been through a great deal. Guess you were in the wreck, too. Here's towels and wash cloths. See that little room? It has a shower. I'll unlock it for you. I'll let you shower; patients are the only ones that should go in them. We are allowed to bend *my* rule, occassionally! Just be quick and quiet!" she warned.

They were caught by surprise and amazed with her concern. Diesel grinned, "Who said New Yorkers are uncaring?"

"Another myth, I reckon. Red loved it here. She says New Yorkers are good people! She's usually right!" smiled Early. "Wonder where she is? She looked bad...Real bad!"

"Here, fellows," replied the nurse upon returning. "I'll check on your wife and be right back."

It didn't take any urging for the two to find

the little room.   It had everything; they certainly
needed the comforts of what a bath could do. Upon
returning to the room, they were met by a policeman.
Early Bird's heart fell to his feet. He sat quickly,
motioning to the officer to do the same.

"Any news about the woman?" the cop asked.

"Not yet!" injected Diesel. "It's all a dead-
end wait now."

The nurse again returned. The slight smile
seemed to indicate the possibility of good news. The
men all stood and watched her prop against the narrow
bed. Finally, she found a whisper of a voice. "The
patient should return to her bed in about an hour or so.
She is in recovery now!"

"Recovery? Recovery from what?" cried out
Early.

"They found bleeding...Internal something...I
can't say just what. They had to take her in for
surgery. You can go to the recovery if you want. We
like for family to be nearby," she whispered again.
"I'm very sorry...She won't recognize you yet."

"Oh, God! Will she be all right?" blurted out
Early Bird. "She has been through so much!"

"Our doctors are the best and I know we have
all been praying! I just believe she will be just fine! I
really believe she will come through!" smiled the
nurse. Then the men could see the nurse's attire she
wore was that of a nun. "Look! See that beautiful
light? The Spirits are with us...Hovering over us and
the Angel of Mercy is in the heavens watching over."

"Oh, God! I pray!" cried Early as his face fell
into his hands.

"Oh, Father, let the mercy of your love abide
with us and have your way in our hearts. Bring us

understanding and healing and your will be done," prayed Diesel loudly. "She had died! They had to revive her once! Sister, tell us!"

The pretty nun shook her head and smiled brightly, "But the angels came and restored her...The doctors brought her back! Come, let me take you to her!"

Early followed her from the room. Diesel sat back down; the cop looked puzzled.

They each could only wait until the powerful medication could run its course. As Early looked into her bandaged face and held one of her bandaged hands, he continued to plead for her recovery.

As the nurse had said, it took time. Finally, Red moved on her own...But just slightly. Then, she tried to murmur.

"Don't talk, Darling, I'm here!" Early soothed. "Everything is going to be all right!"

Again, Red tried to force words and focus her eyes. Then tears began to pour from her nearly closed eyes.

"Baby, take it easy! Don't try to rationalize anything now! You just got out of surgery. You're going to be all right and I'm here! I won't leave you!" Early Bird comforted.

She calmed quickly and squeezed his hand. "I love you," she made her lips say without voice.

Early sat back down to let her rest. The doctor came in and checked her over. Then, nurses returned, telling Red she had to wake up and not talk. They told her she had had surgery and that she would be fine.

Time continued to tick by while the patient slowly awoke from a long, tedious ordeal. Red's first thoughts was how wonderful it was not to have had to feel everything. She squirmed and felt the pressence of Early Bird. It pleased her totally. In fact, she didn't need anything more.

Finally, two men had her to slide onto a gurney and rolled her out of the brightly lit area. She felt the light even through closed eyes. Still, Red was very tired. She just wanted to hang onto Early and sleep.

Diesel was gone but left a note on the bed. The staff rushed around Red High Heels to settle her in. The nun checked her statistics as Early watched while Red lay so acceptantly. She finished, giving him a nod and a wide smile.

"Now, she's in your hands!"

That seemed like a strange thing to say, Early thought. It was as if it were an order for him to give her the reason to go on. He sat gently on the bed clinging to her hand. She looked pitiful against the white sheets. He could see the long gash on the side of her forehead where she had been stitched. Other numerous places had the fine little blue stitches and then some places were pulled together with a strange band-aid. Her head was partially wrapped in a gauze, but at places he could spot her red hair. The multiple deep bruises had deepened with a variety of deep shades of blue and purple. Swelling had deformed her normally beautiful face, creating her to look like another person. Evenso, Early Bird knew this was the form of his special lady. It hurt to think of what she had been through, although, he had yet to hear the whole story. Regardless, it wouldn't be good.

He wanted her to rest, knowing she needed him to take care of her and not let danger touch her again. She was a long way from all that she loved and the things she could do so well. Early remembered a time when he met her on the road. Her help had pulled off in a rest area. They had drank some beer and fell asleep. Red had flipped crazy. The men were quite young but she went off on them. He remembered her yelling, "You little whimps! I'm going to whip all three of you! Get me a switch from that tree!"

"Please! Red, don't spank me! We were tired. We won't ever do it again! Please!" the young fellow started crying and the tears rolled like a tornado. "I want to work. I promise to be good! Remember? We loaded before we left. It made us so tired! Please, give us one more chance!"

He remembered how Red immediately felt sympathy for them and explained the ritual of sticking together on the road and doing the right thing. She ultimately melted, saying, "I guess you were tired. Get back in there and sleep. We'll stay here 'til morning."

The balance of the night Red had spent with Early Bird. They had connected in Virginia earlier and her help had left the truckstop a little ahead. On down the road they couldn't arouse them on the CB so the search was on. Somehow, another driver heard the conversation between their trucks and informed them that he noticed a similar truck at a rest area. This meant doubling back for about sixty miles, plus, the farther they went the more angry Red became. This was what he loved her for. She could fly wild and be calm minutes later. She used to kid and say, "I forgot to be pissed; what am I supposed to be angry about? Guess that's the good thing about getting old!"

"You aren't old! You're just senile!" Early remembered saying. "I'm glad you have that easy forgiveness. I wish I could do that."

"Well, it's much easier to flip out as you go!" she laughed, falling into his arms. "Forgiveness is a form of love. I love life, so it's that which pulls me through."

Early Bird came back to the moment as Red moaned and tried to whisper. Then she clearly voiced, "I love you."

Facing her, he took her into his arms and smiled gently. "Oh, Red, I love you...Oh how I love you! I'm so happy that we're together now. We have it all...I'll never leave you!"

Tears began to stream down her face as she felt him holding her. It was all coming back to her. She focused her eyes across his shoulder to see a cross hanging beside the door. She remembered a verse from many years ago and began to whisper it carefully.

"He restoreth my soul; he leadeth me in the paths of righteousness for his name sake. Yea, though I walk through the valley of the shadow of death, I will fear no evil; for thou art with me; thy rod and thy staff, they comfort me. Thou preparest a table before me in the presence of mine enemies; thou anointest my head with oil; my cup runneth over. Surely goodness and mercy shall follow me all the days of my life and I will dwell in the house of the Lord forever."

"That's beautiful! Absoluetly beautiful," he praised.

"Early, I have been down the road...I'm lucky to be alive! It's by the grace of God that I'm here," she began. "After I talked to you on the phone, I went back into the store. Devil was in there...Lurking and waiting for me. He was set on insane from jump street. That look on his face told me he was planning

311

to kill me. I tried to reason with him but he had already decided that my life was over. He beat me unmercifully for hours. What saved me was my coat; I never took it off. I lost my consciousness, then my memory, for a while; I even thought I was blind. It was so awful!"

Early could feel her tremble. He held her gently. "It's over, honey. Now we can move on. Whatever you need, I'll try to supply. You are so precious and I love you. Don't you need to rest now?"

She shook her head, crying. The tears spattered onto the white sheets but she didn't seem to notice. A nurse appeared and reached for her arm to check her statistics. "You need to stay calm. Its all over now! You came through the surgery real well."

Red whimpered, "Yes, the surgery is over...He'll always come back! Just when you least expect him, he'll find a way back!"

The fear was clear in her eyes. Early knew she was still afraid. Emotionally, she had been brutally battered along with the physical. He found it very difficult to understand how anyone could harm another person for no reason. Even more so, he thought a man had to be a real dog, even worse, a pure low-life, to brutally torcher a woman.

Once the nurse left the room, Early reached for a tissue and dotted her eyes very gently. Soothingly he smiled, "My precious. I can't undo what has happened but I will be here for you no matter what it takes. Right now you are in a lot of pain and so much has happened to you. Don't try to take anything on, just let it all slide for now. When you feel better, then we'll get back to all this. Right now, just know you are loved!"

He thought to himself, "I'll never let him get away with this!"

"You say this...About love," Red winced as she moved, then flipped the covers back. "What about all this?"

Early looked for the first time at the bandages encircling her lower torso and legs. It was almost like a thick pair of gauze panties splotched with blood and tape. It took him by surprise; he gazed open-mouthed.

Once more, the tears poured from her eyes and she covered her face with her one available hand. "I'll never be a woman again! He took it away from me!"

"Don't say that!" he cautioned. "You'll be as good as new!"

"No! No! No! Never!" she cried openly and feeling shameful.

"Did he rape you?" Early nearly shouted, feeling the hatred in his soul. "Baby, tell me, is that what happened?"

Red sobbed and moved her head side to side signaling 'no', then she managed, "Worse!"

"Baby, stop this worrying. It doesn't matter! I just love you regardless!"

"Oh yes it does!" she whimpered. "Oh, Early Bird, he stabbed me in my thighs and put the knife there! You know...Up into my vagina!"

"God, no! That scum! That's what they had to repair!" he gasped. "Sweetheart, you will always be mine! Sex is not what you are to me! I love you! I need you! Just get well and we'll make ourselves a good world without all this trouble. I am here!"

"No! I can't let you..."

"Quiet. You have nothing to say about it. I

will not leave you. You cannot run me off. I love all of the wonderful things you are and all of that is still right here." He took her hand from her face and smiled, "Hey, Red High Heels! Remember, you're tough and you'll overcome all this better than anybody else could!"

Suddenly, she licked her lips and whispered, "Yeah, with you I can do anything! Ready to get us a truck? Want to team?"

"Hell, yes! Baby, anything! Just lean on me while you need to!" grinned Early Bird, feeling better with her change-up. "We'll get whatever rig you want and see it all! We'll do it all!"

As he held her close, thinking to himself, "That cruel bastard. It isn't over!"

*****

Meanwhile, several townships away, in the darkened area of the Long Island Expressway, where current had been interrupted with the downing of power equipment, the bobtail that had been fleeing the police left the road. Built-up snow and frozen water along the roadway was creating spin-outs and uncertin confussion.

The police had long since retreated knowing the danger of a high speed chase. Traffic had mounted in front of them with the on-ramp merging vehicles. In traumatic weather, a speeder was not worth it. The fleeing bobtail had only been parked on the roadside and the big International furniture combination van had been stopped and returned. With another call on their radio, they determined to turn their busy attention to a higher priority.

As the bobtail rammed several smaller vehicles, Devil felt as if he were in one of those 'bumper car' carnival rides. There was no control in a skid; he felt the slipping but couldn't stop it. His own stampede had started this chain reaction.

"Oh, shit! Damn! Get the hell out of the way!" he screamed frantically as the truck continued to surge forward. It seemed so fast yet still in slow motion. He wondered what he had done to get into all this mess. "Yeah! You bitch! Red High Heels! If it weren't for you I wouldn't be into this shit! You ain't nothing but a damn whore! Bitch! You ain't gettin' away with this fuckin' shit! And that big old motherfucker you're with ain't shit!"

Once more, the rig groaned and slid sideways to rest against something. He realized his passenger at this point had flown like a bird out the door, and it was as if he had slammed it behind him. As the truck settled into an unknown place, Devil tried to analize his next move. He waited for the cops or somebody, yet no one came; finally he bailed out of the cab to check it out. Surely he could find a way out! The road traffic was still moving.

Nearby, a woman was looking at the side of her Mercedes stopped in the ice almost beside him, yet she wasn't in the way of his rig.

"You all right? Slick out here!" he mumbled, testing her answer.

She looked at him. "I guess I can just go. Doesn't seem like anything is wrong with my car. You all right?"

"I guess," he smiled. He flipped into his 'good guy nature' and started to look her vehicle over. "I don't know how to get a taxi from here! One might be hard to come by!"

"Here, I'm scared! Would you drive me out of this? Please, I'll pay you! I'm not used to this kind of driving!"

He lit up with her proposal and opened the passenger door and motioned for her to get in.

He settled into the driver's seat of the fancy car and searched for the gear shift. It was more complicated than the old pickup he was familiar with. He grinned, "Pretty lady, I need some know-how! What do I do?"

She smiled, "Just turn that and hold the brake. Have to put on your seat belt or it won't go! You can do it!"

He did all he was told but the vehicle was stuck. He tried everything, then suggested, "Looks like we might have to get into my truck! Maybe it will move."

"I can't do that! I've never been in one of those things. My husband would kill me!" she groaned.

"Well, maybe you'd be better frozen to death. It's cold out here even if you don't think so. By morning, if you don't get help, you would be in trouble. I'm not going to hurt you. I'm just a poor, old trucker. You were going to help me, now it's my turn! Come on!"

"I guess I'll have to. You are so kind! Thank you!"

As they got out of her car, there was a huge scream, "Hey! Come here!"

They looked into it's direction and caught a glimpse of Snag laying on top of a big pile of snow. He looked quite strange hanging in the filthy mass nearly in mid air.

"Damn, how did you do that?" quizzed Devil.

"Come here! Help me down! You always said God takes care of drunks and fools. Reckon I'm both!" Snag offered. "Please help me!"

Without words, Devil and the woman assisted him to their level. The traffic was beginning to move more; others were finding their way back to the roadway. The three of them returned to Devil's warm truck and he started trying to rock it out of its hole. Finally, with a back and forth movement the truck slipped out of its crimped position.

"Yippee! We got it now!" Snag squealed happily. "This heater sure feels good! That wuz wild, flying out in the dark! I just knew I was a real goner!"

"You're lucky," injected the woman.

"Devil's lucky! Out of the clear blue, he's got a woman!" laughed the man.

"She needs help, that's all!" Devil snapped a warning to Snag, indicating for him to shut up. The helper had rolled himself in the quilt in the bunk.

"We could tie to her car and pull it, maybe," assisted Snag.

"Could we? I'm afraid to leave my car her!" she quivered from nerves.

Devil looked at her pleading face. She was thin, sad-like to a point of helplessness. Her coat was expensive, as were the pieces of jewelry. "You stay in the truck and we'll try. We have to hook a rope. Come on, Snag!"

Once on the ground Devil warned, "Don't mess this deal up. We'll move off this road. When we get it out, just follow me and we'll break down again. I'm going to get me some of that!"

They made the motions for assisting; then, the car eased behind the truck. Snag detached the rope and followed.

Devil slowly returned to the road followed by Snag. They drove to a rugged, out-of-the-way ware-house area. Snag stopped her car a half block away from the rig.

"I gotta check a tire!" laughed Devil. "Are you all right? Don't be afraid. Everything will be peachy!"

"I've never been up so high like this; maybe once in a bus," she awkwardly stated. "Are we going to be all right?"

"Of course. Get us a beer off the floor there," pointed Devil.

"Ugh! I don't like beer!" she retorted.

"Maybe not, but you need it for energy and warmth," he grinned as he got out of the truck motioning for Snag to walk to him.

"Stay in that car. She got any gas?" asked Devil.

"Full tank!"

"Good, go get you something to eat but get back here soon. We can't take long. Don't get lost!" demanded Devil then, returned to the truck.

"Things all right?" she inquired.

"I sent for road-service. Hope you don't mind. When he returns you can go home," he attempted to satisfy her curiosity. "How's the beer?"

"Not bad!" she giggled.

"They call it poor man's champaign! Here, get us another!" smiled the man. She reached again for two beers and they drank them down. "We'd better get back there so we can stay warm!"

"In that bed?" she squeaked, seemingly a bit tipsy.

"Sure, just for warmth!" promised Devil. "That's the best place for heat!"

They slipped into the sleeper. Her back was to him. He could smell the fine fragrance of perfume and lotions; this excited him tremendously.

He thought, 'She ain't beautiful but she'll do.' His heavy arm encircled her and he rested his hand on her breast. The woman froze with fear.

"Come on, relax. I ain't going to hurt you. See, I'll move it!" He began to wiggle his fingers and laugh. "See, I moved my hand!"

"Please, not like that! Stop!" she cried out.

"Oh, Come on, Baby! Just let me touch you. It ain't hurtin' nuthin'! You want it as much as I do!" he squirmed against her. "You'll like it! Feel this thang!"

He grasped her hand and placed it on top of his pulsing penis.

She moaned, "Please, I can't do this! I want to go!"

Devil ignored her plea, rolling and roughly grabbing her. "Shut up! You know you want it! You'll do what I tell you!"

The woman began to cry, "No! I said, no!" Then she caught a glimpse of a knife.

Sitting on top of her he deliberately restrained her and laughed; as he placed her hands beneath his knees. "Go on, git up if you want to!"

She wiggled and kicked but realized she was overpowered. She cried, "I can't understand why a nice looking Southern gentleman could possibly need to force anybody. I thought you were a good person!"

"Ha! That's the problem. People think too much! You decided I was a dumb ass! I shared my beer. Wuzzent I nice to you? You got in bed with me, bitch! I figured you wanted it!" grunted Devil. "You got in my bed!"

"I'm married! My husband would kill me! I never thought of another man. I have five children. Please, just let me go. I'll never tell anybody. Maybe I did let you think wrong. Please! Please! Please!" she continued.

"I don't know what to do with this big thang!" he snorted a he unzipped and flipped it onto her stomach. "Pull those britches down!"

"I can't! Please!" she pleaded. "Please! No!"

"Git 'em off!"

"No!"

"Git 'em off, now!" he growled.

"Please! My husband would kill us! Besides, I have my monthly!" she hedged.

Devil snickered, "Ain't stopped nobody I know yet! Pull 'em down!"

Without words, she wiggled under his weight, trying to push her pants down, finally revealing her bare stomach.

He ordered her to stop and began to rub his penis against her. The woman was relieved that he seemed to be satisfied with this. She prayed it would be over soon.

Fortunately, he manipulated himself, demanding her to watch. With a scream, it was over. Devil flopped beside her and began to sweat.

"I let you off! Now you'll have to do without! You'd better not tell this because if you do I'll tell 'em you begged me for it. Nobody would believe you. Do you understand? Remember, I picked you up in a bar."

"Yes! Please, let me go!" she murmured.

"Go on, but leave your clothes here!" he demanded. He could see her car parked behind the truck from the side mirror.

Once nude, she jumped from the truck, falling as she landed on the ground. Struggling to her feet, the woman hurried toward her car. The door opened and Snag got out.

"Damn, you sure look good! Where's your stuff?"

"Let me in my car!" she pleaded. "Please, just let me go! Everything will be all right!"

"Did he screw you?" snickered Snag. "He's got a whopper!"

"Get away from me!" she screamed, pushing him aside. The motor was running so her vehicle was warm and inviting. Although frightened, she forced the gear in place, snapped off the emergency brake, flipped the steering wheel to spin out of the area.

Retracing from memory the route back to the main road, the lady felt she was getting more lost. A police car rolled up behind her and she jammed on brakes. Once more sliding with the car in the rear nearly colliding. The cop got out and ran to her door. He was stunned seeing her sitting there in the driver's seat wearing shoes only.

"You're going to catch cold!"

"Please! Help me!" she panicked.

"I'm sure you need it!" he answered, then listened to her story. Once she finished, he shook his head. "Did he rape you?"

"No! But it was horrible! He had a knife on me, too!"

"Do you have any clothes to wear?" the man asked as he rached for his radio, calling for help.

She wrapped a blanket around herself. The patrolman brought her a rain coat from his car. Very soon, more police arrived. Once the report was complete, a female officer followed her to her home. Again, there was the chain of repeating the events to a very upset husband.

The police were on alert for the bobtail. When it returned to the expressway, they were all over it. With a half dozen cars and many officers in pursuit, Devil pulled to the edge of the road just before the main exit that would leave the Island.

With guns drawn, they carefully approached the big truck. Being familiar with arrest procedure, both men in the truck put their hands forward, waiting for instructions.

Devil swore to his partner, "Remember, it's our word against hers. Nobody touched her! We met her at a bar!"

The cop snatched the driver's door open. "Get out! Keep your hands where I can see them! Hey' you! Get out the other side!"

Both men fumbled to the ground to face the cops. Immediately, they were searched, then ordered into two seperate police cars. While they were being interrogated, another car rolled in back of them.

*****

"What luck!" grunted Diesel Chaser.

He managed to get off to the side of the road.

322

The flashing lights were sparkling like rockets in the dark sky. The big bobtail stuck high above the other traffic. He slipped the car slowly behind the police cars and tried to summarize the situation; seeing Devil in the front seat of the car in front gave him great satisfaction. Diesel needed to be at the airport soon but this delay was a must. He watched as the officer talked to the man.

Apparently things were not going as they should. It wasn't long before they got out of the car. Devil wasn't handcuffed.

"How in hell can that be?" yelled Diesel, bolting to catch up with the officer. "You can't be serious! This bastard has got to be taken in!"

The officer snapped, "I'll handle this!"

"No, I'll handle it! You're under arrest!" Diesel displayed his badge.

The other police officers looked on.

"Fuck you! You pussy! You ain't taking me nowhere!" screamed Devil spitting on the badge.

Anticipating his move, Diesel was on Devil's heels; the police looked down gun barrels waiting. Diesel's adreneline allowed him to soar into the air like a swan in flight. With ease, he landed squarely on the back of the fleeing man and quickly brought him to the ground and placed his knee in Devil's back. Reaching for an arm he yelled, "Give me your handcuffs!"

"You ain't taking me in, bastard! You ain't no law. Just an old 'has been'! I've done been down this road! Git the hell off me!" groaned Devil.

Somehow, Devil moved to push the marshall off his back trying to retrieve a 'go' position. With the cops' eyes upon them, Diesel held Devil into place and jumped to his feet with a bolt and found the solid jaw of the culprit ready to receive his first connecting swing. The sound of shattering teeth and a big *splat* echoed through the area. As Devil fell backward, he mumbled, "Bastard!"

"That's for Red High Heels!"

"Who? Never heard of her!" he sputtered and spit blood. "I'll sue you!"

"I've heard it before! Book him! Attempted murder, assault...The works! This is a real animal!"

Devil was finally arrested, cuffed, then, pushed into a patrol car by an awaiting officer. The others gathered around Diesel and listened to the story. With Red being in the hospital, they would go to her for the fill-in of the complete episode and try to take the man out of action for a long time.

The police could include this to the list of complaints. The woman who had been abducted and assulted was not hiding her situation.

Diesel returned to the mission of meeting Red's family. He felt better knowing the 'animal' was now in custody. The past days had been filled with concern and search for Red. That last punch would make the difference in a job well done.

*****

Later, everyone was united at the hospital. Red was out of the danger from the surgery and managing to return back to a more normal state of being. Seeing her family gave her strength and seemed to bring pink to her cheeks. Early couldn't keep his hand from her hand. Even so, it was an unspoken item. Red was very lucky. No, it was really a miracle that she had survived. Life isn't luck, it's a gift from God.

She handed Early a hand scribbled paper. "Here, I wrote this for you and Diesel."

He smiled at her and kissed her cheek as he unfolded the page and read it carefully.

Ode to Justice

When your faith is shattered
    And life stands still,
Now, nothing much matters
    Seems it's all over the hill.
Fringes of foreign dreams that
    really could come true.
It might take doing, near dying
    before the real issue.
When all else fails
    and your patience goes thin,
Outside the realm encircled
    Kicks the real tiger in.

They take your heart
    Eat away at your soul;
Spell their emotions upon you
    trying to steal your control.
Money seemed to be important
    all before that time,
You go all out for banquets
    while you socially climb.
When the rug snapped from beneath
    and you cling hard not to fall
You look all over and around
    but there's almost no one at all!

They blow fear and savage vice
        to make you tremble inside
Until finally one day it happens.
        You cut loose and go hide.
Time takes its toll as it rules
        Your head into your hands
Someday something to equal,
        they deserve their final dance.
It comes, finally once and for all,
        The hell is ended at last.
The big tiger comes to call
        On those who laid trail for your past.

The tribute to justice
        Finally will come,
Hallelujah it's over
        The tiger has won!
He now lines up the devils
        March them to their tune.
Put them away now
        Like they tried doing to you.
Sing out for freedom and deliverance
        Come from hiding and lift the vale.
When the tiger stalks his prey
        He marches them to their hell.
But patience and time
        May liberty bring;
Only if there's a tiger
        Watching over you and me.
The tribute to justice
        Finally will come
Hallelujah it's over
        The tiger has won!

CHAPTER 14

Red was driving herself physically; the emotional could last a lifetime. It had been several months since she had left the hospital. Trying to pull everything in order, the woman had insisted that Early Bird should return to his own life with a promise of her eliminating the furniture business.

She leaned back in her chair and put her feet on top of her desk as she smiled and whispered in the phone, "Yes! Of course I love you! I need to see you soon!"

Early promised, "Soon! Sooner than you think!"

"Now would be about soon enough!" she laughed. "I don't have black eyes anymore and I feel so good today!"

"Walk to your door, Baby!" he ordered.

Looking outside, she screamed and threw the phone onto the floor. Racing for the big, shining Freightliner parked beside her own truck, Red reached for the open door of the truck as Early Bird slid out and grabbed her swiftly.

"Hey! Oh, girl! I told you that I'd be back!" Early cooed. "I love you!"

"I love you!" Red High Heels matched his mood. "Thank you for coming! I really need you here today!"

"I'm taking you with me! You can't stay away any longer!" he muttered as their lips met and they filled their hands with each other's body. The reunion was filled with the tingling sensation of its excitement.

Early had been patient and understood what a severe ordeal Red had been through. He knew she had needed time to heal in every way. All of what happened wouldn't go away overnight. She had been right, sending him back on the road. This had given them both space. Although time and distance wouldn't change his feelings, Early Bird could only hope Red still felt the same. In his time gone, he had yearned to hear her laugh and smell her sweet perfume. She had always had a wonderful sense of humor, but in the last phone calls, there was no longer the laughter in her voice. She seemed to have turned to a distant sadness.

As he touched her deep red hair and caressed her, he felt the old hot sensation shoot through him. He wanted her to love him and to need him because she wanted him. He passed the first test...He'd come back to her.

"Come in!" uttered Red. "The store is almost

empty!"

Early walked through the glass door and stared in amazement at the lack of product. Prior, the place had been filled to the brim with every kind of furniture available.

"I told you this was coming to an end!" solemnly she informed. "I suppose I will be out of here by the end of the month. We took a bit more time so everybody could find jobs."

"This is amazing!"

"It shouldn't be. I promised you!"

"Yes, but it just doesn't seem right. Are you sure you want to let go of this?" he pondered.

"I can always open another store. I haven't shut all the doors. I just took a loss. You have to when you go out of business!" sadly she mourned.

"Baby, it's in your voice...In your mood. You are different now! I don't want to take your world away from you. That's not what we are about. If you're not happy, then we can't be happy!" Early focused.

"I had to close this anyhow. There is always another possibility that 'he' could come back. I hope not and I think not...Still, it will always be there as a chance!" she began to cry. "He still rules!"

"Oh, baby! It has to be different now! He was arrested and put away!" Early reminded her.

"That's what you think!" she wept. "Devil got out of jail three days after all that! He even called me once and I hung up after I told him there was a restraining order and to leave me alone!"

"God, can't people learn?"

"Not him...He will be through, when he wants to be. He's a freak! After all he put me through, you would think he would just go on with his life!" she stated.

"We should have killed him when we had the chance. Looks like it might take a bullet!" He shook his head as the phone rang.

Red grabbed the instrument and kept saying, "I understand." Then, "Um-huh!" Finally she blurted out, "I will think about it and let you know."

She flipped wild and slung the phone across the room. She kicked a chair, turning it over, then proceeded to fall onto a sofa and pound the pillows as she outwardly cried.

Early watched as she frantically tried to get past her dilemma, then he gently took her into his arms and let her finish crying it out on his shoulder. He could feel her tenseness and the trembling of her body. He sensed her fear.

"Honey, tell me!" he whispered. "That phone call?"

"That was the district attorney's office. There is an attorney that's assigned to my case. They called last week and told me about his deal with that other woman. She dropped her charges. It turns out that the people didn't want to go to court. It would mean a public awareness for them. Since he mostly scared her, they let it go. If we both had cases, it would be better for me. We can't even bring up any of that deal with that woman since it was dropped!" she worried. "I can't believe the law! It's in favor of the criminal. Had I been killed, I would have a solid case!"

"Not really. I can go to court with you...So can Diesel, your friends and family. You're not alone in this. It has to come to an end!" Early smiled, trying to reassure her.

Red moved off to herself and remembered another time and place. Her thoughts roamed to the past as she stared into space.

She could see in her mind's eye, the pistol in her face and Devil foaming at the mouth as he screamed, "I will tell you when it's over! You silly bitch! Sit down, you ain't going nowhere! Where would you go? Everybody hates you! You ain't nothing! The cops laugh at you! Shit, it don't take but a few dollars to get them on another side of town! Ain't that right?"

"Please, I'll do right! Let me cook you some dinner! Please!" she had cried, trying to get him to let go.

He took the pistol and whacked her beside the face making a long cut at the edge of her hairline. The blood oozed freely; he pushed her to the ground as watching neighbors retreated into their houses. She tried to run again, after he had fired the second bullet, he assured her the next one would not miss. She stopped and turned to face him. He galloped to her and slapped her with his open hand. Her ears rang and she fell to the ground again.

"Git up! Git in the house!" he screamed. Then he addressed the neighborhood, "Any of you nosy fucks want some of this? Just call the law!"

Red had gone back into the house, wiped her cuts and bruises just as she had done many, many times before. She forced herself to act as if nothing had happened; even told a couple jokes. His brother came to visit; later Devil left the house with him.

This was her chance. She had to make her move now. The next beating might be the one that would kill her. She had already taken action on 'this'

331

move. She had been getting anything that she felt she wanted out of his place and replacing it with clothes and jewelry from the Goodwill. He hadn't noticed her things missing. He would check her room for such. Her business in New York was set and could sustain her; this was sooner than she had planned, but she couldn't wait. This time, she had to leave for good.

With a visit to her daughter, Red slipped to her truck that had been loaded days before and stashed out at the factory lot. She fumbled with the gate key and finally felt home free. It was a big fear to disobey Devil. He would come looking, she knew...At least in New York she would have a chance. He couldn't get to her so easy.

Red remembered the advise of the SBI. "Don't be alone at any time. Stay in crowds and don't talk to him!"

Still, staring into space, Red coughed, "I'm sorry, Early! I'm still so paranoid!"

"You have a right to be! Tell me, what can I do to help?" he grieved. "You have to tell me!"

Red was wringing her hands with a piece of fabric. "Just don't leave me! Please, just don't leave me! I'll get over this!"

Again, Early Bird gathered her into his arms and tried to soothe her anguish. He sang her his song about "Red High Heels." Ultimately, she relaxed and began to smile.

Dinner and dancing was uncomplicated. They had a beautiful time, totally enjoying each other; talking, laughing, and playing.

The waiter brought the check. Early flipped his American Express card onto the tray and wrote in the tip amount. Red watched admiringly.

"You are fabulous!"

"It's only because of you, baby!" he grinned and kissed her hand. "I want us to move on...But I want you ready. How are you coming along now?"

"Pretty good! Is there room in that truck for my bloomers?" she contended.

"This one is just temporary. You tell me what you want!" he offered. "Team driving is a total commitment. For that, we'll have everything you need and want!"

"Do tell! I guess I need a set of Colonial columns put on the front of the truck!" she finally teased.

"You have to get a straight-truck for that!"

"Oh! Then forget the furniture van! I hate that thirty-five footer! They drive like a rock!" she pouted. "Just see that we have the inside wonderful! Maybe a Jacuzzi?"

"How about we get a 'Y' membership and visit lots of them!" he sparkled. Finally, they were again planning to be together as a team out on the road. They laughed and dreamed like children for the moment.

Arriving back at the store brought a twist of events. The loving stage set was blown to bits. Early drove her delivery van next to his truck and stared. "My Lord! Look at that!"

"Oh! I can't believe anybody would be so awful!" she agonized. "It has to be Devil!"

"Maybe not; he is nuts but surely not stupid!" Early managed with a stern face. "Let's call the police."

All calls were made to the police and Early's company. They waited for the shoe to fall.

"It probably looks worse than it is. Punks paint vehicles in the north all the time. Some of our trailers have all kinds of garbage on them. It's a gang thing!"

"This isn't! It's just to let us know he was here!" wretched Red. "This is how 'Crazy' works. He just can't let go!"

Early was grateful that the police were on the scene quickly. The paint written, dabbled and splashed was still very wet indicating it had only been minutes prior to their arrival that the deed had been done. They started the report and Red kept snapping pictures of the truck from every angle. Suddenly, she caught a glimpse of a shadow that moved at the very back of the trailer. She watched nearly motionless. The truck was backed close to a building and sheltered the rearview. Once again, the figure moved. Again, Red caught the movement. Naturally, anyone there would be the culprit...They would have to be.

Red started to sing, "I need you...Oh, I need you!"

Early and the two cops slipped toward her and caught her motion to be quiet. They all stood and watched the shadow. Shortly, it moved again in an up and down motion. The police drew their guns and ordered the others to stay back. One slipped around one side of the fifty-three foot trailer by going under to cross to the other side, then they met at the back. With a fast signal, they both swung around the backside of the vehicle screaming, "FREEZE!"

Everyone stayed silent for a time; then a voice babbled, "Shit, man, I am about frozen!"

"Get out of there and come here where I can see you!" the somber cop called out. "Keep both your hands in sight!"

"I wuz jest gettin' comfortable. It's cold. My cardboard and the truck knocks off the wind," mumbled the ragged man wearing torn shoes and filthy clothes.

"You know this man?" smiled one cop to the other. "Aren't you Michael?"

The bum nodded his head. Red knew him, too. From time to time he would do odd jobs for 'change.' She had even felt sorry for him and let him fix a place to sleep at the back of her store under a tree.

She smiled at Michael. "Remember when you slept under the mulberry tree and the next day you were spotted purple?"

"Yeah! That worked good, too! People thought I had a terrible disease and handed me all kinds of money. I hated to see them cut that tree down!" Michael gloomily gave way.

"Michael didn't do this!" Red defended. "He's harmless!"

"Did you see anybody out here a few minutes ago?" asked Early.

"Didn't see nobody, but I heard a bunch of people. Didn't come out...You know how it is. The punks pick on us and beat us. They rob us, too!" Michael informed.

"How are they going to rob you?" asked Early.

"They take anything we have away. One time some kids took my baby stroller that I used to carry my stuff in. I loved that thing. It was good storage and women thought I had a baby in it. I'd say he was sleeping but needed milk; that was worth five dollars most times!"

"Which direction did the noisy people go?" frowned a cop.

"Sounded like to the railroad tracks. I heard skateboards!" the bum sneezed, forcing everyone to step backward. "That way, I'm sure."

"Call the railroad and have them look for kids that have paint on their clothes," ordered a lawman in his radio. "This is the tenth time this week those jerks have hit! It's been buildings, too! They use the same kind of paint; see that big splash of green and the yellow? They customize their work. The red letters will come off easily but this other is different."

"They labeled the truck right!" winced Early. "I just don't usually go public with these words!"

Additional enforcement agents arrived. One man held his hand to Early Bird to shake his. "I may have to declare you as a menace! We are getting to know each other quite well."

"This isn't my thing! I just seem to find trouble here!" drooped Early. "I would rather never to come over the George Washington Bridge. Nobody volunteers New York delivery anymore. Some companies even advertise 'No New York' when they are recruiting drivers."

"We found those kids already that did this. They didn't get far away at all! The diner called to report paint tracks on the floor in the entry. Can you imagine one of them had to use the bathroom?" snickered the cop. "It certainly is horrible for them to do this kind of thing; but this is fun for them. Why can't kids like this realize the effect on other people? Here they come now!"

"We got 'em!" smiled the handsome officer.

"Their parents will come to the station for them! Thought they needed a good look at their job!"

Everybody looked at the well groomed young fellows. They sat in the patrol cars, looking at their feet.

"At least they seem to feel remorse!" Red added.

"Their only remorse is they got caught!" replied a policeman. "This is just one more step before they become real criminals. If they don't get help now, they'll move on to a bigger crime. This is an expensive job on this truck and trailer!"

"Probably cost ten thousand dollars in downtime and putting the truck back into service. They didn't miss anything! Everything has paint! The worse thing is they jimmied the door and got the inside, too!" complained Early. "I don't know what I'll do!"

It was then that Red could see the splashed interior from the outside lights. Early used his key and opened the driver's door. He turned on the overhead lights to expose the mess. The windshield had been sloshed with yellow and the seats caught the red paint.

"They got inside!" yelled a cop. "That adds bigger charges that will stick. "Breaking and entering! Anything missing? Anything? That would be theft!"

Early looked and realized his coffee cup was gone. "My mug! It's gone!"

"Good! We have them good!"

This put a new angle into their lives. The rest of the evening was spent with paper work and discovery. All else was set aside. Finally, about three in the morning, Red and Early found a sofa to flop on in the furniture store.

They were awakened by the key in the lock as it made a big *click*. Red jumped and heard footsteps. Then the smell of coffee eased her sudden awakening.

Her old manager called, "Hi there! Brought you some coffee and sweetrolls!"

"What a night!" Red answered. "Oh, thanks!"

"I saw that horrible mess outside! The punks! Who did it? Devil, I suppose!" Puss moaned.

"No...Just punk kids!" Early smiled, walking in to receive his treat. "Some mess, that's for sure."

"You can use my truck to make your delivery," Red suggested.

"All right. That will at least get rid of the trailer. I'm loaded light anyhow. That single axle will do it. My multi-color truck will just have to be taken in. I'll call my insurance company," Early Bird planned.

When Red and Early went to change the trailer around, the true damage appeared. It was all beyond belief. Even so, with furniture pads covering the driver seat, Early got the cab from the trailer and moved it out of their way. "That paint is everywhere!"

Partially dry paint still setting up all over the once beautiful Freightliner gave the task-master a pitiful look. The sun dealt the machine to a sad disclosure. The truck was unusable, undrivable. The buckets of paint had gotten into the mechanical parts, too. It would have to be towed.

"I guess you have a 'boarder' for a few days!" Early teased.

"Your insurance can afford it!" smiled Red,

tossing her hair.

Later, they delivered the trailer to its destination and bobtailed back to the store. Early hit some rough road in Brooklyn.

"Damn! I think I bit my tongue!"

"You are just used to being pampered with your fancy trucks!" laughed Red. "What are you going to do now?"

"Trade it in, I suppose! We can get anything you want!" Early propositioned. "They might have to scrap it! I can't wait for it to be fixed; that could be weeks if I were lucky."

They agreed to go south and find another truck for Early. Red would be able to finish the sale of her store within a month. Timing seemed good. A change of pace seemed in order. They made a second delivery of furniture to the place that was buying all her stock. It was removed from the trailer and they were able to return to the store for the last load that would be sent back south.

"Damaged freight! That is so aggravating. We tear some up and they send us some that is messed up. That sleeper-sofa has its bed whop-sided. Give me that screwdriver. We'll fix it," Red groaned.

This took longer than anticipated but fixed it back into the right place. That meant leaving a special order that could now go to the customer. Again, Red found other items that could be re-worked. Finally, she jumped back into the trailer and unloaded a good part of the items already had loaded. Early Bird didn't question her. He just took orders. It was very late when they finally closed the trailer doors.

"I didn't mean to do all that!" apologized Red. "That's the way furniture is. I can get drawers fixed and mend and replace cushions. It will be easier on the other end."

"That's all right. Makes me appreciate my work. Most of the time all I have to do is drop one trailer and pick up another. Sometimes they send me with several drops. I practically never have to touch freight."

"Ha, ha! I made you work, didn't I?" mocked Red. "Poor baby. Had to exercise those big old muscles! This will keep you thin!"

"That's all right. I'll just get fat!" Early returned. "We going tonight?"

"What do you want to do?" she quizzed.

"Maybe we should at least get out of New York and we can stop enroute. You know how it is with the crazy traffic here," Early pointed out. "Let's eat at the diner then leave."

"Good! I could eat the whole menu!"

One of Red's customers located them in the diner and bounced to the table. "Oh, I'm so glad I found you. I want that dining room suite we talked about."

Another delay put them to leave even later. Once underway, the big decision was which route out would be the best. They agreed on the George Washington and the Turnpike. The old International made the way as if it were gifted and talented. Red was driving.

"I love old Blue! I've been a lot of miles in this thing!" she giggled. "I know it isn't much to you, but what the heck, it does move!"

"That's right and it's paid for!" he assured. "Most of all, it is yours. I have to say, you know your job!"

"Watch this!" smirked Red. "See how these asses have to ride my tail?"

Early looked into the side mirror. He could see a vast number of motorcycles coming up fast. A voice on the CB yelled, "Hey, stickwagon, I'm coming beside you. Stay there! Black Hawk, move on the other side of him!"

"All right! I'm not a him!" Red answered. The two trucks came abreast with her in the middle, like a sandwich.

"Watch those bikers!" called Red. She still had some of them on her rear and they were starting to dive between the trucks.

"All right, now keep in your lane. We're moving in. They won't be able to cut through!" snorted the Peterbuilt driver,

"Watch your right!" yelled Red. "One's between us!"

Quickly, she hit her brakes as did the other two trucks. You could hear the sound of tearing, brakes and clamoring of bikes into each other. The trucks came to a standstill, blocking all the traffic on the expressway.

"Oh, God! Early! Bikes are everywhere! Look!" she sorrowed.

"This is not your fault! Just stay calm and stay in the truck! Here...Take a piece of gum! Just stay calm," Early comforted.

"Somebody might be hurt. Early, there's a bike under my trailer! I see a tire! Oh, God! I see a leg! Oh, no...The leg is by itself! It isn't on anybody!" she suffered. "Look!"

Early Bird slid on top of the box covering the motor and looked from her mirror. "Just keep cool.

Don't look at it! Let me get in the driver's seat. I'll handle this!"

"No, it's my wreck!" she granted. "Maybe we had better get out to help!"

"You can't get out your door, can you? That truck is right on you. This one over here is about the same. Some game they were playing for no reason."

"I can get out the window and go down!" Red stated. "I'm going out there."

The sirens sounded in the near roadway just behind them. Honking and a loud bullhorn was trying to inch toward them.

Red hung from the door and stuck her head back in. "Honey, hand me a couple of those throw-away cameras."

Knowing that the pictures could say a thousand words, Red snapped every angle she could find. Bikes and bodies were all around. She thought to herself, "Guess I'll be making history now! Never thought being a photographer would be my long-suit!"

When the police arrived on horseback, the traffic was well tied for several more hours to come. They freed one lane finally to let the outgoing traffic move just slightly. Each vehicle had to slow down and look. Once the rubber-neckers passed through, more kept following.

Red pitched her cameras into her truck through the window she had jumped from. Early was walking around, checking on the people. He slipped behind her.

"Don't volunteer any information. Just let the authorities investigate! You just are in the middle!"

As people were gathered for the hospital, Red

watched. She tried to think what she could have done differently. She did the only thing possible. Her trailer was skinned with blue paint from the bike under her axle. She wondered where that man landed. Red stooped to her knees to examine the drop-frame. The trailer was about sixteen to twenty inches from the ground. The bike was caught underneath and twisted, but the person driving it was elsewhere. She couldn't look at the leg. At a glance anyone would admire the handsome high boot laying there, lifeless. She tried to squeeze back the tears.

"Honey, its your turn now. They want to talk to you. I'll go with you," he cautioned. "Remember, think and answer slowly!"

"How many did I kill with my truck?" bitterly she quivered.

Looking behind the trailer, Red could only see a pile of bikes, two wrecked cars and another truck. It looked like a mass of junk. People were sitting and laying in the roadway, still. With the slow traffic, firefighters, medical wagons and various aides it was difficult coming or leaving.

"You didn't kill anybody," Early answered calmly. "Nobody is dead! The bikers can't weave in traffic like they were doing!"

"What about the one with the leg...?" she turned so as not to look.

"Come here!" Early was pulling her by the arm.

"No! I can't look!" she shook.

"Look! That's just a boot! There isn't a leg in it. One of the bikers had his riding boots hooked onto the back seat. Nobody lost a leg!" Early coaxed her to look.

"Thank God!" sighed the woman then laughed nervously. "A boot! What a relief!"

After the report and clean up, their truck was finally released but not before the D.O.T. checked it out. Red had been in her lane. Everything was mass confusion and up for grabs as to fault.

"Bikers!" swore one trucker. "They get in your blind spot just so you can hit them. The assholes came up like Trojans! They were everywhere! I figure they have to show off for each other!"

"Lots'a dare-devil in their blood," noted a cop.

"They're lucky they just ran over each other. Three ran into that drop-frame. If it had been my trailer, there wouldn't have been much to stop 'em," grunted a driver. "I looked up and suddenly they're flipping, falling and dropping all over the place."

Getting the Transtar back to the road was not easy. The bike parts laying around wanted to tag along. People kept stopping them until they finally had all the pieces snatched from beneath the rig.

Red gave a big sound of the horn; at last everybody scattered to let the big truck through. The road was wide open and it was late.

"I guess you are tired?" smiled Early.

"Not very...I'm going to get to the Petro in Elkton. We can break there," she offered.

"How'd I know you'd do that?" smiled Early.

"Cause, you know it's my favorite place! They know how to treat us!" Red flashed. "Get in bed and rest. I can drive this. It's only about two hours."

Early obeyed and fell to sleep as he listened to Red sing along with a Patsy Cline tape.

Red drove the speed limit and kept a watchful

eye. A thunderstorm seemed to be waiting ahead. She slowed the truck in the thunderous down-pour. At a given point, a back trailer tire seemed to wobble, then it appeared all right. She looked for smoke in the mirror but water from the road sprayed so that even if a tire was burning it would have been drenched. She was glad when the storm passed and then getting to the end of the turnpike.

Early slept through it. She parked the rig in the fuel island; he rolled out from the bunk to the motor box.

"Wake up, Sweat Hog!" she teased. You snore like a horse!"

Early rubbed his eyes, capturing his memory of time and place. Red was servicing her truck as he found his shoes and shirt. The old cab-over lacked for convenience. He was used to the closet and big sleeper that you stand in. This had to be crawled into.

Red returned with a cup of coffee for him. As he reached for it, she smiled and shrugged her shoulders, "Guess what?"

"Who knows! I'm glad I'm not psychic...I'd be crazy by now! All this action will make a man crazy!" he shrugged and sipped. "This is good!"

"I'll pay for fuel and then pull into the garage!" smiled the woman.

"Garage?" he blurted out. "Why? I checked the truck up the road."

"I had a blow-out during the storm. I thought she wiggled funny. That was a dance I hadn't taught her!" joked Red. "We can eat while they change it."

This was the Petro's favorite task, selling tires. Early jumped into action and played 'Let's Make a Deal'. A complete set of new Michelins were agreed upon.

"Let me buy them for you!" he tried.

"Of course not! This is business!"

"I thought they could be a wedding present!" he crowed.

"Not hardly! I want something womanly for that...not some old masculine thing. I wouldn't give you a brake-job!"

"I don't have a truck! You're one up on me. At least you have wheels!" Early laughed.

They spent an hour eating then returned to receive the rig. Red was excited about the new tires. She had saved almost two hundred dollars buying the single axle van all four tires at the same time.

"Driving a single axle, I figure I need to change-up when they get a little more than half worn. I get a good trade that way and it leaves less possibility for error," she said, handing over her credit card.

Early drove out of the garage and looked for a parking spot near the back. "We can sleep late if we want to!"

"You can. I figured I'd drive on!" her eyes sparkled.

"We are staying here!" Early replied. "Get back into that bed before I spank you!"

Suddenly, he realized he was teasing her about something that would never happen. He stiffened as he tried to undo the word 'spank'. "I didn't mean that...I just want you to sleep!"

"It's all right, Early. I know you're playing. Put it like this. "Let's break in my sleeper! We never have!" she smiled as she touched his hand gently.

"Let me park this rag!" he gleed. Once in the spot, he reached for her and gently placed his lips to hers. She met him anxiously.

"I've got to fix the drape!" she whispered.

Red placed the curtains and adjusted things somewhat. She quickly slipped into a little thin, blue nighty that she had under the edge of the mattress. The small bed didn't matter, they were together.

He clung tightly and breathed softly across her neck. "You are delightful. I love you!"

Feeling the chill of excitement, Red returned the gesture. "I love you, too! You're special...I don't know how I lived before!"

In the little blue Transtar, they found one another as perfectly as in all their other moments. The covers were neat and clean, the starched sheets added a comforting glow as they reached for the stars.

Nestling into Early's arms, Red whispered, "Maybe we should just go on the road in this! It will get us there, too!"

"This is wonderful...Whatever you want!" Early trailed off and began to breathe steadily as he slipped into deep sleep.

Red was wide awake. Being overtired and anxious taxed her possibilities for slumber. She reached for the covers and tucked them around her man. Her hand felt his hair then she comforted him by soothingly caressing his neck. Early smiled slightly and snuggled closer to her.

"I'll always love you, Early," Red whispered aloud. "You are truly my knight in shining armor. I guess a truck would be shining armor!" she laughed at her pun. Tears filled her eyes as the days past re-entered her mind. She could see Early Bird connect a big punch to the side of Devil's jaw that stuffed the man almost under his truck. Then, her memory wandered farther back to the happy sunshine and a picnic along the roadside when Early gave her the diamond pendent. He was always there when she would let him be. He could move the mountains and stop the rivers' flow if needed. And yes, he had bridged the barriers and brought her forward into a new light. Early was wonderful and simple in his needs. He always gave more than he took.

Even though there was all the matched personality exchange, Red felt somewhat uneasy. Something made her afraid to really become completely his. It wasn't him...Never! He was magnificent, a good person and gentle.

The torment of having to face Devil in court was on her mind. This kept her afraid. He had been in jail but somehow made bail. What would it take for that miserable 'pit-in-the-stomach' feeling to go away?

Red could see Early in the stream of light that bore through a crack at the edge of the drape. He was so silent as he slept. She took her hands and caressed his hair to make it stand up in two points above his forehead. This made her laugh.

She whispered, "Poor thing, you let me be so mean to you! I just love you to pieces. Be patient with me! I'm trying to get over all I have been through! I know nothing is your fault. It's all I went through. I just can't help it!"

Early listened to the words but kept her secret. He moaned and sat up, banging his head on the roof. "Ouch! I forgot, we're here! Are you asleep?"

"No!"

"Want something to drink?" he yawned.

"Here!" She produced a cold Seven-Up. "Trucking champagne!"

"Great!" he smiled, reaching for the stemmed glass. "You sure know how to entertain!"

"What are you saying?" Red urged and slapped him with a pillow on the leg.

"Just that your mother must have taught you well...See, the fancy glasses and the cheese! Baby, you planned this!" he said.

"Of course! You're worth it!"

They settled again and Red fell to sleep in his strong arms.

The rest of the trip to North Carolina went normal. The weather was perfect. They left the big truck at the dock and found her little car nearby. It was to her house, phone calls then Early wanted to look at trucks.

"Go with me!" he pleaded.

"You have to make this decision. I can't do it for you!" argued the woman.

"Then, we'll just take the Transtar!" he barked. "Like you said, it'll get us there. You can just sleep when it's my time to drive and I'll sleep when you drive! We can just run, run, run! We don't need anything but..."

"Hush! I'll go with you!"

Later, they entered the beautiful Freightliner facility. The customer service was excellent once they realized your mission. The president of the company walked along as they studied the trucks available.

"Let's forget color right now and pick style!" smiled Early. "I always shop for my features then I paint it!"

He went through the type of motor, transmission and style real fast. The man took notes agreeing he was on the right track."

Red left the men talking and ambled into the yard to look and pick. There was every color with all kinds of features that made one dizzy.

"Here it is!" she screamed, running back into the showroom. "I found it! Early, I found it! Come here! This is the one! I love it!"

"She may not pick what you need..."

"Oh yes she does! Whatever she wants is fine!" Early assured him.

"Come on! Wait until you see the God of Trucks!" she boasted.

"Are you sure?" balked the man wishing to take plenty of time.

"Look, we're dealing with *Red High Heels*," sighed Early.

Red flashed a winning smile and nodded as they followed her. She ran ahead and jumped onto the steps, hanging onto the door. "Look! This is so beautiful! Angel...That's it! Her name is Angel!"

The men looked at each other. The company man muttered, "Top of the line...Great taste! Are you ready for this?"

"I have to be!" collected Early. "I forgot to tell you, mine was ruined in New York...Insurance has to call us."

Red had picked a new Freightliner that just happened to have all the goodies Early wanted, plus the beauty, too. A special paint finish made the elegant truck glisten in the sun. Gold trim was used instead of chrome.

"Why did you pick the cab-over?" asked Early.

"I like it! You want that old, ugly nose pooching out! They look like pigs!"

"No, since last night, I really love a cab-over!" he winked.

"Let's look inside! I saw one similar at the truck show but not this pretty!" she cooed.

The man produced a ring of keys and opened the door wide. "Want to go for a drive?"

"Maybe! We need to look first!"

Early was overwhelmed with the space inside; truly everything you could want. The side steps swung out to make getting in easy. The walk-in sleeper was very new fashion. The bunk was made with sheets and comforter and the refrigerator was filled with goodies.

"Grab some lunch," he smiled. "We show these trucks everyday! It depends on your needs! Schneider just ordered cab-overs."

Red selected a ham and cheese on rye with a bottle of icy cold milk. Early and the man took theirs and each found a place to sit.

"Now, if I can have a lap-top and a sewing machine this would be right!" she laughed.

"If that's what it takes, you can have it!" resigned Early Bird.

"See, I am used to a cab-over. Mine is just old, but this is a Cadillac! It has everything the other trucks have! The shorter frame can help in delivery," noted Red.

"You know, being over the engine inside the truck is objectionable to some people. That shorter nose on the Classic is a real betweener. Where the long nose makes the truck longer, this extension gives more to interior space," pointed out the man, feeling Early Bird should be the decision maker.

"If Red wants a bicycle...It will be fine with me. She likes this truck!" smiled Early and slipped his arm around her. "You like this sleeper? Right cozy!"

"Maybe I am more in love with the color outside. This is still wonderful!" she sparkled. "Let's look at that one over there!"

She pointed to an up-graded Classic, sporting a strange color of plum. They baled out of the cab-over and filed across the path. The door was unlocked enabling them to follow the company sales official. The interior had every possible feature. It was perfectly 'road ready'. The leather seats had a mellow glow, the motor was so quiet it was almost impossible to know it was running. Everything was one notch ahead of anything Red had ever seen. All details of home-life were included...A microwave, refrigerator, stereo, radio, TV and tape deck, double bunk sleeper with flip away upper bunk. Lots of storage drawers and hanging closets. The little toilet-shower addition was especially inviting; as was the desk holding a lap-top.

"Old Purple really has it!" she acknowledged. "This is a huge sleeper. Sure beats the other night in my truck!"

"It is really a custom truck. We can handle anything. Company trucks are one thing; road-teams need more. TriAd Freightliner can make life on the road! That's our specialty!" the fellow assured them.

They looked at each other and smiled. Early's beeper sounded at the same moment Red's cell phone rang. Each responded accordingly.

The men couldn't help but listen to Red's conversation. Only Early could read between the lines. He watched her face turn white as she sank to the sleeper to sit. Her excitement shrank into a composed silence.   The light that danced in her eyes disappeared.

"Yes," she gulped with a dry mouth. "When?"

She whispered to Early, "Write this down!" and addressed the phone once more. "Please, let my friend take this information."

Early took the phone as Red flew from the truck and leaned next to the fuel tank covered area. The mesh steps greeted her as she fought not to be sick. Struggling to keep her composure, the woman breathed deeply, feeling numb. Even her lips tingled from the shock feeling.

The men came to her and the president nodded, "Come, use my office! I'll get you whatever you need!"

Silently, they went into the stately building and found refuge in his huge, comfortable surroundings with all the awards and pictures of superior moments. Red sat stiffly, looking around, trying to collect herself. The official left the room and Early reached to console her, trying to find words that would work.

"Tell me, baby, what is it?"

It was then Red let the storm go. Her eyes turned wet and red as the mascara streaked her cheeks. She pushed him away. "I love you! But, it will never work!"

"Yes it will! Talk to me!" he replied.

"I'm out there trying to tell you what to do when I have no right to!" she sobbed.

"Sure you do! I want you to!" he tried to calm her.

Shaking her head fiercely, she babbled, "Oh,

no! I can't do it! I just can't!"

"Baby, things will work out!" he partitioned.

"Never! I'm destined to live my life dodging the bullet! Once this trial is over...It will start all over again! I won't put you through anymore. You are too good for me!" she pleaded. "I got tied up with that crazy criminal and I will never be rid of him! He always comes back and there aren't enough balls in the land to ever stop him!"

Early tried to reach for her but she stepped back. "Later you'll know I'm right. Just let go! Go on with your life without me! I won't let him ruin you. Just leave it all alone! I can't go on like this! You have to work and live. This'll all fade in time!"

"No! Red, please don't do this to us! We will find a way!" he cried. "Please, girl, I'm begging you! Please don't give it up!"

"I have to Early Bird...I can't fight anymore!" She let him hold her as her heart broke. "I just can't! I just can't do this anymore!"

"Please, Baby! Please!" he wept.

She shook her head, taking the paper from his hand with the information regarding the court date with Devil. Walking away, she couldn't look back. She avoided the eyes on her, while rushing past the line of desks going out the building and to her car. She paused a minute, then got in. Backing up, she saw the image of Early Bird at the glass entrance. With a jerk, the car lurched forward; she disappeared.

CHAPTER 15

Red High Heels was facing one of the most earth shattering dilemmas of her life. The upcoming trial in New York with Devil could sweep her into a cross fire. The summons back to court was devastating to say the least. She felt there were few on her side. A friendly word here and there from friends helped somewhat but was powerless. The District Attorney's office had their routine and drew the case against the man on their findings in the police file. This report covered the word-for-word accusations from Red, her hospital results and bills. There were also a few statements from people who knew she had been stalked, beaten and terrorized by Devil over the past few years.

'*ALLEGED*', the common usage, applied to all his shifty patterns of behavior. Red felt as if she were the criminal from the double questioning, lies submitted under oath by Devil via his lawyers, and the implication that she should have walked away.

She sat nervously waiting for the deposition to once more resume. Finally, everyone gathered at the long table. Some people appeared that she had never seen before. Protocol was followed as it began.

A very large nosed Italian man snorted, "Why did you stay around this man? Did you not realize there was this 'so-called' danger?"

"Which question do I need to answer?" Red calmly ployed.

The D.A. injected, "Don't batter this witness. These are not necessary questions!"

"All right already!" he took the feat and turned to a different form, "I know you feel you have been through a great deal. Tell us what happened to you on the night of the alleged assault."

"I came back to my business that night..." she started.

"Do you usually make it a practice of being out all hours of the night during bad weather?" the man intervened.

"Sir, I sell furniture. I have to handle this; I do what I have to do!"

"I would think you would be afraid!"

"Sometimes I guess I might be...But..."

He laughed, "You mean you can work all these strange hours unafraid, yet you let someone you know force you into a fragile situation?"

"It wasn't like that! He did this! Not me! I've gone out in the middle of the night to the darkest parts of Brooklyn, driven through the rough neighborhoods in the Bronx. Even once I got lost in Harlem.

Nobody there ever bothered me. I was minding my own business then, and I was minding my own business when Devil jumped me from behind in my store! I never let him in! He broke in! He did all that to me that you have in that report! He's twice my weight! I begged him and pleaded with him but he kept beating me, on and on and over and over!" she screamed nearly out of control.

Happy to upset her, the man leaned across the table and smiled, " Didn't it make you feel good in an odd way that this man loved you so much he would do anything to get you back!"

Red flipped; she stood and slung the papers before her. "Nothing about him will ever make me feel good! He stalked me! He beat me! He threatened me! And, do you want to hear the most horrible part? He shoved a knife up my 'cootie' threatening to cut me in half! Why don't you go home and do that to your wife? You're just like him if you can defend his actions! You condone his activities by selling yourself out! You're paid to be a part of him! Arrest me for refusing to do this anymore! I can't take it! Let him go! Put the bars on me! I'd be safer in jail!"

Red fell into her chair and threw her head on the table and sobbed outwardly. "I just can't take this humiliation!"

The attorney replied, "It's just my job! We can take a break!"

They all left the room with Red still glued to the table. Her friend, Puss, touched her back and whispered., "I'm sorry! That son of a bitch! I could hear it out in the hall...Well, my ear was stuck in the door!"

The two women began to laugh, envisioning

an ear hanging in a doorway.

Red cried, "I'm afraid! There is nothing that can be done. Even with the hospital records and his confession, he'll still be free. He might let up, but you know and I know this will just make him madder!"

The District Attorney returned with several glasses of drink. "Here, get hold of yourself!"

"It doesn't matter! We lost before we started!" sighed Red.

"No we haven't! You're a great witness and you're smart! You think great! Emotional...Yeah. You are super! A jury would probably kill him! They know about this!" he assured her.

A finger snapped and the other lawyer called to the D.A. The D.A. joined him in the hallway; then, came back to the table.

"They are through with this deposition. Lawyers need these for discovery so they have a bigger attorney fee. We can go now. Just be nearby. The court date is next Tuesday at nine o'clock. Call my office at eight. We'll meet together before court. I want you on time. By the way, avoid discussing this case to outsiders!"

*****

Early Bird called Greensboro, North Carolina to contact Red's daughter. She had moved to her new house. The phones switched the call automatically, "Hey, little one!"

"Early Bird! I am so mad at my mother! I know she will always love you! Have you seen her yet?" the young woman questioned.

"She says 'No'. So I have to wait and hope!"

he told her. "I'm picking up my new truck tomorrow. I'm in town."

"Then get over here! You need a ride? Lucky Runner will be home soon!" she gleed.

"I have a rental car. Are you certain that I won't be too much trouble? I just need to hear about Red!" he agonized.

"Of course not! Dinner will be like having her here cooking! I just defrosted one of her chicken pies and I have rice and steamed broccoli. I'll make the cheese sauce you and Lucky crave! Oh, you remember her coconut pound cake? I have frozen slices for us all!" she boasted. "This will be like having Mama here but sort of by proxy!"

"You're the best! I'm on my way!" he thanked her.

Kikki's husband slammed the door and grabbed his wife around the waist. "Guess what I'm thinking?"

"What? We have company coming!"

"Oh, no! I'm tired and the day was hectic!" he grumbled.

"Early Bird! He came to pick up his new truck. That hateful mother has not called him or talked to him since she ran him off! The hussy! She's making a big mistake!" griped Kikki.

"You women are crazy...You run us off and dare us to go! That's what Red is doing! They always get back together," he replied as he started to peel the tomatoes. "Early is a fine man. I'm glad he is what you call 'company'. I'm kicking off my shoes! He's family."

*****

Far out on Long Island, almost to the end of the Expressway, a young man was found laying on the steps of a police station. He had busted ribs, bruises in the face and his pants were nearly torn off.

"How did you get here?" asked the policeman who bent over him. "Don't move. We have an ambulance coming."

The horns and noise from the emergency van only blasted a few minutes and stopped below them. Men rushed quickly and slipped the young man away for help.

A detective had glanced in the ambulance before it dashed away. He scratched his head for a moment. "Who was that man?"

"I don't know. He was just laying here! Probably some homeless!" the other cop volunteered. "We sent him to the hospital for clean up."

"I've seen him...Damn! Where have I seen him before?"

The cops returned inside the station house and went about the task of changing shifts and preparing for the coming day. Several hours later the detective jumped up from his computer and yelled, "I remember! That's the guy that was always with that fellow that beat up those women! You know that woman, Red! It's a wonder this cat's alive!"

The partner smiled, "Let's go see the nice young man and take him some flowers! He just might be able to answer some questions!"

"That's right! That busted face might have straightened out his amnesia!" grinned the other cop. "We need to find out his health status first, then squeeze his memory. He knows it all!"

"Want to lay a hundred that the old man went

nuts on him! That's one 'honey bucket'!" he winked. "I'll never forget the bastard outrunning us on ice in that bobtail. Now that's a slick one!"

They slapped each others hands and grabbed their hats.

*****

Devil rotated nervously on the legs of the office chair as the attorney continued his phone call. Finally, his mouth piece flipped the receiver in place and pushed a button, "Bring us some coffee. We're going to be here for awhile. Don't let anyone disturb us!"

"You have the talent!" laughed Devil in a smooth boosting manner.

"Shut up! Don't try to hustle me! You should have been at that damn deposition! That woman is not lying! Is she?" questioned the attorney, giving him a worried look.

"I don't know what you could mean! All women lie...I lie...You lie! So what does it matter. I hire you to fix my shit. I ain't hiring you to fall in love with that bitch! She just wants me in jail. I ain't sure of what she says anyhow. For all I know old Snag might have beat on her. It's like I told you, she slipped on some ice and hit her head. I left after that. Maybe her cop boyfriend did it. They're all crazy!" Devil shuffled the blame and began to sweat. The perspiration poured off his face and hands. "Git me something to drink. I got a pill. I'm having a heart attack! Hurry! Help me!" he coughed.

The woman came with coffee, doughnuts and two glasses of water on a tray. She whimpered, "Oh!

He looks pale. Here, take this water!"

"Devil! Here, the water...Where's the pill?" asked the lawyer.

Gasping for breath, the pale man pounded his shirt pocket as he topple over in the chair. Quickly, the secretary grabbed the phone and called 911. Devil's eyes rolled back as his lawyer forced the pills into his mouth. When the medics arrived, he had managed to sit up and seemed better. They checked him out and warned him to see a doctor. He had had an anxiety attack but since he had a heart condition it could work on that.

Sitting on the sofa, Devil rubbed his head, playing the attack for all it was worth. "I just can't take that abuse! They're trying to get me!"

His attorney looked at him strangely and shook his head. "Neither can I!"

Devil went into a forced coughing fit, seeking added sympathy. Even so, the attorney kept remembering Red's words, *"You condone his activities by selling yourself out as part of him!"* He stood and walked to the mirror across the room and Red's voice echoed, *"Do that to your wife!"* He thought of his beautiful, shapely wife who had never broken a fingernail and lived totally pampered. This could never happen to her. But could it? Here he was working a case for a crazy man. There were many situations where a client went after the lawyer's family if things didn't go to suit him.

Looking at his client, he watched the man performing his act. "He's good," he thought. "This man could go to Hollywood. Now what? What kind of wrath have I bought? Oh, God...What can I do?"

Once more, Red's voice deafened his ears,

"Let him go...Put the bars on me! I'd be safer in jail!"

Again, he tried to sit at his desk when he caught the last words on the composed document. They read...RED HIGH HEELS--*"I can't take this humiliation!"*

He motioned to his client then sat across from him. "You are not going to be able to go through a trial. Maybe we can work out a plea bargain!"

"Naw. She won't do that! It's my blood she wants, the bitch!"

"We can try. There's nothing to loose, lots to gain. This goes on all the time. The court dockets are booked so tight that we have to wait forever to get scheduled. With what we have, I might be able to talk them into something. It will cost a lot of money to drag it on! I'll tell them how sick you are!"

"Do it, if you think you can!" Devil agreed.

The attorney dismissed him, ordering him to come back the next morning for court. Paper work would have to apply even if he were able to pull the deal off. One thing was in his favor. Red High Heels was not stupid. She knew very well that court and a piece of paper would not stop the man. They all had to hope he would go away and play his games in another place and at another time!

*****

The phone went wild at the near empty furniture store. Things were happening in all directions. The buyer for the stock was having a tantrum wanting the five bedroom suites delivered before noon. Red listened, holding the phone by its' cord about three feet from the hand-set. It spun around as she dropped it into a trash can. The voice kept demanding, "I told you I had three customers waiting for this! Miss Red! Listen to me!"

Retrieving the hand-set, she answered, "I'll get it to you as soon as I get this morning appointment out of the way! They'll get started in court and you know they will have to break until next week or something. I just can't do differently...I'm under court order!"

"Court order! Hell, you ought not put yourself in that kind of position! You are a smart woman..."

Red cut him off, "You don't know anything about what I've been through. Don't judge me! Durn! Come get this stuff yourself! I've been going overboard to get your crap to you when you should pick it up yourself. Do you have anything that says I have to do it all? For months I have run for you like I'm your slave! You're like most men, you think a woman is just to take orders! I don't give a flying fart if you ever get any more furniture! Nobody could please you anyhow! Good-bye!"

She slammed the phone down and let it ring when it started back. Finally, the answering machine picked up and the man was trying to get her to answer, "Miss Red, I didn't mean it like it sounded. I'm sorry! Please pick up!"

"All right, I hear you! I'll call you later, after court!" the nervous woman bargained. "I'm sorry, too. I have to go! It's on the truck; they'll bring it!"

The next call on the call-waiting was Early Bird. Finally, she returned to his call. "Hi!"

"I just wanted to say hello. Are you all right?"

His palms were so wet he nearly dropped the receiver. With his mouth being dry, it made talking difficult.

"I'm all right. How about you?" she calmly replied.

"I miss you!" he whispered. "I want to see you again, soon!"

"Maybe after I get the store moved," she endured.

"I saw your kids a few weeks ago. Did you know?"

"Yes. .She told me. That was nice," the woman formally answered.

"Girl, what's wrong? If you don't want to be together, can't we be friends?" Early pleaded with her cold spirit.

"Once you're lovers, you can't be friends! It would hurt too much! I've got to go. I have an appointment that won't wait!" she impatiently clammered.

"Well, let me know if you need me...I'll never be far away! I love you, Baby! I love you. .Just keep that in mind. I'll do anything..." He made her listen to that much before she snapped at him.

"Just go on your way and don't worry about me. I'm taking care of myself. A woman doesn't have to have a man!"

"Yeah, but I sure could come in handy!" he reminded her. "I'll be attached to my cell phone! I love you, Red!"

"I have to go! Bye!" she nearly whimpered and hung up. "I love you too, Early Bird! I will always love you!"

Red forced the tears back, not wanting to wreck her 'court face'. Puss beeped her horn and she raced for the door.

"Wow! You look splendid!" giggled Puss. "Must be some good looking man in the D.A.'s office!"

"Ha! If there were a million good looking jerks out there, it wouldn't matter. They'd all be criminals, assholes or queers!" snapped Red. "I don't need a damn man...It's just trouble!"

"I understand. One day this will all be over!" she comforted.

"No! Everybody believes a man can do as he pleases. I almost got into trouble at the deposition. I really don't care. I told them I'd just as soon go to jail, and I almost would. I have nothing left! People don't believe me and if they do they'll still side with him because they're scared. I've lost my business in the process. It's cost me a fortune to mess with the doctors and miss working. The truck needs a lot of repair now. It's almost like I've never lived; everything has turned out useless; worthless. It has sucked away all my dreams, energy and *will*. I feel numb! There's nothing to look forward to!" blurted Red.

"That's only how you feel now! This is a lot to have to go through!" soothed Puss.

"The truth...I never thought I'd ever have to go through something like this. If he gets by, I'd better disappear! It's so humiliating!" Red strained. "I'll never be the same! Life will never be the same!"

"You should call Early Bird! Go with him! He's a good man!" reminded Puss.

"He needs to forget me! He'll be better off!" suffered Red. "I just don't care anymore. I feel empty and lost. My life's all gone! What really kills me, is I tried for all my life to be respected and do right; but none of that matters. Everybody only remembers the bad and they really don't know how it actually is. They just imagine what they think it is. Like they say, you have to walk in my shoes!"

"I could never have managed to be as strong as you are! You have been through more than I could handle. Just remember, it may not mean much, but I admire you and I care for you. A lot of people care for you. These that are on-lookers don't count anyhow. Just concern yourself with people who do love you and there are lots of us," insisted Puss. "This will be over soon; then it will all be over!"

There was plenty parking since they were an hour early. Slipping the sportscar into a parking slot, they stepped to the street to cross for the coffee shoppe.

"Wait!" ordered Red. "Go in. If *he* is in there, I'm not going in."

"I'll check!" Obeying the sound in her voice, Puss looked in and motioned that things were all right.

The place was filled with other court-bound people. Some looked worried and others seemed cheerful.

Red revealed, "Looks like there's the guilty and repressed here. That girl over there looks so pitiful. Let's sit with her!"

They walked over and placed their tray on the girls' big, round table. "Okay to join you?"

She mumbled as they sat down then yelled, "Give it back! I told you, give it back!"

The room of people stared. The girl continued and started to loudly curse the women. Red and Puss looked at each other and grabbed their treasures, moving to another table. The girl walked over to them and asked, "Are my breasts too big? Look, they said my knockers are too big!" She proceeded to remove her sweater and then her bra. Her chest proudly displayed the enormous excess.

"Damn! Let's go!" whispered Puss.

"No! Those tits might touch me if I have to pass her. Wait!" urged Red.

Immediately, a man rushed to the woman. "Come on, Lucy...Put your sweater on. You can't do that in here!"

"I can't? Oh, excuse me! Where can I?" she smacked her lips over and over, then started flipping her arm. "Suck it! Suck it!" Then, she went into a giggling spree. She kicked off her shoes and started tearing at the rest of her clothes. Two men forced her to go along with them.

They ushered the woman into an office and closed the door. Customers returned to their morning coffee, understanding this girl was just one more of the pitiful; maybe homeless, maybe addicted, or even misplaced.

When they returned to the courthouse, Red and Puss became a part of a line to enter. The check point was similar to that at airports. Puss dropped her purse into a basket and walked through.

Red slipped her's into another basket but the buzzer sounded. Two uniformed personnel walked over and had her to repeat the trip. Again the buzzer sounded. They took her into a small side space and had her to remove her jewelry, coat and shoes.

"What's the problem?" asked Red, embarrassed.

"You!" smiled a young cop. "Here it is!" He held her key chain with a pocketsize mace container.

"Oh, that! I can't carry a gun!" Red cracked.

"This is not legal in New York! You will have to leave it. You can't take this little knife in the court, either. Pick it up when you leave. I could expect that from an out-of-towner!"

"I don't understand how y'all know I'm an out-of-towner!" giggled Red. "I'll be back. Thank you!"

The attorney from the D.A. found them quickly and nearly pushed them into a worn out office at the top of a set of huge steps. "I'm glad you got here early. I need to talk to you!"

"Are we ready?" asked Red. She felt the butterflies jump.

"It's up to you. I had a messenger bring me some papers this morning, early. I need to go over this with you."

He read part of the papers; a woman came in and sat quietly. Then, he finished the pages.

"This is my secretary. We have a copy of your deposition. Do you want to go over it?" he asked kindly.

"No, I remember that!" Red nodded.

"Let me tell you this..." He dryly covered the prospective happenings for the coming day. "Let's go on into the court room."

As quickly as they found the long table, Devil noisily sat at the opposition table across from them. He had a wide grin as if he were a man of means, his usual attitude. He caught Red's glance and winked. She felt violated with his smirk but brushed it off. The two attorneys got up at the same time and met in the middle, between the desks. They conversed and began waving their hands. Walking to the front, they made more motions and returned to their clients.

"They want to make a deal!" Red's attorney whispered. "Are you interested?"

"I'll listen," Red whispered.

The judge entered the courtroom; procedure was carried out.

"Judge, both of us need a short recess to speak with our clients before we select a jury," the D.A. started.

"Approach...Both of you!" he replied. "Don't waste my time with games!" cornered the judge.

"We're not. Maybe we can find grounds to agreement. My client will listen. It might save us a long hearing," replied the D.A.

"All right, take a half hour. I have some things that need handling here. Be ready when you're called again!"

The attorneys returned to their clients and the D.A. motioned for Red to follow. The room was small but had seating and an end table. He dropped his book onto it, speaking. "Red High Heels, I will tell you the proposal. No frills...Just fact. Devil's people want us to let him plead guilty to some lesser charges that will keep him out of jail but away from you. They say in a few words, he is sorry. If you will agree, they will pay your expense...Hospital, court fees and such. You will get an order of protection."

"Sell out! That's what it means!" Red screamed.

"No, this will just keep you from going through all the long days of harressing questioning and embarrassment. This sort of thing gets nasty. You know how it was in the deposition," he tried to comfort.

"I suppose I do! Even if I go through with it, they will insinuate that I made him do it or something. There's no winning with him! And, there's no winning in court. That's the system; so damn careful how we handle our criminals! If they are very mean, then they are considered crazy or insane. Fine! Let him off! Excuse him! One day he'll get somebody else. If he gets me again, I'll be dead!" she trembled and began to cry. Her eyes filled with tears; she threw her hands in the air flipping her wrist with disgust.

"We will make it tough on him. He has to leave you alone. If he bothers you, he will spend time in prison. He has to face the judge. You won't have to go through all this. You make your decision. Do you need more time? I can ask the judge. I'm sorry you ever had to get to this," reasoned the attorney.

"No, just get it over with!" she cried. "I want it behind me. One day, he'll get what he really deserves! You know what? People never really get away with things. Sooner or later they pull the rug from under themselves. You wait! You'll see. He'll do something again. People like him never learn. They just get worse!"

Red straightened up her face and followed the lawyer back into court. Devil was grinning as the two attorneys again approached the bench. Red wanted to cry for having to give anything but she wouldn't have to face him now. The court took another recess and Red was allowed to leave.

Puss threw the little sportscar into gear and roared out of the parking facility. Once on Sunrise Highway, she smiled, "Well?"

"Just the same old thing. He gets off with a slap on the hands. At least it's over for me! I don't think I could stand several weeks in the same room with him. Pull over, now!" She leaned out of the still moving car and threw up her breakfast. Once she was back in the vehicle she grunted, "That's how he makes me feel. Looking at him brings it all back! I'm glad it's about over!"

"We'll have to come for the final disposition, won't we?" Puss asked.

"I suppose. They'll tell us," Red answered.

"You going to call Early Bird?"

"Heck no! He's gone...He accepted it being over!" Red sadly whispered. "That, my friend, is over. He sure was the best love of my life. He probably has someone else, now."

*****

Once back at the store, Red finished her delivery to the other place and returned for another load. This cleaned out the place. She sat on the floor and looked around. There had been many wonderful years here, she reflected, but there's a time for change. She wondered what she would do. Her delivery van was just back from the garage. Red wanted to take a ride to the water. There was a diner she liked there.

When she arrived, it was packed with people in a line out the door. She left her name and left for the pier. The sea gulls were sleeping around the edge. The water was slick; totally calm and a full moon cast a lonely beam across to her feet as if she were staged in a spotlight. Red looked at the stars and made a wish.

"Starlight, star bright...Tell Early Bird I love him tonight!" A tear fell onto the diamond pendent he had given her. She murmured aloud, "I'm sorry, Early...I just put you through hell!"

*****

"You still have the apartment here?" Kikki giggled.

"Of course. I'll unload that soon. Did you come to play awhile?" asked the mother. "We could go into Manhattan like we used to!"

"That's exactly what I want to do! Chinese tonight!" she squealed.

They spent the next few days romping the avenues and streets of their favorite shopping haunts. Kikki sparked, "Mother! Look at that! That wedding dress! It's beautiful! Come on! Try it on for me!"

"Not on my life!" snapped Red.

"Please! For my store!" she insisted.

"Why not! Can't we get it wholesale? It's from *Jasmine*!" said Red, "Let's go there!"

They shifted toward the garment district. The windows were full of great suits and party dresses. Red couldn't deny that she missed the clothing business. But, like everything, it was all different. Life was now a new beginning. Red was not certain what her future would be. Still, she knew it would come together. Things always did. However, this time, there was a real emptiness she had never known. It scared her.

Daughter and Mother dragged all their packages into a cab. They were soon swept through the Midtown tunnel and flying back to the apartment.

Slamming the door, then locking it, Red giggled, "Some trip! You'll kill me!"

"My feet! I think they'll drop off!" Kikki smiled and dropped to the floor. "I love you, Mother!"

The phone rang, Kikki snapped it up. "Hey! Yes! I'm all set!"

The voice begged, "Please, are you certain?"

"Like never before! Went shopping today! Everything is set. Just do your part!" Kikki demanded.

As quickly as she finished the conversation and hung up; the phone rang again. Once more, the young woman answered, "Just a minute!"

Red saw her expression and reached for the receiver and sat down. "Yes?"

"We need you in court tomorrow. There are some things you need to sign. Then, it will be over!" acknowledged her D.A. spokesman.

She agreed to be there and informed Kikki. They called Puss to join them. It was set.

Meanwhile, Kikki slipped into another room and called Early Bird, "Hey, we have to go to court tomorrow on that old bastard!"

"I'll be there anyhow! I'll bobtail to the courthouse."

"Great! This will be even better! There is a perfect place there! Be in the north side parking lot! You'll see Puss' car!"

"I'll be ready!" he answered.

*****

Seven o'clock forced the three women to beat the traffic east to the courthouse again. Red brushed lint from her elegant suit. Her tall heels added the business look. She was happy, maybe because the moon was no longer full. A full moon works on you day and night. At last this part of her anguish was behind; at least for the time being.

Inside the courtroom, Devil was sitting with a sad face. He didn't look when they sat down. The judge entered and everyone hushed. The order was being read; Devil was standing.

The judge called the lawyers again to the front. He talked, then motioned for them to return to their seats.

"We will suspend active jail time. In the event you break probation, the order will come back and you will serve all of this time. This is very serious and you cannot take it lightly! The most important part of this order is that you stay away from Red High Heels; no calls, no intimidation...Leave her alone completely. This is in force at this very minute, as we speak. Do you understand that? This is a permanent order. Any violation of any kind will result in this being retroactive and you will serve this time. You will pay these expenses listed. Can you do that?"

"Yes, sir! I will stay away from her. I'm sorry for all of this!" Devil slipped in. He looked at Red and smiled. She looked away and stared in front of her.

Soon, it was all over and the women walked out of the room. They stood by the door, waiting for the attorney. A loud bang from the gavel got everyone's attention.

The judge shouted, "Order in the courtroom!"

The three women looked inside and watched a sheriff hand the judge a paper to read. He handed it back and the sheriff who walked in front of Devil, then said, "You are under arrest for MURDER! You

Early Bird, do you take this woman to be your wife?"

"I do. I promise to love and keep you forever; anywhere you go, I will be there. Anything you need I will try to provide. Forever, I will love and cherish you. My whole being belongs with you. I will climb our mountains and walk by your side until death parts us."

The judge asked, "And Red High Heels, do you take this man?"

"Oh, yes! Early Bird, I will honor and obey...Love and cherish you. I want to be with you until the day I die. Forever, let me hold and belong in the heart of your soul."

A huge crowd had gathered as the judge asked for the rings and gave each of them one, saying, "This ring is only as meaningful as what it represents to you. However, the round circle signifies the full circle of your love. Place them on each other's fingers."

They slipped the wide bands on each other and looked at their entwined hands. The judge smiled and said, "By the powers vested in me, I pronounce YOU Early Bird, husband, and YOU, Red High Heels, wife...Let me be the first to congratulate you and say, don't let *anything ever* come between you! You may kiss your bride!"

The crowd screamed. cheered; jumped and cried. They threw hats and papers into the air. Women cried and men shook hands around.

Early Bird and Red High Heels held each other and gently kissed. They rushed to his big Freightliner with the people following. He swept Red into his arms and tenderly kissed her lips. The truck door was opened by Lucky and Kikki.